"What ... bina-
tion of ... earch,
and a p ... glad
there wi ...

... mbly

"Utterly absorbing. Vividly alive characters in a setting so
clearly portrayed that one could step right into it. A very
clever plot in which each clue is clearly offered and yet the
identity of the murderer is a complete surprise. I look forward to many more books in which Nell Sweeney and Detective Cook work together toward justice."

—Roberta Gellis

"*Still Life with Murder* is a skillfully written story of intrigue
and murder set during Boston's famous Gilded Age. Nell
Sweeney, governess and part-time nurse, is a winning heroine gifted with common sense, grit, and an underlying
poignancy. With its rich sense of place and time and a crisp,
intelligent plot, readers will speed through this tale and be
clamoring for more." —Earlene Fowler,
bestselling author of *Steps to the Altar*
and *Sunshine and Shadow*

"P. B. Ryan captures an authentic flavor of post–Civil War
Boston as she explores that city's dark underbelly and the
lingering after-effects of the war. The atmosphere is that of
The Alienist, but feisty Irish nursemaid Nell Sweeney is a
more likable protagonist. I look forward to seeing her in action again." —Rhys Bowen

"P. B. Ryan makes a stunning debut with *Still Life with Murder*, bringing nineteenth-century Boston alive, from its teem-
ing slums to the mansions on Boston Common, and populating
it with a vivid and memorable cast of characters. The fascinating heroine, Nell Sweeney, immediately engages the reader
and I couldn't put the book down until I discovered the truth
along with her. I can't wait for the next installment."

—Victoria Thompson,
author of *Murder on Mulberry Bend*

STILL LIFE
WITH MURDER

P. B. RYAN

BERKLEY PRIME CRIME, NEW YORK

STILL LIFE WITH MURDER

A Berkley Prime Crime Book / published by arrangement with the author

PRINTING HISTORY
Berkley Prime Crime mass-market edition / July 2003

ISBN: 0-425-19106-0

Berkley Prime Crime Books are published
by The Berkley Publishing Group,
a division of Penguin Group (USA) Inc.,
375 Hudson Street, New York, New York 10014.
The name BERKLEY PRIME CRIME and the BERKLEY PRIME CRIME design are trademarks belonging to Penguin Group (USA) Inc.

PRINTED IN THE UNITED STATES OF AMERICA

10 9 8 7 6 5 4 3 2 1

For my agent, Nancy Yost, who's represented me for nearly a decade . . . and we're still speaking to each other! Nancy's business smarts and good humor are what make us work, and for that I'm supremely grateful.

Many thanks to Martha Bushko for knowing how to polish a novel without grinding away the good parts—a gem among editors.

Thanks also to the warm and generous Susan Uttal for twenty-five years of unwavering friendship, and most recently for her enthusiastic service as my personal Boston tour guide.

Finally, my deepest appreciation to Nick Dichario, Kathryn Shay, Tim Wright, my evil twin, Pamela Burford, and my husband, Richard Ryan, for taking the time to read and sometimes reread this manuscript as it took shape. Your insights were valuable, your encouragement and support priceless. This book, and the experience of writing it, wouldn't have been the same without you.

A guiltie conscience is a worme that bites and neuer ceaseth.

—NICHOLAS LING, *Politeuphuia*, 1597

Charlestown

Chas. River

Charles River

Boston Common

Public Gardens

Back Bay

Boston Harbor

Tully's body found
in alley outside Flynn's

Boston, Massachusetts

1. Flynn's Boardinghouse
2. Hewitt Home
3. Division 2 Police Station
4. County Jail on Charles St.
5. Deng Bao's Hop Joint
6. Pelham Hotel
7. Jack Thorpe's House
8. Maynard's Apothecary
9. Tremont Temple
10. Molly & Pearl's Flat

~ N.S. Feb. 1868

September 1864

Cape Cod, Massachusetts

"IT'S going to be a bad one." Dr. Greaves said it so quietly that Nell, sitting across from him in the Hewitts' glossy black brougham, almost didn't hear him.

Nell squeaked an end of her paisley shawl across the foggy side window. Trees writhed against a purpling sky as they rumbled past; raindrops spattered the glass. "The storm, do you mean? Or . . ." She eyed the flat mahogany surgical kit on the seat next to him, the cracked leather doctor's satchel by his feet.

"The delivery," he said. "*And* the storm." A flare of lightning lit his face, making him look, for one jolting moment, strangely old. She'd never thought of him that way, despite being half his age. Cyril Greaves remained lean in his middle years, and was taking his time in turning gray. And then there were those benevolent eyes, that ready smile.

He wasn't smiling this evening.

"There must be something terribly amiss for them to have sent that fellow to East Falmouth for me." Dr.

Greaves cocked his head toward the brougham's front window, through which the Hewitts' coachman, who'd introduced himself as Brady, was just visible as a smear of black hunched over the reins. "Families like the Hewitts don't bother with physicians for mere chambermaids. Not for routine births, anyway. It's only when disaster strikes that they fetch one, and by then it's usually too late."

All too true. How Nell dreaded the difficult calls— especially when something went wrong with a birth.

Crossing his arms, Dr. Greaves stared out at the passing countryside as it grew dimmer and more turbulent. A white-hot rivulet crackled down from the heavens; thunder rattled the carriage. Nell turned to gaze out the other side window, thinking she might draw this landscape tomorrow if she wasn't too tired after her chores. No, she'd paint it, on a sheet of Dr. Greaves's best writing paper, in ink—great, bruising stains of it, black for the trees and a near-black wash for the sky.

Brady halted his team at a massive iron gate, which was hauled open for them by two men in macintoshes. Snapping the reins, he drove the brougham past a shingle-sided gatehouse and up a long, undulating roadway. Nell had all but decided this couldn't possibly be the Hewitts' estate; there was just too much of it. But then a pulse of lightning illuminated a building in the distance—a huge, sprawling edifice adorned with turrets and a hodgepodge of steep gambrel roofs.

Her breath came out in an astonished little gust.

Dr. Greaves smiled at last; she often made him smile, but rarely when she meant to. "They call this place Falconwood. The Hewitts spend about six weeks here every summer, usually mid-July to the end of August. I wonder why they're still here."

"*Six weeks?* This . . . *castle* is for one family to live in for six weeks?"

"The Hewitts call it a cottage," he said, "but it's got over twenty rooms. Those in back look out on Waquoit Bay. The boathouse is larger than most people's homes."

Nell stared at the mansion as they neared it, at the scores of warmly lit windows, picturing the two-room hovel she'd shared with her entire family for the first eleven years of her life.

Her expression must have reflected her thoughts. "Nell," Dr. Greaves said softly. "You, of all people, should know that life isn't fair. And yet, somehow, you always manage to muscle through. Most people follow the path wherever it leads them. Others hack their own way through the brush and always seem to end up on higher ground. You're of the second sort."

The clattering of horses' hooves drew her attention back to the house, which they were circling on a paved path. Like the gatehouse, it was sided in shingles that had weathered to a silvery gray.

"The Hewitts have been summering on the Cape for about twenty years," said Dr. Greaves as he gathered up his satchel and surgical kit. "Not the most fashionable vacation spot, but I understand they like the solitude. Their main house is in Boston, on a Brahmin enclave they call Colonnade Row—that's a section of Tremont Street built up with mansions that make Falconwood look like a gardener's shed."

"Brahmin?"

"The first families of Boston—the venerable old blue-bloods." Dr. Greaves answered even the most uninformed query without scoffing at her ignorance. Nell had learned a lifetime's worth in her four years with him. "They tend to worship at the altar of high culture, and August Hewitt is no exception, though he's unusually sanctimonious for that breed. The wife's English, I think. There are some sons. The local girls would swoon for days whenever one of them showed up in town. They haven't been round the past few summers—except for the youngest. I see him at church every Sunday, along with his father. Perhaps the rest are off fighting Johnny Reb."

The carriage shuddered to a stop on a flagstone court behind the house, near an attached leaded-glass greenhouse with a domed roof. Passing the reins to a waiting groom, Brady unfurled the biggest black umbrella Nell had ever seen, opened the brougham's door, and handed her down. "I'd best be takin' you folks in through the greenhouse," he said in a wheezy Irish brogue, raising his voice to be heard over the drumming rain. "The drive's flooded out up ahead. Watch that puddle, miss."

Taking a lantern from the brougham, the coachman gestured them toward an imposing arched entryway. Nell followed him through the unlit greenhouse, which she'd expected to be filled with plants, but which instead housed . . .

Paintings? She gawked as she wove through a forest of canvases propped on easels, each executed in loose, vibrant brush strokes. Some were seascapes featuring picturesque Waquoit Bay, and there were one or two still lifes, but most were of people—not posing formally, but lounging in opulent surroundings, exquisitely attired; jewels glinted, silks shimmered. They materialized out of the darkness, these sublime apparitions, only to dissolve back into it as the coachman's lantern swung past. The lamplight shifted and swayed just enough to make it seem as if they were inclining their heads ever so slightly toward Nell, eyes alight, mildly curious, before looking away.

The women dazzled, but it was the young men whom Nell found most arresting. There were perhaps three who had been painted repeatedly, golden creatures with luminous skin and expressions of languid ease. A particularly large canvas, which stood half-finished near the back wall, depicted two of them. One, an adolescent with hair the color of champagne and quiet, watchful eyes, sat tucked into one end of a maroon settee, while his brother—for surely these were two of the Hewitt sons—sprawled in elegant repose across the other. This older one's hair was a slightly darker blond, his smile more careless. Collar loose, tie undone, he had both arms draped across the back of the settee, a brandy snifter cupped lightly in one hand.

On a folding table nearby sat a palette crusted with dried oil paints, a jar of brushes, a wadded-up rag; some preliminary sketches were tacked to the easel's crossbar. Nell detected only the faintest whiff of linseed oil and turpentine; she would have expected the smell to be stronger.

"That's the one I see at church." Dr. Greaves pointed to the younger brother.

"Aye, that's young Master Martin. He's right pious." Gesturing them through a multipaned door into the house, Brady winked at Nell and whispered, "For an Episcopalian."

Nell winked back. She didn't think she looked particularly Irish, but those from the old country always knew.

"I'm to hand you over to Mrs. Mott, the housekeeper," the coachman said as he led them into a dim, cavernous kitchen, where he pulled a bell cord. Cocking his head toward a lamplit hallway, he said, "They've got Annie down there in the cook's room. That's Annie McIntyre, the girl what's havin' the baby. She sleeps up on the top floor, ordinarily, with the rest of the maids. But when her time comes, Mrs. Hewitt, she said to put her down here where it's more cozy and private-like."

There materialized before them an old woman who looked to have been rendered in hard pencil on smooth vellum, so devoid of color was she: pale bespectacled face, scraped-back gray hair, unadorned black dress with a heavily laden key ring dangling from her belt, hands like carved bone clasped at her waist.

"Evenin', Mrs. Mott," Brady said. "I'm to go fetch

Father Donnelly now. When you're ready for me to take you back, Doc, just—"

"We'll find you, Brady. Thank you."

"This way." Mrs. Mott turned and led them down a hallway, at the end of which slumped a young woman in a black dress with white collar, cuffs, and apron. Red hair frizzed out from beneath her cap—not just a rusty brown, like Nell's, but a smoldering, red-hot red. She eyed them while gnawing on a thumbnail.

Pausing at a closed door halfway down the hall, Mrs. Mott turned to the maid. "Mary Agnes, shouldn't you be turning down beds?"

"Mrs. Bouchard wants me here in case I'm needed."

"You don't answer to Mrs. Bouchard, though, do you? You answer to me. For pity's sake, girl, stop chewing on that—"

"Oh, God." From behind the door came a woman's ragged moan. "Oh, God. Oh, Jesus." She was young, her voice high and thready. Another woman started to say something, but her words were drowned out by a wail that trailed off into whimpers. Mrs. Mott shrank back from the door. Mary Agnes looked at the ceiling as she started back in on the thumbnail.

Dr. Greaves knocked. "It's Cyril Greaves, the doctor. May I—"

The door swung open. "Thank the Lord." Stepping aside for them was a solidly built Negro lady with a great copper bowl of a face and hair like hoar frost on gray moss. "My name is Mrs. Bouchard," she said in a sonorous voice seasoned with a peculiar accent, not quite Southern and not quite French. "I'm Mrs. Hewitt's nurse. She asked me to help."

"Yes, thank you." If Dr. Greaves shared Nell's curiosity as to why Mrs. Hewitt should employ a nurse, he gave no hint of it. Nell followed him into the room, noticing as she turned to close the door that Mrs. Mott was already halfway down the hall, her tread as silent as if she were barefooted, although Nell couldn't imagine that was the case.

Leaning over the narrow bed, Dr. Greaves felt the forehead of the young woman lying in it, a heavily pregnant, china-doll blonde with big, panicky eyes. "How are you holding up, Annie?"

"N-not so good," she panted. "Something's wrong."

Mrs. Bouchard said, "The baby's lying transverse, Doctor. Hasn't budged through fourteen hours of labor." It wasn't a servant's uniform the nurse wore, but rather a fine but severely unadorned black dress that looked to have been dyed from some other color. Her only jewelry was a small enameled watch pinned to her bosom. Was the household in mourning for some reason? Nell, in her faded blue basque and plaid skirt—hand-me-downs from Dr. Greaves's niece—felt suddenly rather shabby and conspicuous.

Dr. Greaves whipped off his frock coat and handed it to Nell, who laid it, along with her shawl and bonnet, on a chair in the corner of the small, tidy room. Rolling up his shirtsleeves, he nodded toward a wash basin in the corner. "Is that water clean?" he asked Mrs. Bouchard.

"I boiled it."

"Annie," he said as he soaped and rinsed his hands, "I'm going to have to examine you, but it shouldn't hurt. This nice young lady"—he nodded to Nell as she turned back the bedcovers from the bottom up—"is Nell Sweeney, my assistant. She's about your age, I should think."

"Let me guess." Nell smiled at Annie as she sat on the bed next to her. "You're . . . twenty?"

"Twenty-two."

"Exactly my age, then."

Annie grimaced, her head thrown back. *"No . . ."* she groaned.

"Ride it out," Nell softly urged, holding her hand and

smoothing damp tendrils of hair off her face. "This will all be over soon, and then you'll have a lovely baby to—"

"Oh, God . . . oh, God." The girl cried out hoarsely during the contraction, trembled as it subsided; she was clearly exhausted.

Noticing Annie's wedding ring, Nell said, "Tell me about your husband." She'd learned not to ask *Where is your husband?* in case he was lying in a grave near some far-off battlefield.

"He . . . he . . ." Annie hitched in a breath and glanced down at Dr. Greaves, who must have begun his examination.

"Annie, look at me," Nell said gently. "What's his name?"

"M-Michael. Only . . ." Annie swallowed. "Only everybody calls him M-Mac, on account of his last name—McIntyre."

"He's one of our drivers," offered Mrs. Bouchard as she straightened a stack of clean sheets on the dresser. "Or was, till he signed up with the Boston Volunteers."

"The Eleventh R-Regiment," Annie managed.

Mrs. Bouchard said, "He lost a leg at Spotsylvania in May. Been in the hospital since then, but he wrote to say he's coming home next month."

"Then you'll be seeing him soon!" Nell said.

Annie's head whipped back and forth on the pillow. "I'll be dead. Something's wrong."

Dr. Greaves said, "Annie, I'm not going to lie to you. Something *is* wrong. But it's nothing I can't fix. Nell." He gestured for her to stand. "I want to show you this so you'll know it next time we run across it. See how wide her abdomen is from side to side?"

She let him position her hands on either side of Annie's distended belly, over her linen chemise.

"Feel that?" Dr. Greaves asked. "The head's on one

side, buttocks on the other—the worst position a baby can be in for delivery. Cord's prolapsed, too." Folding the bedcovers back down, he asked Mrs. Bouchard, "How long since her water broke?"

"Around dawn, just as she was going into labor."

"I'll need to operate as soon as we can get things set—"

"Operate!" Mrs. Bouchard exclaimed.

"Oh, Jesus," Annie moaned. "You're going to cut it out of me? I *am* going to die!"

"Annie." Dr. Greaves turned her face toward him. "If you try to deliver this baby normally, your womb will very likely rupture, and either you or the baby—or both of you—will assuredly die. I'll use chloroform. You'll sleep through the whole thing."

"But, Doctor . . ." Mrs. Bouchard cast him a look that said she knew exactly what happened to women who underwent Caesareans.

"I've had excellent success with this procedure," Dr. Greaves assured her. "The secret lies in suturing the uterine wall. And no, it doesn't cause infection to leave the stitches in, so long as you keep things clean. Do you have any experience with surgery, Mrs. Bouchard?"

Her chin shot up. "My father was a surgeon in New Orleans. I assisted him for twenty years, through hundreds of operations. I won't faint dead away, if that's what you're worried about."

"Good—you and Nell can both help me, then."

" 'Excellent success,' " Annie said. "W-What does that mean? Some of them still die, right? The mothers? When you do this operation?"

Dr. Greaves's hesitation was telling. "It's your only hope, child. And you're young and strong. There's no reason to think you won't make it, and . . . well, the baby almost always does."

"Do it," she rasped. "But first I need to speak to . . ."

She mewed in pain as another contraction mounted. "Send for . . ."

Mrs. Bouchard patted her hand. "Father Donnelly's on his—"

"Mrs. Hewitt. I need to speak to M-Mrs. Hew—" Annie broke off with an agonizing howl.

Nell held her hands and comforted her until the pain had eased. Mrs. Bouchard said, "I'm sorry, Annie, but I'm not about to disturb Mrs. Hewitt at this hour. If you've got something to say to her, tell it to me and I'll give her the—"

"*No!*" Annie was trembling again, badly. "I have to speak to her myself, alone. Just her and me."

"Out of the question," Mrs. Bouchard said resolutely. "With everything that's befallen that poor woman of late, she doesn't need you troubling her with—"

"Then there will be no operation."

The nurse sighed with exasperation. "Annie, for—"

"Just do as she asks," Dr. Greaves quietly implored her.

Mrs. Bouchard marched out with a hiss of crinoline, hands in the air as if there were a rifle to her back.

"We can operate in the kitchen," the doctor told Nell, "on that big tiled table. See if there's someone who can't improvise some sort of stretcher. I'll need the gas jets turned up, and some lanterns hung from the rafters. Here." He dug the square-sided bottle of carbolic out of his leather bag. "You know what to do. Get that creature out in the hall to help."

"WHAT *is* this stuff?" Mary Agnes winced at the tarlike stink of the rag Nell had given her to wipe off the table.

"Carbolic acid," Nell said as she scrubbed down a big enameled butcher tray that would hold the surgical instruments. "It'll get that table as clean as it can get."

"What's the use, if he's fixing to cut her open on it? It'll be a right bloody mess by the time he's done."

"He says it helps."

"Are you a nurse, like Mrs. Bouchard?"

"Not like Mrs. Bouchard. He's trained me in that sort of thing, but mostly I just . . . help with things. I go on calls with him, keep his books, do a little cleaning and cooking . . ."

"Don't he have a wife for that?"

"She's been ill for some time." That was what Dr. Greaves called it, anyway—an illness. But Nell knew that the Boston "hospital" in which his beloved Charlotte had spent the past eight years was, in fact, some sort of fancy lunatic asylum.

"What does he pay you?" Mary Agnes asked. "Or is it just room and board?"

"Room and board," Nell said. "But he teaches me things, too. Not just about medicine, but about history and music and how to speak and conduct myself with people. He's taught me how to read real books and write a proper letter and work with numbers. He—"

Mary Agnes cleared her throat as she speeded up the pace of her scrubbing. Catching Nell's eyes, she glanced meaningfully toward the door.

Nell looked that way to find a woman entering the kitchen in a Merlin chair, something Nell had seen only in pictures until now. Mrs. Hewitt was wheeling the upholstered wooden chair herself despite the presence behind her of Mrs. Bouchard, who could presumably have pushed it for her.

Viola Hewitt was tall—even in the chair, you could tell that—and aristocratic, with black, silver-threaded hair in a braid draped over one shoulder. In lieu of a dressing gown, she wore a purple and gold silk robe of Oriental design over her nightdress, much like those worn by the women in Dr. Greaves's book of Japanese prints; kimonos, he'd called them. She was a handsome woman, striking even, despite being an apparent cripple, and of a certain age. There was, however, an aura of melancholy in her eyes, in the set of her mouth, in her very posture, that robbed her of any claim to true physical beauty.

Mrs. Hewitt glanced once in Nell's direction as she rolled through the kitchen toward the hallway, wheels rattling over the slate floor; Mrs. Bouchard brought up the rear. Two ivory-handled canes and a needlework bag were hooked to the back of the Merlin chair.

"That's not what I would have expected her to look like," Nell said when she was out of earshot. "Aren't her sons fair?"

"The three younger ones are." Mary Agnes smiled dreamily. "You never saw such lovely men, like angels in a painting. They got their coloring from Mr. Hewitt. He's the kind of blond that looks almost white. He really *is* going white now, but you can hardly tell the difference from before."

Nell shook out a tea towel to lay on the instrument tray, thinking back to one of the paintings in the greenhouse, the only one whose subject was standing. He was an older gentleman in white tie, holding an opera hat and gloves in one hand, walking stick in the other. He had hair like tarnished silver, radiant blue eyes, and a grimly regal bearing: August Hewitt.

Dr. Greaves and Mrs. Bouchard entered the kitchen, having been asked to give Annie and her employer some privacy. Mrs. Bouchard sent Mary Agnes off for three clean bib aprons and as many freshly washed towels and dish cloths as she could carry. Taking the surgical kit from Dr. Greaves, Nell gathered up the ivory-handled instruments to be doused with carbolic: scalpels, bistouries, tissue retractors, artery forceps . . .

A muffled wailing, just barely audible over the pattering of rain on the windowpanes and the slight hiss of the turned-up gas lamps, made them turn toward the hallway. At first Nell thought Annie was having another contraction, but it soon became clear that she was crying.

"That girl has no business bringing any more woe on that woman's head," lamented Mrs. Bouchard as she unfolded a sheet onto the table. "She's aged a decade this past month as it is."

"Why?" Nell asked. Too late, when Dr. Greaves cut his eyes toward her, did she realize her tactlessness. She asked too many questions; he always said so. One could often learn more, he claimed, by keeping quiet and fading into the background.

Thankfully, Mrs. Bouchard didn't seem to mind. "The Hewitts lost their two oldest boys, both of them, just a day apart. They were captured back in February, at Olustee—that's in Florida—and thrown in that godforsaken hellhole down in Georgia."

"You mean Andersonville?" Dr. Greaves asked. Even Nell, who had little time for newspapers, had heard about the notorious Confederate prison camp, a fenced-in sea of tents housing three times as many Union soldiers as it could accommodate. Rumor had it thousands had already starved to death or succumbed to one of the many forms of pestilence that thrived in such conditions.

Mrs. Bouchard nodded, dabbing her eyes with the edge of her apron. "They died last month, of dysentery—Robbie and Will. *Dysentery.* Lord, what a wretched way to go. It isn't right. It just isn't right."

"Both sons were in the same regiment?" Nell asked as she lined up the disinfected instruments one by one on the tea towel. Dr. Greaves was asking questions; why shouldn't she?

"They enlisted together in the Fortieth Massachusetts Mounted Infantry, on account of being such good horsemen."Mrs. Bouchard smoothed down the sheet with a bit too much vehemence. "Robbie, he was a regular volunteer. The older one, Will—he signed on as a surgeon."

Dr. Greaves, washing his hands at the sink, glanced over his shoulder. "He was a surgeon?"

"Just finished up medical school over in Scotland. University of Edinburgh."

Dr. Greaves let out a low, impressed whistle.

Mary Agnes returned with a towering stack of linens, including the three aprons, which Mrs. Bouchard distributed to Dr. Greaves and Nell, keeping one for herself. "Poor Mrs. Hewitt hasn't done much of anything since she got the news, which isn't like her. I've told her she must rise above it, get on with things. After all, she still has Martin and Harry—those are the two younger ones. She was painting them when the cable came about Robbie and Will."

"Martin's the youngest, yes?" asked Dr. Greaves as Nell helped him on with his apron. "The one I see at church?" The one with the champagne hair and insightful eyes.

Mrs. Bouchard nodded. "He was all fired up to enlist next month, when he turns eighteen, but now his father's forbidden it. Says it'd kill his mother to lose another son. Mr. Hewitt, he pulled some strings and got Martin into Harvard so he can stay at home with his mama. He's already gone back to Boston, so as not to miss too much of the first term."

"And Harry?" Nell prompted.

Mrs. Bouchard turned away to fuss with the sheets on the table. "Oh, Mister Harry's needed at his father's woolen mill in Charlestown."

It would appear that Harry Hewitt had chosen, like so many other young sons of wealthy families, to sit out the war and let his neighbors and servants—and brothers— fight it for him. Nell thought back to his image in the big

unfinished painting—the beguiling grin, the lax fingers
cradling the snifter.

From the direction of the greenhouse came men's
voices. Opening the glass door, Nell greeted portly old
Father Donnelly, her parish priest, and relieved him of his
sodden overcoat.

"You'll have to wait your turn, Father," said Mrs. Bouchard. "Mrs. Hewitt and Annie are—"

"Mrs. Hewitt and Annie are done talking," Dr. Greaves
declared. "If I wait much longer to operate, it will be too
late. Father, do you think you can . . . do whatever you
have to do while we're moving Annie to the kitchen?"

"I . . . suppose—"

"Good. Mrs. Bouchard, if you would give me a hand
with Annie . . . Nell, make sure we're all set up in here."

It took mere minutes to get Annie settled on the table
and prepared for surgery, with Father Donnelly muttering
over her all the while. The poor girl, her face red from
weeping, shivered with fear despite their reassurances.

Banishing everyone but Mrs. Bouchard, Nell, and himself from the kitchen, Dr. Greaves said a brief prayer—a
Protestant prayer, but Nell and Mrs. Bouchard crossed
themselves just the same. He attached the drip spout to
the tiny brown bottle of chloroform while Nell fitted the
inhaling mask with fresh gauze.

"Close your eyes, Annie," Nell murmured as she
placed the mask over the girl's nose and mouth. "When
you wake up, you'll have a baby."

"I say—she's a beautiful little thing, is she not?"
    Nell, cradling the swaddled infant in her arms,
smiled across the kitchen table at Viola Hewitt. "All babies are beautiful."

It was well past midnight; the gas lights were low
again, casting the immense kitchen into amber-tinted semi-

darkness as the storm continued to rage outside. Dr. Greaves and Mrs. Bouchard were down the hall with Annie, watching for postoperative complications. Mrs. Hewitt, ignoring her nurse's exhortations to turn in, had lingered in the kitchen to oversee Nell's bathing and diapering of the newborn.

"They're not all as beautiful as that one." Mrs. Hewitt returned Nell's smile, her melancholic fog having dissipated over the past couple of hours. She had a distinctive voice, deep-throated and a little gritty, its rough edges burnished a bit by the remnants of a genteel English accent. "She's so plump and pretty, with that big, lovely round head. My boys all had a rather squished, stomped-upon look, as I recall."

"The round head is because of the Caesarean. She didn't have to pass through the . . ." Nell looked away, chastising herself for having made such a reference in polite conversation, especially with the likes of Viola Hewitt; what would Dr. Greaves say?

Mrs. Hewitt chuckled. "I'm afraid I'm not particularly easy to shock, Miss Sweeney. Mr. Hewitt is of the opinion that I ought to be a bit more prone to swooning, but I could never quite get the knack."

The baby yawned, quivering, then settled down again, weighty and warm in Nell's arms; how it gladdened her heart whenever she had the chance to hold a baby. She tried to fluff the thatch of black hair, but it was still matted, despite her bath. "Is her father dark?" she asked, thinking of Annie's golden locks.

Mrs. Hewitt frowned slightly. "No, Mac is . . . sandy-haired, I suppose you'd say. But newborns are funny that way. My Martin was born with a full head of thick, black hair, but now he's the fairest of all of my . . ." She trailed off, no doubt reflecting that "all of" her sons now numbered just two.

"I'm sorry for your loss," Nell said.

"Yes. Well. We're usually back in Boston by now, but I've been putting it off because—" Her voice snagged. "I've been saying it's because of Annie, because she couldn't travel in her condition—she's part of our Boston staff, you know. But we could have gone on ahead and sent for her after the baby came. It wasn't that. It was going back to that house on Colonnade Row, where those boys were little . . ."

The baby squirmed in Nell's arms, mewing and smacking her lips, her head jerking this way and that.

Mrs. Hewitt watched with interest as Nell dipped her little finger in the teacup of boiled sugar water with which she was keeping the hungry infant appeased. "She's ravenous, that one. I do hope Annie's up to feeding her soon."

"Me, too," Nell said as she slipped her fingertip in the baby's mouth. There was fresh milk in the ice closet, and an old baby bottle to put it in, but giving it to her at this point could spoil her for the breast.

"I would ask to hold her again, but she'd only fuss, as she did before. She's happiest with you. I've rarely seen anyone handle a baby with such . . . tender assurance."

Gratified by the praise, Nell murmured her thanks as Dr. Greaves returned to the kitchen. "Our new mother is awake and doing splendidly," he reported with a smile. "Why don't you bring the baby to her and see if she'll nurse? And then perhaps we should locate that Brady fellow and ask him to drive us back to East Falmouth. Mrs. Bouchard will sit up with Annie tonight, and I'll return in the morning to—"

"You mean to travel in this rain, and at this hour?" Mrs. Hewitt asked. "I've got half a dozen guest rooms, all standing empty—I can certainly spare two for the night. I'll have you brought nightclothes and whatever else you need, and then Brady will take you back to town after breakfast."

Dr. Greaves accepted her offer of hospitality, to Nell's relief; why endure a late-night carriage ride in such weather?

In the cook's room, she found Mrs. Bouchard propping pillows behind Annie's back. "Look who's here," said the nurse as Nell sat on the edge of the bed with the baby. "It's your—"

"Take it away," Annie moaned, whipping her head to the side.

Nell looked inquiringly toward Mrs. Bouchard, who appeared dismayed but unsurprised at this reaction. "Now, Annie, don't be that way. You're her mother, after all, and she needs—"

"I don't want to see her. Take her away. *Please.*"

Mrs. Bouchard nodded resignedly to a stunned Nell, who left with the child, closing the door behind her. Walking down the hallway toward the kitchen, she heard Mrs. Hewitt say, "Four years? And you've been pleased with her?"

"More than pleased," Dr. Greaves responded. "Nell's a hard worker, and clever. Nothing slips past her."

Nell stilled near the entrance to the kitchen.

"She's got a great deal of common sense, too," he continued, "and a strong stomach. I never have to worry about her keeling over at the sight of a gruesome injury."

"From a good family, is she?" inquired Mrs. Hewitt.

Nell held her breath for the long seconds it took Dr. Greaves to answer. "Her parents were from the old country, ma'am. Came over when Nell was about a year old. They're both gone now, first him and then the mother, when she was just a child." Nell's father was gone, all right, but it wasn't his Maker he'd met; it was that greasy-haired barmaid from Dougal's Tavern.

"And there's no other family?"

Nell steeled herself, wondering if he'd mention Duncan.

"She had a number of younger siblings—that's how she learned to care for children. Disease took most of them—cholera, diphtheria—but one brother lived to adulthood. She assumes he's still alive, but it's been years since she's seen him. James—she calls him Jamie."

Nell released a pent-up breath.

There came an interval of silence punctuated by the muted *bong* of a clock somewhere off in another part of the house, striking one.

"She seems . . ." Mrs. Hewitt paused. "I found myself telling her things . . ."

"Yes," said Dr. Greaves; Nell could hear the smile in his voice. "She has that effect."

"I don't suppose she has any Greek or Latin."

A pause. "No, ma'am. She's quite proficient in French, though."

"Any Italian or German?"

"None to speak of. But she's got a better command of the three R's than I do, and she reads whatever I put in her hands. Lovely penmanship, and a fine hand with the drawing pencil."

"She's of good character and chaste habits, I take it?"

"She's never given me any reason to censure her, ma'am." Which didn't precisely answer the question.

"That little scar near her left eyebrow—may I ask how . . ."

"An old injury. I stitched it myself." As he had the several others that weren't so readily visible. Before Mrs. Hewitt could ask him to elaborate on his vague answer, he said, "May I inquire as to the nature of your interest in her?"

"I just . . . I need to consult with my husband first, and I'm not sure if he's still up reading. If I don't get the chance to speak to you again tonight, perhaps . . . after breakfast?"

"As you like, ma'am."

Nell heard the wheels of the Merlin chair rolling away over the slate floor. She listened as the sound grew softer and disappeared, then reentered the kitchen to find Dr. Greaves staring at the door through which Mrs. Hewitt had just departed. He turned to look at Nell as she came up behind him, his expression contemplative, and perhaps a little sad.

"What was that about, do you suppose?" Nell asked.

He sighed. "Eavesdropping, Nell? I'm surprised at you." Before she could protest that he might have done the same had he found himself the subject of a similar conversation, he said, "Let's finish cleaning up in here. It's been a long night."

N ELL hastened to the guest room door as a second knock came, her fingers fumbling with the mother-of-pearl buttons on the dressing gown she'd found laid out for her when she was shown to this room about an hour ago.

Must be Mary Agnes, with another down pillow to heap upon the bed, another little perfumed soap or lush towel, she thought as she reached for the knob. But in fact, it was Viola Hewitt, not in her chair but standing with the aid of the two ivory-handled canes. "It's dreadfully late, I know, but I saw the light under your door, so I thought perhaps . . . May I . . . ?"

"Yes, of course." Stepping aside, Nell held the door open for her visitor, whose gait, although halting, had an odd, birdlike grace about it. A metallic scraping could just be heard beneath the silken swish of her kimono and nightdress.

"Leg braces," she explained. "They get me up and down stairs, but it's an ordeal. I say, how very pretty your hair looks down. *You've* no need of the curling tongs." She nodded toward the dressing gown. "Not too long? It's mine, you see."

"Oh, no, it's lovely." It was, in fact, the loveliest thing Nell had ever worn, a satin-trimmed cashmere peignoir the color of butter, worn over a matching silk nightgown. Now that she'd finally felt the liquid slide of silk over her bare skin, Nell understood why women prized it so. The ensemble was a far cry from the patched cotton nightdress and threadbare wrap hanging in her little dormer room back at Dr. Greaves's.

"You're comfortable here, I hope?" Mrs. Hewitt embarked on a torturously slow tour of the room, smoothing the counterpane on the tall half-tester bed, adjusting the angle of the cheval mirror. She opened and closed the dressing table's single drawer, rearranged the roses in a fat Chinese urn. Their fragrance mingled with a whisper of lemon oil. The room smelled sweet and exotic and a little old; to Nell, it smelled like wealth.

Nell couldn't help wondering why she was being treated to such luxury. Most people in Mrs. Hewitt's position would have berthed her upstairs with the servants.

"I went to Dr. Greaves's room, thinking I'd speak to him first, but he's not there. Perhaps he's downstairs unwinding after the evening's ordeal. I did tell him where he might find the sherry." Mrs. Hewitt glanced at the door to the dressing room, which stood slightly open.

"How is the baby faring?" Nell asked. Mrs. Hewitt had had a cradle fetched from the attic and put next to her own bed.

"Fast asleep, with a nice, full belly. I'm so glad she took to the bottle. Good heavens." She crossed to the little writing desk in the corner. "Did you do these?" Lowering herself into the chair, she lifted the two drawings Nell had inked on paper she'd found in the middle drawer—thick, creamy vellum embossed with a single word: FALCON-WOOD. They were sketchy portraits, one of the baby and the other of Viola Hewitt herself.

"They're just rough," Nell said, heat sweeping up her

throat as Mrs. Hewitt studied them. "When I have time, I'll add some more detail and—"

"Don't. They're perfect fleeting impressions, just as they're meant to be. I must say, though, it's remarkable how well you captured me—both of us—just from memory."

"I don't have a great deal of time to draw from life. I've learned to fix things in my memory and draw them later. It's almost like . . . making a photograph in my mind."

"It's a gift, being able to do that." Still contemplating the sketches, Mrs. Hewitt said, "Annie doesn't want the baby. At all. She means to give her up."

"Ah."

"Do you know why?"

Nell paused to choose her words carefully.

Mrs. Hewitt said, "I can't be shocked, remember?"

"Is it because her husband isn't the father?"

Mrs. Hewitt laid the sketches down carefully. "It was a year and a half ago that Mac enlisted in the Boston Volunteers, and he hasn't been able to get home since then. I've forbidden the servants to speak of it. These matters are . . ." Nell thought she would say "unseemly." Instead, she said, ". . . complicated. But we live in a world that likes to pretend such things are simple."

Too true, Nell thought; still, the older woman's acceptance of the situation struck her as bizarre.

"I'm adopting the baby." Viola Hewitt's smile evolved into a full, girlish grin when Nell's mouth literally dropped open. "Mrs. Mott doesn't approve. Neither does my husband, but he's humoring me because of . . ." Her expression sobered. "Because he knows it will make me happy to have a baby round the house. And a baby girl! I always wanted a daughter, but I ended up with four sons instead. Not that I didn't love them more than life itself, God knows. But there's something about a little girl . . ."

"Yes, there is." Still, rationalizations aside, for a society matron to adopt a maid's bastard . . . It was outrageous.

"Annie doesn't want her, and she doesn't want her husband or family to find out about her. If I don't take Grace, she'll be . . ." Noticing Nell's puzzlement, she smiled. "I'm calling her Grace. It was my mother's name. If I don't take her, she'll be doomed to some squalid orphan asylum, or worse yet, the county poor house. That's where they put the absolute dregs, the type of paupers who would simply die on their own—drunks, lunatics, people with the most dreadful contagions, all thrown in with the motherless little children. I've done charity work in those places. My dear girl, if you'd ever seen the inside of one . . ."

If only I hadn't, Nell thought.

"Annie will leave my employ and relinquish all legal claim to the child. Our attorney will draw up the necessary papers. In return, I'll ask Mr. Hewitt to recommend her to the Astors in New York—making no mention of the baby, of course. It will be an excellent position for her, and I'll see to it that they hire Mac, as well. They can always use another driver."

"Won't her husband question the scar on her abdomen?" Nell asked.

"She can tell him it was an appendectomy."

"You've thought it all through."

"More completely than you know," said Viola. "We'll be returning to Boston next week, with the baby, and . . . Nell, I'd like you to consider coming with us."

Nell stared at her. "As a . . . nursemaid, you mean?"

"We actually have one of those—well, she's been retired for some time, but she still lives with us in Boston. Miss Edna Parrish. She was my nanny back in England, and I brought her here for the boys. The thing of it is, she's quite elderly, and somewhat infirm. She'll be insulted if I don't ask her to take care of Grace, but she can't possibly manage on her own. I'd do it myself, but I've got these useless legs to deal with. Infantile paralysis, you know. Caught it in Europe right before the war."

"I'm so sorry," Nell said, but in truth, she was somewhat intrigued by the exotic ailment; she wished it wouldn't be considered rude to ask about it.

"I was thinking perhaps you could assist Nurse Parrish in her duties while Grace is little. Then, when she gets older and needs to be educated and learn comportment and so forth, you'd be more of a governess."

"A *governess*? *Me?*" A nursemaid might hail from the working classes, but Nell had read enough governess novels to know that their heroines were nearly always, despite their reduced circumstances, as wellborn as the families that employed them—and always well educated. "I'm not equipped for a position like that."

"I think you are," Mrs. Hewitt said. "You're intelligent, capable . . . and you seem to adore children."

"But governesses are teachers, and I've had so little formal schooling. And I'm . . . I'm not from your world, Mrs. Hewitt. I don't know anything about your way of life."

"You're clever. You'll learn. Besides, for the first eight years or so, you'll be what's known as a nursery governess, and to be perfectly frank, one doesn't generally expect as much of them as one does of a preparatory governess. You'll have plenty of time to fill any gaps in your own tutelage before taking on the more rigorous aspects of Grace's education. Even then, one does expect to hire outside masters in various subjects . . . languages, piano, dancing . . . A good governess is as much a moral guide as an instructress, and I can't help but think you would excel in that role."

If only she knew. "Mrs. Hewitt, I . . ." How to put it? "You may be harboring illusions about me that—"

"Gentlewomen have no monopoly on virtue, Nell—a minority view in my particular circle, but I'm accustomed to being regarded as an eccentric. I suppose I am—but I'm also, if I do say so myself, an astute judge of people. I know in my heart you'd be wonderful for Grace."

"I . . . I appreciate your confidence, Mrs. Hewitt, I truly do. But—"

"Have you ever been to Boston, Nell?"

"No, ma'am."

"Well, there's no place like it in the world. Our house is right on Boston Common, which is some forty-five acres of parkland. You'd have your own room on the third floor next to the nursery. I shan't lie to you—it's a rather plain room, but large and bright, and it has windows facing the Common, and a little nook off to the side that can serve as a sitting room. The nursery can be converted into a schoolroom when the time comes. You'll get ten dollars a week, and of course room and—"

"Ten . . ." *Ten dollars a week?* "For *myself?*"

"To spend any way you'd like. You'll need a proper wardrobe. My dressmaker will run some things up for you—at my expense, of course. Three or four day dresses to start with, I should think. At least one tea dress, and a nice walking dress, for when you take Grace out and about. Perhaps a simple black taffeta for dinner. Something to wear to church on Sundays." Looking down, she brushed an invisible speck off her kimono. "Mr. Hewitt did ask me to discuss the issue of religion. We're Anglican, you know—Episcopalian you call it here. Mr. Hewitt switched over from Congregationalism when we married. And I would assume you're . . ."

"Quite Catholic, I'm afraid."

"Yes, well, I had a Catholic governess myself—Mademoiselle D'Alencour, my finishing governess. I re-

minded Mr. Hewitt of that just now when he . . . well, he
had some concerns. Grace will, of course, be brought up
in our faith. You're welcome to attend Mass with the
house staff, but once Grace is old enough for church, it's
got to be King's Chapel. And as for . . . doctrinal matters . . ."

"You don't want me putting papist notions in her
head."

"In all other matters, I bow to your discretion. You'll
be free to deal with her as you see fit, for the most part,
without a lot of second-guessing from me. All I really
expect is that you rear her with the same care and love as
if she were your very own. Naturally, I would prefer that
you remain unwed while Grace is young, in order to de-
vote your full attention to her. And of course, your conduct and reputation must be above reproach—you're
responsible for the upbringing of a young girl, after all.
But I can't think you'd let me down in that regard. Does
this sound like something you'd be interested in?"

Having a baby to hold and feed and kiss anytime she
wanted? A child to raise as her own—almost—after
thinking it would never happen? "Yes," she said earnestly,
remembering how the infant Grace had felt in her arms,
so warm, so right. "Yes, I . . . Oh, yes, I would love it!"

Mrs. Hewitt seized Nell's hand and squeezed it. "I'll
speak to Dr. Greaves in the morning about releasing you
into my employ."

Nell nodded, although she knew in her heart that Dr.
Greaves wouldn't stand in the way of an opportunity like
this. He wouldn't like it, but he would do what was best
for her.

It took some effort, and Nell's help, for Mrs. Hewitt
to rise unsteadily from the chair. As she was leaving, she
turned and said quietly, "You mustn't judge Annie too
harshly. She does love him, you know—her husband,
Mac. She wept for weeks after he left. But people get

lonely. They . . . seek comfort where they can find it."

"I know."

That statement was met with an indulgent smile. "You may think you do, my dear, but you're really such an innocent. Perhaps someday, when Grace is old enough, you'll marry and gain some understanding of these things."

Marry to gain an understanding of loneliness? But then Nell thought of her mother, gaunt and shivering in her little hut with her many mouths to feed after her husband ran off. Had she never married, she never would have ended up so forsaken.

Closing the door, Nell rested her forehead against it. *You're really such an innocent.* Unfortunately, one doesn't remain innocent for long with the kind of life in which she'd been thrust. One does what one has to, just to survive. But Viola Hewitt didn't know that. To her, Nell was a simple Irish Catholic girl of working-class stock and unblemished virtue. There would be much to keep hidden if she took this position, the worst of it having to do with Duncan.

Nell didn't relish the notion of harboring secrets from a woman she'd already come to like immensely. But she could if she had to. And if she took this position—and dear God, how she wanted it—she would have to.

Turning, Nell looked toward the dressing room. "Did you hear?" she asked softly.

The partially ajar door creaked open as Dr. Greaves emerged from where he'd secreted himself, hair slightly mussed, braces dangling. His shirt, which Nell had been unbuttoning when the first knock came, hung open.

For a moment he just looked at her, and then he raised his glass of sherry in a kind of toast, his smile so sad it seemed to reach around her throat and squeeze.

"To higher ground," he said.

Chapter 1

February 1868: Boston

IT was a shocking turn of events, both wondrous and devastating; a miracle or a tragedy, depending on how you looked at it.

The news came while Nell was relaxing in the Hewitts' music room, listening to Martin sing his new hymn for his parents. Accompanying him on the gleaming Steinway in the corner was Viola Hewitt in her downstairs Merlin chair, one of four she kept on different floors of the Italianate mansion that overlooked Boston Common from the corner of Tremont and West Streets.

August Hewitt lounged in his leather wing chair by the popping fire, arms folded, spectacles low on his nose, his *Putnam's Monthly* lying open on crossed legs. Nothing pleased him more on a Sunday afternoon than to bask in the bosom of his family circle in this richly formal room, his favorite. The Oriental-influenced Red Room, a silken refuge visible through an arched doorway flanked by six-foot stone obelisks, was his wife's preferred sanctuary.

Ancestral portraits lined the music room's rosewood-paneled walls, six generations of Hewitt "codfish aristoc-racy," most of them in the shipping trade; copper and cloth went to China, ice to the West Indies, and rum to slave-rich Africa on ships that came back laden with silks, teas, porcelains, sugar, cocoa, tobacco, and the molasses with which to make more rum. But the real merchant prince among the bunch was Mr. Hewitt's father, scowl-ing down from above the black marble fireplace, who'd diversified into the textile trade by founding Hewitt Mills and Dye Works, thus greatly augmenting the family for-tune.

And then, of course, there was August Hewitt him-self, represented by his wife's monumental full-length portrait—flanked by modestly draped, life-size statues of Artemis and Athena—who had negotiated a lucrative con-tract to produce U.S. Army uniforms back when almost no one seriously envisioned a war between the states. His foresight had heaped the family coffers to overflowing.

Little Grace, in her favorite apple green frock and pin-afore, lay curled up on Nell's lap, two middle fingers still somehow firmly lodged in a mouth gone lax with sleep. The grosgrain bow adorning the child's dark hair tickled Nell's chin, but not unpleasantly. Gracie's somnolent breathing, the lulling weight of her, her soapy-sweet little-girl scent, all filled Nell with a sense of utter well-being.

Across the room, Miss Edna Parrish sat propped up with pillows in her favorite parlor rocker—head back, eyes closed, mouth gaping, archaic mobcap slightly askew—looking for all the world like a strangely withered baby bird. Gracie had climbed out of her nursemaid's lap at the first wheezy snore and clambered up onto Nell's, dozing off almost instantly.

Through the velvet-swagged windows flanking the fire-place, Nell watched snow float down out of a pewter sky, her book—*Miss Ravenel's Conversion from Secession to*

Loyalty by Mr. DeForest—neglected in her hand. She
loved watching snow lay its glittering blanket over the
city—so opaque, so pristine, as if absolving the streets
beneath of their years of grime.

Boston had been a shock to her upon her arrival here
three years ago—so huge, so raucous, a buzzing hive in
which she'd felt not just lost but utterly invisible. How
she'd longed for the rustic familiarity of Cape Cod—at
first. Over time, the city gradually lost its daunting new-
ness and began to feel like home—*her* home. Just as she
became a part of Boston, so she became a part of the
Hewitt family. Gracie was the child of her heart, if not
her womb, and time had only served to cement her sense
of kinship with Viola Hewitt.

That kinship notwithstanding, it was rare that Nell
joined the family for these Sunday afternoon gatherings,
Viola having exempted her from her duties for the better
part of every weekend. On Saturdays, Nell often prowled
the Public Library, the Lecture Hall, or—her favorite—
the Natural History Museum. There were several other
Colonnade Row governesses with whom she'd struck up
an acquaintance as their charges played together in the
Common, and from time to time they would meet for
Saturday luncheon or a lingering afternoon tea—but as
Nell had little in common with them, no true friendships
ever sprang from these outings.

Every Sunday morning, Nell went to early Mass, a too-
brief low Mass for which she had to awaken and dress in
the predawn gloom, so that she would be free to watch
Gracie while Nurse Parrish and the Hewitts attended services at King's Chapel. After that, she was once more at
liberty to go her own way. If the afternoon was mild, she
might take a long walk—even in wintertime if the sun
was bright—or perhaps settle down with a book on a
bench in the Public Garden. When the weather was less
agreeable, as today, she often read or drew in her room.

She would be there now had Viola not specifically re-
quested her presence today.

*Gracie is better behaved with you than with Nurse Par-
rish,* Viola had told her, *and you know how Mr. Hewitt
gets when she starts fussing. He'll send her to the nursery
if she makes so much as a peep, and I so long for her
company this afternoon. You'll be home anyway, because
of the weather. Please say you'll sit with us.*

Unable to refuse much of anything to Viola, who'd
come to hold as dear a place in her heart as her own long-
departed mother, Nell had agreed. Mr. Hewitt had cast a
swift, jaundiced glance at Gracie when she abandoned
Nurse Parrish's lap for Nell's, but otherwise ignored her—
as he did her governess.

Nell tried to recall the last time she and Mr. Hewitt
had occupied the same room, and couldn't. That their
paths rarely crossed was due to his distaste for children
in general and—from all appearances, although it made
little sense—to Gracie in particular. At his insistence, the
child took all her meals, with the exception of Christmas
and Easter dinners, in the nursery with Nell. On weekdays
he put in long hours at his shipping office near the
wharves, dined at home with his wife and Martin—Harry
almost always ate elsewhere—then spent the remainder of
the evening at his club. He came and went on the week-
ends, as did Nell; on those rare occasions when they
passed each other in the hall, they merely nodded and
continued on their way.

"It's different," Mr. Hewitt said when the hymn ended.
"Not bad, actually, but that bit about God bestowing his
grace on all the sons of man, welcoming them into his
arms and what not . . . You might think about rephrasing
that."

Martin, standing by the piano, regarded his father with
a solemn intensity that might be interpreted by someone
who didn't know him well as simple filial deference. At

a quick glance, the flaxen-haired, smooth-skinned Martin looked younger than his twenty-one years; it was those eyes, and the depth of discernment in them, that lent him the aspect of an older, wiser man.

His mother closed the piano softly, not looking at either her husband or her youngest son.

From the front of the house came two *thwacks* of the door knocker. Nell heard the butler's purposefully hushed footsteps traverse the considerable length of the marble-floored center hall; a faint squeak of hinges; low male voices.

In the absence of a response from his son, Hewitt said, "It's just that one could interpret 'all the sons of man' as encompassing, say, the Jew, or the Chinaman. Edging awfully close to Unitarianism there."

Long seconds passed, with Martin studying his father in that quietly grave way of his. "Thank you, sir. I'll give it some thought." His gaze flicked almost imperceptibly toward Nell.

A soft knock drew their attention to the open doorway, in which Hodges stood holding a calling card on a silver salver. "For you, sir."

Motioning the elderly butler into the room, Mr. Hewitt snatched up the card. "It's Leo Thorpe. Dear, weren't you just saying we hadn't seen the Thorpes in far too long? Show him in, Hodges."

Just as August Hewitt looked to have been chiseled from translucent white alabaster, his friend Leo Thorpe could have been molded out of a great lump of pinkish clay. Florid and thickset, with snowy, well-oiled hair, his usual greeting was a jovial "How the devil are you?" Today however, he was much more subdued.

"Ah." Mr. Thorpe hesitated on the threshold, looking unaccountably ill at ease as he took them all in. "I didn't realize you were with—"

"I was just leaving." Martin offered his hand to the

older man as he exited the room. "Good to see you, sir."

Mr. Thorpe dismissed the sleeping nursemaid with a fleeting glance before turning his attention to Nell. Rather than rising from her chair, and thereby waking Gracie, she simply cast her gaze toward her open book, as if too absorbed in it to take much note of anything else. He hesitated, then looked away: the governess tucked back in the corner with her sleeping charge.

Nell didn't mind, having become adept not so much at mingling with Brahmin society as dissolving into it. Dr. Greaves was right: It could work to one's advantage for people to forget you were there. The formal calls and luncheons to which she often accompanied Viola Hewitt, with or without Gracie—Mrs. Bouchard having little tolerance for them and Viola needing help getting about—afforded, despite their tedium, the most remarkable revelations. Nell had innumerable sketches upstairs of fashionably dressed ladies and gentlemen whispering together over their fans, their champagne flutes, their teacups. They hardly ever whispered as softly as they should.

"Leo," Viola began, "we were just saying it's been far too long since we've had you and Eugenia over."

"Hm? Oh, yes. Quite."

"Why don't you join us for dinner Saturday? Ask Eugenia to call on me some morning this week, and we'll work out the details."

"Yes. Yes," he said distractedly. "I, er . . . That sounds splendid."

"Everything all right, Thorpe?" inquired Mr. Hewitt. "It isn't your gout acting up again, I hope. Here—have a seat."

Viola offered her guest tea, "Or perhaps something stronger," but he shook his head.

"This isn't really a social call, although I dearly wish it were. It's about . . . well, your son." Thorpe fiddled with the brim of his top hat, upended on his knee with his gloves inside. "But you see, Hewitt, I was actually hoping we could speak in private."

Viola's smile was of the long-suffering but taking-it-well variety. "You can talk in front of me, Leo. What mischief has Harry gotten himself into this time?" As August Hewitt's longtime confidant and personal attorney, Leo Thorpe had been most accommodating, over the years, in sweeping the worst of Harry's libertine excesses under the carpet. Mr. Thorpe was also, as of the last city election, a member of Boston's Board of Aldermen, and thus responsible, along with the mayor and members of the Common Council, for all facets of the municipal government.

"Not another row over a woman, I hope," said her husband. "It *was* awfully late when he came in last night—or rather, this morning. Heard him crash into something down here, so I got up to check on him. Found him reeling drunk, of course, and he'd lost his new cashmere coat and scarf somewhere—or had them stolen off him, or gambled them away. Slept through church, as usual. Had a bath drawn around noon, and his breakfast tray brought up to him while he soaked in it—must have spent over an hour in there."

"It's not about Harry." Rubbing the back of his neck, Mr. Thorpe informed his hostess that he would perhaps, after all, appreciate a nice, stiff whiskey.

She rang for it. "You can't mean that our *Martin* has done something . . . ?"

"Absurd." Her husband banished the notion with a wave of his hand.

"I couldn't imagine it," the alderman agreed.

"We only have the two sons, Thorpe," Hewitt said. His wife fingered the primitive turquoise necklace half-buried in the froth of blond lace at her throat, her mouth set in a bleak line.

Thorpe looked toward the doorway as if hoping the drinks tray had materialized there.

"If it wasn't Martin or Harry . . ." Hewitt persisted.

"A man was arrested last night on Purchase Street in the Fort Hill district, outside a place known as Flynn's. It's a . . . well, it's a sort of boardinghouse for sailors, among"—his gaze slid toward Viola—"other things. Gave his name as William Toussaint. That's how they—"

"Toussaint?" Viola sat up straight. Her French pronunciation was a good deal better than Mr. Thorpe's. She looked away when her husband cast her a quizzical glance.

"That's right," Thorpe said. "So that's the name they booked him under at the station house, but then this morning, when the shift changed, he was recognized by one of the day boys—Johnston, a veteran." He took a deep breath, eyeing the couple warily. "Please understand—it came as a shock to me, too. The man we arrested last night is William—your son William."

The Hewitts gaped at him.

"Seems Johnston hauled him in back in July of 'fifty-three," Thorpe explained, "along with almost a hundred others, when they raided those North End bawd"—he glanced at Viola—"houses of ill fame. That's how he knew him."

Finding his voice, Hewitt said, "That . . . that was fifteen years ago. How could he possibly re—"

"He remembers the raid because it was the biggest one they ever staged, next to Saint Ann Street in 'fifty-one. And he remembers your son because, well . . . he was a Hewitt."

Viola stared at nothing, as if in a trance. "Will was home for the summer, and we hadn't left for the Cape yet. It was the day after his eighteenth birthday. He'd gone out for the evening with Robbie. Your Jack was probably with them, too," she told Leo. "But Robbie came home without him around midnight . . ."

"Impossible," declared Mr. Hewitt. "Must just be some passing resemblance. William is dead."

Dennis, one of the Hewitts' two handsome young blue-liveried footmen, came with the drinks, which he offered, unsurprisingly, to everyone but Nell. Had Viola noticed, she would have said something, as she invariably did when Nell was slighted by one of the staff. Governesses, because they were often treated more like family members than employees, tended to draw the wrath of a house-hold's domestic staff; but at least most of them had been born into privilege and were therefore nominally deserv-ing of a show of respect. Not so with Nell, who was widely scorned by servants with similar working-class back-grounds since they regarded themselves as her equals—or in some cases, her betters—and resented having to serve her. Particularly scornful were Mrs. Mott, Dennis, Mr. Hewitt's valet, and most of the maids—especially the sul-len Mary Agnes.

Thorpe took his whiskey neat and swallowed it in two gulps. "Captain Baxter—he's in charge of Division Two, which covers Fort Hill—he sent for me this morning, be-cause of, well, who you are, and knowing I'm your at-torney—and your friend. I went down to the station house and saw him. August, it's William—your William."

"He's alive," Viola said tremulously. "I don't believe it."

"I *can't* believe it," insisted her husband. "If he's alive, why is he only surfacing now? Why did he never let us know? And why on earth would he be listed on the An-dersonville death roll? It said he died of dysentery on August ninth, eighteen sixty-four. Why would it say that if it weren't true?"

"I asked him that," said Thorpe. "I asked him a great many things, but he wasn't what you'd call forthcoming.

If you don't mind my bringing this up, has anyone gone to the prisoners' graveyard at Andersonville and seen his—"

"Robbie has his own grave," Hewitt replied. "As for William . . ." He glanced at his wife. "It seems there were a great many prisoner fatalities on that particular day. He was interred in a mass grave."

"Cursèd business," Thorpe muttered.

"I would assume, Thorpe, that you asked this fellow point blank if he was William Hewitt."

"Certainly—just to make it official. He wouldn't answer, but I knew it was him. He's a surgeon, yes?" Thorpe reached into his coat for something swathed in a handkerchief. Unwrapping it, he revealed a strip of tortoise-shell with a crack in it.

Viola sucked in a breath as he unfolded from the object a slender, curved blade stained with something dark. Nell craned her neck slightly for a better view.

Turning it this way and that, Thorpe said, "I gather it's some sort of folding scalpel."

"A bistoury, actually," Nell said.

Thorpe turned and blinked at her.

She scolded herself for calling attention to her presence, but the damage was done. "Bistouries are surgical knives that are quite narrow," she explained, "and sometimes curved, like that one. And very sharp at the tip." Gracie stirred, but settled back down when Nell rubbed her back.

"It's obviously a well-used blade," Thorpe said, "but he's kept it honed. The blade is stamped TIEMANN."

"That's the manufacturer," said Viola. "That scalp—bistoury is part of a pocket surgery kit I gave Will for Christmas when he came home that last . . . well, it was his last Christmas with us, in 'sixty-three. He and Robbie were both granted two-week furloughs. Robbie was with us the whole time, but Will only stayed two days. The last time I spoke to him was Christmas night, as he was heading up for bed. The next morning, he was gone. I never saw him again."

"A *pocket* surgery kit?" Thorpe said.

"Yes, it was this little leather roll with the instruments tucked inside. He had his full-size kit, of course, but I thought a portable set might come in handy. Where did you get that?"

"From the policeman who arrested your son. William . . ." Wrapping the bistoury back up, he said, "I'm sorry, Viola. William used it to cut a man's throat."

Color leeched from her face. Her husband sat back, slid off his spectacles, rubbed the bridge of his nose.

The alderman poured himself another whiskey. "Your son—or rather, William Toussaint—has been formally charged with murder. He killed a merchant seaman in an alley next to the boardinghouse late last night. Fellow by the name of Ernest Tulley."

"No," Viola said dazedly. "No. I don't believe it. Why on earth would he do such a thing?"

"He wouldn't say, even after the boys . . . well, they, uh, interrogated him at some length last night, but he wasn't talking. As near as they can figure, it was a frenzy of intoxication. The other sailors say he'd come there to smoke opium. There's a room set aside for—"

"*Opium?*" She shook her head. "My Will . . . he would never . . ." Her normally throaty voice grew shrill. "He's a *surgeon,* for God's sake! August, tell him." She pounded the arms of her wheelchair. "Tell him! Will could never—"

"Viola . . ." Her husband rose and went to her.

"*Tell him,*" she implored, clutching his coat sleeve. "Please, August."

Nell stared, dumbfounded. Never in the three years she'd known Viola Hewitt had she seen her lose her composure, even for a moment.

"Viola, I'll take care of—"

"There's been some horrible mistake," she told Thorpe, her voice strained, clearly struggling to get herself in hand. "I know my Will. He . . . he was always . . . spirited, but he could never take a life. He's a healer. Leo, please . . ."

Her husband took her by the shoulders, gentling his voice. "Do you trust me, Viola?"

"*You* know he didn't do this, don't you?"

"You must get hold of yourself, my dear. Giving vent to one's emotions merely makes them more obdurate— you know that. Now, I'm going to take Leo upstairs, to the library, to sort this thing—"

"No. *No!* Stay here. I'll stay calm. I'll—"

"You've too delicate a disposition for such matters, my dear. I'll take care of everything, but I must caution you not to make mention of this to anyone—and that includes Martin and Harry."

"I can't tell them their own brother is alive? And arrested for murder? For heaven's sake, August, they'll find out sooner or later."

"Just trust me, Viola. Thorpe." Hewitt motioned his friend to follow as he left the room.

"August!" she cried as the two men headed for the curved stairway that led from the back end of the center hall to the upper floors. "What do you mean, you're going to 'take care of everything'? What does that mean, August?"

"Mrs. Hewitt . . ." Nell began.

"I've got to get upstairs," she said in a quavering voice as she grabbed the folding canes off the back of her chair. "Where's Mrs. Bouchard?"

"It's Sunday. She's got the day—"

"You help me, then." Yanking the canes open, she planted them on the Oriental rug. "Hurry!"

"Ma'am . . ." Nell looked from the sleeping child in her

arms toward the ceiling, where footsteps squeaked; the
library was directly overhead, right off the second-floor
landing.

"You're right. By the time I got up there . . . You go!"

"Me? They'll never let me—"

"Tiptoe upstairs and listen outside the door."

"Eavesdrop?"

"Just don't let anyone see you. Be on the lookout for
Mrs. Mott. She can be quiet as death, that one."

"Mrs. Hewitt, your husband will dismiss me for sure
if he catches me." He'd sacked employees for far less.

"He won't if I make enough of a fuss. You know he
can't bear to distress me. Nell, please." Tears trembled in
Viola's eyes. "I'm pleading with you. I've *got* to find out
what he's planning to do. I'm so afraid . . . *Please.*"
Plucking a lace-edged handkerchief from her sleeve, she
blotted her eyes and held out her arms. "I'll take Gracie.
Hurry!"

Gracie mewed like a vexed kitten when Nell rose and
carried her across the room. "No . . ." the child griped
sleepily, no doubt assuming she was being taken upstairs
to finish her nap in the nursery. "Want Miseeney." She
jammed those two fingers in her mouth, eyes half-closed,
pinkened right cheek imprinted from the double row of
tiny covered buttons on Nell's bodice.

"Miseeney has to go now," Nell said softly as she
tucked the child in her adoptive mother's lap. "Nana will
hold you." Having Gracie call her "Nana" had been Viola's idea; it would inspire too many raised eyebrows in
public, she reasoned, for such a young child to call a
woman of her advanced years "Mama."

Nell stole upstairs as quietly as she could, thankful for
the carpeted stairs and the plush Aubusson on the landing.
Muffled voices grew louder as she neared the slightly ajar
library door, where she paused, sketched a swift sign of
the cross. *Please, Saint Dismas, please, please, please*

don't let him open that door and find me lurking here.
Funny how she still directed her prayers to the patron saint of thieves, after all these years.

"He could hang for this, you know," said Leo Thorpe.

"Has he been arraigned yet?" asked Hewitt.

"Yes, and he was utterly uncooperative. Waived his right to counsel, made no attempt to defend himself. Refused to plead, so the court entered a not-guilty plea on his behalf. He did ask for bail, though, and I understand he seemed quite put out when it was denied, as is customary in cases that warrant the death penalty. He'll be detained until trial."

Hewitt grunted. "Arrogant bastard didn't think he needed a lawyer. Serves him right."

"Of course . . . given your position and influence, if you were of a mind to get the bail decision overturned . . ."

"I'm not about to grease some judge's palm just so that damnable blackguard can be free to cut some other poor bastard's throat."

This was the first time Nell had ever heard coarse language spoken in this house. She would not have expected it from the rigidly proper August Hewitt, even with no ladies present.

"Are you . . . quite sure, old chap? He is, after all, your son. I mean, I appreciate that you're less than sympathetic right now, but given time to reflect—"

"*Not one red cent.* Damn him," Hewitt said shakily. "*Damn him* for doing this to his mother. To go three years—*over* three years—without letting us know he was alive, and then this . . . this . . . By Jove, he committed murder! If he was innocent, he would have pled not guilty right from the start. And opium? He was always a bad egg. Sad to say, but even as a little child, I knew he would come to no good."

"Heartbreaking, when they're born that way."

"Of course, Viola is soft-hearted when it comes to William. Understandable. He's her firstborn, and women are sentimental creatures."

"Quite."

"What address did he give?" Hewitt asked.

"Some hotel. He doesn't have a permanent address."

"Well, not here in Boston, but surely—"

"Anywhere. He appears to be something of a nomad."

"A Hewitt wandering around homeless. Never thought I'd see the day."

"Hmm . . . yes. Quite so." Thorpe cleared his throat. "Say, Hewitt, is it true you've got a bottle of hundred-year-old cognac locked up in that cabinet?"

"It is, but you're daft if you think you're getting any. It's the last of a case my grandfather bought from Hennessy's first shipment to New York in seventeen ninety-four, and I'm saving it for the birth of my first grandchild. There's a nice tawny port in that decanter—help yourself."

"I do believe I will."

"Cigar?"

"Capital!"

To occupy herself in the ensuing silence, and to rationalize her presence there, should she be discovered, Nell perused the paintings hung close together on the darkly paneled walls—Mrs. Hewitt's portraits of her family, bordered in ornate gilt frames. Here on the landing there was one of her husband with his three younger sons and several of those sons posing separately and in pairs. Achingly handsome men, in particular the late Robbie, with his thick, gilded hair and dramatic black eyebrows. Around the corner, in the corridor leading to the family bedrooms, were many more of her paintings, most of the Hewitt scions ranging in age from infancy through their twenties. Notably absent from the collection was any depiction of their eldest son. All Nell really knew about

William Hewitt was that he'd been schooled, from early childhood, in England.

When Hewitt spoke again, his tone was contemplative. "There was always a William Problem, from the moment he was born. I must say, Viola handled his youthful misdeeds with remarkable aplomb, but this . . . He's gone too far. I won't have her exposed to him. Her health's been fragile, you know, ever since she fell ill in Europe. It's not just her limbs—she tires so quickly. I don't think she could endure the strain, if I were to let William back in her life—not with what he's become."

"Damn fine cigar," Thorpe muttered.

"Rest assured, Thorpe, it is my intent that William be prosecuted to the fullest extent possible—but under this assumed name, mind you. What is it, again? Something French."

"Toussaint," Thorpe replied, still mispronouncing it. "But won't he be recognized for who he really is?"

"Unlikely. William grew up in England, remember, except for summers, and he always went with us to the Cape. He actually spent very little time in Boston, and Viola could never get him to go calling with her, or to dinners and dances, so he met hardly anyone. Robbie was the only one he spent any time with—and your Jack, of course. Robbie wouldn't go anywhere without him—remember?"

"Yes, quite. Oh—! Did I tell you Orville Pratt and I are bringing Jack aboard as a junior partner in the firm? We're going to make it official when we announce Jack's engagement to Cecilia Pratt—probably during the Pratts' annual ball."

"Excellent! Jack's a fine young man—as was Robbie, despite William's efforts to corrupt them both. But as to his being recognized, rest assured there's not a soul in Boston—aside from Jack, I suppose—who would know him if he saw him on the street. Except, of course, for those fellows at the station house. They're the ones who trouble me. How many are there?"

"Well, Johnston, of course—the one who remembered arresting him. He told one or two others, including Captain Baxter, and Baxter summoned me. I gave orders for no one else to be told until I could speak to you, and I had him put in his own cell, away from the other prisoners."

"Those who know must be silenced. From what I hear, there isn't a single member of the Boston Police Department who wouldn't sell his mother into white slavery for the price of a pint of ale."

Even through the door, Nell heard Thorpe's deep sigh.

"Offer them whatever it will take for them to forget who William Toussaint really is," said Hewitt. "And of course I expect a certain zeal in bringing him to justice. Perhaps a bonus for those involved once he's found guilty and sentenced. Have this Captain Baxter handle it. But talk to him soon, before he and the others start opening their mouths."

"It will be done within the hour."

"I don't want my name mentioned, Thorpe, or yours. It goes no further than Baxter."

"What about the girl? That pretty little governess?"

"Nell? She's devoted to my wife. She'll keep her mouth shut if I explain to her that it's in Viola's best interest—which, of course, it is, although Viola won't see it that way. As for William, I want him out of that station house and away from prying eyes as soon as it can be arranged."

"He's to be transferred to the county jail on Charles Street tomorrow to await trial."

"Good. Bury him as deep in that bloody mausoleum as you can get him." Now it was Hewitt's turn to sigh. "Damn him."

"Miss Sweeney?"

Nell whirled around, her heart kicking. "Master Martin." He'd come around the corner, evidently on his way downstairs. "I was just looking at your mother's paintings," she said as she walked past him, into the corridor proper, so as not to be heard by the men in the library.

"Extraordinary, aren't they?" He looked about fifteen when he smiled like that. "I keep telling her she should hang them downstairs, where visitors can see them, but she thinks that would be vulgar."

Taking in the myriad paintings lining the long, high-ceilinged passageway, she said, "I was wondering why there are none of your brother William."

"I assumed you knew." Martin shoved his hands in his trouser pockets. "He was the black sheep of the family."

"I suppose I suspected that. Nobody ever talks about him."

"Father doesn't like to hear his name—even now that he's gone. I find it hard to understand. I mean, he can't have been any worse than Harry, and Harry's always in one fix or another—either it's his drinking, or his gambling, or his . . ." Martin looked away, clearly discomfited.

"His mill girls?" This from Harry himself as he emerged from his room down the hall, teeth flashing, tawny hair well brushed and gleaming. The only evidence of last night's excesses would be his complexion, which had that bleached-out Sunday morning look to it, and a certain puffiness around the eyes. "Say it, Martin. Our lovely Miseeney is much like Mother, you know—unshockable." Surveying Nell's dress from neckline to hem, he said, "And doesn't she look fetching this morning. Is that a new shade of gray?"

"Morning?" Martin scoffed. "It's two-thirty in the afternoon, Harry. And I hardly think Miss Sweeney appreciates your mockery."

"Miss Sweeney recognizes a good-natured jest when she hears it. Are you saying you're the only one who's allowed to flirt with her? Hardly seems fair."

"I wasn't . . . We weren't . . ." Even in the dimly lit corridor, Nell could see Martin's ears flare crimson.

"If he takes any liberties," Harry told Nell as he sauntered past, "you must call me at once." With a wink, and leaning conspiratorially close, he added, "I'd give anything to witness that."

THIS was the first time Nell had ever seen Viola Hewitt cry. It wasn't gentle weeping, either, but great, hoarse sobs that shook her to the bones as she sat hunched over the writing desk in her pink and gold sitting room. "It's all my fault," she kept wailing into her handkerchief. "All my fault . . ."

"Of course it's not your fault," Nell soothed as she kept half an eye on Gracie in her Nana's adjacent boudoir, dragging hatboxes out of the closet while Viola's lady's maid, Paola Gabrielli, sat in the corner sewing a veil onto a purple velvet bonnet. "How could it be your fault?"

Viola shook her head, tears dripping onto the letter in front of her, a letter that began, *Dear Will . . .* "Oh, God. I'm a horrible mother."

"You're a wonderful mother."

"No, you don't know. You don't know. And now . . . and now my baby, my Will . . . They're going to h-hang him. And it's all my fault."

Her fault? Did she knife that man outside Flynn's boardinghouse? Did she tell Alderman Thorpe to bury her son "as deep as you can get him" in the Charles Street Jail? There were people responsible for begetting this situation and making it worse, but it seemed to Nell that Viola Hewitt was as blameless a victim of it as Ernest Tulley.

Heedless of the tearstains dotting the letter, Viola folded it and tucked it into an envelope, on which she

STILL LIFE WITH MURDER 47

wrote, in her signature violet ink, *Dr. William Hewitt* before drawing up short. She jammed the pen back in the crystal inkwell, tore the envelope away, and replaced it with a fresh one, which she addressed to *Mr. William Toussaint*. She heated a stick of violet sealing wax in the flame of her desktop candle, melted it into a tiny silver spoon, dripped the molten wax onto the envelope's flap, and imprinted it with her monogrammed insignia.

"You must take this to Will," she told Nell.

"What?" Nell exclaimed as her employer shoved the letter in her hand.

"You're the only one who can do this, Nell. God knows August won't. He won't even acknowledge Will as a member of this family. He doesn't care if he hangs— you told me so yourself. And he'll be livid if I bring Martin or Harry in on this."

"Mrs. Hewitt, I—"

"Do it this afternoon. Once they transfer him to the county jail, you'll have a hard time gaining access to him. Right now, he's at the Division Two station house, which is on Williams Court. I used to bring blankets and Bibles to the prisoners there. Each holding cell has a sort of anteroom for visitors. You'll be able to talk to him without anyone overhearing you."

"What if Mr. Hewitt sees me leave? Or Hitchens?" The devoted valet reported everything to his employer. August Hewitt would cast her out in a heartbeat if he found out she'd gone behind his back. Nell's most harrowing nightmare—the one from which she literally awoke in a sweat from time to time—was the one where she found herself back in her old life, with no home, no family . . . and worst of all, no Gracie. "Won't it look suspicious, me going out after deciding to stay home because it was snowing so hard?"

"If anyone asks, you can tell them you're planning to

paint Boston Common in the snow, and you need to see how it looks."

It was a good lie; Nell was grudgingly impressed. But what if it didn't work? Going behind August Hewitt's back this way was far worse than eavesdropping at his library door. She'd never heard him sound so furious— or determined. If he found out what she'd done, he would fire her, and Viola would be helpless to prevent it. Nobody defied August Hewitt and got away with it, ever.

And, too, the notion of walking into a police station filled Nell with a cold dread all its own. "I don't think I could handle this, Mrs. Hewitt."

Misjudging the reason for her trepidation, Viola said, "Nell, believe me, you have nothing to fear from my Will. He's incapable of doing what they say he did. And he would die before he'd let an opium pipe touch his lips. He thinks it's a blight on humanity—he once told me so himself. He said they should outlaw it here, as they have in China. He's a good man, a *surgeon*. He would never . . . cause you harm, if that's what you're thinking, or—"

"It's not that. I just . . . I . . ."

"I need to find out what really happened, from Will himself. Obviously I can't go myself, much as I wish I could. I've dreamed of seeing him again—literally. I wake up sobbing from those dreams. But I have to think of Will. If I were to visit him, everyone would notice me. They know who I am there. Someone would figure out who Will really is, and he's obviously gone to great pains to prevent that. And, too, if Mr. Hewitt were to find out I'd defied him . . ." Her brow furrowed. "He mustn't find out you've been there, either. Use a false name. Say you're doing charitable work. Talk to Will alone if you can. Tell him I'm going to try to overturn the bail decision tomorrow so he can get out of there."

"Can you do that? Without Mr. Hewitt finding out?"

"The husband of an acquaintance of mine is a judge in

the criminal court. Horace Bacon is his name. I happen
to know she likes to live beyond her means, and I've
heard rumors Horace has accrued a fair amount of debt.
I can't see him turning down my request if it's accompanied by a nice, fat envelope. And if it's fat enough, I
imagine you can convince him to expedite the process and
keep my name off any paperwork having to do with—"

"*I* can convince him?"

"You're the only one I can ask to do any of this, Nell."
Frowning, she said, "I'll need to hire a lawyer, too."

"Won't the court appoint a public defender?"

"No, we need our own man, someone very good and
very discreet, who'll agree to keep Mr. Hewitt out of it.
That will be trickier than the business about the bail. My
husband knows just about every lawyer in Boston."

A flurry of nonsense babbling drew Nell's attention to
the bedroom, where Gracie was gamboling in circles,
arms outstretched, an ostrich-plumed bonnet jammed low
over her face. Paola—Nell's only real friend on the Hewitts' staff—caught Nell's eye and smiled. A darkly beautiful woman about Viola's age, although she looked much
younger, Paola was known as "Miss Gabrielli" despite
being married—assuming her husband was still alive, for
she hadn't been back to Italy in the thirty or so years she'd
served as Viola's lady's maid. By the same token, tradition regarding housekeepers dictated that Evelyn Mott, a
spinster, be addressed as "Mrs. Mott." None of it made
much sense to Nell, but she'd long ago stopped trying to
understand Brahmin customs.

"I can't leave," Nell said. "Who'll keep an eye on Gracie?" She was a child who got into everything and needed
frequent running after, which was why Viola was unequal
to the task.

"Nurse Parrish will awaken from her nap soon enough.
In the meantime, Paola can set aside her work long
enough keep a proper watch over her. Please, *please*,

Nell—I beseech you. I *must* find out what really happened last night. I won't rest until I do." Fresh tears pooled in her eyes. "You're the only one I trust, and I know you can do this. You're so strong, so clever and capable. And people respond to you. *Men* respond to you. You'll have no trouble getting in to see Will."

Nell pressed the heel of her hand to her forehead, feeling trapped and woozy and increasingly resigned. If not for Viola Hewitt, she would still be in East Falmouth, wearing frayed castoffs as she tended to Cyril Greaves's needs. Not that she'd begrudged him any of it, God knew. She'd been fond of Dr. Greaves, very much so. He'd quite literally saved her life—only to remake her into the kind of woman who could function in a world of glittering privilege. He'd let her go regretfully, but with a measure of grace that had touched Nell deeply, because she'd known he was doing it for her. For all that, she would be eternally grateful; but she was grateful to Viola Hewitt as well, exceedingly so, for having invited her into this world—and for giving her Gracie, the only child she would ever have.

In a quiet voice still rusty with tears, Viola said, "You're lucky in a way, you know that?"

"Know it? I think about it every morning when I awaken and every night as I'm falling asleep."

"I don't mean that. I mean . . . You're so much freer than I am, really—freer than any woman of rank. We're all kept shrouded in cocoons of propriety lest we somehow bring scandal upon our families—and there are more ways of doing that than you can imagine. Ah, but the governess . . . neither servant nor pampered gentlewoman, but something quite apart. Do you have any idea how blessed you are to be able to come and go as you please? The demands of my class have crippled me more surely than the affliction that put me in this chair. You, on the other hand, have no cocoon to bind you."

Reaching out, Viola stroked Nell's cheek. "You're a butterfly. How I do envy you."

Chapter 2

"A lady to see you, Toussaint," announced the pock-marked guard through the iron-barred door of the holding cell.

"I don't know any ladies." The voice from within—drowsy-deep, British-accented, and vaguely bored—did not belong here. It was a voice meant for the opera box, the ballroom, the polo field . . . not this fetid little police station cage.

Nell's view of William Hewitt was limited by her position against the wall of the cramped visitors' alcove and the fact that it was only the cell's door that was comprised of open grillwork; the walls were solid brick. From her angle, all she could make out through the barred door were two long legs in fawn trousers, right ankle propped on left knee. A hand appeared and struck a match against the sole of a well-made black shoe. The hand was long-fingered, capable—a deft hand with a scalpel, she would guess.

Or a bistoury.

"Her name is Miss Chapel," said the guard as he hung Nell's snow-dampened coat and scarf on a hook on the alcove wall. "She's from the Society for the Relief of Convicts and Indigents."

The aroma of tobacco wafted from the cell. "I don't suppose it would do any good to point out that I am neither a convict nor an indigent."

"You'll be a convict soon as they can manage to drag your sorry"—the guard glanced at Nell—"drag you in front of a jury. And then you'll be just another murdering wretch swinging from a rope over at the county jail."

Nell clutched to her chest the scratchy woollen blanket and Bible she'd brought. She hated this. She hated being in this monstrous brick box of a building, surrounded by blue-uniformed cops who all seemed to stare at her as if they knew who she really was and why this was the last place she should be. She hated the way Gracie had cried and reached for her, squirming in Paola's arms, as she'd put on her coat to come here. And she *really* hated having to confront this man who may or may not have cut another man's throat the night before in a delirium born of opium—or lunacy.

"You can give him them things, ma'am, but I'll have to check 'em first." The guard held his hand out. "The blanket, then the Bible." He unfolded and shook out the former, fanned the pages of the latter, and handed them back.

"You can sit here if you've a mind to pray or what have you." The guard scraped a bench away from the wall and set it up facing the iron-barred door from about five feet away. "You'd best keep your distance. If he tries anything, like grabbing you through the bars or throwing matches at you, you give me a holler—make it loud, 'cause I'll be all the way down the hall."

Matches? Nell thought about the flammable crinoline shaping her skirt, and the newspaper stories of women burned alive when their dresses brushed candles or gas jets. She stood motionless after the guard left, listening to the receding jangle of his keys as he returned to his station at the far end of the hall.

"I'll take the blanket." The long legs shifted; bedropes squeaked. "You can keep the Bible."

With a steadying breath, Nell stepped away from the wall and approached the door to the cell, staying a few feet back, as the guard had advised.

Its occupant was standing now, his weight resting on one hip, drawing on a cigarette as he watched her come into view. He was tall, somewhat over six feet, with hair falling like haphazard strokes of black ink into indolent eyes. His left eyelid was swollen and discolored, with a crusted-over cut at the outer edge. Two more contusions stained his beard-darkened jaw on that side, and his lower lip was split. *They interrogated him at some length last night.*

Even unshaved and unshorn, his face badly beaten, there could be no mistaking that this man was Viola Hewitt's son. It wasn't just his coloring—the black hair and fair skin—but his height, his bearing, the patrician planes and hollows of his face.

His gaze swept over her from top to bottom as he exhaled a plume of smoke, but it felt different than when Harry did it. With Harry there was always a speculative glimmer behind the roguish audacity in his eyes, a spark of real heat that he could never fully disguise. The eyes of the man assessing her at the moment betrayed no such illicit interest. He took her measure as indifferently as if she were a mannequin in a shop window.

Nell felt like a mannequin sometimes, or a doll, given Viola Hewitt's enthusiasm for dressing her. *I'm too old and too crippled to wear the newest styles,* she would tell Nell, *so you must wear them for me.* The dresses she ordered were always of the latest Paris fashion, but discreet in cut and color, as befitted a governess—no stripes or plaids, no swags, ruffles, bows, or rosettes, no feathered hats. Today's costume was typical: a gunmetal day dress with the sleek new "princess" skirt and a small, front-tilted black hat. The only jewelry she wore on a regular basis was the pretty little gold pendant watch Viola had given her their first Christmas together. Just this morning, Viola had praised her "restrained elegance." Nell didn't think she would ever understand how rich people could interpret such dreariness as elegant.

As for William Hewitt, he might have passed for something akin to elegant this time yesterday, but now . . . He was in his shirtsleeves; moreover, his shirt was flecked near the top with brownish-red stains—whether his own blood or Ernest Tulley's, she had no way of knowing. His collar and tie were both missing, giving him a decidedly disreputable air. Adding to the effect was the cigarette, which Nell had never seen a man of his station smoke, although she'd heard they were catching on in certain fast circles.

He came toward her, hand outstretched.

She stumbled back, dropping the Bible and knocking over the bench.

He looked at her through the bars, not smiling exactly, although there was a hint of something in his eyes that might have been amusement. *Idiot!* Nell berated herself. She knew not to show fear around dangerous men. A man with the predatory instinct was like a wolf; if he sensed your weakness, you were done for. It was a hard lesson, but one she'd learned well. She was out of practice, that was it; too much soft living among civilized people.

He gestured toward the blanket wadded up in her arms. "I was just reaching for the—"

"Of course. I . . . Here." Swallowing her trepidation, she stepped just close enough to push the blanket through the bars. The unbuttoned cuffs of his sleeves, which should have been white, were stiff and brown, as if en-crusted with mud; but of course it wasn't mud.

He took the blanket, shook it out, and draped it over his shoulders, chafing his arms through it—curious, since it was quite warm in there, thanks to a wood stove out in the hall. "Good day, Miss Chapel." He turned his back to her in brusque dismissal.

Retrieving the Bible, she stammered, "I . . . I actually need to—"

"Trust me when I assure you that any time spent pray-ing over me would be quite wasted." He crossed with a slight limp to the cot he'd been sitting on before, one of two against opposite walls of the windowless cell. Both mattresses were sunken and lumpy, their ticking soiled with a constellation of stains that didn't bear thinking about. There was no pillow, no furniture—just an empty stone-china chamber pot in one corner and a tin bowl of gruel studded with cigarette butts in the other.

He flung his cigarette into the gruel and sat again, stiffly. Tucking the blanket around him, he leaned back against the wall, yawned, and closed his eyes.

"I didn't come here to pray over you, Dr. Hewitt," Nell said.

If he had any reaction to her use of his real name, he kept it to himself.

"Your mother sent me," she said.

He opened his eyes, but didn't look at her.

"She's brokenhearted over what's—"

"Go away, Miss Chapel." He shut his eyes again.

"It's Miss Sweeney, actually."

"Go away, Miss . . ." He looked at her, interest lighting his eyes for the first time since she'd arrived. It was the Irish surname, she knew. He glanced again at her fine dress, her kid gloves, and chic hat—and for the first time, he really looked at her face. "Who are you?"

"My name is Nell Sweeney. I work for your mother. I

gave a false name because . . . well, she sent me here secretly. Your father doesn't . . . he doesn't want anyone to
know who you really are."

It took a moment, but comprehension dawned. "He just
wants William Toussaint to be quietly tried and hanged,
thus solving forever the William Problem." When Nell
didn't deny it, he chuckled weakly, but something dark
shadowed his eyes, just for a moment. "So you work for
my mother, eh? As what, some sort of companion? Or are
you a new nurse? Did she finally oust Mrs. Bouchard for
having a backbone?"

"No, I was trained as a nurse, but it's not what I do—
Mrs. Bouchard is still there. And although I do believe
your mother has come to regard me as a sort of companion, officially I'm a governess. Your parents hired me to
help Nurse Parrish care for a child they adopted."

"Adopted?" He sat up, staring at her. A bitter gust of
laughter degenerated into a coughing fit. "Haven't they
ruined enough sons?" he managed as he fumbled inside
his coat.

"It's a little girl, actually. Gracie—she's three."

"I pity her." Dr. Hewitt produced a small, decorative
tin labeled BULL DURHAM, which contained prerolled cigarettes, and put one between his lips. "I mean, I'm sure
you're a capable governess," he said as he lit it. In the
corona of light from the match, his face had a damp,
candle-wax pallor. "You strike me as a sensible woman,
in spite of the knocking over of the bench. But it is my
opinion that people should recognize when they're hopeless at something, and give it up—and if there were ever
two people utterly hopeless at parenting, it's Viola and
August Hewitt."

He bundled himself in the blanket again and leaned
back against the wall, coughing tiredly as he puffed on
the cigarette, his face sheened with perspiration.

"Are you sick?" Nell asked.

"Not strictly speaking."

"It's been my observation that surgeons are ill equipped to diagnose themselves."

"If I were still a surgeon, I suppose that might be a consideration."

"You're not a surgeon anymore?"

"Christ, look at me!"

Rattled by his vehemence—and by the blasphemy, which her ears were unused to of late—Nell turned and busied herself righting the bench. She sat, smoothing her skirts just to have something to do with her hands.

"As I said, Miss Sweeney, when one is hopeless at something, the wisest course is to just give it up. Better for all concerned."

She decided to redirect the conversation to her reasons for coming here. "Your mother really is very distraught over your arrest, Dr. Hewitt. She sent me here to . . . well, among other things, to find out what actually happened last night."

He regarded her balefully. "If I didn't tell the men who did this to me"—he pointed to his face—"why on earth would I tell you?"

"For your mother's sake?"

A harsh burst of laughter precipitated another coughing fit. "You will have to do much, *much* better than that, Miss Sweeney."

Why, oh why couldn't Viola have found someone else to do this? Changing tack, Nell said, "She intends to hire an attorney to represent you."

"A singularly idiotic notion."

"I beg your pardon?"

He covered another yawn with the hand holding the cigarette, which was quivering, she noticed. "Why waste the fellow's time?"

"A rather nihilistic outlook, considering your life is at stake."

"Nihilistic?" Dr. Hewitt regarded her with amused incredulity. "Where the devil does a girl like you learn about *nihilism?*"

Nell sat a little straighter, spine and corset stays aligned in stiff indignation. "It isn't only surgeons who learn to read, Dr. Hewitt. There was a German philosopher named Heinrich Jacobi who—"

"Yes, I'm familiar with his work—it was assigned to me when I was reading philosophy at Oxford. What I'm wondering is why *you* read it."

"The physician I was apprenticed to—the one who trained me in nursing—he took it upon himself to tutor me in various disciplines."

"Did he, now." Before Nell could ponder what he meant by that, he said, "What's this fellow's name? I know most of the physicians in the city, at least by reputation."

"He lives on Cape Cod, near your parents' summer cottage in Waquoit. His name is Cyril Greaves."

"Is that where you're from, then? Waquoit?"

"Near there—East Falmouth. Dr. Hewitt, I didn't come here to talk about myself."

"Yet I find you suddenly fascinating, given your unexpected dimensions, and I've been so frightfully bored. Was he an older man, this Dr. Greaves, or . . ."

"Forty-four when I left his employ."

"Not that old, then. How long were you apprenticed to him?"

"Four years, starting when I was eighteen."

"And before that?"

Nell lifted the Bible from the bench next to her and placed it on her lap like a talisman, all too aware of how defensive she looked. "I'm afraid I don't really see the point of—"

"Indulge me. I've been quite starved for conversation in this place." He took a thoughtful pull on his cigarette.

"You had a family, presumably. Parents? Brothers and sisters? What did your father do?"

What didn't he do? "He worked on the docks, mostly— cutting fish, unloading ships, that sort of thing."

"A day laborer, was he?" The lowest of the low, taking whatever job was available for whatever pittance was offered.

"That's right," Nell answered with a carefully neutral expression.

"A hard life, I daresay."

"You've no idea." Nell had the disquieting sense, as he questioned her, that he was slipping an exploratory scalpel into her mind, her memories, her very self—a dangerous proposition, given what he might unearth if he ventured deeply enough. Too much was at stake—far too much—for her to permit that.

She said, "Let me save us some time here, if I may. I had a family. They're gone now. The details are really none of your concern. I'm sorry if you're bored because you've ended up here after taking your wonderful life with all of its blessings and tossing it in the trash bin. That was your choice to make, though, and I hardly think it should now be my responsibility to provide jailhouse entertainment for you at the expense of my privacy."

Sticking the cigarette in his mouth, Dr. Hewitt clapped listlessly. "What a very impassioned speech, Miss Sweeney. Have you ever considered the stage as a vocation?"

She looked away, disgusted.

"No? I suppose I'm not surprised. Actresses have to be willing to bare their souls—and somewhat more than that, from time to time." His gaze skimmed down to the knife-like toes of her black morocco boots, just visible beneath the hem of her skirt, and back up. "If there was ever a woman buttoned up more snugly than you, I've yet to meet her."

"Must you keep turning the conversation back to me?" she asked.

"And yet I sense, if you loosened just one or two of those buttons, the most extraordinary revelations would burst forth. That's the last thing you want, though, isn't it? To be exposed. It terrifies you."

"As I said," Nell continued tightly, "your mother plans on hiring a lawyer to—"

"Go away." Sitting up, he hurled the cigarette into the bowl of gruel, where it sizzled, and tugged his blanket more tightly around himself. "Just go away, if that's all you can prattle on about. And tell Lady Viola to abandon this foolish notion of getting a lawyer. Some people are meant to hang."

"Guilty people are meant to hang."

"Precisely." Sweat trickled into his eyes; he wiped it away with the blanket. "Not that I'm too keen on that particular method of execution. I saw six men hanged at the same time once. It took a full ten minutes for them to stop writhing. One of them broke his neck, but he still struggled. Hellish way to go. I wouldn't mind a firing squad—or perhaps a syringe full of morphine. Quick, fairly painless . . ."

"Are you saying you killed that man?"

"Boorishly put, Miss Sweeney. You're cleverer than that."

"Your mother believes in your innocence, Dr. Hewitt."

"Why, for God's sake?"

"Because you're her son," Nell said quietly. "Because she loves you. Why else would she have sent me here?"

He laughed wheezily, and without humor. "Because she's addicted to philanthropic projects—it helps to ease her remorse over her lack of a soul. Trust me when I tell you that woman is incapable of maternal love. You think you know my parents, Miss Sweeney, but you really have no idea."

Rising from the bench, Nell retrieved Viola's letter from the petit-point chatelaine bag hanging from her waistband—a more practical alternative to a mesh reticule—and reached through the bars to hand it to Dr. Hewitt, who leaned toward her to take it. "She asked me to give this to you."

"Still using the violet ink, I see." Turning the envelope over, he rubbed his thumb across the dab of sealing wax. "She always did like to do things handsomely." He crushed the letter in his fist and tossed it into the chamber pot.

Gasping in outrage, Nell clutched the iron bars that separated them. "Your mother *wept* as she wrote that," she said with jittery fury, feeling close to tears herself on Viola's behalf. "She *sobbed*. And you just . . ." She shook her head, appalled at the sight of the crumpled-up letter in the stoneware pot. "Then again, I don't know what else I would expect from a man who would walk away from his own family—his own mother—at Christmas, without even saying goodbye. Not to mention letting them think you've been dead all this time. It's you who've lost your soul, Dr. Hewitt, and I pity you for it, but I despise you, too, for bringing this grief upon a woman who's shown you nothing but a mother's true, heartfelt love. Perhaps you really do deserve to hang."

Uncoiling from the cot, he closed the distance between them with one long stride, the blanket slipping to the floor. Tempted to back away, Nell held her ground, hands fisted around the bars, not flinching from his gaze. For a moment he just stared down at her with his bloodied shirt and battered face, eyes seething, a hard thrust to his jaw. Reaching inside his coat, he produced a match, which he scraped across one of the iron bars; it flamed with a crackling hiss.

"You were told to keep your distance," he said softly.

Chapter 3

NELL'S heart thudded in her ears as she considered the prospect of her skirts bursting into flame, and what to do about that if it happened. She didn't step back, though, nor did her gaze waver from his.

He looked away first, at the burning match, and then again at Nell. "You *are* a cool one, when you want to be." Turning, he tossed the match into the chamber pot. The letter ignited. Nell lowered her head and closed her eyes as it burned, the smoke stinging her nostrils.

"It was a two-week furlough," he said quietly, with little remaining of his former rancor.

Nell opened her eyes to find him leaning a shoulder against the bars, thumbs tucked in his leather braces, his gaze on the floor.

"Robbie and I arrived home the morning of December twenty-fourth—Christmas Eve. I made it through that day and the next without too much familial melodrama, but on the day after Christmas, I was, shall we say, discovered in an indiscretion. A minor thing, really, or it would have been, had it not been that monster of morality August Hewitt who discovered it."

"Indiscretion?"

"He came into my room that morning to wake me for a shooting party and found a pair of ladies' drawers on the floor next to my bed."

He glanced at her, no doubt wondering if he'd shocked her, or perhaps hoping he had. Nell kept her expression bland and refused to step back, although he was unnervingly close, mere inches away. From this vantage point, she could see how he shivered, despite the sweat that soaked him.

"He went into one of his quiet, cold rages about my having smuggled a woman into the house. In fact, he was crediting me with initiative where none existed, since the woman in question had merely slipped down the service stairs during the night. Of course, if I'd told him that, he'd have sacked the poor wench on the spot and tossed her into the street like so much rubbish. Not quite what she deserved just for having had the poor judgment to favor the likes of me."

"She was one of the house staff?" Nell asked.

"A chambermaid—my first and only, if you can believe it. Some men are enchanted by those white, ruffled aprons, but they were never quite my cup of tea. Of course, as far as Saint August was concerned, it may as well have been my hundredth offense as my first. He ordered me out of the house forthwith, but not before informing me, rather starchily, that his precious Robbie would never have done such a thing. He was right. Robbie was a good son, a good man. He was the only one of us who was worth anything—except perhaps for young Martin. He had possibilities. Harry was always"—he shook his head— "a bit too much like me, I'm afraid. My fault, to some extent."

"Why do you say that?"

Dr. Hewitt rasped a hand over his unshaven jaw, his gaze still trained on the floor. "I never had very much time for him, during my visits home. He was three years younger than Robbie—*six* years younger than me—so taking him along on our . . . evening adventures was out of the question, although he begged to be included. And, too, I saw something of myself in him—those of us with an appetite for sin always recognize it in others—and I didn't like what I saw. I could have offered him counsel, of course—led him away from that treacherous path I knew so well. But I was too preoccupied, too disgusted by him, and by myself, to offer him any meaningful guidance. So he continued down that road with only himself for a guide. He travels it still."

"He may not have a guide," Nell observed, "but he does have rescuers—rather too many of them, if you ask me. Perhaps if he'd had to answer for his sins now and again, he would have learned to avoid them."

"Spoken like a true daughter of Rome."

She bristled.

"Your quiet indignity is most impressive, Miss Sweeney, but you're squandering it. I don't single out your faith for special scorn. They're all the same to me." His expression grew wistful. "Robbie was devout. Not like Martin, but he believed. He used to crouch down in our little hole at Andersonville and pray. Yet still he was taken, at the age of twenty-five, and in a way that no man should have to . . ." He shook his head, his eyes gleaming. "But in my more philosophical moments, I've thought perhaps it was almost a blessing. He'll always be young, always good. He won't ever be ruined by that hollow, gold-plated world we were born into."

With a grim smile, he added, "For that matter, neither will I. I was supposed to set up a medical practice here in Boston after the war—something on Beacon Hill, perhaps. My only regret is that I'll have to wait months before that little appointment with the hangman. May as well just get it over with, all things considered."

He scooped up the blanket, scrubbed it over his sweat-slicked face, and wrapped it around himself again. Limping over to the cot, he seated himself with a grimace and lit another cigarette with unsteady hands.

"Are you going to be all right?" she asked.

"What did you say your Christian name was? Nell?"

"That's right."

"Short for . . . ?"

"Cornelia."

He drew on the cigarette and studied her as he exhaled, a haze of smoke blurring his ravaged face. "You should probably leave, Cornelia."

She buttoned on her coat, draped her green woollen scarf over her shoulders, gathered up her Bible. "I may come back tomorrow."

"Tuck your scarf in—it's bitter out. And don't come back tomorrow. You might not find me here, in any event. At some point they'll be throwing me in the back of the Black Maria and—"

"The what?"

"It's a closed wagon, painted black. They use it for transferring prisoners from the station houses to the Charles Street Jail. They won't let you in to see me there—you'll be wasting your time if you try."

"Your mother's asked me to try to get you out of here tomorrow. She thinks she can convince a judge she knows to grant bail."

" 'Convince' meaning 'bribe,' I assume. Can she afford that out of her pin money? That's the only way Saint August won't find out about it."

"I'm going to pawn some jewelry for her."

"She's sending you to a *pawnshop*?" A choking little cough escaped him.

"No, she told me about something called the Pawners'

Bank of Boston. It's for ladies with jewelry and other high-value items. They're honest, and they keep the rates low."

"What will those noble Bostonians think of next?" he asked wryly. "Well, God knows she won't miss the jewelry, and I daresay I'll be desperate for my freedom by tomorrow." He studied his quaking hand as he raised his cigarette to his mouth. "But tell her to send someone else for me. Not you."

"There is no one else."

"Then leave me be. As I have made my bed, so I must lie in it. *Vous l'avez voulu, George Dandin.*"

"You may have brought this on yourself, Dr. Hewitt, but I'd hardly think to compare you to a ninny like George Dandin."

"Your Dr. Greaves found Molière worth teaching, I see."

"I read it on my own, actually."

Surprise lit his eyes; she found that absurdly gratifying.

As she turned to leave, he hauled himself to his feet—a nicety she wouldn't necessarily have expected, given the circumstances and his apparent indifference to matters of decorum; he had, after all, smoked in front of her. With a courtly little bow, he said, "This has been a most diverting conversation, Miss Sweeney. It was worth being arrested just to pass the last half hour in your company."

Her face prickled.

"I didn't mean to make you blush," he said.

"Of course you did."

He smiled, really smiled, for the first time, and shook his head a little. Pulling the blanket more snugly around his shuddering body, he said, not unkindly, "Do go away."

As she was stepping into the hallway, he said, "Miss Sweeney."

She turned.

He wasn't smiling anymore. "Don't come back."

"THAT'S her, Detective," muttered the guard to a dark-haired hulk of a man standing near his desk as Nell walked down the hall.

The detective turned toward Nell, assessing her with the trenchant facility of a seasoned cop. He was like a bear in a gray sack coat, all mammoth shoulders and out-sized head, the most prominent feature of which was a jaw that looked as if it could snap iron girders. He had a tweed overcoat slung over his shoulder, a bowler tapping absently against his leg. "You're the one that was visiting Toussaint?"

"That's right."

"I'm Detective Cook—Colin Cook." He spoke with the faded brogue of someone who'd come over in late child-hood, probably one step ahead of the famine. "I've been assigned to the Ernest Tulley murder."

She inclined her head in response to his cursory bow, surprised to encounter an Irish detective in a police de-partment that had only grudgingly begun admitting his kind in recent years. "How do you do, Detective?"

"I'll do just fine once I find out why William Toussaint done what he done last night."

"*If* he did it."

Cook smiled indulgently. "How long have you been contributing your services to the Society for . . . what is it, Prisoners and . . ."

Nell clutched the Bible to her chest as she foraged in her mind for the wording she'd given when she'd signed in.

"The Relief of Convicts and Indigents," said the guard as he consulted the sign-in log.

"Quite some time," she hedged.

"You're to be commended for your benevolence, though why you'd want to waste it on a murdering cur like William Toussaint is beyond me."

"You're that convinced of his guilt?"

"We know the murder weapon belonged to him. Granted, that's circumstantial, but he was there in the alleyway with the body, reeling on opium, and he didn't even try to deny his guilt. We know he done the deed, he's just not talking."

"Not that you didn't do your best to force a confession out of him last night."

Cook held his hands up. "Wasn't my doing, Miss . . . Chapel, is it?"

Did he look amused, or was that her imagination? "Yes."

"I never touched the man. Not that I wasn't tempted, but I tend to slam a body out cold on the first punch, which makes them less than talkative. It was the fellas that arrested him who worked him over, plus one or two boyos from the night shift who had nothing better to do. But can you blame them? A confession would have saved everybody involved a world of trouble."

" 'Everybody' meaning you?"

"My captain did assign me the job of establishing a motive for the murder."

"I thought opium intoxication was the motive."

"You ask me, that's the long and the short of it. Who knows why an opium fiend does what he does? It don't have to make sense to sober types like you and me. But orders are orders, so I've got to try and scare up a witness or two who saw the murder or what led up to it. Thing is, everybody at Flynn's scattered like rats last night before I even got there. I know most of them fellas, the sailors that rent beds there and the ones that just come for the sport—they get pinched for public intoxication on a regular basis. They're none of them exactly partial to chat-tin' with the cops. Better if I show up when they aren't expecting me."

"If they don't want to talk to you, they won't." Nell knew that type.

"Probably not, but you got to remember, we caught Toussaint in the act, or all but. Motive or no, witnesses or no, he's bound to hang. Only, my captain doesn't want to take any chances with this one, so he's making me go through the motions. Speaking of which—time to pull up my socks and get to work. A pleasure to make your acquaintance, Miss Chapel." Donning the bowler, he told the guard to sign him out. "I'll be at one seventy-five Purchase Street."

Purchase Street? "Flynn's Boardinghouse?" Nell asked. "You're going there now?"

"That's right. How do you know about Flynn's?"

"I . . . I think Mr. Toussaint must have mentioned it. Would you mind if I tag along?"

Cook looked at her as if she were demented. "Miss Chapel, I'm not sure you understand what kind of a place this is. It's not just a boardinghouse. It's more what we call a free-and-easy."

"I know they smoke opium there."

"And gamble and consort with women of the worst description."

"I'm not easily shocked," she said, thinking how very much like Viola Hewitt she sounded.

"Well, I am. And the idea of a lady like you in a place like that is just about enough to stop my heart. So I'm sorry, but . . ." Raising an apologetic hand, he turned away.

"You haven't asked me about my visit with Mr. Toussaint, Detective."

Cook paused for a moment, the great wall of his back very still, before turning to face her again. He regarded her in expectant silence, as if to say, "Go on."

"We did chat a bit."

"What about?"

"All sorts of things. He's actually a rather engaging conversationalist."

"Funny, he didn't strike me that way when I questioned him this morning—or tried to. Perhaps if I'd been a little green-eyed lass with a Bible in my hands and a blush upon my cheek, he'd have paid me some mind."

The guard sniggered.

"Did he tell you anything of import as regards the case?" Cook asked.

"He told me so many things," she said. "Some fresh air might revive my memory. Perhaps if I were to walk with you over to the boardinghouse . . ."

He emitted a heavy, exasperated sigh. "Why?"

She lifted her shoulders. "Curiosity, perhaps? This may be the only chance I ever get to see a place like that." The truth, of course, was that she would sooner step through the gates of Hell than through the doors of a place like that; after her long, grueling climb out of such squalor, she had little desire to revisit it. Unfortunately, this might be her only chance to glean the information Viola had begged her for, but which her son refused to impart. *I must find out what really happened last night. I won't rest until I do.*

"Curiosity," Cook scoffed. "What, like one of those gaslight tours, where the nabobs get a taste of the lowlife? You want me to lift up the rock and let you watch the bugs and worms crawl about so you can go back and tell your friends you were in an honest-to-goodness hop joint?"

"Hop joint?"

"It's only newspapermen that call them opium dens, Miss Chapel. Those that are on the hip . . ." He paused, noting her puzzlement. "Hopheads. Opium drunkards. 'Cause you've got to lie sideways, on this"—he patted his

hip—"to smoke the stuff. Those that are on the hip call
them hop joints."

"Are there many of them?"

"Four in Boston that I know of, and that's four too
many. There's one in the South Cove that's a proper lay-
down joint with all the fixings, like what they've got in
San Francisco. Then there's the one in Flynn's, another
on Ann Street, and one on Mount Whore—uh, that is on
the slope behind Beacon Hill. They're nothing but seedy
little back rooms with a couple of couches or beds for
laying down on. There's not much to see, Miss Chapel.
You'd be wasting your time."

"But not yours, if the walk there were to freshen my
memory about my conversation with Mr. Toussaint."

He glowered as he buttoned up his coat. "Just mind
you keep up with me. I'm a fast walker."

"So am I."

She was, but she still had to practically sprint so as not
to fall behind as he crunched determinedly along side-
walks packed with trampled snow, puffing like a loco-
motive. It still snowed, but lightly, airy flakes drifting out
of a darkening sky. Vehicles were few and far between
on this early Sunday evening—an omnibus, a rickety old
hack, the occasional private carriage or sleigh. Spectral
figures beneath black umbrellas passed by on the sidewalk, their numbers thinning as she and the detective
worked their way eastward. Soon they were well into the
grimy Fort Hill district, where Nell had never ventured.
Beneath a gas lamp stood a woman whose vermilion
cheeks and risqué attire left little doubt as to her calling.
The watery fetor of nearby Boston Harbor mingled with
whiffs of grease, cooked meat, and sewage to produce a
miasma common to impoverished quarters everywhere.

It dawned on Nell that Colin Cook might have been
promoted to detective as much on the weight of his Irish-
ness—Fort Hill being dominated by his countrymen, who

tended to gravitate to waterfronts—than in spite of it. Not that he wasn't well qualified. Despite his ambivalence toward this case, Nell sensed a capable brain tucked deep inside that bulldog skull.

"May I ask you a question, Detective?" she asked as they crossed Belmont Street, dodging a pung hauling snow to the harbor.

"Long as you don't slow down."

"Are you absolutely convinced of William Toussaint's guilt? Do you have no doubts at all?"

Cook glanced at her as he walked. "We're alone now. You can call him by his real name."

Ah.

"Yes, I am convinced of William Hewitt's guilt," he said, "and no, I don't have any doubts. Now, since we've progressed on to real names, mind telling me yours?"

Her heart raced, and not just from struggling to match his pace.

He said, "You couldn't remember the name of the charity that sent you, which as far as I know doesn't even exist. And *Chapel*? You might have picked something a bit more believable. O'Malley, perhaps. Or Cassidy. Or Quinn."

They always knew, those from the old country.

"At least tell me who sent you," Cook demanded. "Thorpe? Or was it the great and mighty August Hewitt himself?"

Nell cast him a sharp, dismayed look. Captain Baxter was supposed to have shared Mr. Hewitt's bribe money with the men who knew their suspect's true identity—Detective Cook and that Johnston fellow, presumably—but without disclosing where that money had come from.

"I'm a detective," Cook said. "I detect things. Wasn't much of a challenge. Baxter's thick as clotted cream. Ask a leading question, keep your mouth shut, and he can't help but fill the silence with noise."

It was the same technique he'd used on her back at the station house, Nell realized with a pinch of shame. This was bad, very bad. She'd be sacked for sure if Mr. Hewitt were to find out about her visit to his son, never mind that she'd done it at his wife's behest. He wouldn't find out directly from Detective Cook, of course; they moved in different worlds. But if Detective Cook were to tell Captain Baxter, and Captain Baxter were to tell Alderman Thorpe . . .

She said, "I . . . I've let Mr. Hewitt down, I'm afraid."

"So it *is* him that sent you. Trying to make sure his son's actually guilty, is he, before hurling him under the wheels of justice?"

"Something like that. But he expects me to conceal my true purpose, and you've figured it out. If you could find it in your heart not to tell your Captain Baxter . . ."

"Why the secrecy?"

"I don't think Mr. Hewitt wants the captain—or especially Alderman Thorpe, because they're friends—to feel that he's second-guessing the police. He just wants to be absolutely sure he's doing the right thing."

"Only God can judge that—I mean, it's his own son, and murderer or no, you've got to wonder why he's so eager to see him hang. Least with me, it's my job, and I've got the comfort of having the good book on my side—an eye for an eye, you know."

"Not to mention those forty pieces of silver." She winced; too late to take it back. Dr. Greaves would have asked her what she was thinking.

Cook stopped walking; so did Nell. He faced her with a hard-set jaw, hands thrust deep in his pockets, breath smoking in the frosty twilight. "Judas was a friend to Jesus. William Hewitt is no friend of mine. And I'm hardly betraying him, Miss . . . What the devil *is* your name, anyway?"

"Sweeney. Nell Sweeney."

"I'm bringing him to justice, Miss Sweeney."

"Because it's your job?" She'd already stepped into it; may as well wade through.

"That's right."

"A job for which you're being paid twice—once by the Boston Police Department and again by August Hewitt—with a bonus if his son hangs. Don't get me wrong," she quickly added, mindful that she was alleging to be Mr. Hewitt's agent. "You'd be a fool to refuse the money. It's just that I find it hard to listen with a straight face when you profess to be doing this for noble motives."

"That's it." He seized her arm and strode toward a narrow path between two buildings, hauling her roughly along with him.

"What . . . what are you—"

"You're a difficult woman, Miss Sweeney." He propelled her ahead of him into the murky passage, walled on one side by an old brick commercial building, and on the other by a dilapidated house. From somewhere came the incessant yelping and whining of dogs. "A fella can't help but want to take you down a peg."

"Let me go." She strained against his grip, against the raw, meaty bulk of him, cursing the thread of panic in her voice.

"Not till you take a look at this." He pointed to a darkened patch of snow, barely visible in the gloom. "See that?"

Nell stilled. What had looked at first like a shadow on the snow was, in fact, a sprawling, rust-tinged stain.

"That's blood seeping up from the pavement," he said.

Chapter 4

NELL looked around. "Is this . . . ?"

"Flynn's Boardinghouse." Cook nodded over his shoulder at the adjacent two-story house, sided with peeling clapboards. What looked to be years' worth of refuse lay in snow-frosted drifts against the side wall, amid old wooden crates and jumbles of firewood; the aging garbage added a stale note to the cold evening air. Lamplight shone through greasy windows. A barrage of shouts and laughter momentarily drowned out the yapping of the dogs. Somebody yelled, "Lucky bastard!"

"At a little past midnight last night," Cook said, "Patrolman Danny Hooper was walking his beat along the wharves, one block that way"—he pointed behind the house—"when he heard a woman scream. He cut through the back alleys, so it took him less than a minute to get here. When he did, he found Ernest Tulley laying there in a pool of blood, and William Hewitt crouching over him, finishing the job."

"Finishing . . . you mean . . . with the bistoury . . . ?"

"I'll spare you the sickening details," Cook said, "but yes, he was being quite thorough. There was blood all over his hands, even some on his face. Tulley was dead, but only just."

Nell crouched down to study the blotchy stain, which extended the width of the alley in both directions. It was the only indication that anything untoward had occurred here last night, today's snowfall having done away with any footprints or signs of struggle. No, not the only indication, she saw, glancing around: the deteriorating clapboards on the side of the house were streaked where someone had tried to scrub away blood that must have spurted several feet.

"Arterial bleeding," she murmured.

"You hack a man's throat open, better do it outdoors or plan on buying new wallpaper."

"Hack?" Nell had been picturing it as a single slice, something akin to a surgical incision.

"Took a bit of effort to get the job done."

"Did he say anything at all—Dr. Hewitt?" She stood, smoothing her skirts.

"He asked if he might smoke a cigarette," Cook said. "Other than that, he pretty much kept mum. As for why he done it, I know he'd been smoking opium, according to the fella that owns this place—fella name of Flynn, Seamus Flynn. If there was any other reason for what he done, he ain't sharin' it—not that it'll make any difference in the long run."

"And every last witness fled?"

"All except for Flynn and his daughter. She's the one that let out that scream last night. Steps out for a bit of fresh air and finds a dead man laying in a pool of blood and the murderer still hunched over him. *That'll* perk you up. Her old man had spent most of the night down in the rat pit, supervising the . . ." He paused when he noticed

Nell's look of bafflement. "You hear them dogs? Come with me."

Cook gestured for her to follow him around back and through a rusty gate to a treeless, trash-strewn stable yard. The stable itself was a tumbledown affair with a sagging roof; she smelled horseflesh, rancid hay, and manure, heard a low equine whinny. The barking emanated from a rambling structure fashioned of waste wood and broken furniture; dogs snarled and paced in the attached chicken-wire run, its floor littered with snow-covered droppings.

"Flynn keeps about a dozen terriers in that there kennel," Cook said. "Bloodthirsty little demons. On Saturday nights he takes 'em down to the basement"—he pointed to the rear of the house, which had two doors, one open to reveal a crumbling cellar stairway—"and he drops 'em one by one into an eight-sided wooden pen filled with rats. No cards or dice on Saturday nights, just the rats. Every fella in this town that fancies himself a sporting type, be he Brahmin or beggar, he heads on down to Seamus Flynn's basement on Saturday night to bet on how many rats each dog will dispatch. Little mustard-colored bitch named Flossie set the record last year—twenty rats in twelve seconds."

"My word."

"He boards horses, too," Cook said, cocking his head toward the stable. "Between that and the opium and his cut of the wagering, plus three dollars a week for every bed he fills and payments from the, uh . . . the women who solicit in his establishment, he don't do half bad for himself."

"If you know about the prostitution and the gambling, why don't you arrest him for it?" The answer was so evident that she answered before he could. "He's paying you off."

"Not me personally—they don't trust my kind to play bag man. Let's just say I've been told to look the other way. It's not too hard. Flynn don't want no trouble, and he's careful not to attract any. Tell you one thing, he's none too pleased over the little drama that unfolded in his alleyway last night. Bad for business, having us coppers sniffin' around, 'specially given the clientele he attracts."

"Did *he* see anything last night?"

"Not much. Like I said, he was down in the pit most of the night, but he did come upstairs once or twice to sell gong to—"

"Gong?"

"Opium. There was a handful of pipe fiends came and went, but William Hewitt was there all night. Must have gotten good and boiled on the stuff, to have done what he done."

"Are you absolutely sure he'll be convicted?"

"I'd stake my badge on it—and you can go back and tell that to Mr. August Hewitt. What's more, I'll be there cheering them on when they string him up, 'cause it's no worse than what he deserves. As for the money, I certainly *would* have been a fool to refuse it, and not just because they don't pay me enough to begin with. Would have gotten Captain Baxter nervous as a cat if I'd turned it down. He would have wondered why, maybe worried that I was fixing to finger him for accepting payoffs. He never has liked having me around, uppity mick that I am. I'm sure a high-reaching little lace curtain colleen like yourself knows how that feels."

Nell didn't bother responding to that, "lace curtain" being something of an epithet among Boston's Irish. "Why *does* he have you around, then?"

"It was the chief's idea to have Irishmen policing their own, but Baxter thinks of us as foreign riffraff, and he's been achin' to can me ever since I got promoted—and me with a brand new house and a wife I happen to worship, who deserves better than to end up out on the street. Tell me, Miss Sweeney, have you never compromised yourself even a little bit, never done something you wouldn't want to admit even in confession, 'cause it was the only way to make your life a little more bearable?"

She looked away, the bitter air stinging her cheeks.

"There's none of us that are blameless," he said. "Yes, I took August Hewitt's money, and I'll take the bonus once his son's sentenced. But it makes no difference in terms of how I treat this case. I know a guilty man when I see him, and William Hewitt is as guilty as they come."

"He just doesn't seem . . ." She shook her head. "Something about him . . ."

"The damnedest people . . . Begging your pardon, miss. The strangest people turn out to be murderers, folks you'd never suspect. Given a good enough reason, just about anybody could do the deed, even you or me. That don't make it right, though, and when it happens, it's got to be punished."

"Yes, but if you'd talked to him . . ."

"And whose fault is it that I wasn't able to, eh? All he'd tell us was his name, and that turned out to be hooey. Only reason he talked to you is 'cause his father was clever enough to send a bonny little thing like yourself. Knew his son's weakness, he did."

Inside the house, men shouted and cheered.

"Come on," he said. "I know them boys in there. If we wait much longer, they'll be too soused to talk to us—or rather, to me. You're to hold that quick tongue of yours and let me do the questioning."

A ramshackle wooden staircase crawled up the outside of the house in back, starting between the cellar entrance and the other, blue-painted door. Landings on the second and third floors provided access to the house through doors with cracked windowpanes; a window on the second floor was half boarded up. There were footprints around the bottom of the staircase and on its snow-covered treads.

"Watch the ice on the stoop," Cook said as he opened the blue door, ushering her through a cluttered little vestibule and into a kitchen redolent with frying onions. A tall woman in an apron and head rag stood at the cook stove; she didn't turn when they came in.

Cook doffed his hat to her back. "Evening . . . Kathleen, is it?"

"That's right," she said without turning around. Her Irish-accented voice was thin and girlish, in contrast to her sturdy build and big, efficient hands.

"Where's your da this evening, Kathleen?"

Her shoulders twitched. "Saw him headin' upstairs earlier. Ain't seen him come down."

"Your boarders sound like they're feeling their oats," Cook observed. "What is it this evening? Cards or chuck?"

"Chuck. Drawing room." Kathleen glanced over her shoulder, her gaze lighting with interest, and perhaps a touch of envy, on Nell's fine coat and hat. The girl had pleasant features rendered homely by a raw abrasion on her left cheek, surrounded by discolored swelling. The bruising stood out bluish-purple against her milky skin; it had happened within the last day or two.

"Follow me," Cook murmured as he guided Nell down a long hallway, the boisterous voices growing louder as they neared the front of the house.

"What happened to that girl's face?" Nell whispered.

"I asked her last night. She claims she slipped on the ice, but I suspect it's her father's handiwork. He's a hard-chaw if ever there was one."

To their right was a staircase to the second floor; to their left, two doorways, the first of which he gestured Nell through. She found herself in a dismal little back parlor furnished with two threadbare couches and a scarred old leather chaise lounge. A blanket-covered mattress occupied the middle of the floor. Faded old paper imprinted with cabbage roses was curling off the walls.

"This is the hop joint, or what passes for one," he said, gesturing with the bowler. "Told you there wasn't much to see. Flynn keeps the opium and pipes and what-not locked up in there." He pointed to a built-in cupboard against the wall. "Sailors acquire the habit in foreign ports, and they're willing to pay to satisfy it. There's others that come here besides them, like Hewitt, but it usually doesn't pick up here till nine or ten at night."

"It's chilly in here," Nell said.

"Flynn keeps the windows cracked open for air—otherwise the whole house would stink of burning gong."

Through the two partially open windows, hung with yellowish, tied-back lace curtains, Nell had a pretty good view of the alley she'd just been in, and the brick building next door. A rattle of dice came from beyond the wall to the front drawing room, followed by roars and whoops. Crossing to a pair of pocket doors, Cook yanked them open.

Silence swept through the smoke-hazed drawing room as its inhabitants—perhaps a dozen men and one woman—looked toward Nell and Detective Cook standing in the wide doorway. Most of the men were gathered around a chuck-a-luck table scattered with coins and crumpled bills—roughly dressed sailors with the exception of two who appeared to be, not boarders, but gentlemen seeking "free-and-easy" diversion, as William Hewitt had last night. Another well-dressed young man sat in the corner with the woman—a painted hussy—perched on his lap, a silver flask in her hand. The air was thick with stale sweat, staler gin, and cheap tobacco.

Cook held up a badge. "Detective Colin Cook, Boston Police. Any of you jack-tars around last night when that fella got his throat cut in the alleyway?"

A couple of the men shook their heads; most looked away, exchanging sneers, rolling cigarettes, fiddling with their money. One bearded behemoth with overgrown black hair sprouting from beneath a leather cap ogled Nell while gulping whiskey from a bottle.

"You. Noonan." Cook pointed to the giant in the leather cap. "Where were you around midnight last night?"

"At church," Noonan said, still watching Nell, "prayin' for a Bible-totin' angel to come save me from my wicked ways. Looks like my prayers was answered."

When the chuckles had died down, Cook said, "We arrested a fella last night—tall, black haired. Calls himself William Toussaint. He'd been kicking the gong around in there." The detective nodded toward the back parlor. "Anybody notice him?"

There were some shrugs, some shakes of the head; for the most part, the inquiry was simply ignored.

"You're new here, aren't you?" Cook addressed this to the hussy on the young swell's lap, a buxom creature with washed-out yellow hair whose face powder didn't quite conceal her flaccid jowls and crepey neck. The lace trim on the bodice of her too-tight green satin dress was coming loose, as if it could no longer bear up under the strain.

"That's right," she said, her gaze wavering slightly as she handed the silver flask back to the young dandy.

"She's Molly's friend Pearl," someone offered, blanching when Noonan turned his flat-eyed glare on him.

"Where *is* Molly?" the detective asked; no answer. "Was she around last night?" A few shrugs, some whispers. To Nell, Cook said, "Molly works out of here almost every night—knows all the regulars. There's other girls that come and go—they pick up the overflow on busy nights—but Molly's always around. So . . . Pearl, is it? Were *you* here last night?

She hesitated. Finally: "I didn't see nothin'."

"I know you girls like to ply your trade to them with the deepest pockets. Toussaint gives the appearance of a man of means. I don't suppose you cozied up to him."

Noonan turned to look at the whore over his bottle as he took another swig.

She held the bearded sailor's gaze for a moment, her crimsoned lips pressed together like a knife slit, then looked back at Cook. "Can't say as I noticed him."

"No? He was in there all night." Cook nodded toward the back parlor.

"I spent most of the night standin' round out back with the other girls."

To the group as a whole, Cook said, "The fella that got killed, Ernest Tulley—was he around much last night?"

A few men exchanged looks. Someone spat on the floor.

"I'm sure you all knew him, at least by sight," Cook said. "He was a deckhand on a Liverpool packet ship called the *Evangeline*. Mr. Flynn tells me he rents a bed here whenever his ship's in port. I find it hard to believe no one saw him last night."

"I'm pretty sure I *smelt* him," said a sailor smoking a cabbage leaf cigar.

That statement was met with a flurry of laughter.

The man who'd spoken had purplish streaks under each eye and a badly distended nose. "What happened to you?" Cook asked.

The sailor tapped his cigar onto his trouser leg and rubbed the ashes into the wool. "Met with an accident."

"And you?" Cook pointed to another man in back, cradling a bandaged hand as if to hide it.

"Accident."

"Seem to be a lot of them around here," Cook observed dryly. "Anybody know whether Tulley and Toussaint exchanged words at all?"

"They didn't." This from a swarthy young sailor with blue-black hair.

"Shut your mouth, you ignorant wop," someone hissed, more in a warning tone, it seemed to Nell, than in anger.

"Castelli don't know nothin'," Noonan said. "It was Rat Night last night. He was down in the pit with everybody else."

"All night?" Cook asked.

"That's right," Noonan said.

"No it ain't." Castelli said something to Noonan in Italian, punctuating the rebuke with a brusque hand gesture Nell had never seen before. "They didn't talk, Tulley and that guy they arrested," Castelli told Cook. "Far as I could tell, they didn't even know each other."

"Anybody else have any observations from last night they'd care to share?"

Noonan gave the dice cage attached to the chuck table a lazy spin. Its clattering was the only sound in the room.

Cook shook his head disgustedly. "Does it mean nothing to you that one of your own took a knife in the throat for no good reason at all?"

"That fat, miserable yellow jacket weren't one of us," Noonan growled, to murmurs of agreement from his companions. "You ast me, he had it comin' to him, and ain't a man among us'll argue with that."

"Why?" Nell asked, ignoring Detective Cook's glare. "Because he was Southern?" *Yellow jacket* had been Yankee slang for a Confederate soldier.

Every face in the room turned toward her. Noonan looked amused at her temerity. "Ain't none of us gonna stab a man in the throat just fer that, sweet pea. War's over, last I heard."

More for some than for others, Nell knew. There were men whose scars—those you could see and those you couldn't—were terribly slow to heal. "Why did he have it coming to him, then?" she asked.

Noonan gave her a big, stump-toothed grin. "You come on upstairs with me, I'll explain it to you—nice and slow and easy, just the way you sweet little angels like it."

"That's enough of that," Cook protested over the ensuing snickers and hoots. Drawing Nell toward the hall by her arm, he said, "Any of you jackanapes feel like talking—without an audience—you'll find me at Station Two on Williams Court."

To Nell's surprise, the detective didn't escort her outside, but upstairs to the second floor, explaining that he wanted to find Seamus Flynn and get the name of every man who was there last night. "I wish you'd held your tongue, like I told you. They were starting to talk." He pounded a fist on the nearest door off the dimly lit hallway. "Flynn?" He swung the door open. It slammed against a cot, one of perhaps a dozen crammed together in a dreary room strewn with clothing, rucksacks, and the occasional battered sea chest.

"Does it matter so much whether they talk or not?" she asked. "I thought you were just going through the motions. Which is just as well, because those men downstairs obviously loathed Ernest Tulley. Why should they help you convict his killer?"

He glared at her as he stalked to a door at the end of the hall, she struggling to keep up. "It would look better, is all, if I could produce a body to put on the stand," Cook said. Baxter would just love to see me come up empty-handed."

He swung the door open after a perfunctory knock, revealing a much smaller, dimly lit room with bright pink walls. A big four-poster bed strewn with pillows and rumpled blankets stood against the back wall next to the door to the outside stairs and beneath the partially boarded-up window Nell had seen from the stable yard. "Flynn?"

"He was here, but he left," said a red-headed sailor sitting on a straight-backed chair in the corner, smoking a cigarette. "Said he had some rats to catch."

"He went out thataway," added a female voice as an

arm rose from the unkempt bed to point at the door on the back wall. Squinting, Nell saw that some of what she'd taken for heaped-up bedcoverings were, in fact, the disarrayed clothing of a couple locked in carnal embrace. They seemed as indifferent to the interruption as to the presence of the red-haired man, who was presumably waiting his turn.

Cook slammed the door shut, his face boiling red. "Jesus, Mary, and Joseph."

Biting her twitching lip, Nell spun around as if scandalized.

"Miss Sweeney, I . . . Dear God. I don't know what to say."

She cleared her throat as she turned back to face him, wishing she had the capacity to blush at will. "That would be Molly, I take it?" It struck her as funny, when it didn't utterly exasperate her, how solicitous people could be over maidenly sensibilities she'd never really possessed— such sensibilities being a luxury she could ill afford, growing up as she had. So expert had she become at feigning them, though, that they almost felt real, from time to time.

"I don't suppose you know where Mr. Flynn would go to catch rats?" Nell asked, hoping to refocus him on their purpose for being here.

He shifted his jaw for a moment. "Come with me."

"JAYSUS, not you again!" snarled a ruddy-faced, matted-haired man as he stepped out of a stall at the end of the stable's central aisle, some unidentifiable tool in one hand, a roiling, squeaking sack in the other.

Seamus Flynn had a deep-chested, thick-brogued voice that reminded Nell of her father's; the same bread-dough gut, too, despite his ropy leanness. A lantern hanging overhead illuminated the gold crucifix around his neck, as well as bits of straw clinging to his long-sleeved under-shirt and sagging hemp trousers, making it look as if he'd been dusted with flecks of gold. Grinning at Nell, he said, "Don't tell me the coppers are hirin' birds as well as bog-trotters now. What's this town comin' to?"

"This here's Miss Chapel," Cook said. "She's with the Society for the Relief of Criminals and Indigents."

"*Convicts* and Indigents." *Now* she remembered.

Cook shot an amused little glance her way. "She was praying over the fella we arrested last night, so I thought she might like to visit the scene of the crime, as it were. Give her a better idea of the sins that need forgiving."

Straw crackled; Flynn ducked abruptly back into the stall, quick as the vermin he hunted. "There y'are, ya little bastard!" There came a series of panicked squeals. "Got-cha!"

Detective Cook, clearly fascinated, strode forward to watch. Nell followed him warily, arriving at the empty stall in time to see Flynn stuff a squirming rat into his sack with the tool, which turned out to be . . .

"Curling tongs?" she exclaimed.

"Nothin' works better." Flynn squeezed the pair of tongs to separate the hinged arms, one shaped something like a tuning fork, the other like an elongated sugar scoop. "Little buggers don't stand a chance."

The bag in his fist churned and squalled. Cook looked impressed. Nell's stomach clenched. Perhaps she really *was* becoming delicate. It should have gratified her to think she might be turning into a proper lady at last, but in truth it just made her feel weak.

"Say, Flynn," Cook began, "I wonder if I couldn't trouble you for a list of the men who were here last night—your boarders and any visitors you happen to know by name."

"Right, and have you pester 'em till they decide it's

just too much trouble to give Seamus Flynn their business anymore? Not likely, Detective."

"I could force you to hand it over."

"You'd be wastin' your time. They was all downstairs bettin' on the rats, 'cept for them that was rollin' the log in the back parlor there, and they was too hopped up to be of much help to you."

"Are you sure all the men stayed in the basement the whole time?" Nell asked. "Surely some of them availed themselves of the women who work out of here."

"That's right," Cook said, having apparently forgotten his prior injunction about holding her tongue.

Flynn looked both intrigued and amused that the Bible-toting Miss Chapel had chosen to bring that up. "The girls conduct their business up on the second floor, in a room at the end of the hall. I painted it pink for 'em and put a nice big bed in there to make it more homey-like. Rat Night's a busy night, so there's sometimes four or five chippies waitin' out back by the cellar stairs for fellers to come up lookin' for a different kind of sport. The girl that gets picked, she usually just brings him up the outside stairs there. So, you see, anything takin' place on the first floor—such as between that Ernest Tulley and whoever killed him—the dollies wouldn't know nothin' about."

"What does a girl do if the pink room is already occupied?" Nell asked.

"Then they use any empty room. They like the back parlor, if there ain't nobody smokin' gong in there, 'cause of that mattress on the floor, and all them couches. The girls'll double up in there if their customers don't mind. Only place they ain't allowed is up on the third floor, 'cause that's where me and my daughter—"

Flynn stilled, head cocked, grinning slowly. Nell heard an almost imperceptible rustling and backed out of the stall into the aisle. Whirling around with surprising grace, the Irishman kicked the straw heaped in the corner, tongs

poised. A huge rat darted out; Flynn plucked it up deftly
and held it aloft as it thrashed and squealed. "Oh, what a
fine big brute you are!" he praised, depositing the writhing
rodent in his sack. "Mind you give my Miss Flossie a
good tussle next Saturday. She gets bored when it's too
easy."

Swallowing down her bile, Nell said, "I, uh, I understand you came upstairs yourself a few times to sell opium
to your customers who were smoking it."

Flynn nodded. "Yeah, I like to keep an eye on things
in there, make sure everybody has what they need.
Weren't much to do last night, though. That one they
arrested—Toussaint—he was there all night, but he was
real quiet-like. Just shoved some money in my hand, laid
hisself down, and lit up bowl after bowl—I rarely seen
anybody go through it like him."

"There were others in there with him, right?" Nell
asked.

"Couple of sailors early on—regulars whenever they're
in port—but they just had a bowl or two apiece and left.
Next time I checked, there was just Toussaint, who'd
more or less dozed off—the gong does that to 'em—and
one other feller. I asked him if he wanted somethin' to
smoke, but he says nah, he ain't no hop fiend, and then I
seen he was suckin' on a bottle. The swells, they like to
bring their own. The gin I sell here ain't good enough for
'em."

"Why did he come to your place," Nell asked, "if not
for opium or the rat pit? He could have done his drinking
anywhere."

"There's them that'll show up on a Saturday night for
cards or chuck, not knowin' about Rat Night, or maybe
forgettin' about it 'cause they're already in their cups. The
rats ain't for everybody. Some of 'em take off then, and
some just sit and drink. This feller just wanted to sit and
drink."

"What did he look like?" Nell asked.

"Can't rightly say." Flynn scratched his soft belly with the tongs. "I keep it dark in there, 'cause that's the way them gowsters like it, and all I seen was the back of his head, 'cause he was settin' on the couch that faces away from the door. Sounded like a swell, though, and I think I saw a top hat on the arm of the couch."

"Do you happen to know when he left?" she asked.

"He weren't there when I came up the last time," Flynn said. "Nobody was—the room was empty. That's when Kathleen screamed. I wouldn't have heard her if I'd still been downstairs. Ain't nothin' noisier than a rat pit, 'cept maybe a cockfight. Blood sport brings out the howlers. I look out the window and what do I see in the alley but ol' Ernest Tulley layin' there in a pool of blood." He sketched a cursory sign of the cross with his curling tongs.

"And William Hewitt finishing him off," Cook prompted.

"Well . . ." Flynn lifted his shoulders. "Can't rightly say that's what he was doing."

"He was crouching over the body," Cook said.

"With his back to me."

The detective glowered. "Seems like lots of fellas had their backs to you last night."

"All I'm sayin' is I never seen him do the deed. Neither did Kathleen, when you come right down to it. And like I told you last night, there was some boyos in the house across the way who seen somebody tearin' out of that alley and down Purchase Street *before* Kathleen screamed, so you might well be jumpin' to—"

"Someone was seen running away?" Nell turned to face Cook. "What else haven't you told me?"

The detective cast his weary gaze to the ceiling. "They were hooched-up on homemade bark juice, those fellas. Within minutes, just about everyone in this entire place had up and run off, so who knows what they really saw, or when?"

"Want to know what I think?" Flynn asked.

Cook said "No" as Nell said "Yes."

Flynn scowled, his nostrils flaring. "I think nothin's been right in my house since that Roy Noonan started comin' here. When them others run out of money to gamble with, they borrow it from him, and they're too ignorant—or desperate—to ask how much it's gonna end up costin' 'em. If they're slow in payin', he gives 'em a taste of those big fists of his, and promises worse."

"I think I saw a bit of his handiwork in there," Cook said.

"On the one hand, they look up to him like he's Lord God Almighty, but most of 'em are scared of him, too—and if you ask me, they're right to be. They say he killed a man aboard a whaler couple-few years ago and dumped the body overboard, and not a crewman willing to finger him for fear he'd be next. I ast him myself if it was true, and he just grinned at me in that dead-eyed way of his."

"If you hate him so much," Cook asked, "how come you let him stay here?"

"The one time I tried to tell him we was full up and I couldn't rent him a bed, he whips out a knife like you use to gut fish and starts diggin' under his fingernails. He asks me am I sure about that? What am I supposed to say then?"

"Did Ernest Tulley owe Noonan money?" Nell asked.

"Seems to me I heard he did," Flynn said as he knelt down to tie off the sack. "Heard he owed him quite a bit, and when Noonan demanded payment, Tulley just laughed at him. Noonan don't like being laughed at."

"What are you implying?" Nell asked.

Flynn raised his gaze to her. "You seem like a smart lass. You figure it out. And when you do, maybe you'd like to share it with the good detective here."

Cook shoved his bowler on with a little too much force. "Good news for you, Mr. Flynn. I've had about all I can stand of this place for the time being. I don't relish having to go back empty-handed to my captain, but I did warn him it was pointless, sending me here. If you come up with any more fascinating theories, write them down and send them to Miss Chapel, care of Station Two—assuming you can write."

Flynn grunted something under his breath as he stood.

Nell was halfway down the aisle when she turned and said, "One thing I was wondering, Mr. Flynn. How did your daughter get that black eye?"

Hefting the bag over his shoulder, he said, "I'm thinkin' it's that dago she's so sweet on."

Cook said, "You mean Castelli?"

"Are they sweethearts?" Nell asked.

"I know she meets him in here at night," Flynn sneered. "I say he's the one dealt her that shiner—they're a hot-blooded race—but it's no more'n she deserves for gettin' mixed up with his kind. Prob'ly brought it on herself, anyway, headstrong as she is."

"Kathleen?" Nell thought about that childlike voice, those big eyes lingering on her hat and coat.

"She don't look it," Flynn said, "but believe me, she can be as much of a bitch as my Flossie when she's riled. One of these Saturday nights I should throw *her* in the pit with the rats. She'll set a new record—see if she don't."

It was a good deal darker when Nell and Detective Cook left the boardinghouse than when they'd entered it, in part because it had stopped snowing. They stood under a street lamp, Cook's hands stuffed in his pockets, his expression shadowed by the brim of the bowler. "I've held up my end of our bargain, Miss Sweeney. Now tell me about your conversation with William Hewitt."

"Was Ernest Tulley a heavy man, Detective?"

He cocked his head, as if thrown by the non sequitur. She said, "Noonan called Tulley 'that fat, miserable yellow jacket.' *Fat.* I just wondered if he actually was."

"He was a stocky man, I'll grant you that, but no more so than Noonan himself. They bore a certain resemblance, now that I think of it—both with that dark, shaggy hair and full beard—and that barrel chest. You might have thought they were brothers—twin brothers, even—except I understand Tulley had quite the Georgia drawl."

"Was he as tall as Noonan?"

"Taller—he was monstrous. Dressed shabby, like all the rest of 'em."

"I'd like to see him, if I may."

"Ernest Tulley?" A disbelieving little huff of laughter escaped him. "You can't be serious."

"Why not? He's in some morgue, I would assume."

"You must be mad if you think I'd bring a lady into—"

"I'm a sort of nurse." Or was at one time, if one stretched the definition of "nurse." "I've seen my share of dead men." That much was true.

"Nevertheless . . ."

"And afterward you can ask me anything you want about my conversation with William Hewitt."

He regarded her sullenly, working that great jaw back and forth. "You're really a very difficult woman, Miss Sweeney."

She smiled. "So you've said."

NELL *had* seen dead men, many of them, but none in recent years, and never one who had succumbed to such savagery. Ernest Tulley's throat had been carved open like meat. Pushing his beard aside, Nell counted seven haphazard slashes, some shallow, some deep and gaping. One had severed the carotid, hence the copious bleeding and a death that was almost certainly swift— blessedly so.

Almost as hard to look upon as the dead man's throat was his face. With his grayish skin, protruding tongue, and wide, startled eyes, he resembled nothing so much as a gargoyle on some medieval cathedral.

"Have you located his next of kin?" Nell asked.

"I've got the boys working on it. I'd like to get some background on him, anyway. Oftentimes it turns out the seeds of a murder were planted long ago—they just need the right conditions to sprout."

Pointing to the slashed neck, Nell asked, "Does this look to you like the work of a surgeon, Detective?"

"That wasn't surgery, Miss Sweeney. It was a mindless attack by a man in the grip of opium intoxication."

"Yes, but still, one would think—"

"Then one would be thinking too much—something that seems to be a bad habit of yours, if I may be so bold."

"Did you notice the blood on Dr. Hewitt's shirt?" she persisted. "Those few little spatters? Given these wounds, and the violence with which this man bled out, the killer should have been saturated with it."

"He was wearing a long frock coat and vest. A tie, too. Most of the blood would have ended up on them."

"He didn't have them in his cell." Otherwise he wouldn't have had to wrap himself up in that blanket when he started shivering. "Were they put aside as evidence?"

"Should have been, but the boys don't always see to the details like they should. Things tend to get a little confusing when a fella gets arrested for murder. Stuff gets misplaced. There's no question Hewitt had blood on him, though. His hands were red up to the wrists."

Nell closed her eyes, remembering the dried blood encrusting William Hewitt's shirt cuffs. She filled her lungs with chilled air tainted with death and carbolic, let it out.

"Seen enough?" asked Detective Cook from behind her.

"Almost." Had Tulley been ambushed and dispatched before he realized what was happening, or had he struggled with his attacker? She eased the sheet down to expose the huge man's burly crossed arms. "He tried to ward off the blade," she told Cook, pointing to the lacerations on his wrists and hands where he'd raised his arms or made grabs for the weapon; indeed, the little finger of his right hand was nearly chopped off.

"Where did you learn about defensive wounds?" Cook asked. "From some book?"

From witnessing knife fights, actually, and patching up the survivors, but she could hardly tell him that. "From a book, yes. There was a whole chapter on it."

"Are you done now?" he asked.

Nell whipped the sheet back over the dead man. *How I wish I were.*

"So, what did you and William Hewitt talk about this afternoon?" Cook asked when they were outside on the street again, breathing in the clean night air.

She scoured her mind for something innocuous, something he couldn't use to help build a case for the prosecution. "He's estranged from his parents."

"I think I already guessed that." The detective blew on his ungloved hands and rubbed them together.

"He doesn't want an attorney."

"Which he made abundantly clear last night."

"He did say he doesn't consider himself a surgeon anymore."

Cook shoved his hands impatiently in his coat pockets. "Did he say anything about Tulley? Give any hint why he done it?"

"He never admitted having done it. I imagine he knows that the burden of proof rests with the commonwealth. He *is* innocent until proven guilty, regardless of your own prejudices."

Cook studied her in the dark. "Where on earth did August Hewitt find the likes of you, anyway?"

"I'm the governess for a little girl they adopted."

The detective barked with laughter. "A governess! That's perfect. The demure little Irish miss who knows just what to do and say. You know, you remind me of my wife, Miss Sweeney. Not in looks so much, though you're almost as pretty as she is. No, it's that brain—" he thumped a finger on his own broad cranium "—that seems to know everything except when to back off."

"I hardly think—"

"Back off, Miss Sweeney," he said with quiet fervor. "Heed a word of warning from someone who's been dealing with miscreants of all stripes for far too many years. William Hewitt may be well born, and he may be educated and amusing and all the rest of it, but that don't mean he didn't rip Ernest Tulley's throat open like a rabid dog last night. In fact, it's often those young Brahmin princes who do the worst, 'cause they've been raised to do as they please, and never mind the consequences. There's always someone willing to clean up their messes."

Too true, Nell reflected, thinking of Harry, and so many others like him.

"You think William Hewitt's different somehow, but he's just another rich young bounder who takes what he wants when he wants it—and what he wanted last night was opium, and plenty of it. Whether it was that alone that drove him to do what he done, or whether he's a little bit gone in the head, or even if there's some better reason on top of that, the fact remains that he's a vicious man—a vicious and *charming* man. Take it from me, they're by far the most dangerous kind."

"As I'm all too well aware," she said sincerely. "Don't worry, Detective. I've been exposed to that breed. I'm quite immune now."

"For your sake, I hope that's true."

UPON arriving home that evening, Nell headed straight for the Red Room to report the day's events to Viola, only to pause outside the door when she heard Mrs. Mott's voice from within.

"As you know, Mrs. Hewitt, my duty is to the house-hold rather than to any one member of it. And when a situation arises that upsets the balance of the household, well, I reckon it's my duty to say something. Now, as regards the Sweeney girl . . ." To Mrs. Mott, Nell was "the Sweeney girl." Mrs. Bouchard, of whom she also heartily disapproved, was "the Negress." "You know my feelings on the matter. The girl is underbred for her position, and that causes enough problems right there, but to let her lark about as she does . . . Meaning no disrespect, ma'am, but it sets a poor example to the other servants."

Viola's tone, when she spoke, was very quiet and even in that way that meant she was holding herself in check. Mrs. Mott was the third generation of her family to serve the Hewitts, and August wouldn't hear of dismissing her despite her testy relationship with his wife. "Nell is not a servant."

"A matter of semantics, ma'am. She's—"

"And therefore not under your jurisdiction."

"Not officially, but—"

"Will there be anything else, Mrs. Mott?"

There came a strained pause. "No, ma'am."

Nell stood right where she was until the door opened. Mrs. Mott's parchment-pale face lost a bit more of its color when she encountered the subject of her little diatribe staring her in the face. Stepping aside to let her pass, Nell said, "Good evening, Mrs. Mott."

The housekeeper brushed past her and receded down the central hall, her footsteps utterly silent on the marble floor.

Chapter 5

"Y OU here for William Toussaint?" the pockmarked guard asked as Nell approached his desk at Station House Two the next morning. "You're too late. Sorry."

"Too late?" Nell remembered how pale Dr. Hewitt had been when she'd left him yesterday, how shaky. "You don't mean—"

"He took sick after you left yesterday, real sick."

"Oh, God." The floor felt as if it were shifting under her feet. She braced her free arm on the desk to steady herself, the other being burdened with the coat Viola Hewitt had sent for her son.

"We got him out of here around dawn. If he's fixing to go under, better he does it at the Charles Street Jail than here. Let *them* file the report."

Nell closed her eyes, weak with relief. He was alive— ailing, but alive. The first thing Viola had asked when Nell joined her in the Red Room yesterday evening was *How is he? Is he all right?*

He'll be fine, she'd hedged, loath to reveal the true extent of William's condition. Viola was reeling emotionally; first the revelation that one of her two dead sons was actually alive, followed immediately by the news that he'd been arrested for murder. How much more could she take?

Tell me everything, Viola had implored. Nell had told her as much as she dared, hating that her well-meaning prevarications put her in the same league with August Hewitt, who coddled Viola to a fault. She did tell Viola that her son had burned her letter, but not how badly he'd been pummeled, nor how ill he'd appeared toward the end. *Are* you *all right?* Viola had asked her as their conversation wound down. *I'm asking a great deal of you, I know. Is it too much?*

No, Nell had said, surprised to find that she meant it. She didn't relish this mission Viola had set her upon; not only did it imperil the life she'd come to cherish so dearly, it dredged up a past she'd thought was long behind her. But she could do it. She was not just the only candidate for the job; she was the best candidate for the job. That had come to her as she lay in her too-large bed last night, curled up with her head beneath the covers, waiting for the sheets to absorb her body heat. Her life experience encompassed two very different worlds—the world William Hewitt had forsaken and the world he now embraced—for she moved as effortlessly today among the silk stocking set as she once had among thieves and cardsharps and whores.

Nell might pass today for as fine a lady as any in Boston—by other ladies, if not by their servants—but she understood criminals and gamblers and fallen women. She understood men who maddened themselves with intoxicating poisons and then reached for their knives. She understood the police, both the good and the bad among them.

"You all right, miss?" asked the guard. "You aren't fixin' to faint on me, are you?"

"I'm not a fainter, no."

"What's that you got there?" he asked, pointing to the papers in her hand. "A bail order? I thought bail was denied."

"That judgment was overturned." Through no small effort of her own. First thing this morning, Nell had visited the Pawners' Bank on Union Street, a surprisingly dignified establishment where she'd traded two brooches, a ring, and a string of pearls for the thickest stack of greenbacks she'd ever seen. Then on to the courthouse chambers of Judge Horace Bacon, who'd been, as Viola had predicted, more than willing to overturn the bail decision in exchange for about an inch and a half of that stack. And now here, only to encounter this vexing little detour.

"You're bailing him out?"

Nell turned to find Detective Cook looming like a grizzly in a doorway behind her.

"I . . . yes, as a matter of fact, I—"

"You're not immune after all, are you?" Cook said disgustedly. "He's worked his charm on you, and you've gone and convinced his father that he may not be—"

Nell cleared her throat and slanted a look in the guard's direction.

Cook ground that great kettle of a jaw, shook his head. "Tell you what, why don't you step in here for a minute? There's someone I want you to talk to."

The someone turned out to be Daniel Hooper, the young blond patrolman who'd been the first cop on the scene of Ernest Tulley's murder. He stood in a corner of the detective's office, a closet-sized nook rendered all the more cramped by the books and files stacked around its perimeter. The windowless walls were papered with newspaper articles, photographs of crime scenes, and leaflets illustrated with drawings of menacing-looking men.

"May I take your coat?" Cook asked.

She shook her head. "I can't stay long. I've got to get to the Charles Street Jail as soon as possible."

Gesturing Nell into a leather chair facing his cluttered desk, Cook took a seat behind it and folded his arms. "I've been thinking I should let Patrolman Hooper tell you exactly what he saw Saturday night, just like he told it to me. I'd meant to spare you the details, but it strikes me it might serve to enlighten you a bit about the accused and what he's truly capable of. And seeing as how you're not one of these wilting blossoms who carries the smelling salts around with her, I'm thinking you can handle it." He nodded to the patrolman. "Go ahead, Danny. You were in the vicinity of Foster's Wharf when you heard a woman scream . . ."

"So I come runnin'," Hooper said. "Didn't take me but a minute to get to the alley, and I seen that Toussaint fella crouching over a dead man—or maybe he wasn't quite dead yet, I'm not real sure. Actually, I wasn't even sure it was a man at first, 'cause his hair was kind of long and tangled, and there was a big mat of it laying over his face. There was—begging your pardon, miss, but there was blood everywheres. I mean, on the ground, on the side of the building . . ."

"Was he actively bleeding when you got there?" Nell asked.

Hooper hesitated. "Um . . . I'm not rightly sure."

"If there was still arterial bleeding, you would have noticed," she said. "It would have spurted out in rhythm with his heart. If it wasn't, he was probably already dead."

"I guess he was, then. But Toussaint was hollering at him anyways—cursing, calling him names. I pulled my Colt and ordered him to stand up, but I don't even think he heard me. He just keeps on doing what he was doing—"

"What, exactly, *was* he doing?" Nell asked. "Or could

you see well enough to tell? There wasn't much moonlight Saturday, and no snow to reflect light."

Cook said, "There was light coming from the boardinghouse windows—not much, but some. I remember that."

"That's right," Hooper said. "I could see that the dead man had his throat laid open, and a knife sticking out of it, a little one. Turned my stomach, if you want to know the truth."

"Was Mr. Toussaint actually cutting him?" Nell asked.

"He was choking him."

"*Choking* him!"

"Yeah, it was like he'd done as much as he could do with the knife, but he couldn't stop. You should have seen his eyes. They were like a wild animal's, and his face was spattered with blood. He's got his hands around the fella's throat, and he's squeezing so hard he's all red in the face. Still he's swearing at the poor guy, saying he deserved worse than he was getting, stuff like that."

"What else?" Nell asked. "Can you remember his exact words?"

"Yeah, he called him . . . something bad, something I don't like to repeat in front of a lady. He said 'You should choke to death, you . . . ' That's when he said the bad word. 'Or down in the mud.' "

"Drown in the mud?"

Hooper shrugged. "That's what it sounded like to me. He said, 'You're getting off easy, you . . .' Well, you know."

Nell sat back, dismayed and bewildered. Hard as she tried to envision William Hewitt murdering a man so savagely, the image wouldn't form in her mind.

"I finally just walked right up to him and put the barrel of my gun right smack against the side of his head and told him to stop what he was doing and put his hands in the air," Hooper said. "He calmed down some then."

"A gun to the head will have that effect," Cook observed.

The patrolman said, "By then, someone had raised the alarm, and they were pouring out of that boardinghouse like roaches when you light the gas jets. Only ones that stuck around till Detective Cook came was the owner and his daughter—and one other fella, a dago, I think."

Cook's gaze lit on something over Nell's shoulder. "Yes, Ferguson."

"There's a woman here to see you, Detective," said the officer standing in the doorway. "Says her name is Pearl Stauber."

"Really!" Cook sat forward, smiling. "That's the new chippy from the boardinghouse," he reminded Nell. "Send her in. Danny, you're dismissed. Unless Miss Sweeney has anything further to . . . ?"

Nell shook her head. "Thank you, Patrolman."

Except for the addition of a voluminous red shawl, Pearl looked much the same as she had yesterday evening: same green satin dress, peroxided yellow hair *sans* hat, and tired face paint. She paused in the doorway, steadying herself with a hand on the jamb as she took in the tiny office and its inhabitants with a gaze that looked a bit too unfocused for midmorning. A sour-sweet fusion of gin and rose oil wafted from her.

"Here." Rising, Nell offered the other woman her chair. "I'll be leaving soon."

Pearl sat heavily, tucking her shawl around her. "I don't suppose you've got a bit of the hair of the dog," she asked Cook in a slightly thick-tongued voice. "I've got the devil's own morning head."

"Gave up the bottle for Mrs. Cook when I got married," the detective replied, rising and heading out the door. "But most of the boys have a little taste tucked away somewhere. I'll be right back."

Pearl turned to squint blearily at Nell after Cook left. "Who the hell *are* you, anyway?"

"I'm Nell . . . Chapel. With the Society for Criminals and . . . I mean the *Relief* of Criminals and . . . No, *Convicts* and Indigents. I, uh, I've taken a personal interest in this case, so Detective Cook is letting me observe the proceedings."

Cook returned then with a nearly full pint of whiskey, from which Pearl eagerly gulped. "That's enough," Cook said, taking it back. "You're not hung over, you're drunk. Did you spend the whole night that way, or was it that you needed a little Dutch courage before you came here?"

"A bit of both, I guess," Pearl said as she dabbed her mouth with her shawl, staining it with whiskey and lip rouge. "That Roy Noonan wouldn't like it one little bit if he knew about this. He don't see as how none of us should tell the coppers nothin', even if it don't concern him."

"Not fond of the constabulary, is he?" Cook asked dryly.

"He's got a brother in New York went simple in the head after the cops worked him over a little too rough. If he knew I was here . . ." She frowned. "You won't let it get back to him, will you?"

"Course not."

"It's just, you said if anyone had somethin' they wanted to say without an audience, they was to come here," Pearl said. "So I came." She gazed longingly at the bottle in Cook's hand. "Just one more sip to—"

"After you tell me what you came to tell," he said. "I take it you know something about the murder?"

"I know about something that happened a few hours before—maybe around eight o'clock. I was upstairs in the pink room. That's where we take, uh . . ." She glanced uncomfortably at Nell.

"I know about the pink room," Nell said. "Who were you there with?"

Pearl rolled her eyes. "Noonan, God help me. So, anyway, we're . . . doin' what we're doin', when all of a sudden there come this racket from right above us like to wake the dead. They was screamin', slammin' furniture around. I half expected the ceiling to fall in."

"Did you recognize any of the voices?" Nell asked.

"One of 'em was that Kathleen Flynn, which makes sense, seein' as how that's her bedroom up there—only her pa, he don't allow no one up there but him and the girl, so I was surprised to hear them others."

"Were they male voices?"

Pearl nodded, her gaze on the bottle of whiskey. "Yeah, it was that Ernest Tulley, the one that ended up dead in the alley, and the other one—the one they arrested."

"William Toussaint?" Nell asked, thinking, *No . . . please don't let it have been him.*

"That's right," Pearl said.

Nell asked, "You knew for sure it was them? Just from their voices?"

"Toussaint's got that limey accent, right? Plus, I seen 'em. They come tearin' down the outside stairs, first Tulley and then the other one, trying to catch him. Tulley tripped and fell halfway down to the second floor and ends up sprawled on the landing. It was dark out, but I had a real good view through the window above the bed, 'cause I was facin' it on my hands and—"

"Thank you," Cook said, "I get the picture. What happened then? Did Toussaint catch up with him?"

"Oh, yeah, he leaps off the stairs and lands on him hard. They tussle a bit, and then Tulley slams that fella right through the window."

Nell winced, visualizing the boarded-up second-floor window.

"Toussaint lands on the bed, right in front of us, glass flyin'. It's a wonder none of us was cut. Tulley, he goes poundin' down the stairs. Noonan's fit to be tied. He starts throwin' punches at Toussaint, but Toussaint's already headin' for the door and Noonan's got his pants around his ankles. Anyway, by that time, Tulley was long gone. Toussaint looked for him, but it's a tangle of alleys over there near the wharves—no tellin' which way he may have gone."

"Do you have any idea what they were fighting about?" Cook asked.

"It was the girl," Pearl said, as if that should be obvious. "They was fightin' over that cow like she was Helen of Troy."

"Are you sure?" Nell asked. "Did you hear what they were saying?"

"Didn't have to. They both ended up in her bedroom at the same time, which sounds like bad planning on her part, but what can you expect from an ignorant little drab like that? I thought it was just that Eye-talian she was lifting her skirts for. Turns out she's givin' free rides to anything in pants. No wonder I can't make enough to live on."

Cook said, "Toussaint returned, presumably."

"Yeah, and heads straight back to the parlor, which was where he'd been before all the hubbub. Back to his gong—I seen him cookin' up another bowlful when I come back down."

"Was anyone else there with him?" Nell asked.

"Couple of fellas—looked like sailors. I went back out to hang around the cellar stairs with the other girls, but it was freezing cold out there, and I wasn't gettin' picked, so I come back inside. I headed for the back parlor to lay down on one of them couches, 'cause us girls had been passing around a bottle to keep warm, and I was feeling a little woozy. The sailors was gone, but that Toussaint was still there—he'd nodded off between bowls. There was another fella there, too, and he was a gentleman—

real fine clothes. Me and him started conversatin'.''

Cook grunted. "I'll bet you did."

Pearl answered that with an expression of frosty disdain. "He let me drink some of his whiskey, and then I just couldn't keep my eyes open one more minute, so I laid myself down and dozed off. When I woke up, they was talkin' about Tulley."

"You mean Toussaint and the other man?" Nell asked. "Did it seem as if they knew each other?"

"Oh, yeah, I'm pretty sure they did. They seemed real friendly. The one fella, the whiskey drinker, I think he might of been in politics. The city government, maybe, somethin' like that."

"What made you think that?" Cook asked.

Pearl shook her head distractedly, as if trying to remember. "I can't rightly say. Course, I'd had a snootful by then, so who knows? What I *do* remember was Toussaint sayin' he was gonna make Tulley pay for what he done."

"Are you sure?" Nell asked. *Oh, God...*

"Yeah, and he sounded like he meant business. They didn't know I was awake, 'cause it was real dark in there, so I just laid real still and listened. 'I'll make that bastard pay.' He musta said it a dozen times. I knew it was him 'cause of the accent. 'He'll pay for it, damn him. He'll pay with his life.' That sort of thing."

Nell shook her head, her gaze on the floor, her mind whirring. *He'll pay with his life...* Over a woman? She couldn't see it. But perhaps when one considered that Tulley was a Southerner... William Hewitt had, after all, suffered greatly at the hands of the Confederates. Could a man ever be the same after enduring what he'd endured? Was that enough, along with the opium intoxication, to induce a murderous rage in an otherwise civilized, if somewhat dissolute, man?

Cook took down Pearl's address on Milk Street—a little flat a few blocks from Flynn's, which she shared with her friend Molly—and instructed her to stay in touch. "Buy yourself a dark, plain dress and a decent hat—something you can wear to court without lookin' quite so much like what you are."

Pearl rose to her feet, eyeing the whiskey. "You said I could have some more of that after I told you what I come to tell."

Holding the bottle out of her reach, he said, "That was before I realized you had such valuable testimony to present. You're going to need to sober up and stay that way. Won't be much use to us in the shape you're in now."

"Don't know what I was thinkin'," Pearl muttered as she huffed out, "trusting a cop to keep his word."

"So," Cook began after Pearl had left and they were all alone. "You've got August Hewitt thinking that murdering cur might be innocent after all, eh?"

"Not at all. He's as determined as ever to see him hang." Nell wanted to make sure Cook didn't doubt this, lest he say something to Captain Baxter about Mr. Hewitt's change of heart, which would be disastrous once it got back to Mr. Hewitt himself.

"Then why on earth would he bail him out?"

"I gather Mrs. Hewitt insisted on it," Nell replied, thinking the best lie was one that echoed the truth as closely as possible. "She's planning on retaining an attorney, too."

"Ah. Of course. She has no idea her husband's out to see her son writhing at the end of a noose, eh?"

"That's right."

"Well, writhe he will," Cook said with a smug grin, "bail or no bail, attorney or no attorney, now that all the pieces are falling so neatly into place."

"Are you going to have Noonan testify, too? I know he won't want to, but you could subpoena him."

"It's up to the prosecutor, but I'll advise against it. First

of all, all's he witnessed was that tussle on the stairs between Hewitt and Tulley. Pearl's the only one who heard
Hewitt say that about making Tulley pay. Secondly, even
if we could bully him onto the stand, he'd be more of a
liability than an asset. Pearl we can clean up and coach.
Noonan, forget it. The jury's bound to distrust him and
anything that comes out of his mouth. We don't need him,
anyway. Pearl's testimony clinches the case against William Hewitt."

"Not quite," Nell said. "Did it occur to you to ask
yourself why she went to the bother—and risk—of coming here to tell you this? People like her don't go out of
their way to court trouble, Detective, and they only tell
the authorities what they want them to know, I can assure
you of that."

"Oh, you can," Cook cheerfully sneered. "And what
would you know of it, eh?"

Careful. "It's just common sense," Nell bluffed. "But
I daresay it might be useful to find out why Pearl Stauber
is so eager to incriminate Dr. Hewitt."

"And how do you propose to do that, seeing as how
people like that only tell us what they want us to know?"

"You have to ask?" She plucked the bottle of whiskey
out of his hand and strode out of the room, leaving him
staring after her.

"PEARL!" Nell, clutching the bottle and frock coat while
holding her skirts above the slush, caught up to her
quarry on the corner of Williams and Congress. "Wait!"

Pearl turned, shielding her eyes with her hand, her
grimace sweetening when she saw the bottle.

"I thought that was terribly unfair of Detective Cook,"
Nell said, hoping it didn't take too long to find out what
she wanted to know. She had to get to the Charles Street
Jail; God knew how badly William Hewitt's condition had

deteriorated since yesterday. "A promise is a promise. Do you suppose there's anyplace we can go . . . ?" Public drinking was a surefire way to get arrested in Boston.

Pearl looked around and spotted an alley between a bank and a small hotel. "In there."

It was chillier out of the sun, but they found relatively clean fruit crates to sit on, and they were away from prying eyes. Pearl went through the motions once of offering the bottle to Nell, who politely declined, then set about steadily emptying it. "That hits the spot." In the shadowy light between the two buildings, the prostitute seemed to be wearing a crudely painted plaster mask.

"How long have you been . . . doing what you're doing?" Nell asked conversationally.

Pearl looked at her over the bottle, wiped her mouth. "This the first time you ever talked to somebody like me?"

Would that it were. "Well, yes. And I must say, I'm a bit curious."

"Least you admit it." Pearl smiled knowingly as she took another swallow. "I been liftin' my skirts for a livin' maybe nine, ten years, but I've only been at Flynn's about a week. Molly said it was easier money than the street, and warmer, but I don't care for it one bit. I still have to stand out in the cold on Saturday nights, and them other girls get most of the business, 'cause they're younger. I like the rich young swells, when I get one of them—they smell good, and they finish up quick, if they're not too drunk—but them sailors, they're a rough bunch. That Noonan? Mother of God."

"A tough customer, eh?"

"You can't see it," Pearl said, pointing to her right cheek, caked with paint and powder, "but I'm black and blue under here."

"Oh. Did he do that Saturday, when you and he . . . ?"

Pearl swallowed down some more whiskey, nodded. "He kinda lost his, uh, interest after all that ruckus with

Tulley and Toussaint. Blamed it on me, though. Said I was too fat and ugly to be in the business, and it was my fault he couldn't come. I made the mistake of lookin' him up and down and saying at least I get *paid* to do it with the fat, ugly ones. There's some of you so desperate you have to pay *me*."

Nell winced through her laughter, knowing what came next.

"He told me he'd pay me, all right, and then he back-handed me into the bedpost. Said he'd stop there 'cause I was nasty lookin' enough without havin' my face bashed up, but if I crossed him one more time, he'd make sure no man would ever want to pay for me again."

"And yet," Nell said carefully, "you came to the station house this morning, which would be bound to infuriate him if he found out."

"He won't."

"But still, it's a risk. I'm just wondering why you took it."

Pearl tilted the bottle to her mouth; it was less than half full now. She stared at nothing in particular for a minute, her gaze unsteady, then took another drink. When she spoke again, her words were noticeably slurred. "I seen him come in Saturday night, Toussaint. First thing I think is, there's one deadly handsome devil. Then I realized who he was."

"You knew him?"

"Long time ago, back in 'fifty-six or 'fifty-seven, before I was . . . doing what I'm doing now. I was assistant wardrobe mistress for the stock company out of the Boston Theatre over on Washington. We were doing *Romeo and Juliet* and *Fortune's Frolic* that summer—same cast, one show right after the other, six nights a week plus matinees. Our Juliet was Virginia Kimball."

"Oh, I've seen her picture." A raven-haired beauty with

porcelain skin and slumberous, kohl-rimmed eyes. "Very
pretty."

"*I* was pretty back then. *She* was ravishing—you
wouldn't believe it if you saw her in the flesh." Pearl
sounded as wistful as if she were talking about a man,
one hand lightly stroking her throat. "And some actress.
The critics loved her. So did the men. That's when I first
seen William Toussaint. There was about a week that
summer where he practically lived backstage, tryin' to
make time with Mrs. Kimball—even though she was
probably a good ten years older than him, maybe fifteen.
She called him 'Doc' for some reason."

"*Mrs.* Kimball? Was she married?"

"If she was, no one ever saw him. But there *was* this
Italian count who'd bought her a house on Beacon Hill
and all them diamond necklaces she was so famous for.
Course, he was hardly ever around either, seein' as he had
a wife and another mistress and about a dozen kids in
Italy."

"Oh, dear."

"Mrs. Kimball, she'd get lonely, and she did love to
be wooed—and Doc was good at it, let me tell you—but
she just strung him along, batted him around like a kitten
with a ball of string, watchin' him unwind bit by bit. She
couldn't do nothin' more than flirt, see, 'cause if the count
found out, that'd be it for the house and the diamonds.
But Doc, he thought he had a fighting chance. He found
out different when the count cabled Mrs. Kimball that he
was on his way, and she told Doc to run off like a good
boy and quit pestering her."

"She said that?"

"In so many words, and after all them flowers and gifts,
and him being so . . ." Pearl sighed. "Damn, he was something. A little younger'n me, but not by much. Tall, elegant . . . Not real talkative, but when he did say something,
it was worth hearing. And he had these eyes that looked

like they could set you on fire if he stared at you hard
enough. Always treated me so nice—not like most men,
who only act that way to get you to drop your drawers.
Course, I woulda laid down in a heartbeat if he'd asked
me—he probably knew it, too. I swear I thought Mrs.
Kimball was touched in the head, to turn her nose up at
him, count or no count."

"How did he take it when she sent him away?" Nell
asked.

"He didn't make a scene, but I could tell he'd had his
heart ripped right out of his chest. He walked out of her
dressing room like a man in mourning. I told him he
looked like he could use a drink, and he said could he
ever. I didn't drink then like I do now, but I kept a bottle
of port in my little sewing alcove. We went in there and
pulled the curtain and tossed back a few. And then he sat
me on the edge of the cutting table and . . ."

Pearl drew in a tremulous breath, gulped down some
more whiskey. "It should have been bad like that, me on
that table with my skirts thrown up, him standin' there in
his evening clothes, just unbuttonin' what had to be unbuttoned, but he made it . . . Christ, I thought my heart
was damn near gonna burst. Do you know I had to bite
my lip so hard to keep from screamin' that I actually drew
blood?"

"My word."

"And he sent me the prettiest little pearl ear bobs the
next day," Pearl said, "with a note sayin' as how their
luster couldn't compare to mine—somethin' like that.
You know—'cause I'm called Pearl?"

"Yes."

"Course, I never saw him again, 'cept once the next
summer from a distance. He was in the audience for *King
Lear* and *The Guardian Outwitted*, with a couple of other
fellas. They left during one of the musical numbers we
added to *Lear*. Wasn't long after that I started runnin' out

of money and took to chargin' for it—just every once in a while at first, and then . . . Well."

"I don't understand," Nell said. "You recognized Toussaint. You'd liked him. Why on earth would you come here and give Detective Cook ammunition to prosecute him for murder?"

" 'Cause he did it." Another swig of whiskey.

"Even if you think that, you wouldn't have fingered him unless you had some reason to want to punish him. What happened Saturday night, Pearl? He came to the boardinghouse and you recognized him. Then what? Did you talk to him?"

"Not right away. I was aimin' to—I seen him there in the back parlor—but then Noonan drags me upstairs, and just when he gets goin', Tulley and Toussaint kick up that racket and I end up with nothin' to show for my time but a black-and-blue mark. By the time I got it covered up and went back downstairs, Toussaint was back to rollin' the log. I told him I was surprised to see the likes of him smokin' gong in a place like Flynn's, and I asked him how'd he been all these years. He looked at me the way folks look when they're tryin' to place you. I said, 'Boston Theatre, about ten, twelve years ago, remember? My hair was brown then.' He didn't remember—or if he did, he was pretending he didn't."

"I'm sorry."

"No, I know I've changed. I didn't hold it against him. Them two sailors was there, so I whispered in his ear that I wanted to take him upstairs and do him for free—anything he wanted, on me. He turned me down. Fed me some soft solder about how pretty I was, and it wasn't me, but his parts don't work like they should, and I'd be wastin' my time."

"He said that?" Nell asked incredulously. "That he couldn't . . . ?"

"Yeah, sounded fishy to me, too—'specially since I

knew from personal experience that his parts worked just fine, and then some. Plus which, hadn't he just been upstairs tryin' to do to Kathleen Flynn what he's now sayin' he can't do at all? I ain't no genius, but I can put two and two together, and what it added up to was he wanted a woman, he just didn't want me." Pearl's voice snagged; her chin quivered.

"Pearl, maybe he—"

"Do you know how many times," she asked in a rusty-damp voice, moisture welling in her eyes, "when I was layin' under some stranger, waitin' for it to be over, I would close my eyes and pretend he was Doc? It made me feel so good about myself, every time I remembered that a man like that had wanted me once. It was just about the only thing that ever did make me feel good about myself." She shook her head; tears spilled down her cheeks, trailing rivulets of eye paint. "Damn him."

Nell handed her a handkerchief. She dabbed at her face. "Didn't help my frame of mind none to spend the next hour out there in the cold, tryin' to catch the eye of some fella half my age. I didn't really go back to the back parlor to take a nap, like I told the detective. I was aimin' to give that Toussaint a piece of my mind for conjurin' up a boldfaced lie and thinkin' I'd believe it, but he'd nodded off, so I struck up a conversation with that other fella. He was a real charmer, and his whiskey wasn't half bad. I offered to do him French-style for a half-buck, right there, 'cause Molly had someone upstairs in the pink room, and there was another girl waitin' for it after that."

"You were willing to . . . do that with Toussaint still in the room?" Nell asked.

"Toussaint was asleep when I started in on the other one, but it took forever, so I was still goin' at it when he woke up. He seen what was goin' on, but he didn't pay us no mind, just smoked him another bowlful, then dozed off again. Finally, I just had to stop. I thought the fella'd

be mad, but he said it was all that whiskey he'd drunk,
and he gave me a three-dollar gold piece for my trouble!
Now, *that's* a gentleman."

"Indeed."

"I drank some more of his whiskey and fell asleep on
one of the couches. When I woke up, Toussaint was
sayin' that about Tulley payin' for what he done."

Nell said, "What did he look like, the other man?"

Pearl shrugged. "Young. Nice lookin'. They're all nice
lookin', them types."

"You'd recognize him if you saw him again? Even
though it was dark in there?"

"My eyes had gotten used to the dark, and I got a real
good look at him. Yeah, I'd recognize him." Pearl shook
the bottle, sloshing the remaining ounce or so of whiskey
around inside. "I've had a pretty wasted life, I guess. I
used to think I was gonna be a seamstress, open up a shop,
something like that. I grew up on a farm, you see, and we
was dirt poor. All my sisters went to work in the mills
just north of here, in Charlestown, but I wanted something
better, so I come to Boston." She laughed harshly and
drained the bottle. "More the fool me."

Chapter 6

"THIS is highly irregular, Miss Chapel." Lloyd Cavanaugh, a sallow little man with slick black hair who was deputy warden of the Suffolk County Jail on Charles Street, squinted at Nell's bail order through diminutive spectacles. "First I'm told to put him in solitary confinement—which is, by the way, utterly contrary to policy here, a fact which nobody seems to care about but me—and then six hours later I'm to let him go?" He ruminated over the papers for far too long, as if looking for a reason to challenge the order.

Please, Saint Dismas, don't let this dreadful little man ruin everything.

Cavanaugh slapped the papers down with a grimace. "Reichert!"

A lumbering uniformed guard appeared in the doorway of Cavanaugh's office, a ring of keys in one hand, a short club tethered to the wrist of the other. "Sir?"

"Go fetch William Toussaint."

"That's the one that's sick," Reichert observed.

"Well, he won't be our problem anymore, will he?"

The guard shambled away, sorting through his keys. Cavanaugh sat back, fingers laced on his chest, his gaze—bug-eyed through the tiny eyeglasses—fixed unwaveringly on Nell. With a glance at the coat folded over her arm, he asked, "What, if I may ask, is your interest in this prisoner?"

"He's a charity project of the lady I work for."

"And that would be . . . ?"

"Mrs. John Amory Lowell." The Lowells were August Hewitt's main competition in the textile business. Although indisputably one of the First Families of Boston, Mr. Hewitt regarded them as relative newcomers, their presence in His City dating from barely over a century ago. They were, in his estimation, "avaricious parvenus who got where they are by marrying their cousins," and he did not receive them. He would be furious, of course, that a Lowell matron with philanthropic pretensions had arranged for his son's release, but his pride—and the risk of exposing William Toussaint's true identity—would leave him no choice but to let it go.

"Mrs. Lowell, eh?" The little man's eyes filled the thick lenses. He sat up, tucked his chair in, straightened some papers. "Most kind and generous of her to take an interest in the . . . less fortunate."

"I quite agree."

"Yes. Yes, indeed."

He fussed and fiddled until Reichert returned—at a trot this time, and breathless, keys clattering. "What's the matter, man?" Cavanaugh demanded. "And where the devil is William Tou—"

"I think he's dying," the guard panted. "He was having some kind of fit when I went in there, and then he just . . . He's laying there, gasping for air, and he don't answer when I—"

"I've got to see him," Nell said. "Let me—"

"Out of the question," Cavanaugh retorted. "Ladies aren't permitted in the men's cellblocks."

"I—I'm a nurse. I can help him. *Please.*"

The deputy warden shook his head resolutely. "It's strictly against procedure. If I make an exception for you, I'll be compelled to make it for—"

"How do you suppose Mrs. Lowell will react when I tell her you allowed this man to die rather than bend the rules just this once?" Nell demanded.

Streaks of pink stained Cavanaugh's cheeks. "Take her back there," he ordered Reichert. "But make sure the prisoners are all in their cells first, and don't leave her side for a moment."

The big guard ushered her through the administrative core of this cruciform granite monstrosity to a door fashioned from iron bars and wire lattice, which was locked and manned by two keepers. Their jaws dropped when they saw Nell. She and Reichert had to wait while the prisoners were herded into their cells, whereupon the door was unlocked and she was escorted into a long, cavernous atrium lined with four stories of cellblocks. It was surprisingly bright, sunlight from tall windows reflecting off whitewashed walls—a far cry from any jail Nell had ever seen the inside of.

Some voices rose above the drone resonating in the vast corridor. "Look what Reichert done brung us!" someone bellowed from one of the cells, to the accompaniment of snickers and lascivious moans. "A late Christmas present, d'you reckon?"

"Bring her up here," someone called from the tier above. "I'll do the unwrappin'."

There followed a cacophony of wolf whistles, guffaws, and suggestive remarks, most of them far more lewd than anything she'd heard at Flynn's Boardinghouse last night. "Sorry about them animals, miss." Reichert shook his head as he rummaged among the keys on his ring. "This

is one of them *modern* prisons"—he sneered the word—
"where they let 'em run around in the yard all day and
feed 'em beefsteak for supper. *I* don't have it that good.
You ask me, we should burn this place down, and the lot
of 'em with it. How's *that* for progressive?"

Unlocking a cell door toward the end of the row, he
called out, "Toussaint?"

Nell stepped around the guard and into a good-sized,
sun-washed cell, sucking in a breath when she saw the
inert form of William Hewitt in a fetal position on the
narrow bed, chin tucked to his chest, arms locked around
his middle. His bruise-mottled face was pallid, his eyes
half-closed and bleary. He looked like every corpse Nell
had ever seen.

She made a feverish sign of the cross as she leaned
over him. "Doc—" *Careful.* "M-Mr. Toussaint."

"Toussaint!" Reichert nudged the insensate man with
his truncheon. "You still with us?"

He was answered with a strangled breath, such as a
victim of consumption might produce in his death throes.
William Hewitt was alive, after all—but in even worse
condition than Nell had anticipated. This close to him, she
could see how he trembled. A sudden spasm gripped him;
he clutched at his stomach, groaning.

Laying the coat on the foot of the bed, Nell fumbled
in her chatelaine—the small bag bulging with its contents
today—for the little bottle she'd brought with her. "Mr.
Toussaint, can you sit up?"

She touched his arm; he flinched. "Take *me*!" he cried
hoarsely. "I'll do it! I'll do it, you bastard!"

Nell edged closer with the bottle—warily, given his
delirium. "I have something to make you—"

"Christ, no." He shuddered convulsively, his eyes
glazed and watery. "No, no, no . . . I would have done it.
I *would* have."

"Mr. Toussaint. *William.* Listen to me. I've got—"

"Damn you to Hell," he rasped, "So help me God, I'll make you pay for—"

"Will." She touched his arm.

He flung her aside with one fierce sweep of his arm. Nell yelped as her head struck the wall, thrusting her hat down over her eyes. She tore it off to find Reichert looming over Will, snarling, "You dog. Is that how you treat a lady who's trying to help you?"

"No!" she cried as he slammed his club into Will's stomach. Will groaned and curled into a ball, retching violently but bringing nothing up; Nell suspected he hadn't eaten since his arrest. "Don't! He doesn't know what he's doing."

"Animals, the lot of 'em," Reichert muttered, shaking his head.

"Here." Sitting on the edge of the bed, she uncorked the bottle. "This will make you feel—"

"It'll kill me." Struggling to a sitting position, he backed away from her. "Stockade Creek's full of typhoid."

Stockade Creek? "It's medicine, not water. Here." Curling one hand around the back of his rigid neck to hold his head still, she brought the open bottle close to his nose. "See?"

He stopped fighting her as the distinctive scents of camphor and aniseed wafted from the open bottle, which contained an opium tincture familiar to just about everybody who'd ever sought relief from a bad cough or a bout of diarrhea.

Will's rheumy gaze met hers for a fleeting moment. There was recognition, surprise, and unless she was very much mistaken, a glimmer of gratitude in his expression as he wrapped his hand around hers and tilted the bottle to his mouth.

"Stop!" she exclaimed as he gulped its contents. "You'll kill yourself, taking that much!" Prying his fingers open, she loosened his surprisingly strong grip and wrested the bottle away, appalled to find he'd half-emptied it.

He sank back against the wall, eyes closed, dragging in wheezy breaths that grew gradually slower and less erratic, until she couldn't hear them at all anymore.

Reichert leaned over him, prodded his shoulder. "Is he . . . ?"

"William?" she said anxiously. "Will?"

There was no response.

"This don't look good," Reichert said. "What *was* that stuff?"

"Oh, God," Nell whispered. Had she just helped William Hewitt to commit suicide? "Will? *Will?*" She patted his face.

He stirred, his breath coming in stertorous little hitches that alarmed her until she realized he was chuckling. "I'd have to drink a quart of paregoric to do myself any harm—or much good, for that matter." He raked both palsied hands through his hair.

Oh, thank God. "I know it's not very strong, but it was all I could find at home." It was laudanum she'd been looking for as she'd rummaged in vain through the Hewitts' medicine cupboard; the most popular opiated tonic on the market, laudanum contained more than twice as much morphine as paregoric.

"It'll do," he said, reaching for the bottle, "assuming I get enough of it."

"No!" Nell stood, tucking the bottle securely in her bag. "You've had too much already, and I need to get you out of this place. Here, put this on." She shook out the fine, double-breasted black frock coat and helped him into it. It was a castoff of his father's that Viola had intended to donate to charity. Mr. Hewitt had them made on Saville Row in London; they all looked exactly alike.

"I'll show you out the back way," Reichert said as Will

rose awkwardly to his feet, holding on to the wall for support. "So's you don't have to run that gauntlet again."

Will's progress out of the building and across the yard to the brick wall surrounding the prison was slow and erratic, with Nell supporting him most of the way. Not only was he woozy, but there was that limp of his to contend with. Despite his leanness, he felt heavy and unwieldy, frequently stumbling and having a hard time regaining his feet. It called to mind all those black, frigid nights Nell had had to walk her father home from Dougal's Tavern, with him swaying and lurching and crooning his mournful "Kathleen, Mavourneen."

Reichert escorted them through the front gate and returned to his post, leaving them on bustling Charles Street, blinking against the glare of sunlight off yesterday's snow. Will slumped against an iron horse trough, a wavering hand shielding his eyes. Hatless, collarless, and grimy, with a pale, bruised face and two days' growth of beard, Dr. William Hewitt looked every bit the quintessential derelict; a casual passerby would assume the elegant coat was stolen.

He doubled over, fingers digging into his stomach, groaning a cloud of vapor into the frosty air.

"Are you all right?" she asked. "Dr. Hew—"

"I told you not to come," he gasped, gripping the trough with rigid hands. "You should have listened to me."

Was it that he hadn't wanted her to see him like this, ailing and humbled? Or had he been trying to protect her from an experience he knew she would find disturbing, even sickening? Was it pride or a deeply buried chivalry that had motivated him? The latter was not impossible. A man might be capable of murder, yet harbor a perverse spark of nobility in his breast, as she knew all too well. Such men were the most dangerous of all.

"Yes, well, I didn't much want to come either but your

mother didn't give me much choice." Nell spied an empty
hansom cab half-hidden behind a streetcar rumbling
through the graying slush of Charles Street, and hailed it.
"Come," she urged, gesturing for Will. "I'm to see you
home."

"I've no money for a cab," he said as the compact
black coach drew up in front of them. "The Station Two
gendarmes cleaned me out quite thoroughly, I'm afraid."

"They stole your money? The police?"

"My money, my watch, my cigarette case . . . Let's
see . . . coat, vest . . . oh, yes, my sleeve buttons . . ."

"They stole your coat and vest? Are you sure they
didn't just set them aside to use as evidence?"

He shook his head. "One of them tried them on and
said his wife was good at getting bloodstains out. I left
my hat and overcoat at the boardinghouse, but no doubt
they've been filched by now."

Shaking her head, Nell prodded him toward the waiting
vehicle as its driver, seated high up behind the open-
fronted cab, tipped his hat to her. "Don't worry about the
money. Where are you staying?"

"Not far from here. You needn't come."

"Your mother insists. She wants to know where you
live and to be assured that you've gotten there safely."

Despite Will's condition, he gestured for Nell to enter
the cab first and supported her elbow as she stepped up
into it, settling herself at the far end of the tufted leather
seat. No sooner had he climbed in beside her than he
slumped down, wrapped his arms around himself, and
closed his eyes. He was shivering, but she suspected it
was more from the opium sickness than from the cold.
The paregoric had eased his misery only marginally, it
would seem.

"Where to?" the driver asked.

"Dr. Hewitt." Nell shook his shoulder. "You need to
give the driver an address."

"What did you mean," he asked blearily, "don't worry about the money?"

She withdrew a fat envelope from her bag and handed it to him. "There's about two hundred dollars there, I think—what was left over from the Pawners' Bank after paying your way out of jail. Your mother wanted you to have it."

He sat up straight, thumbing through the bills.

"You folks want me to take you someplace?" the driver asked. "If not, I'd appreciate it if you'd—"

"Corner of Tyler and Kneeland," Will answered, stuffing the money in his trouser pocket. The driver flicked his reins. Turning to Nell as the cab started rattling down the street, Will said, "Tell Lady Viola I'll pay her back as soon as the cards start falling my way."

"Is that how you've been supporting yourself?" Nell asked.

"I assumed you knew." A shudder coursed through him; he rubbed his arms.

"Here in Boston, or . . ."

He shook his head. "There are gaming hells aplenty in other, less troublesome cities—New York, Shanghai, San Francisco . . ."

Shanghai?

"I'd been steering clear of London and Boston—too many people one wouldn't care to run into . . . postmortem, as it were." Ruefully he added, "But then I followed a high-stakes faro game here a couple of weeks ago, much against my better judgment. Thought I could keep to the shadows, win a pocketful of rocks, and slip away quietly. Should have listened to my gut, eh?"

He gave her a mild little smile that disconcerted her, inasmuch as it seemed to suggest some sort of understanding between them, not to mention his presumption that she sympathized with his plight: arrest for murder.

Hunkering down in his corner of the seat, Will folded

his arms, crossed his legs, and closed his eyes. He fell utterly still and remained so, despite the jouncing of their vehicle as it wove and dodged among the horse cars, carriages, carts, and pedestrians jostling each other in the narrow cobblestone lanes of Beacon Hill. As they rounded the King's Chapel Burial Ground, quaint brick row houses gave way to elegant granite buildings with canopied shops at ground level: *S.A. KING, Photographist; A.B. CHILD, Dentist; EMIL F. NOLTE, Hairdresser; C.F. POTTER, Ladies' Boots*. The shop fronts grew humbler as the main business district gave way to the South Cove, their windows devoid of awnings, their signs—COAL, FISH, JUNK, IRON FENCES, BACON, LUMBER—crudely lettered. Even when the modern granite-block roadbed retrogressed to archaic brick, causing the cab to jiggle maddeningly, the man beside her did not stir.

Hearing a little *hmph* of laughter, Nell turned to find Will studying her through drowsy eyes. "I must say I'm surprised to see a proper little thing like you without a hat," he said. "Or indeed, with your hair in such agreeable disarray."

Nell raised a hand to the curlicues springing loose from her chenille-netted hair, momentarily puzzled by the absence of the brown velvet bonnet she'd donned that morning—puzzled and dismayed. Only a certain kind of woman went about hatless. "Oh . . . it came off when you . . ." *When you hurled me into that wall.* "That is, it must have fallen off back at the—"

"When I what?"

She hesitated. "You weren't yourself. It wasn't your fault."

He stared at her a moment; she thought he was going to say something, but he turned away with a grimace and slammed a fist on the roof of the cab. "Pull over!"

Chapter 7

STEAM gusted from the horses' nostrils as the driver reined them in at the corner of Harrison and Beach, their hooves clattering on the uneven bricks.

"What? No." She tugged at Will's sleeve as he unfolded himself from his seat, but he wrested himself free with a force that hurled her back.

Staggering to the edge of the street, he dropped to his knees, his back heaving. By the time Nell made it to his side, what little his stomach had held was in the gutter.

The driver eyed him with distaste. "Is he drunk?"

"No," Nell said as she helped Will to his feet. "Just ill."

The fellow looked skeptical; given Will's appearance, she could hardly blame him. He raised his reins as if to take off. "I don't need some sot making a mess of my—"

"He won't," she promised as she guided Will back to the cab. "He's done being sick. We'll pay you double."

The driver looked on warily as Nell wrestled Will back into the leather seat, where he crumpled with a series of ragged coughs. He grunted in evident pain as the cab lurched forward, his body racked with tremors. "Give me the paregoric."

"I'm afraid to," she said, grabbing her chatelaine as he reached for it. "You've had so much already."

"Which I've just thrown up, in case it escaped your notice."

"Yes, but—"

Seizing her wrists painfully to pry her hands off the bag, he tore open its flap and fished out the bottle. He drained it in one long swallow, wiped his mouth with the back of a trembling hand, and returned the empty bottle to her.

She watched as he settled back into the seat, dragging a hand through his lank hair. He closed his eyes, breathing in great, harsh lungfuls of air.

"Does it help?" she asked.

"It's not enough, by a long shot." He sounded winded, and looked half-dead, which she supposed he was. "But it will . . . get me where I need to go." He regarded her with quiet curiosity. "How did you know to bring it?"

"Once, back during the war—it was the summer of 'sixty-three, I think—Dr. Greaves was summoned by a family whose son had been discharged from an Army hospital with a chest wound. I went with him. Tommy was the boy's name—that's all he was, really, just a boy, no more than eighteen. At first they'd thought it was his wound acting up, then they began to suspect appendicitis, because of the abdominal pain. By the time we got there, Tommy could barely breathe, and he was convulsing so badly they'd had to tie him to his bed. He kept screaming for his pills, but he'd run out. His parents got new ones from the druggist, but they were the wrong kind."

Will sank deeper into the seat, rasping both hands over his face; his eyes were red-rimmed, as if he hadn't slept in days. "All those opium pills I dispensed in field hospitals—thousands of them, great, rattling floods of them . . ." he said, his voice weary. "I often wondered what would happen when some of those lads got home. But when you saw a man's leg off . . . and I sawed them off by the score after every battle, sometimes by the hundreds, arms as well . . . Minié balls expand when they hit bone, smash it to bits. Nine minutes per leg—that's all it took me. When you do that to a man, you've got to give him *something*, something that works. Say what you will about opium, it kills pain like nothing else. One minute they're screaming and sobbing and thrashing, and the next . . ." His expression grew oddly contemplative; he almost smiled. "Blessed oblivion." He looked at Nell. "I take it your Dr. Greaves correctly diagnosed the boy's affliction?"

"Oh, yes. He tried giving him some laudanum, which was all he had with him, but by that time, it was too late— he couldn't keep anything down. If Dr. Greaves had had a hypodermic syringe and some morphine . . . but he didn't used to carry that sort of thing with him. He does now."

"The boy died?"

"Horribly. I hadn't known that could happen. I mean, I knew it was possible to die from too large a dose of opium. There's always a warning," she said, squinting at the small type on the empty paregoric bottle. "Same with laudanum or Godfrey's Cordial or Atkinson's Infants Preservative or any of the pills or powders. But it had never occurred to me that one could die from being used to it and then not having it."

"One can if one's dependence is profound enough."

Like yours? she wanted to ask. Will's condition, when she'd first encountered him today, had seemed every bit as dire as Tommy's.

"Opium withdrawal can produce respiratory distress, as you've witnessed," he continued, sounding an awful lot like Dr. Greaves instructing Nell in the medical arts, "and in the worst cases, cessation of heart function. But more often than not, it's just a week or so of . . . unpleasantness."

An understatement if ever Nell had heard one. "Have you ever gone through it?" she asked. "I mean, all the way through it?"

"Dear God, why would I want to?" He sat up as the cab pulled to the curb at the corner of Tyler and Kneeland. "This is my destination. I'll pay the driver to take you back to Colonnade Row."

"Your mother expects me to see you inside," Nell said as she gathered her skirts.

"I don't recommend it, but suit yourself."

Nell looked around as Will helped her down from the cab and paid the driver his double fare. This was a block of unassuming shops similar to those they had passed on the way, except that one—the one Will headed toward, with Nell on his heels—bore signs written in Chinese rather than English. There was a display of Oriental curios in its front window, along with open crates of turnips, rice, oranges, and limes.

Walking into this bizarre little grocery store, to the glassy tinkle of chimes, was like stepping out of Boston and into Hong Kong or Shanghai—or rather, into Hong Kong *and* Shanghai all compressed into one small shop, for it was a veritable riot of clutter and color. Floor-to-ceiling shelves held a dazzling array of Chinese-labeled jars, crocks, bundles, and boxes, every inch of remaining wall space being occupied by Oriental artwork, banners, and placards inked in baffling rows of calligraphy. Paper lanterns of every configuration dangled from the ceiling, along with clusters of herbs, garlic, onions and what appeared to be desiccated fowl of some sort. Snugged together atop lacquered chests were trays packed with figs, ginger, sticky-dark sweetmeats, and various obscure varieties of produce, including some peculiar little nuggets wrapped in leaves.

"Betel nuts," Will said when he noticed her looking at them. Pointing to other trays with a still-trembling hand, he said, "Sugar cane . . . salted bamboo shoots . . ."

"People eat these things?"

"*I* eat these things. There's a whole, vast world beyond Boston, Miss Sweeney."

Nell nodded, dazed by the alien surroundings, the strange, foreign smells. A slight movement in the back of the shop caught her eye. It was an old man—so old he looked mummified—wearing a gray smock like a stableman's, loose trousers, and a brimless black cap over his single braid. Nell had never seen a Chinaman before, not in person. He sat quietly in a darkened corner, next to a counter bearing a scale, a dented tin lockbox, and a pistol. He nodded unsmilingly to Will, his gaze lighting on the blackened eye and split lip.

"Good day, Deng Bao." Will dipped his head while gripping a counter for support.

The old man grunted something, his voice dry as ground bones.

"*Hsiang yen?*" Will raised two fingers to his lips and inhaled.

Deng Bao aimed a quaking finger at a shelf. Will foraged among cigar boxes and pouches of tobacco, sighing in relief when he came up with an exotically decorated tin labeled TURKISH ORIENTALS, which he pocketed. He paid the proprietor, who made change from his lockbox, handing him a box of matches along with the coins.

Will pointed to a curtained doorway in the corner behind Deng Bao. "We go upstairs?"

The old man scrutinized Nell, taking in her elegant though soiled costume with a studied lack of expression. Pointing to Will and then to the doorway, he nodded and spoke a few cordial-sounding words in his native tongue.

But his tone sharpened when he returned his attention to Nell. He held up his palm as if to say, "She stays here."

Will startled Nell by curling an arm around her waist and drawing her close. *"Jinu,"* he said.

The old man's wiry eyebrows twitched upward. He scrutinized her for a long moment, his gaze lingering for some reason on her disheveled hair. Finally he gave one quick little nod and gestured toward the doorway.

"Come, before he changes his mind again." Guiding her with a hand on her back, Will urged Nell through the heavy draperies—several layers of them—that hung over the door. "I'd best go first."

"What was that all about?" Nell asked as she followed him up a creaky staircase. She breathed in a sweet, sooty aroma from above. It reminded her of roasting hazelnuts, but wasn't. Burnt treacle? Not that, either.

"He probably suspected you were just here to gawk—or even worse, preach," Will said, pausing halfway up to catch his breath. "You look too respectable."

"I didn't know that was possible."

"Obviously," he grunted, clutching the banister hand over hand until he reached the top step and another curtained-off doorway.

"What did you say to convince him to let me come up?" she asked.

"I told him you were a whore."

"What?" She gaped at him in outrage. *"Why?"*

"Because," he said mildly as he held the curtains aside for her, "only whores come to places like this."

The room Nell stepped into—a sort of reception parlor apparently, fashioned from the second-floor landing—was downright austere compared to the shop beneath them. The walls and floor were unpainted, the only furniture a small table behind which sat another Chinaman, albeit a good deal younger than the shopkeeper, and sporting a moustache and spectacles. Although traditionally garbed from the neck down, in a yellow-sleeved scarlet smock with frog closures, his headgear consisted of a rather rumpled black pork pie hat.

Spread out on the table before him were perhaps two dozen little glass spirit lamps, which he was refilling from a jug of oil. Nell caught a whiff of something that reminded her of a cake the Hewitts' cook liked to make—coconut?

"You back!" The Chinaman leapt to his feet, arms outstretched, his smile fading as he took in Will's cuts and bruises. "What happen you?"

"My own fault, Zhou Chiang. Had a bit too much absinthe and took a spill."

"Absinthe! Vile green piss!" Zhou Chiang's sour expression changed into a smile as he turned to Nell. "Who this?"

"My keeper."

"Welcome, Miss Keeper," greeted the Chinaman with a little duck of his head; not a full bow, and the pork pie stayed put. *Only whores come to places like this.* He gestured toward an open doorway, through which Nell could see four men—three white and one Chinese—sitting in a fog of cigar smoke around a table lit by a mammoth and ornate paper lantern. "Poker today." He made a shuffling motion with his hands, winking conspiratorially at Will. "Rich suckers. You play? Win big."

"Not today, old man. Got the *yen-yen*." Will held out a quivering hand.

"We fix that." Zhou Chiang crossed to a closed door on the other side of the landing and swung it open. *"Lau!"* he barked, motioning Will and Nell into the dimly lit room. An adolescent Chinese boy dashed over to them, murmuring assent in response to Zhou Chiang's unintelligible commands.

The door closed behind them; Nell felt her stomach tighten. The room in which she found herself was large,

and lined on three sides with wide, double-tiered wooden
bunks covered with straw matting. None of the top bunks
was occupied, but several shadowy figures reclined on the
bottom. A handful of flickering little lamps provided the
only light in the dusky room. The air was sultry, thick,
and permeated with that scorched sweetness she'd first
detected in the stairwell.

The boy called Lau cocked his hand toward Nell in a
"give me" gesture.

Nell looked toward Will, who said, "He wants to hang
up your coat. Let him. It gets awfully close in here." He
shucked off his own coat and handed it to Lau, who hung
it on a peg.

"I can't stay," Nell said. "Neither can you. I need to
take you home, Dr. Hewitt."

"I need this more, Miss Sweeney."

"No, you don't understand. It's a condition of your
release on bail that you avoid all public houses and establishments of ill fame. Gambling and opium are specifically prohibited." Along with "purveyors of strong liquor"
and "houses of assignation."

Lau pointed to Will's shoes. Squatting to untie them,
Will said, "Telling me not to come to places like this,
Cornelia, is like telling me not to eat and breathe."

She said, "I would actually appreciate it very much if
you didn't call me that."

He looked up at her with a wry expression as he loosened his laces. "You've seen me vomiting in the gutter. I
should think we might properly be on a first-name basis."

"I'd rather leave things as they are, if it's all the same."

He appeared to mull that over as he stood and kicked
off his shoes for Lau to line up against the wall next to
several other pairs. "Yes, I suppose I would prefer that,
too, if I were you."

Lau turned to Nell a little shyly, glancing in the direction of her feet.

She backed up a step. "I'll keep mine, thank you."

"At least let him take your overcoat," Will said. "Wouldn't want you fainting on me."

"I never faint," she protested, even as she relinquished her coat, wishing she hadn't sworn to Viola that she would stay with Will until he was safely ensconced in his lodgings.

Lau hung up the coat and turned to Will. *"Yen gao?"*

Will dug a shaky hand into his trouser pocket. "Absolutely."

Lau held his hand out. "Two bit."

"Two bits' worth won't do, I'm afraid." Will counted out six dollars. *"Hop toy.* And a smoking pistol—*yen tsiang*—a good one this time. Bamboo, not wood. Understand? Bamboo?"

"Bamboo." The boy took the money and disappeared through a door in the corner.

Will walked to an empty bunk on the left, ducking under the top tier to seat himself on the bottom. Extracting his cigarettes and matches, he set them on a pair of nested lacquered trays laid out with an assortment of curious implements, including an unlit oil lamp like those Zhou Chiang had been filling. The lamp's base of tarnished brass was engraved with what looked like poppies.

There's one in the South Cove that's a proper lay- down joint with all the fixings, like what they've got in San Francisco.

"Have a seat, Miss Sweeney." Will indicated the bunk on the other side of the tray.

"I'd rather stand."

"You'll only draw attention to yourself," he said as he rolled up his bloodstained sleeves. "Is that really what you want?"

Nell surveyed the room. On the bunk kitty-corner from theirs, two Chinamen drowsed on their sides, their heads supported by odd little concave wooden benches. At first

she thought that the bunk directly opposite was occupied
by a lone woman, a wanton judging by her painted face
and tawdry dress, unfastened at the neckline to display an
indecent swell of bosom. But then Nell noticed a white-
sleeved arm embracing her from behind and realized it
belonged to a man tucked up against her. A mound of
pillows served in lieu of wooden headrests—a concession
for non-Chinese customers, perhaps? The man lay unmoving, while the woman busied herself by twirling
something that looked like a knitting needle over the
flame of her lamp. She glanced icily at Nell, as if to ask,
What are you *looking at?*

Nell sat. The ceiling formed by the top bunk was
inches above her head; it felt strange and somehow illicit
to be sharing this cramped space with this man. "I can't
be here, Dr. Hewitt."

"Nobody's holding a gun to your head, Miss Sweeney." He lifted a pair of dainty little scissors from the tray
and used them to trim the lamp wick. Furrows formed
between his brows as he strove to keep his hands steady
and snip the wick just at the right point. He struck a match
and touched it to the wick, bathing them in an aura of
golden light that seemed only to magnify the intimacy of
their little niche.

It was as he was replacing the lamp's bell-shaped glass
cover that Nell noticed a ring of livid abrasions around
each of his wrists. They were the scars left by manacles,
or rather by his hands straining against them. She knew
that because her brother Jamie had ended up with marks
like that back in 'fifty-nine, after the Falmouth constabulary ran him in for robbing that livery driver. They'd
yanked his hands behind him and shackled them to a chair
rung before they started working him over; his feet had
been bound, too, so he couldn't kick at his tormenters.
Was that how it had been with Will the night before last?
She imagined him fettered like that, unable to ward off

the blows, yet refusing to explain how Ernest Tulley had ended up with a certain folding bistoury in his throat. Perhaps, knowing Will, he'd even gotten in a droll gibe or two. And knowing the police—for they were the same everywhere—they would have responded by redoubling their punishments.

Nell looked away, sweeping the image from her mind, or trying to. The last thing she should be feeling for this man was pity. Perhaps "Saint August," with his interminable harangues about mastering one's emotions for one's own good, had a point after all. For Nell to allow herself to feel sorry for William Hewitt would serve only to give him power over her. She had herself to think of. He could go to the Devil, as he seemed so determined to do.

With the added lamplight, and with her eyes growing accustomed to the gloom, Nell could see just how dreary this place really was. The ceiling was smoke-blackened and dappled with water spots; the walls as well, to a lesser extent. Chinese scrolls had been tacked up here and there in a vain attempt to cover gaps in the plaster where the laths were exposed. There were windows, but they were all shut tight and papered over, no doubt, for privacy. The very air felt heavy and rank in her lungs.

"Relax, Miss Sweeney." Will slumped against the wall, coughing weakly. "You're propped up like a fashion doll on a shelf."

"Forgive me if I don't know how to comport myself in a hop joint."

"If you recall, I advised you to stay away. You're free to leave whenever you wish."

"I promised your mother I'd see you safely home. You led me to believe that was where you were taking me."

He smiled blandly. "You led yourself to believe that. You infer too much, Miss Sweeney—far too many facile assumptions. It's the only flaw I can discern in an otherwise sterling intellect."

Lau reappeared, placing upon Will's tray a little cylindrical horn box and what could only be a pipe—although it didn't look like any pipe Nell had ever seen. It was crafted of a two-foot length of bamboo stained with a glossy black patina. The small terra-cotta bowl, several inches from the pipe's ivory-tipped end, took the form of an enclosed chamber shaped somewhat like a doorknob, with a tiny hole in the center of the flattened upper surface.

Lau offered a pillow to Will, but he waved it away.

"Too soft. *Chum tow.*"

The youth retreated with a nod.

"Stay or go," Will said as he twisted the lid off the horn box, revealing a soft black paste, which he sniffed approvingly. "It's your choice. If you choose to stay, I promise not to hold you down and force a smoking pistol into your mouth. In return, I would simply ask that you stop blathering on about how I've lured you to this lair of corruption when, in fact, I'd just as soon you were on your way."

"Chum tow." Lau returned with a headrest, which he set near the tray. Will pressed a coin into his hand and sent him away.

Taking up a long steel spindle—what had looked before like a knitting needle—Will scooped up a pea-sized dab of opium paste on its tip. He reclined on his side, his head on the *chum tow,* and rotated the tarry little mass just above the oil lamp's flame. His movements were halting, his breathing labored, his hands still quite unsteady.

The woman on the opposite bunk whispered something to her companion, drawing Nell's attention. Casting a discreet glance in their direction, Nell saw that the man had awakened and lifted his head to watch her draw on her pipe. He was handsome and well groomed, with a clean-shaven face and fair, lightly oiled hair—probably some young swell out for a little illicit afternoon exploit. His arm was still curled around the trollop, but he'd shifted his hand to cradle her right breast, as nonchalantly as if they were alone in bed.

Will, preoccupied with his preparations, didn't seem to notice. The little nugget bubbled and swelled as he spun it above the flame.

In a near-whisper, Nell said, "I can't imagine why that old man believed you when you told him I was a . . ." She couldn't bring herself to say the word, one which she'd uttered freely in her former life, when half the women she knew earned their living on their back; only by the grace of God had she avoided that fate.

Will cast her a fleeting, amused glance before returning his attention to the seething opium, transmuted by fire into something that looked and smelled as enticing as molten caramel.

"I don't look like a . . ." She pressed her lips together, embarrassed by the priggishness he brought out in her, and at him for thinking it was funny. "I *don't.*"

"That just shows your naïveté. There are whores plying their trade in this city—in every city—who look as if they could be taking tea with the Queen. They're often the best ones, though you'd never guess it to look at them."

How often, when others treated her like the innocent little Irish governess without a past, had Nell thought, *If only you knew* . . . Yet it mattered not a whit how straight-laced she acted—and felt—with William Hewitt; he saw right through her. He talked about things every well-bred man knew not to bring up in the presence of a lady, but she couldn't quite decide whether to be insulted or gratified. Did he feel free to discuss whores, for instance, because he viewed her as occupying a lower moral plane, or because he deemed her intelligent and enlightened enough not to swoon with indignation?

Will withdrew the opium from the flame and, retaining it on the tip of the spindle, proceeded to knead and stretch it upon the roof of the pipe bowl, dipping it from time to time in the flame to keep it pliant. *They're often the best ones . . .* No wonder he knew the Chinese word for "whore." He probably knew it in any number of different tongues.

"If your position as a governess ever falls through," he said as he rolled the opium once again into a pea-sized ball, "you might consider that line of work yourself. I daresay you could be very successful at it."

"What are you implying?"

"There you go drawing inferences again. You should watch that. You give far too much away."

Impaling the little morsel on the tip of the needle, he thrust it into the bowl's tiny aperture, extracting the instrument with a twisting motion in order to leave the pea there with a little hole in it. He leaned forward then, slanting the bowl across the flame while maneuvering the opium with the needle to keep it in place. It sizzled into vapor as he sucked on the pipe, drawing so deeply of the treacly fumes that his cheekbones stood out like a Chinaman's. Nell found it hard to believe that he could inhale as long as he did; fifteen full seconds must have passed before he slid the pipe from his mouth.

Sweet white smoke trickled from his nostrils as he lowered the pipe with an arm gone utterly slack. He sank down bonelessly onto the bunk, eyes slitted, lips parted, exuding an otherworldly repose. No longer did he tremble; his chest rose and fell in a slow, steady rhythm.

"Dr. Hewitt?" Nell said softly.

His hand twitched, but slowly, as if he were underwater; his eyes drifted shut.

"Are you . . . are you all—"

"Shhh," he breathed.

Chapter 8

For the second time in one day, Nell was struck by William Hewitt's resemblance to a corpse—only this time, despite his wounds and bloodstained shirt, he looked like a man who'd died happy instead of anguished. Moreover, there was a kind of languid masculine grace in the way his body had settled, all long limbs and interesting angles. Perhaps, when she got home this evening, she would sketch him like this.

Will's eyes opened halfway, his dreamy, opalescent gaze seeking out hers before closing again on a sigh.

Perhaps not. Turning away from him, Nell fluffed and smoothed her skirts. She set about tidying her hair as best she could, but the wayward tendrils didn't seem to want to get tucked back into the netting.

Across the room, the harlot with the pipe had also fallen into a stupor, her head slumped forward on the pillow, her lips—so darkly rouged as to look black in the half-light—slightly parted. The man behind her, his face fully visible now, caressed her languorously.

Three and a half years had passed since Nell had felt the touch of a man's hand. A lifetime might pass without her feeling it again. Such was the price of respectability— a respectability William Hewitt might find laughable, but which she cherished for making possible her new life with all its many boons, the chief of which was Gracie. Nothing worthwhile came without a price, and Nell was willing to pay for her blessings. Still, sometimes, especially late at night as she lay in her big bed by herself, she found herself reflecting that the cost was really rather cruel.

Nell roused from her musings to find the man on the opposite bunk still fondling his ladyfriend—only he wasn't observing his own actions anymore. He was observing Nell.

She drew in a breath, scooted back on the bunk.

He kept his gaze fixed on her, his eyes dark and knowing as he slowly squeezed and stroked. Oh, God, had he been watching her watch him?

Nell looked away from his impudent gaze, cheeks stinging. Still he stared at her, even as he dipped his head to nuzzle his companion's hair.

"Dr. Hewitt." Nell reached out tentatively to nudge his shoulder.

Without opening his eyes, he grumbled, "Christ, but you're a bloody nuisance."

"Are you done?" she asked. "Can we go now?"

"Am I *done*?" he chuckled incredulously. "You're joking, surely." Pushing himself upright, he reached for his cigarettes. A certain torpidity dragged at his speech, as if he'd just awakened from a long night's sleep, and his eyes were heavy-lidded.

"I'm feeling a little light-headed," Nell said; she was, in fact. "There's not enough air in this place."

"Leave, then." Will lit a cigarette and dropped the match in a little square-sided stone dish. "Because I'm afraid I'm nowhere near done." He leaned back against the wall, one arm resting on a cocked leg, looking drowsy and comfortable as he expelled a lungful of smoke. His hands were steady, his breathing regular, his expression contented. Quite the metamorphosis.

"Then . . . when will you be ready to . . ."

"When I start answering you with gibberish because I've finally smoked enough gong to make your bloody *nagging* sound like gibberish. That's when I'll be ready to leave."

"I don't think that's such a good idea, Dr. Hewitt."

"Oh, I think it's an excellent idea, Miss Sweeney." Balancing his cigarette on the edge of the stone dish, he plucked a little sea sponge from a dish of water and used it to wipe down the pipe bowl, steam rising from it as he worked. When it was cooled to his satisfaction, he lifted from the tray a small, ivory-handled knife, scowling when he ran his thumb across the blunt-looking curved blade. He felt around in a trouser pocket, muttering "Where the devil . . ." Revelation seemed to dawn. He hissed something under his breath, then summoned Lau, sitting on a stool in the corner. The boy leapt up and came over.

"*Yen ngow* dull," Will said, flicking the blade with an expression of disdain. "No good. Bring me one that's sharp. Sharp—understand?" Lau nodded and sprinted away.

"Was it your bistoury you expected to find in your pocket?" Nell asked.

He looked at her, lifted his cigarette, took a long pull on it. Smoke swirled in the wavering lamplight.

She said, "I've been wondering why you held on to it. You're no longer a surgeon—you said so yourself."

"A pocket knife comes in handy from time to time. Mine just happens to be a bistoury. Or it was. Don't suppose I'll ever see it again."

Curious, Nell thought, how sober he seemed, when just a few minutes ago he was completely insensible.

Lau came back with a better knife, with which Will proceeded to shave bits of opium dross from the tip of the spindle.

Nell glanced covertly toward the opposite bunk to find the man who'd been staring at her absorbed in scooping opium paste onto his spindle from a little clamshell; the two-bit serving, presumably. The Chinamen were talking softly to each other in their own language, one smoking a cigarette while the other twirled his spindle over the flame. She sat back against the wall and tucked her legs under her, arranging her skirts so that they were well away from the oil lamp. Having stripped the long needle of its residue, Will set about doing the same to the pipe bowl.

His hair hung in his eyes as he worked, cigarette clenched in his mouth. So fierce was his concentration that he might have been performing surgery. The grating of the knife as it scraped across the bowl made Nell's teeth hurt.

"What happened to you?" she asked quietly.

He stabbed his cigarette into the stone dish, blew out a plume of smoke, and kept scraping.

She said, "According to your mother, you used to view opium as a blight on humanity."

"I still do," he said without raising his gaze from his work. "One need look no farther than me for proof of it— but it gets worse. I've seen men starve to death on the stuff, because it was all they wanted . . . all they loved." Pausing in his efforts, he used the back of the knife to scratch the stubble on his chin. "One fellow in Shanghai offered to sell me his daughter—not just prostitute her, mind you, but sell her outright, for me to own, just so he could keep himself in gong awhile longer."

"What did you do?"

"I bought her."

"What?"

"As I said before, Miss Sweeney, there's a whole, vast world out there beyond—"

"Yes, but—"

" 'When in Rome,' and all that. Things are different in China."

"Evidently," Nell said, taking in the shabby room and its denizens with a shiver of distaste.

"Before you go blaming the Chinese for this odious custom, you should know that opium doesn't even come from there. Most of it comes from Turkey."

"Still . . ."

He smiled grimly. "Have you ever met the Astors, William and Caroline? They're friends of my parents from New York, somewhat younger."

"Yes, they've visited." They were the most prominent and powerful couple in New York, overweeningly proud of their Knickerbocker lineage—and wealth.

"A while back, William's grandfather, John Jacob Astor, launched himself in the opium trade by shipping ten tons of it to Canton."

"Ten tons?"

"This despite its having been banned by the Chinese government. We Westerners have been foisting opium on the Chinese—sometimes at gunpoint—for quite some time. At least those of us who come to places like this do so of our own free—if somewhat flimsy—will." He tapped bits of black ash from the bowl into the stone box. "How did you know these places were called hop joints?"

"That's what Detective Cook called—"

"Who?"

"Detective Cook. He's in charge of your case."

"Oh, yes." He shoved the tip of the knife in the little hole and twisted it around. "Big Irishman. Giant head. Smarter than he looks."

"He took me to Flynn's Boardinghouse to—"

Will looked up sharply. "He took you to Flynn's? *Why?*"

"I led him to think your father had sent me to make sure you were really guilty. I wanted to hear what the witnesses had to say, maybe try to piece together what actually—"

"You have no business meddling in this," he said, a sort of confounded anger vanquishing his good humor.

"I have no choice. Your mother is determined to find out what happened Saturday night, and I'm the only person she can turn to. I tried to get answers from you yesterday, if you recall, but you put me off completely."

"I don't recall, actually. The *yen* was coming on pretty fast. Was I rude?"

"Occasionally."

"Good. You oughtn't to pry into such things." He whacked the pipe against the stone bowl again, so hard she was surprised it didn't break.

"What did you fight about with Ernest Tulley?" she asked.

"Oh, do spare me, Miss Sweeney."

"You chased him down the stairs, and kept pursuing him even after he hurled you through a window. Were you fighting over Kathleen Flynn?"

"Who?"

"Seamus Flynn's daughter. He owns the boarding-house."

"Ah, her," he said. "Yes, that's it. Clashing horns over a woman. Oldest story in the book."

"No, but really—"

"Yes, indeed. It was the strangely beguiling Kathleen Flynn. Now will you kindly shut up and leave me to my gong?"

"Who was that other man in the back parlor with you?" she persisted. "The one who was drinking whiskey while you were smoking opium?"

He closed his eyes; the air left his lungs.

"Was he a friend?" she asked. "Or—"

"No. I barely—I didn't know him. He just . . . wandered in there. We struck up a conversation."

Ah—a semisolid answer, at last. "You talked about Ernest Tulley," she said. "You made some fairly strong statements. You must have made friends pretty quickly."

"Gong and booze will do that to you."

"You said something about making Tulley pay."

"Did I? I must have been quite enamored of the enchanting Miss Flynn."

"Are you protecting someone?"

"Do I seem the type to go to the gallows in someone else's stead?"

"I don't know," she answered honestly. "What are you afraid of, Dr. Hewitt? That I'll discover you really did it? Or that you didn't?"

"If you're hoping the opium has loosened my tongue to that degree, I'm afraid you're in for a disappointment. It takes a good deal more than one bowl to deprive me of my wits."

"How much *does* it take? More than twenty-five cents' worth, presumably. As much as what's in there?" She pointed to the little horn box.

"Good lord, that much taken at one sitting would kill even me. No, that's a supply to take with me. Suffice it to say the more I smoke, the more it affects me. A bowl or two at regular intervals, or a tincture of opium if there's no gong to be found, will keep the shakes and aching at bay so that I can function fairly normally. More than that will gradually strip me of my senses, but in a most . . . seductive way. No one can appreciate the allure of the poppy until he has experienced it."

"Do you usually smoke enough to affect your senses?"

"Nearly always. It takes quite some time, and a great

deal of gong, but I find it's the only way I can tolerate
myself."

"They say you killed Ernest Tulley in a frenzy of
opium intoxication."

"What do *you* think?"

She looked around at Will's fellow pipe fiends, all of
whom were in some stage of deep repose. "I should think
it would be a miracle if someone under the influence of
this drug could summon up the energy for a proper
frenzy."

"Then I suppose I must have killed him calmly, in cold
blood," Will said as he slid aside the tray that separated
them. "I just followed him into the alley—or perhaps I
cleverly lured him there, and then trapped him." Bracing
an arm on the other side of Nell, he leaned toward her,
forcing her back against the wall. He was so close she
could feel his breath on her face. "And then . . ." Steel
flickered in the lamplight as he raised the knife to her
throat.

Nell held his gaze, reeling inside as if she were looking
down off the edge of a steep cliff at night. Evenly, quietly,
she said, "Put that thing down. The others will see.
They'll fetch the police."

"They've all nodded off."

"That boy Lau will see."

"He can't see the knife from where he's sitting. He just
thinks I'm kissing you."

She swallowed.

He drew the weapon slowly across her throat, its blade
a hair's-breadth from her skin. She didn't flinch, didn't
avert her gaze from his.

"Well done," he murmured as he turned and leaned
against the wall. "You might actually have been quite brilliant on the stage."

She glanced across the room at Lau, seated on his corner stool. He quickly looked down, fiddling with some-

thing in his hands—the coin Will had given him.

"Why did you do that?" she asked, her voice quavering a bit despite her efforts to steady it.

"Just a friendly demonstration," he said, dipping his spindle once more into the horn box. "Who's to say I couldn't have dispatched Ernest Tulley with sober deliberation?"

"I suppose you could have, if you'd had any reason to kill him. But you didn't even know the man. Why would you want to murder a perfect stranger?"

"It doesn't matter why. I'll hang whether I explain myself or not. My guilt is a given. No one doubts it."

She started to speak, then thought better of it.

He noticed. "Don't tell me *you* doubt it."

"You may well be guilty," she said. "You probably are. But I've been thinking you don't quite seem the type—notwithstanding your friendly little 'demonstration.'"

"My dear Miss Sweeney," he said as he fizzled the opium on the tip of the spindle. "Properly provoked, anyone could be the type."

That was what Detective Cook had said. "Then why wouldn't you enter a guilty plea at your arraignment, Dr. Hewitt?"

He shrugged without looking up, occupied with kneading the caramelized opium on the red clay bowl. "Perhaps I just didn't want to make it easy on them."

"Or perhaps your thoughts were too muddled from that"—she pointed to the pipe—"to allow you to follow the proceedings."

"Clever you."

"So, then, you *were* intoxicated?"

He sighed heavily. "Too bad women can't be police officers. You're quite the interrogator."

"You should have spoken to a lawyer before your arraignment. It may not be too late, if you retain one now, to undo some of the damage you've done."

"Lawyers make everything so complicated," he said as he collected the opium on the end of his spindle.

"Lawyers keep people from hanging."

"It would appear I'm misplaying my hand rather badly, then, wouldn't it? I'd bet against me if I were you."

Will implanted the dab in the bowl's tiny orifice, withdrawing the needle with a deft twist and then using it to tend the dissolving opium while he sucked. He was quite dexterous now that his trembling had abated, deploying the long needle with sure, nimble fingers. He did have a surgeon's touch; what a sin for it to be employed to such a purpose.

The pipe fell slowly to the bunk, cradled in his lax hand. He blinked listlessly, gazing in glassy-eyed reverie at nothing. Nell slid the "smoking pistol" out of his hand, curious about its construction.

He clutched at it feebly, muttering, "I need that."

"I just want to look at it."

"That's my saw," he murmured groggily. "I'm not done yet."

Saw? The only type of saw Dr. William Hewitt was ever likely to have owned would be a bonesaw. She set the pipe back in his hand; his fingers closed possessively around it as his eyes drifted shut.

"WHO gave you that?"

Nell opened her eyes with a start, having very nearly dozed off herself while waiting for Will to revive from his second pipeful. "What?"

Lying faceup on the headrest—how long had he been watching her?—he lifted a hand to point at the small scar near her left eyebrow. "That," he said sleepily. "Who gave you that? Your father?"

"No."

He frowned. "Not Dr. Greaves."

"No, of course not."

"Who, then?"

"Perhaps I had a bit too much absinthe and took a spill."

"Into a knife?" He muscled himself into a sitting position. "That's a knife scar."

She touched it. It wasn't very big, perhaps half an inch long. "How did you know that?"

"I didn't." Will sat back heavily and sighed. "I do now." He lifted his cigarette tin, put it down, clawed both hands through his hair. "Look, about before, my . . . baiting you with that knife. That was . . ." He glanced again at the little scar, looked away, scraped a hand over his bristly jaw. "You may very well have saved my life today, bringing me that paregoric and getting me out of that blasted . . . I had no business . . ." He grabbed the cigarette tin. "Anyway, I owe you an apology and a debt of thanks."

"I appreciate that, Dr. Hewitt." She did—yet part of her wished he hadn't said it. His occasional courtesies, hinting as they did at the gentleman beneath the wretch, were strangely unsettling.

He nodded distractedly and lit a cigarette.

"I want to show you something." Sorting through the contents of her chatelaine, Nell located the little velvet picture case she'd slipped in there this morning. She opened it, displaying a photographic portrait—hand-tinted by Nell—of Gracie in her best frock, and handed it to Will.

His expression softened. "Is this the child you care for? She's lovely."

Nell said, "I believe she's your daughter."

On a gust of laughter he said, "Is that what *she* told you—my mother? Because I assure you I've never fathered any children. I'm careful about that sort of thing."

"Gracie's mother is a chambermaid who used to work

for your parents," Nell said. "Annie McIntyre."

Will turned away and drew on his cigarette, but not before Nell detected a flicker of recognition in his eyes.

"Gracie was born nine months after your Christmas furlough in 'sixty-three," Nell said. "Look at her, Dr. Hewitt. The black hair, those eyes, even her mouth. She looks just like you."

He contemplated the picture through a haze of cigarette smoke. Nell saw it dawn in his eyes—the acknowledgment that it was true, that he'd fathered this child.

She said, "My suspicions were aroused yesterday, when you told me about . . . the incident with the chambermaid. I asked your mother about it last night. She told me she's known Gracie was yours since the night she was born."

"Of course she's known. That woman knows everything. Why else would she have taken in a maid's bastard unless she knew it was her own flesh and blood?"

Nell thought back three and a half years to the stormy night of Gracie's birth . . . Annie's insistence on speaking privately with her employer, the muffled sobs, Mrs. Hewitt's eagerness to adopt the baby. *These matters are complicated,* she'd said that night. *But we live in a world that likes to pretend such things are simple.*

"Saint August will have figured it out, too," Will said. "He probably threw poor Annie out on her ear after that."

"On the contrary, he recommended her to the Astors, her husband as well, and made a generous settlement on them."

"To keep her quiet."

"Annie was even more concerned about that than your parents. And I thought your mother acted admirably. If not for her, your own child could have ended up in an orphan asylum, or even some . . . some county poor house. When we spoke last night, she gave me permission to tell you about Gracie." Nell nodded toward the photograph. "You can have that if you'd like."

Will snapped it shut and handed it back. "You should have kept this particular revelation to yourself, Miss Sweeney." He stabbed out his cigarette.

She slipped the case back in her bag, remembering with a pinch of guilt how Gracie, still in her night dress, had clung to her this morning as she was leaving. *Miseeney stay! Don't go 'way again.* "You have a child, Dr. Hewitt, a perfect little daughter. How can you not care—"

"Will you stop making your bloody assumptions?" He grabbed the pipe and gave it a desultory sponging.

"What am I to think when you tell me you'd rather not even know she existed?" Nell said. "For someone who heaps such scorn upon the shallowness and venality of his class, you can be remarkably self-indulgent."

"Self-indulgence," he said as he set about scraping the bowl clean. "Is that what it is?"

"You like to think you're so different from the rest of them, but you're not. You're just another"—how had Detective Cook put it?—"rich young bounder who takes what he wants when he wants it, and never mind the havoc it wreaks on the lives of others. It was left to Annie McIntyre to deal with the consequences of your . . . 'indiscretion.' She told your mother she'd intended to keep quiet about your having fathered the baby and just try to find a good home for her after she was born. She felt your mother had done her a great kindness in being so understanding about the pregnancy, and that it would ill repay her to reveal to the world that her own son was responsible. But when she found out she'd need a Caesarean, she was afraid she'd die and the baby would end up—"

"She had a *Caesarean*?" He looked genuinely shaken.

Nell nodded. "The baby was transverse. It was lucky for Annie—and Gracie as well—that Dr. Greaves was there."

Will was rubbing his eyes with the hand that held the cigarette. He sighed and shook his head. "You may not credit it, Miss Sweeney, but I'm sorry for Annie's anguish, and for any part I may have played in causing it."

Steeling herself against the grudging sympathy she felt for him, Nell said, "I should say you played quite a significant part."

"Not that it's any of your affair, but this wasn't some tawdry melodrama wherein the innocent serving wench is ravished by the . . . what was it? . . . rich young bounder. If you want to know the truth, and not some dime novel version of it, it was . . ." He ran his thumb thoughtfully over the pipe bowl, as if to gauge how good a job he'd done cleaning it. "It was Christmas morning," he said in a subdued voice. "I'd gone to the butler's pantry for some brandy to help me bear up under the festivities and found her in there on the floor, weeping."

"Annie?"

Will nodded as he leaned back against the wall. "At the time, I didn't even know her name. I was hardly ever there, remember. I asked her what was wrong. She told me she missed her husband, who'd been off with the Eleventh Regiment since March. She'd been hoping he could be furloughed for Christmas, as Robbie and I were, but he wasn't. I offered some poor words of comfort—I'm not really very good at that sort of thing. She pulled herself together and returned to her chores. That night, I heard a soft knock on my door as I was falling asleep."

"It was her?" Nell asked.

Will nodded, gazing in an unfocused way at the pipe in his hand. "It wasn't the lovemaking she wanted, not really. That was the price."

"The price for what?"

"For what comes after. Being held, feeling someone else's heartbeat, knowing that there's someone in whose arms one can fall asleep. I suppose I knew that was all she really . . . needed. She needed it, but I let her pay for it anyway. I'd been too long at war. I had needs of my own." He glanced at Nell and looked away, rubbing the back of his neck. "And in case you're wondering, Miss Sweeney, I did wear a French letter. It had grown brittle from disuse. It broke."

Nell's cheeks grew warm.

"I've made you blush again," he said, sounding amused. "You really are rather conventional after all. Or is it my mention of the French letter? Are you outraged on religious grounds?"

"Not . . . outraged."

"Discomfited, then. Your priests disapprove."

"As do yours," she pointed out.

"I have no priests."

"Then I'm sorry for you."

He seemed to ruminate on that as he tapped ash from the pipe into the stone bowl. "Curious that my mother would choose someone like you as her . . . Well, you're obviously more to her than either a governess *or* a companion. This is, after all, a rather challenging and delicate mission she's sent you on. 'Trusted retainer'—how's that for a title?"

"I'm quite content with 'governess.' "

"You would say that. It's the right thing to say, and you're good at that—saying the right thing, doing what's expected, acting the part of the straightlaced little governess. You'd get a standing ovation at the Howard Athenaeum."

"That's actually quite insulting, Dr. Hewitt."

"Perhaps, but that doesn't make it untrue. You're not altogether what you seem. That's what I meant when I said I was surprised my mother employed you, even just as a governess. She's quite a perceptive woman, despite her faults, and I find it hard to believe she doesn't at least suspect your true nature."

Her true nature? Nell couldn't even fathom how to respond to that. "I . . . I don't know what you . . . mean to imply, but—"

"I only meant," he said mildly, "that there are facets to you that aren't apparent until one . . . lifts you up and turns you round in the sunlight." He smiled. "You're just a bit too quick-witted beneath all those tiny little buttons, a bit too tough and canny and wise for your years. You remind me of all those young soldiers who started out as pink-cheeked youths and ended up . . ." He lifted the horn box and the spindle. "Well, the ones who lived might still look the same on the outside, but in here"—he tapped his bloodstained chest with the tip of the spindle—"they've changed. They've seen things, done things, that boys like them should never have seen and done. They've been cast into Hell and survived to crawl out again, but you don't go through something like that without ending up singed. Which is to say wiser but sadder. You're like them."

He didn't wait for a response, but commenced the laborious ritual of cooking and kneading the opium.

Even half-intoxicated, William Hewitt was far too incisive for comfort. There seemed to be no way Nell could keep him from scratching open glimpses of her miserable past. If his mother was perceptive, he was doubly so. It was a quality that must have served him well in the practice of medicine.

"What would possess a person like you to enslave yourself to this drug?" she asked.

"The same thing that possessed your doomed Tommy."

"Pain? Were you injured?"

"Don't tell me you haven't noticed the bum leg."

"I assumed it was from the beating the police dealt you."

"That didn't help—one of them took a baton to my legs—but it's an old bullet wound, actually."

"From the war? I thought surgeons weren't supposed to be fired upon."

"I wasn't—not in battle."

"When, then? At Andersonville?"

"This conversation is becoming tedious," he said as he gathered the gummy little mass on the tip of the spindle.

"It *was* at Andersonville," she said, the bits and pieces coming together in her mind. "You escaped, didn't you? That's when you were shot."

He lay on his side, snugging his head into the *chum tow*.

"Why would they have reported you as dead?" she asked. "They said you had dysentery."

"I did. We all did. I didn't die of it, though."

"Obviously."

"I died during a thunderstorm in the middle of the night." He seated the dab of opium in the bowl, leaned over the lamp, and brought the pipe to his mouth, flames twitching in his heavy-lidded eyes. "I died facedown in the mud."

"I don't understand," Nell said as Will roused into wakefulness after a particularly long period of insensibility.

He groaned, draping an arm over his head. "You do know how to ruin a perfectly good stupor."

"You're obviously still alive."

"Christ, but you're literal. Perhaps I *should* hold you down and force a smoking pistol into your mouth. A little gong might do you a world of good."

"As it's done for you?"

He sat up, reaching for his cigarettes. "I don't limp after a couple of bowls."

"You don't appear to do much of anything else, either. A man like you, with your background, your education . . ." She shook her head. "You don't belong here."

"Do stop hiding behind that kneejerk respectability, Miss Sweeney—at least with me. I'm growing weary of it."

"Go home, Dr. Hewitt," she said with feeling.

"No, I think you're the one who should go home, Miss Sweeney." He lit the cigarette, flicked the match into the little stone dish, and settled against the wall. "Go back to Palazzo Hewitt. I daresay you *do* belong there."

"Your mother made me promise to take you home."

"She would understand your not wanting to remain in this den of sin while I gradually smoke myself into oblivion, which could take a while."

She would, at that. "All right, just . . . tell me where you're staying, at least, so she has some way to get in touch with you."

He expelled a heavy sigh. "Very well, if it'll buy me a little peace. I've got a room at the Belmont."

"Where is that?"

"My mother knows it."

"Be careful, Dr. Hewitt. If the police find out you're frequenting places like this while you're out on bail, you'll be thrown right back in the Charles Street Jail, and you'll stay there until your trial."

"If you don't tell them, I won't."

When Nell rose to leave, Will insisted on walking her downstairs and out to the street, where he hailed a hack that had just turned onto Tyler from Kneeland. His limp had, indeed, all but disappeared; no wonder he'd become so enamored of opium.

"Dr. Hewitt," she began as the old blue-curtained carriage drew up.

"Yes."

"Did you really buy that girl in Shanghai?"

"I did."

"How . . . how old was she?"

"Thirteen, but she looked older, and she was very

beautiful. If I hadn't snapped her up, someone else would have beaten me to it." Will greeted the hack driver and handed him some money. "The lady is going to Colonnade Row."

He opened the door for Nell and held out his hand. She faced him patiently, making no move to enter the carriage.

He smiled. "I took her to a convent and arranged for her to be schooled there. She lives there still. Is that what you wanted to hear?"

"If it's the truth."

"I am many despicable things, Miss Sweeney, but I am not a liar."

"Are you quite sure . . . Mr. Toussaint?"

He nodded as if to acknowledge her point. "I am not often a liar. I was weaned on lies and secrets and genteel fabrications, and as a result, I've developed an aversion to pretense—except on the stage. I'm actually quite fond of the theater. You know, I really do think you'd make a brilliant actress—if it weren't for that dreadful propriety you wear like armor around your soul."

She let him hand her up into the hack then, closing the door behind her once she'd gotten her skirts gathered in.

"Miss Sweeney." He reached in through the open side window to tug at her loosely draped green scarf, warmly chafing the back of her neck. "Do tuck this in. You'll catch your death."

Chapter 9

A knock came at Nell's bedroom door that night as
she sat at her drawing table in the sitting room
alcove, putting the finishing touches on her sketch
of the hop joint above Deng Bao's grocery store. She
glanced at the clock on the mantel, noting it was almost
eleven, and wondered who could be stopping by so late.
The only person who ever came to her room was Mrs.
Hewitt, but Nell had already reported to her on the day's
events—quite an intense conversation this afternoon, during which she'd revealed Will's opium addiction, and the
fact that he made his living through gambling.

She stacked her sketches—this evening's and those
she'd drawn last night after Viola's visit—and covered
them with a blank sheet of paper before she rose to answer
the door, mindful of all she had to lose should the wrong
person find out what she was up to.

"I'm so glad you're still up," said Viola, seated in her
rather rickety old third-floor wheelchair, when Nell
opened the door and ushered her into the room. She had

on one of her many kimonos, the lime green one; on her lap was the bulging needlework bag she used for toting things around the house. "I'm not disturbing you, am I? Oh, were you about to turn in?" she asked when she noticed that Nell was in her dressing gown.

"Not at all. I was just finishing up a sketch, but I'm so tired I'll just ruin it if I keep going." Was it Nell's imagination, or was Viola a little tipsy? Her speech, normally so crisp and refined, sounded suspiciously thick, and there was something about her too-bright eyes and ruddy nose—although that could easily be from all the crying she'd done of late. Nell had never known her employer to have more than a glass of wine at dinner, two at the most.

That speculation was put to rest when Viola withdrew from her bag a bottle of amber-colored liquid, about three-quarters full. "Do you have a couple of glasses? I left my snifter downstairs. Anything will do."

Nell fetched a small water glass and empty teacup off her night stand and brought them to the drawing table, thinking this would be the first time strong spirits had touched her lips in over seven years. She exclaimed in protest as Viola filled both glass and cup nearly to the brim.

"I'm trying to finish it," Viola explained.

Um ... "Do you think that's such a good idea, Mrs. Hewitt?"

"No, it's a terrible idea. We'll both have blinding headaches tomorrow." Handing Nell the teacup, she raised her own glass toward the half-open door to the darkened nursery, where Gracie was fast asleep. "To Grace Elizabeth Lindleigh Hewitt."

"To Gracie." Nell took a sip; the liqueur tasted sweet and nutty and a little musty, but pleasantly so. "This is good."

"It should be."

Something in Viola's tone gave Nell pause. She held

the bottle in the light from the oil lamp on her drawing table to read the brittle old label through its fine, finger-smeared powdering of dust; it was a Hennessy cognac. "This isn't . . . you wouldn't . . . Um, how old is this cognac?" she asked, taking another small sip.

"It spent twenty-six years in an oak barrel." Viola smiled. "And another seventy-four in this bottle."

Nell choked as she was swallowing. "This . . . this is Mr. Hewitt's hundred-year-old cognac!"

"It is," Viola said as she took a generous swig.

"But he's saving it for the birth of his first grandchild!"

"So you reminded me yesterday. So, last night I reminded *him* that our first grandchild was, in fact, born three and a half years ago. I asked him if it wasn't past time to uncork Grandpapa's cognac. He gave me *that look*." Tilting her chin up just slightly and peering down her regal nose, Viola fixed Nell with a subtle but altogether withering disdain.

So flawless was the impression, and so surprising—Viola never criticized her husband, and certainly never mocked him—that Nell burst out laughing.

Viola laughed, too, and they clinked their glasses. Nell silently prayed, as she drank, that August Hewitt would never discover the part she'd played in polishing off his precious cognac—not to mention bailing out his son! Her position here, her charmed life . . . Gracie . . . It was vulnerable, all of it. She'd begun to take it for granted, but it could all be snatched from her in a heartbeat, and then where would she be?

"What are you drawing?" asked Viola as she wheeled closer to the table. Nell lifted the blank sheet and handed Viola the gloomy little charcoal sketch she was working on. "Is this the opium den he took you to? I can hardly make anything out."

"It was dark."

"So I see." Viola shuffled idly through the stack

of drawings: Flynn's Boardinghouse; the alley outside
Flynn's, rendered in pencil except for a dilute ink wash
to indicate the bloodstained snow; a map of Boston she'd
traced out of the city almanac, with her notations scrawled
on it . . . "Ah, you've finished this one." Viola picked up
the meticulous pen and ink drawing of Deng Bao's grocery store to examine it more closely.b "The detail is extraordinary. Was it really this . . ." She stilled, her gaze
on the drawing at the very bottom of the stack. "Oh, my
God. Is that him?"

"Oh . . . Mrs. Hewitt," Nell said as Viola lifted the
sketch, a pencil portrait of Will, pale, unshaven, and battered. "I'm sorry. Yes. That's him."

Viola's eyes reddened as she brushed a fingertip over
the contusion surrounding his left eye. "My poor Will."
She gazed at the portrait through a shimmering glaze of
unshed tears. Laying the drawing aside, she opened her
needlework bag and produced two flat, embossed leather
cases, which she handed to Nell. "This is who he used to
be."

Nell opened the top case to reveal a smoky-silver da-
guerreotype of a woman and two children framed in an
oval of golden scrollwork. The woman, seated with a baby
in her lap, was a very young, very pretty Viola; she wore
a flower-sprigged dress, with her hair center-parted and
ringleted in the style of the late thirties. Leaning up
against her, his arm resting protectively on the baby, was
a boy in knickers with neatly combed black hair, huge
eyes, and a beguiling smile.

"The little one is Robbie," Viola said as she tilted her
glass to her mouth. Robbie was one of those big, sturdy
babies who was undeniably male despite his pale curls
and elaborate, lacy, christening gown. "And of course, the
boy is Will. He's about four there."

"He looks older."

"It was his height, those long, gangly limbs. August

always thought of him as older, always expected so much of him, but he was really just a little—" Viola's voice caught. She took a gulp of cognac.

"He looks so happy," Nell said. There was something heartbreaking about that guileless smile, the solicitous little hand on his baby brother.

"Will adored Robbie. He was never jealous, like some older siblings. All he wanted was to play with him and take care of him." Viola's hand shook slightly as she snapped open the second case. "This was taken in June of 'fifty-eight, before a ball to benefit the Children's Aid Society."

The photograph was of four handsome young men in white tie, lounging in what Nell recognized as the Red Room downstairs. Robbie, looking like a gilded young god at about twenty, was seated on his mother's favorite piece of furniture, the thronelike Japanese chair elaborately carved with "guardian lions." The adolescent Harry sat perched on an arm of the chair, his grin precociously cocky, a hand resting on Robbie's shoulder. In contrast to the older three, whose evening wear was classically austere, Harry wore a waistcoat of gaudily patterned brocade. Will and another young man, whom Nell didn't recognize—light brown hair, fair skin—stood in back, framed by an enormous Japanese painting of a hawk in the snow.

"That fellow standing next to Will is Leo Thorpe's son, Jack," Viola explained. "He was Robbie's best friend, about a year older. They were still in their teens when Will started dragging them to saloons and gaming hells and God knows where else. For the week or two every year that Will was in this city, it was always just the three of them."

"I heard Mr. Thorpe say something about making his son a partner in his law firm."

Viola nodded. "Poor Jack, he really never wanted that, but Leo has his ways . . ." She sighed and took another sip of cognac. "Jack joined the Fortieth Mounted Infantry along with Will and Robbie right out of law school. When the war ended, he took a job in Washington instead of coming back here to join Pratt and Thorpe, which greatly upset Leo, since he's the only son. But this past Christmas he moved back to Boston, and the next thing I knew, he was unofficially engaged to Orville Pratt's daughter Cecilia. Leo and August have their differences, but they're very much alike in one respect. If there's something they want, they eventually get it."

Too true, Nell thought, studying the photograph. "Were Harry and Robbie close?" she asked, taken by the fraternal affection of that hand on the shoulder.

"Oh, yes, Harry adored Robbie—everybody did. He was one of those people who just . . . shines. There was something about him, a special grace, a light. Harry was three years younger. Mind you, he was a little wild even back then, but he worshipped Robbie."

"Was he jealous of Jack?" Nell asked. "Because of how close he and Robbie were?"

"I think so, but he managed to keep that under wraps fairly well. He never got into any serious trouble until the war, but then, without Robbie around to try to please, well . . ." Gravely Viola added, "When he heard about Robbie's death, he went a little mad, I think. Started drinking and didn't stop for days, wouldn't go to the mill. He hasn't been quite the same since then." She shook her head. "I feel responsible. I should have done more for him."

"William feels the same way. He regrets not having guided him more effectively."

"He shouldn't. They were so far apart in age, he and Harry. And Harry was a hard one to guide. He still is. He'll do something utterly outrageous, and seem so contrite about it, even devastated, but then the next day it's as if none of it ever happened. Do you know he started a fistfight over a woman after a service at King's Chapel last year? He beat the poor fellow unconscious right there in front of the church. An hour later, he was laughing about it over Sunday dinner. It cost August five thousand dollars to keep him from being prosecuted."

Nell nodded as she sipped her cognac. "I heard about that."

"Did you hear about the time he got arrested for public indecency?" When Nell shook her head, Viola said, "It was about five or six years ago. He went for a little midnight swim in the Frog Pond with two . . . women of the town, and by the time the police arrived, they were . . . well . . . no longer swimming."

"Oh, dear."

"Leo handled it," Viola said, her words slurring together. "Leo handles everything. All those ghastly little dramas with Harry's mill girls . . . The pregnancies to be dealt with, the husbands to pay off, the gambling debts, all those fines for public intoxication . . . I just worry that someday Harry will do something money can't put right. Will was no angel either, but at least he was only arrested the once that I know of, when they raided that brothel back in 'fifty-three."

"Until now," Nell reminded her.

Viola drained her glass and reached for the bottle.

"Was *William* ever jealous of Jack's friendship with Robbie?" Nell asked.

"Oh, no. Will was . . . well, not so much above such petty emotions as . . . apart from them. I don't know if that makes any sense."

"Yes," Nell said. "I know what you mean."

Touching the photograph thoughtfully, Viola said, "I think this was the only time I'd ever managed to talk Will into attending one of the charity balls. Frankly, I was hoping he'd meet some suitable girls. His taste ran to . . . well . . ." She took another sip of cognac.

What a sensation he must have caused that night! Nell thought. The "suitable girls" would have gone wobbly in the knees; their mothers, if they had any sense, might have steered them toward safer prospects.

"He disappeared from the ball after about twenty minutes," Viola said. "Came home the next morning with his tie gone and his shirt open, reeking of whiskey and perfume. August was seething, of course. Will calmly packed a few things, as he always did, and left. We didn't see him for days, but Robbie eventually found him and talked him into coming to Cape Cod with us. Will loved those summers at Falconwood—although he usually stayed by himself in the boathouse. He said he liked the lapping of the water against the dock. It infuriated August, of course, but I think it was preferable in his mind to having Will in the main house, where he'd have to deal with him."

"Mr. Hewitt . . ." Nell began carefully. "He seems to . . . I mean, it seems as if he . . ."

"Loathes Will?"

"Well, yes."

"And why do you suppose that is?" Viola asked.

Nell hesitated.

Viola lifted the glass to her lips, smiling over its rim. "I can't be shocked, remember?"

It was what she'd said the night Gracie was born, when she'd asked Nell why she thought Annie would choose to give up her own child. *Is it because her husband isn't the father?* Nell had asked.

Viola was waiting.

Nell couldn't say it.

Viola drained and refilled her glass.

"Mrs. Hewitt," Nell said. "Do you really think you should be drinking this much?"

Viola turned away, maneuvering her chair rather clumsily, given the glass in her hand and her mounting inebriation. She wheeled squeakily over to Nell's bed, a far too big four-poster, and adjusted a pillow; it was a nervous habit of Viola's to conduct these little inspection tours when she had something on her mind. "I heard the story of Frankenstein from Mary Shelley's own lips when I was seven years old—did I ever tell you that?"

It took Nell a second to digest this conversational detour. "No."

"Mary's father, William Godwin, lived near my father in London, and they were friends." Viola straightened the lace runner on Nell's dresser, sipped some more cognac. "My mother died of childbed fever after I was born, and Father never remarried. He was a respected man, a baronet, but something of a freethinker, like Godwin and his crowd. He brought me up with the same education and opportunities as if I were a son."

Viola moved on to the fireplace, where she took a poker to the smoldering embers. It was a handsome hearth with a carved oak mantel, the centerpiece of a spacious room that was flooded with sunlight during the day, thanks to tall windows on two sides.

"I grew up questioning everything," Viola said as she stirred the embers into ashes. "Religion, the monarchy, marriage . . . in the abstract, mind you, from an academic perspective. It was one thing, in my father's view, to espouse, say, free love, and quite another to practice it. His dream was for me to travel and paint and meet fascinating people, and then marry for love—some enlightened aristocrat with a tidy income, preferably. He adored me. He wanted the best for me. And he . . . he trusted me. He always told me I deserved the freedom he gave me because he knew I would never do anything foolish."

She shook her head. "When I was twenty-two, I went to Paris to study painting. The École des Beaux-Arts didn't admit women, so I spent over a year just copying paintings at the Louvre. But then I met . . . Someone introduced me to . . ." She sighed and took another drink. "Emil Toussaint."

"Toussaint?"

"He was a painter," Viola said without looking up from the glowing ashes. "It was an extraordinary world, Paris in the thirties. Poets and writers and artists flocked there, and we were all trying to challenge the old order, to do something new and fresh and outrageous. We were la Bohème, and Emil Toussaint was one of our princes— but the critics scorned him because he wasn't mired in the past. He believed in capturing a moment on canvas, a fleeting impression."

"It's the same thing you're always telling me," Nell observed.

"Oh, he was brilliant, he truly was, quite ahead of his time, despite his . . . well, he could be terribly imperious, quite full of himself, but I worshiped him anyway. Not only because of his work but because of his . . . presence, his . . . mystique. He was a commanding man, very tall and well built, with this great mane of jet black hair. I got stupid just looking at him."

Nell chuckled as she raised her cup to her lips, not because it was particularly funny, but because she recognized the feeling. It was precisely how she used to feel with Duncan. His beauty had stung her heart; so had everything else about him.

"Emil invited me to study privately at his atelier in the Latin Quarter," Viola said. "I was so proud to have been one of his chosen. And oh, how my heart would pound when I noticed him gazing at me . . ." Suddenly she looked very sad. "I didn't know—until too late—that he was in the habit of seducing his female students, and that he had a wife in Boulogne."

"Oh."

"By the time I returned to London, I was four months pregnant. I was desperate, and devastated, and far too mortified to tell my father—he would have been so ashamed. My sister Bertha was the only person I confided in, and she was appalled. So was I. I didn't feel remotely enlightened or sophisticated, quite the opposite. I'd been weak and gullible and wanton. Another month passed, with me fretting in secret over what would become of me. Bertha gave me the name of a French midwife who would . . . cure such dilemmas for a price, but by then I'd felt the baby move and I just . . . I couldn't."

No wonder Viola had been so understanding of Annie McIntyre's predicament, Nell thought.

"Father had begun to tease me about growing plump," Viola said as she took another drink. "My panic had reached the level where it was almost paralyzing. I rarely left my room, took all my meals there. Father had a deuce of a time convincing me to join him for Easter dinner. We had company, you see, and he didn't want to entertain them alone. One of his guests turned out to be a young man from Boston whom I'd met two years earlier, while he was making his grand tour."

"August Hewitt," Nell guessed.

Viola nodded. "He'd tried to court me back then; but I'd put him off. He was handsome enough—quite dazzling, really, with that silver-blond hair and those blue eyes. But he'd seemed so staid at the time, so ridiculously pious, while I, of course, had fancied myself quite the free spirit. But that evening, over Easter dinner, he struck me as . . ." She shook her head. "He seemed so *good,* so fundamentally decent—especially as compared to Emil. It was a mild night, so I slipped away after dinner and went into the garden to be alone. He followed me there. He told me . . ." Viola smiled. "He said he always used to think I was a bit too thin, but it appeared that my appetite had improved, and I was all the more beautiful for it. I burst into tears. He led me to a bench and offered me a handkerchief. I blurted it all out, about being pregnant and at my wits' end and Father not knowing."

"Really? What . . . what did he . . ."

"At first he just stared at me, in utter shock. I instantly regretted having told him. He asked who was responsible. I told him only that it was someone I'd known in Paris, a married man of low character who'd deceived me. August assumed I'd been all but forced . . . plied with absinthe, perhaps, and taken against my will, and God help me, I let him believe it. He stared off into the dark for about a minute, and then he asked me to marry him."

"Oh."

"He told me he loved me, that he'd always loved me, and that he didn't blame me for what had happened to me, and would put it entirely out of his mind and raise my child as his own. It was the answer to my prayers. Within weeks, we were man and wife. We spent the next two and a half years touring Europe. Will was born in Tuscany. When August brought me back to Boston, people just assumed the baby was his. August let me bring Paola back with me, even though he felt I should have a proper French lady's maid, like his mother and sisters. And he had this house built in the Italian style to please me—I'd loved Italy, and he wanted me to be happy here."

"Have you been?" Nell asked, although she thought she knew the answer. Viola Hewitt was an iconoclast whose youthful indiscretion—and the marriage that had saved her from it—had effectively imprisoned her for life in the granite-walled bastion of propriety that was Brahmin Boston. Like her son William, Viola felt a measure of contempt for this "hollow, gold-plated world," a world that Nell would give anything to have been born into.

"Happy?" Viola mused. "I was happy when Will was little and still living here with us. I was astounded by the depth of my love for him. August . . . he tried to love Will—I truly believe that. He wanted to be a good father to him. He didn't want to rear his sons as he'd been reared, with whippings and beatings. He tried to discipline Will with . . . he called it 'firm reason.' "

"Did Will need disciplining very often?" Nell asked.

"He wasn't routinely willful—not in my estimation—but August felt that young boys should be taught to be mannerly and in complete command of their passions. If Will became excitable in any way—if he laughed out loud at the dinner table, for example—he would earn a lecture on the evils of intemperate behavior and be isolated from me for the rest of the day. That was awful for Will—and for me, as well, because we were very close. The next morning, August would order Will to get on his knees and ask for forgiveness, but even when he was very young, Will would never kneel. That incensed August, and he would send him back to his room. I would be in tears, but Will was always dry-eyed."

Viola drank in silence for a minute. "When August first suggested that we send Will to live with my sister Bertha in London, I refused to consider it. But the more I thought about it, the more sense it seemed to make. I knew Will and August would never get along. The older Will got, the worse it would be for him—for all of us. So I finally gave in. He was five when he left—Nurse Parrish accompanied him on the crossing. That morning, on the dock, waiting for him to board . . ." Her voice broke. "Oh, Nell. He begged me not to send him away. I started crying. So did he. He . . . Oh, God." She swiped roughly at the tears welling in her eyes. "He knelt. He did it, finally. He ran up to August and got down on his knees and pleaded with him. He told him he knew he'd been bad, and that was why he was being taken from me and Robbie, but he'd be better from now on. He promised. He'd be everything August wanted him to be. August finally had to haul him forcibly onto the ship. He screamed and sobbed all the way up the gangway. God forgive me."

At a loss for words, Nell lifted her cup to her mouth, but her throat was too tight to swallow. This, then, was the source of Viola's terrible maternal guilt, having allowed her husband to cast away the child he'd sworn to raise as his own.

"Will's first couple of years in London were fairly uneventful," Viola said when she'd pulled herself together. "I think he was trying to be good so that August would let him come back. He didn't get on with his cousin, though—Bertha's son Archie—so she sent Will off to boarding school when he was eight. He was a model student then, but he became a real hellion in his teens—he'd get caught drinking, or sneaking women into his rooms, or playing cards for money. Eton expelled him, and Harrow came close. August tried to discipline him during his summer visits, but it was no use. He'd run off for days at a time, and only Robbie could find him. He finally settled down a bit at Oxford. I was pleased when he decided to study medicine at Edinburgh, but August felt it was unseemly for someone who carried the Hewitt name to go poking and prodding at other people's bodies. Of course, Will didn't care one whit for August's opinions. He excelled in his medical studies, and when the war broke out, he came back and enlisted as a surgeon."

"I take it he knows Mr. Hewitt isn't his real father," Nell said, "otherwise he wouldn't have called himself Toussaint."

Viola nodded. "My sister let it slip to her son, and of course he took great relish in telling Will he was the bastard of some failed French painter named Emil Toussaint. Will was about thirteen then, and getting ready to enter Eton."

"That would be around the time he started cutting up."

Viola nodded. "Yes. I thought of that. I thought of everything—just a bit too late. I failed him. What Will is, he is because of me. If he hangs, he'll hang because of me. And he *will* hang, even if he's innocent. If August Hewitt wants it to happen, it will happen. He has all that power, all that money. He has his reputation, his connections. He has Leo Thorpe. All I have is you. You've got to help me save him from the noose, Nell."

Nell buried her face in her hands, wanting so desperately to shuck off this burden—but how could she? She'd come to love Viola Hewitt like her own, long-deceased mother, and she owed her so much. "What if I find out that he's guilty?" she asked.

A pause, then: "Do you think you will?"

"The evidence is there, but I still find it hard to believe."

"If he *is* guilty, it's as much my fault as his."

"Have you given any more thought to retaining a lawyer?" Nell asked. If nothing else, it might take some of the pressure off her.

"Some. I wish August didn't have Leo in his back pocket. He's so discreet, so good at making problems disappear."

"What about his son?" Nell asked.

"Jack?"

"He and William were friends, yes? They served together, before William and Robbie were captured. Perhaps he'd feel enough loyalty toward an old chum to represent him in a murder case even if William makes it difficult. That's assuming he practices this kind of law, and that he's any good."

"He was a prosecutor in Washington, but he does defense work now, and I understand he's excellent. But if his father found out—*when* his father finds out, because he can't keep it a secret forever—he'll be furious."

"Still," Nell said, "I should think it would be worth broaching the subject, don't you?"

"It would, indeed. I obviously can't make an appointment for a consultation, though, and I don't think it would be wise to put anything in writing. I'll tell you what. I've already asked Leo and Eugenia to dinner Saturday. She's supposed to stop by sometime this week. When she does, I'll ask her to bring the whole family—Jack, his sisters, their husbands. And I'll invite Leo's law partner, Orville Pratt, and his family. We'll make it a real dinner party. I'll have my dressmaker work up something special for you to wear. We've got five days—that should be enough time."

"*Me?* Governesses don't attend formal dinners."

"Unless their charges are present."

"Gracie's far too young. Everyone knows that."

"They also know I'm a bit of a queer bird. No one ever questions the peculiar things I do—at least, not to my face. At some point during the evening, I'll arrange for you and Jack to speak privately."

"Mrs. Hewitt, don't you think it would be better if *you* handled this end of things? After all, you know Jack Thorpe, and I've never met him."

Viola shook her head resolutely. "It'll be easier for you to sneak away. August is so solicitous of me—he follows my every move. And as I've said before, men respond to you. You're likely to have better luck talking Jack into this than I would."

Nell felt as if she were sinking deeper and deeper into a quagmire of William and Viola Hewitt's making.

"Assuming Jack does agree to represent Will," Viola said, "he'll need to know where to find him."

"He's staying at the Belmont."

Viola cocked her head. "Is that a hotel?"

Uh-oh . . . "I think so. He said you knew it."

The older woman raised her gaze to the ceiling and poured some more cognac. "There *is* no hotel called the Belmont. This is what he would do whenever he and August had a row and he ran off by himself. He'd leave word he was staying at some hotel I was supposed to know about. I would pretend to August that I did, but there was never any such place. I don't know how Robbie used to find him."

Perfect. Nell took a healthy swallow of cognac. "He told me he doesn't lie."

"Oh, he's always hated to lie, but if he feels he's got no other choice, he will. And making up this hotel . . . It's not so much a lie as a . . . dig, a way to let me know he's still in control. And a bit of a jest, I suppose. He always had a fairly droll sense of humor. He made light of the oddest things."

"He still does."

"Find him," Viola implored, reaching out to grasp Nell's hand. "And help him. Please. Don't let him hang, Nell. Promise me you won't let my son hang."

Chapter 10

"HAS anyone seen the new production of Offenbach's *Bluebeard* at the Tremont Temple?" inquired Mrs. Thorpe as she daintily prodded her meringue à la crème with a pastry fork. Eugenia Thorpe was fine-boned and drearily elegant, in striking contrast to her husband Leo. So dusty pale was she from head to toe—hair, skin, gown—that she might have faded away altogether in the rosy-gold haze of candlelight were it not for the glitter and snap of her jewels, the flashing stab of that fork.

"We saw it!" replied Winifred Pratt, a chittering little sparrow of a woman. "We thought it was smashing!"

"We have tickets for next Friday," Viola said, "Mr. Hewitt and the boys and I. I'm so looking forward to it." Her spirits had risen steadily in the five days since her cognac-fueled tête-à-tête in Nell's room, bolstered by the prospect of securing Jack Thorpe's help in freeing her son. Her good spirits seemed to have rubbed off on her husband as well. When she'd confessed to him, in the midst of a searing hangover Tuesday morning, that she'd drunk up his hundred-year-old cognac, he'd stared at her for a long moment, then calmly forgiven her. It was his fault, he'd said. She'd been distraught; this had simply been her way of making him see that.

At Viola's request, Nell had made inquiries at dozens of hotels and rooming houses this past week in an effort to ferret out her son, but to no avail. Still, Viola remained optimistic, as did Nell, at the prospect of recruiting Jack Thorpe's help in finding Will and saving him from the hangman.

Having evidently judged the meringue and found it lacking, Mrs. Thorpe laid down her fork and lifted her glass of sherry. "Yes, well, we saw *Bluebeard* in Paris when it opened two years ago, and I must say, I was unimpressed. I understand it's intended to be a comic operetta, but at times it bordered on the burlesque. You must let me know what you think of it, Viola. Your taste is so much more . . . eclectic than mine."

"Tasty!" Gracie, seated on Nell's lap in her best organza frock—which made her look like a faerie child emerging from a chrysanthemum—pushed a spoonful of glacé pudding into her governess's mouth. "Yum?"

"Yum." It *was* yum, as had been the entire meal, the courses for which—served one after the other, *à la Russe*, by a hushed battalion of servants commanded by Hodges—were beautifully inked on menus propped against salt dishes at each place: *Raw Oysters, Champagne; Green Turtle Soup, Sherry; Salmon in Hollandaise Sauce, Chablis; Vol-au-vent à la Financiere, Champagne; Pâté de Foie Gras Suisse, Madiera; Roman Punch; Roast Fillet of Beef with Mushrooms, Burgundy; Salad, Italian Style, Cheeses; Quails à la Maître d'Hôtel, Port; Pastries, Ices and Jellies, Sherry; Fresh Fruits, Claret; Nuts, Candied Ginger, Sugar Plums, Coffee, Liqueurs.*

August Hewitt's scowl—a reflex with every noise or movement from Gracie's direction—softened when he noticed his wife smiling at him from the other end of the long, flower-heaped dining table. Sixteen men and women in evening dress sat around that table, including the Thorpes' daughters and their husbands—and of course their only son, whom Viola had seated, quite deliberately, directly opposite Nell.

Jack Thorpe was slim and pale and gravely handsome in white tie and tail coat, despite an errant lock of light brown hair that kept falling across his forehead, much to the amusement of his soon-to-be fiancée. Cecilia Pratt was the quintessential Brahmin marriage prize, as bright and golden as a freshly minted double eagle, with a giggle that could burst lead crystal. She drew many an admiring look from the gentlemen at the table . . . as did Nell.

Nell assumed it was her gown that prompted those swift, covert glances, the gown for which Viola had chosen an opalescent silk that shimmered like peacocks' feathers, reflecting a different burnished hue with every shift of the candlelight. Viola's primary dictate to her dressmaker was that it be fashioned with a "décolletage just this side of indecent." Unused as Nell was to such a display, she'd consented to the low-cut bodice and even to the tight lacing required to pinch an extra couple of inches off her waist, but she'd had to put her foot down when it came to an off-the-shoulder cut. She'd pleaded modesty, when in fact the problem was the nine-inch scar that crawled like a worm from the scapular end of her left clavicle over the outer swell of her breast on that side— the worst of her souvenirs from Duncan.

Even Jack Thorpe had appraised her once or twice over the rim of his wineglass, despite how sedate, even pensive, he'd seemed all evening—a reaction, no doubt, to the incessant toasts being offered up regarding his impending engagement and law partnership. The footman Peter, assigned to Jack's section of the table, had been quick to refill his frequently emptied glass; he drank like a man who wished he were elsewhere, yet he showed little sign of inebriation. *Poor Jack, he really never wanted that, but Leo has his ways . . .*

Viola caught Nell's eye and gave her an infinitesimal nod; Nell nuzzled Gracie's hair and said, "Time for bed, buttercup."

"No . . ." Gracie moaned around the two fingers anchored in her pudding-smeared mouth. "Want to stay with Miseeney."

"I know, but it's well past your bedtime," Nell said as she rose, aided by one of Jack's young brothers-in-law, who leapt up to pull her chair out. "You'll be cranky tomorrow if you don't get enough sleep tonight."

"I won't! I won't!" Gracie swore frantically, squirming and struggling as Nell carried her upstairs.

Overtired as Gracie was, and excited from having attended her first dinner party, she took a good deal longer than usual to settle down and be put to bed. Nell kept glancing at the ormolu clock on the nursery mantelpiece as she rocked the restive little girl, fretting over how long this was taking: forty minutes, forty-five . . .

It would take perhaps half an hour, no more, for the fruit course and coffee to be served. At that point, Viola would retire with the ladies to the Red Room for bonbons and demitasse, while the gentlemen lingered at the table for an extra fifteen or twenty minutes to enjoy their cigars and brandy. While wheeling out of the dining room, Viola would pause to tell Jack how much she'd missed him, whispering that Miss Sweeney was waiting for him in the solarium to discuss a private matter.

Having finally rocked Gracie to sleep and tucked her in, Nell sprinted down the service stairs in her soft-soled satin slippers, uneasily aware that Jack must have been waiting for a quarter-hour or more—assuming he hadn't given up and joined the others by now. The footman Dennis passed her on the stairs with a sneering little bow, as if to say, *I served you at dinner tonight only because I had to. You're no better than the rest of us, and we know it.*

Making sure she wasn't seen—God knew what rumors would start flying in the servants' hall if they saw her and Jack Thorpe meeting secretly—Nell squeaked open the door to the solarium, finding it lit only by a thin wash of moonlight from the floor-to-ceiling leaded glass windows. Clicking the door shut behind her, she made her way through a shadowy maze of paintings that were either partially finished or in the process of drying. Her silken skirts rustled so loudly as they brushed against easels and table legs that it sounded as if she were wading through a field of dried corn.

"Miss Sweeney?" He materialized in front of her, a brandy snifter in one hand, unlit cigar in the other.

She pressed a hand to her chest to slow her tripping heart. "Mr. Thorpe. Thank you for meeting me. I'm so sorry to have made you wait."

He waved away her apology. "I was grateful for the excuse to get away by myself for a bit."

"How did you explain your absence to the other gentlemen?"

"I said I wanted to see what Mrs. Hewitt had been painting lately." His slightly thick-tongued speech was the only evidence of how much he'd drunk during dinner. Looking around, he said, "She's been busy."

"Some of them are mine. She lets me work here."

"Yes? Which ones are yours?"

She pointed. "I just finished that one, but it's too dark to see."

Setting his glass and cigar on a worktable, he retrieved a box of matches from inside his coat and lit one, holding it in front of the canvas, a loose-brushed depiction of Gracie and Martin walking down Tremont Street in the snow, hand in hand. In the wavering light of the little flame, she noticed that he'd combed back that stray lock of hair. "Oh, that's extraordinary!" he said.

"Thank you."

Jack studied the painting until the flame began to singe his fingertip, then he flicked it out. "You're extremely talented."

"That's very kind of you." She nodded toward his cigar. "You should light that."

"Oh, no . . ."

"Please do." She emptied some pencils and charcoal sticks out of a ceramic dish and handed it to him for an ashtray. "I enjoy the smell of a good cigar."

"In that case . . ." He moistened the cap of the cigar with a drop of brandy, withdrew a clipper, and carefully snipped the end.

Nell said, "I wanted to speak to you about a matter concerning an old friend of yours—the Hewitts' eldest son, William."

Twirling the cigar over a lit match, he asked, "Did you know Will?"

Nell took a steadying breath. "I do know him. I met him a few days ago."

He looked at her, held her gaze for a moment, shook out the match. Frowning, he blew lightly on the tip of the cigar until it glowed. "I'm sorry, Miss Sweeney, but surely you're mistaken. Will Hewitt died during the war. He and his brother both, at a Confederate prison camp in Georgia."

"Robbie died," she said. "Dr. Hewitt escaped."

He studied her as he drew in a puff of fragrant smoke and let it out. His movements had a slightly drawn-out, measured quality to them, as if the world spun more slowly for him than it did for others. "Surely his family would have heard from him before now."

"He didn't want them to. He's been calling himself William Toussaint, but I've met him, and he's definitely

William Hewitt. Your father's confirmed his identity, too, so—"

"*My father?* My *father's* spoken to him?"

"He interviewed him in jail. Dr. Hewitt's been arrested for murder."

Jack lowered the cigar, stared at her.

"A merchant seaman named Ernest Tulley had his throat cut outside a place called Flynn's Boardinghouse on Purchase Street Saturday night. Dr. Hewitt was caught literally red-handed. They intend to hang him."

Smoke fluttered from his mouth; he closed his eyes, rubbed the bridge of his nose with the hand that held the cigar. "Will . . ." He slumped against the table, his face unnaturally white in the moonlight. "Jesus, what have you done?"

"I'm not convinced he really did it—nor is Mrs. Hewitt."

"No. No, I didn't mean . . ." He kneaded his forehead, as if trying to force his brain to process this new reality. "God, I'm not saying he did it. It's . . . it's not in his nature. I just meant . . . I suppose I meant that trouble just seems to *embrace* Will. Perhaps . . . I don't know, perhaps because he doesn't avoid it the way most men do. He courts it, in a way. He always has."

"We first heard about his arrest last Sunday afternoon . . ." She told him everything up to the point where she and Viola decided to ask Jack to represent Will. Best, perhaps, to ease into that.

He was still leaning against the table, staring at nothing, when she finished her chronology. He didn't seem to notice when a column of ash broke off from his cigar to crash noiselessly on the tiled floor.

"I know you were Robbie's best friend," she said. "But you were friends with Will as well, yes?"

Jack nodded dazedly. "We served in the same regiment, the three of us. Signed up together, swore to stick

together no matter what happened." He brought his cigar
to his mouth again, but lowered it without taking a draw.
"Will was a good . . . *is* a good man. The best. And he
was the best battle surgeon in the Union Army. General
Grant himself told our commander that. He was fearless,
too, took insane risks, exposed himself to enemy fire time
and again to retrieve wounded men. He saved a great
many lives before he was captured."

"How did it happen?"

He gestured haphazardly with the cigar, seemed to notice his brandy as if for the first time, and took a sip. "The
battle was ending, Robbie was injured—badly, he couldn't
be moved. Will wouldn't leave him. There were some
other wounded men, too, but I knew it was Robbie he
didn't want to leave. He stayed with them and let himself
be captured. He told me to retreat with the rest of our
regiment." With a sneer of self-disgust, he said, "I don't
have to tell you I did just that." He swallowed the entire
snifter of brandy in one tilt.

"Of course you did. Your regiment was—"

"No." He shook his head, held up a hand as if to fore-
stall such sophistry. "No. We'd sworn to stick together,
the three of us. *Sworn* it. I should have done whatever I
had to do to stay with them. Don't think I haven't kicked
myself over that."

"You might have died if you'd stayed with them."

"Indeed I might have. I happen to know a great deal
about Andersonville because of the work I was doing in
Washington after the war. They buried a hundred men a
day there. But perhaps I was meant to be one of them."

"A hundred?"

"We're talking about an enormous outdoor pen, Miss
Sweeney, comprised of hewn pine logs, with sentry boxes
every thirty yards, housing some thirty-two thousand
men." His speech lost its torpor and took on the resolute
tone of a lawyer addressing a jury. "There was a diseased

creek running through it for bathing and washing down
the occasional spoonful of rice and peas, sometimes a potato—nearly always rancid. The prisoners were forbidden
to build shelters. There were a few tents, some lean-to's,
but most of them lived their lives completely exposed to
the elements, day and night, all year round. In the summer
it could get to a hundred degrees on a regular basis, and
in the winter there was often freezing rain, and sometimes
even snow. After a bad rainstorm, they would just pull
the bodies out of the mud and bury them in a mass grave."

Nell said, "I saw photographs of emaciated prisoners
in *Harper's Weekly* after the Union Army arrived at the
end of the war." She wished she hadn't. They were little
more than skeletons with skin stretched over them, those
men—eyes vacant, toothless mouths gaping. The images
of their suffering still haunted her.

"That was the issue that came out in June of 'sixty-
five," Jack said. "It's what sparked the general outcry over
Andersonville—that and the fact that every Union veteran
one meets either spent time there or knows someone who
did—Andersonville was so populous that it was actually
the fifth largest city in the Confederacy. The North wanted
retribution. *I* wanted retribution. That's why I went to
Washington after the war, instead of back here. I went to
work for the Adjutant-General's Office of the War Department, to help them prepare the case against Andersonville's commandant, Captain Henry Wirz. There was
a great deal to do. The trial lasted sixty-three days."

"I read about that. He was executed, wasn't he?"

"That's right," he said as he drew on his cigar. "Hanged by the neck November tenth, eighteen sixty-five.
Took him a while to die, but he still got off easy—a good
deal easier than those poor fellows who lived and died
inside that pen. 'Wanton cruelty,' that was our charge
against him. And never was a man more guilty. If there
was any justice in the world, any *real* justice, he would

have been made to suffer the way those prisoners suffered."

"Why do you suppose the Andersonville death roll lists Will as having died of dysentery, when he actually escaped?"

Jack turned his cigar this way and that, contemplating it from various angles. "Perhaps they found a body they thought was his. Or perhaps it was just poor record-keeping. In any event, 'dysentery' was what they'd put down when they weren't sure of the real cause of death, because almost all of them had it. But there were innumerable ways to suffer and die there—scurvy, malaria, smallpox, typhoid, pneumonia, starvation, gangrene . . . plain old exposure. They said you could choke on the stench in that pen, and every man was crawling with lice. The 'hospital' was a shanty, with men lying in their own filth. The blow flies didn't bother waiting for death. Most of the men were infested with maggots by the time they . . . My God," he said, looking up with an abashed expression. "I don't know what I'm thinking, telling you such things. Please forgive me."

"I'm not easily shocked," she said, thinking giddily that perhaps she should have a badge made up that said that. "I was a sort of nurse once."

"Still. . . ." He rubbed his temple. "It's just that my outrage gets the better of me when it comes to that place. So many fine young men, like Robbie, dying in such awful ways."

"Those who lived through it must have died a little bit, too," Nell said. "Look at Dr. Hewitt. The opium, the fatalism. He obviously doesn't care what becomes of him. If he did, he would have denied his guilt by now. He would have retained a lawyer, a good one, instead of just waiting to see who the commonwealth appoints."

Jack smoked his cigar, brow furrowed, as Nell counted off the seconds. Nell found that she actually was enjoying its aroma, which mingled pleasantly with the familiar scents of linseed oil and turpentine. A little over a minute passed before he met her eyes and said, "I want to represent him."

Nell forced herself not to smile in triumph. "Are you sure? Your father's bound to disapprove, and I doubt Dr. Hewitt will make it easy for you."

Pushing off the table, Jack crossed to the wall of glass and gazed out into the moonlit back garden. "I've spent nearly my entire life following the path of least resistance, Miss Sweeney. Somehow I suspect you have no idea what that's like."

Too true.

"Will used to joke about how I was living my life according to 'Papa's Rulebook,' " Jack said. "But I wasn't like Will. The only time I ever displayed any real backbone was when I took that job with the adjutant-general instead of coming back to Boston after the war. I was going to spend the rest of my life in Washington, make my own way. Father begged me to come back and join the firm, started making offers that grew ever more generous. I told myself I could never be bought. Now look at me."

He turned, shoved a hand in his pocket, and puffed thoughtfully on his cigar. "I've taken the easy way, the expected way, once too often. This is my opportunity to make up for that. Yes, Miss Sweeney, I mean to represent Will—whether he wants me to or not. And I'll do what I can to help you sort through this mess. I don't have much in the way of contacts in Boston—not yet—but I've got a fair measure of legal expertise, and I can gain access to certain kinds of information, go places that might be dangerous for you."

If he only knew the places she'd been! "Thank you, Mr. Thorpe. You don't know how much this will mean to Mrs. Hewitt. She'll want to pay you a fair fee for your services."

"Absolutely not!" he exclaimed, sounding truly offended. "I wouldn't dream of charging her for this. If she tried to, I would consider it an insult."

"Very well," Nell said with a smile. "I'll let her know."

Jack rotated his cigar carefully in the clay dish to roll off its excess ash. "Let's see if I understand this correctly. Will is supposed to have killed this man because of an altercation over a woman."

Nell nodded. "Kathleen Flynn, the owner's daughter."

"Is she beautiful?"

"I . . . she's . . ." Nell shrugged. "I'm not really sure, from a man's perspective. Why?"

"Will's women were always magnificent. And very sophisticated. He liked them smart and a little dangerous."

"Kathleen is none of those things. Although her father did compare her to his most vicious rat terrier."

Jack chuckled. She hadn't seen him smile before, and it was quite the transformation, affording Nell a glimpse of the carefree young man he must have been before the war. "I must say, she doesn't sound quite like Will's type. And although I've seen him come to blows over a woman, it was only once, and with good cause. The notion that he would murder a man over some chippy they both wanted to"—he paused uneasily—"court . . . strikes me as—"

"*Court?*" Nell couldn't help laughing. "I hardly think courtship was at issue, Mr. Thorpe, but yes, that's the idea. That and what the police refer to as a 'frenzy of intoxication.' But whoever came up with that theory has obviously never seen anyone under the influence of opium. It's not like being drunk on whiskey. One tends to do a great deal of lying about and dozing off. I can't imagine someone committing murder after smoking it—especially such a vicious murder."

Jack nodded distractedly. "The trick will be convincing a jury of that, and with all the lurid newspaper stories about opium dens, that might be a bit of a challenge. What about this Noonan fellow? He seems a likely culprit."

"He is—especially if it's true that Tulley wouldn't pay him the money he owed him. But I've also been thinking about the second man in the back parlor. He *had* been drinking. We should try to find him. Perhaps Pearl could help us. She lives at one sixty-four Milk Street, a ground-floor flat. She did say she'd recognize him if she saw him again."

"Yes, but assuming that fellow didn't know Tulley, he would have even less reason than Will to murder him. At least, with Noonan, we have a motive."

Nell said, "I just wish Dr. Hewitt weren't being so difficult. He must know how incriminating it looks for him to refuse to enter a plea, or discuss what happened that night, even under police interrogation. You should have seen him the next day, after they worked him over. His face . . ."

Jack whispered something under his breath. "I'm glad I didn't."

"If he *is* guilty," she said, "I assume he's keeping quiet in order to avoid the noose. Why help the prosecution build a case against him? I get the impression he wouldn't mind dying—he seems to view himself as despicable—but he loathes the idea of hanging."

"He's not guilty," Jack said. "He can't be. You don't know him as well as I do, Miss Sweeney. Believe me—he didn't do this."

"Then why won't he hire a lawyer and encourage an investigation?" she asked. "If he establishes a reasonable doubt as to his guilt, he *could* be acquitted . . . couldn't he?"

"I hope so, because that's exactly what I'm going to try to do. As for why he's being uncooperative . . ." Jack looked down, frowning meditatively. "I've often found Will Hewitt to be something of an enigma. Perhaps if I speak to him in person, it will start to make sense. Did you find out where he's staying?"

Nell groaned. "He gave the name of a hotel, but I've since found out there is no such place."

"Ah, yes," Jack said with wry smile. "That was an old ruse of his to get away from his family now and again. Only Robbie knew how to figure out his whereabouts. He and Will revealed the secret to me one night when we were sharing a bottle around a fire. It had to do with his current actress."

"Actress?"

"They were actresses, most of them, the ladies he, um . . ."

"Courted?"

He returned her smile with a rather endearing little duck of his head. Clearing his throat, he said, "The name of the hotel generally had some connection to the play she was currently appearing in, or the featured play if there was more than one. Robbie didn't always know who Will was keeping company with, but he'd seen and read a great many plays, and he had a good memory for details. For example, Will once left word that he was staying at the Shelby. Robbie recalled that Tom's owners in *Uncle Tom's Cabin* were named Shelby. This was back in 'fifty-three, when it was playing at the Tremont, so Robbie bought a ticket, picked out the prettiest member of the cast, and cornered her in her dressing room after the show. It turned out Will had spent the past three days in her flat on Prince Street."

"Why didn't Will just *tell* Robbie where he was staying, if he wanted him to know?"

Jack contemplated Nell over his cigar as he brought it to his mouth. "You don't know Will very well, do you?"

"I met him less than a week ago."

He smiled, smoke curling from his mouth. "An enigma, as I said—but an enigma with his own, peculiar sense of humor. What hotel did he say he was staying at?"

"The Belmont."

"The Belmont . . ." He stared at the floor, eyes narrowing in concentration. "Belmont . . ."

"Portia lived in Belmont," Nell offered.

He looked up.

"In *The Merchant of Venice*? Portia. She lived in Belmont."

Jack smiled at her the way Will had when he'd first begun to detect her *hidden dimensions*. "There's a version of *The Merchant of Venice* playing at the Boston Museum Theatre."

"Really?"

He nodded. "Do you have any plans for tomorrow?"

"Well . . . church in the morning."

"Yes, of course—for me, too."

"And then I need to watch Gracie while her nursemaid goes to church."

"What are you doing after that? Say, around one o'clock?"

She smiled. "I think you and I are going to the Boston Museum Theatre."

Chapter 11

"ARE you sure you wouldn't rather wait downstairs in the lobby?" Jack asked Nell as he prepared to knock on the door of the apartment that occupied the entire third floor of the posh Pelham Hotel.

"I've already answered that," she reminded him. "More than once." Four times, to be precise, during the six-block walk from the Boston Museum Theatre near the old Burying Ground to the corner of Tremont and Boylston. Jack's reluctance to have Nell accompany him into the home of the actress with whom William Hewitt might be living at the moment—a concession to her maidenly sensibilities, presumably—was amusingly ironic. After all, hadn't Nell herself spent some four years living in sinful cohabitation with Dr. Greaves? But her good humor, strained from having gotten too little sleep last night, waned with every repetition of his offer to handle this encounter himself.

Not that she'd minded his taking the lead during their conversation with the stage manager for the theater's stock company—a chinless troll with a trailing moustache who'd leered openly at Nell while Jack scrutinized a handbill illustrated with drawings of the cast.

Her, Jack had said, pointing. *She looks familiar.*

The stage manager had grinned lasciviously. *Not bad, eh? That's Mathilde Cloutier. She plays Portia's servant, Nerissa.*

Jack had met Nell's eyes with a look that made it clear they'd struck pay dirt. *Where does she live?* he'd asked the troll.

Well, now, I can't just be givin' out company members' addresses without their . . . His eyes had glinted as Jack pressed a couple of shiners into his palm. *Pelham Hotel. That's them French flats on the corner of Tremont and Boylston. Third floor.*

"I really don't mind doing this alone," Jack persisted as he stalled outside the apartment door.

With a groan of frustration, Nell raised her fist to knock, only to have him capture her wrist before she could do so. "She's not French," he said.

"I'm sorry?"

"Mathilde Cloutier. You probably think she's from France, because of her name. But she's actually from the French West Indies. She's, um . . . they call her the . . . Ethiopian Enchantress."

"Ah."

"You're shocked."

"A little." Her gaze lit on his hand, still gripping her wrist.

Jack released her abruptly, muttering an apology as a faint pink stain crawled up his throat. He knocked on the door and said, without meeting her gaze, "Will saw her on and off for several years before the war. I met her once or twice in passing. She performed with Buckley's Minstrels then, wearing blackface."

"But isn't she already . . . ?"

"Yes, but the audience didn't know that. It was the only work she could get at the time. Things are different now."

As footsteps approached from the other side of the door, Jack whispered, "Remember me mentioning a woman Will came to blows over once? That was Mathilde."

The door swung open on a lissome creature whose most outstanding feature was a great froth of corkscrew curls tumbling just past her shoulders. Mathilde Cloutier had huge, heavy-lidded eyes, bold cheekbones, and smooth-burnished skin the color of coffee laced with a dollop of cream. So swiftly did she size up her visitors that Jack had barely opened his mouth to greet her when she said, "I hope you're here to take him away." Her accent, while nominally French, was seasoned with a sing-songy Caribbean lilt. Opening the door wider so they could enter, she added, "I am sick to death of him."

She turned and motioned for them to follow her through the vast, opulent apartment—room after room papered in watered silk, layered with Oriental carpets, furnished with Turkish-tufted fainting couches, French gilt mirrors, lushly overgrown rubber trees . . . none of it more gorgeously exotic than Mathilde Cloutier herself. She didn't walk so much as strut, her long legs propelling her with a graceful underwater languor as her dressing gown—a wisp of amethyst silk—floated along behind her like an empress's court train.

Nell breathed in the sooty-sweet aroma of opium mingled with a whiff of patchouli as Mathilde called out, "Company!" Sweeping aside a curtain of tinkling glass beads, she ushered them into a boudoir that might have housed a sultan's harem, so lavishly bedecked was it in jewel-toned draperies and mounds of pillows.

Looking quite at home in this silken seraglio was William Hewitt, reclining on his side atop a colossal bed tented in sheer netting. Drowsy-eyed and naked from the waist up—his lower body being concealed beneath a rumpled sheet—he had his head propped on one hand while the other cradled a bamboo smoking pistol. A silver tray on the floor held the attendant paraphernalia—spirit lamp, spindle, sea sponge, knife . . . Nell noticed the cylindrical horn opium box he'd purchased at Deng Bao's hop joint, which lay open on its side. It had been full when he'd bought it on Monday; now it was nearly empty.

Will went very still when he saw Jack. He stared at his old friend through the netting, looking suddenly wide awake. The cuts and contusions on his face were healing, but Nell was sobered by the bruising to his torso—fading but extensive, especially around his ribs.

"Will," Jack said with a nervous little smile.

Pushing the netting aside, Will looked from Jack to Nell, his expression grim. Quietly he said, "Miss Sweeney, I do wish you hadn't done this."

"Take him away." Snatching up a leather traveling case from the corner, Mathilde proceeded to cram into it various items strewn around the room—a man's shirt, a china shaving cup, a pair of leather braces . . . "Take him out of my sight. I cannot bear another moment of this."

"You cut me to the quick," Will said wearily.

"Take your filthy gong and go!" she yelled at him. "Poison yourself if you must, but don't do it here. I've put up with it as long as I care to!"

"Save it for the stage, Mattie," Will drawled.

She began berating him in French—although it didn't sound much like the French that Dr. Greaves used to drill into Nell—hurling abuse and imperious commands as she stuffed the bag with his possessions. Will responded in the same language, but with a good deal less volume and emotion.

"*Get out!*" she screamed, hurling the luggage at his head.

He ducked lazily to avoid it as it tumbled onto the bed behind him.

"Go away and kill yourself someplace else." She departed the room with icy majesty, the silken robe flowing to the hypnotic sway of her hips.

Will sat up, rubbing his face as if he'd just awakened. "What the devil did you say to set her off?" he asked Nell.

"*Me?* Nothing! Not that I don't sympathize with her. In her position, I'd probably kick you out, too."

He turned to his friend. "*Et tu*, Jack?"

Jack hesitated, glanced at Nell. "I . . ." He spread his hands.

"Still traveling with the herd, eh, counselor? Seems I'm outvoted. Right, then." Whipping aside the sheet, Will threw his legs over the side of the bed and stood, completely and utterly nude.

"Will!" Jack gasped. "For pity's sake!"

Nell whirled around and fled from the room, the rattling of the beaded curtain not quite drowning out Will's groggy chuckles. Heat scalded her face; her legs quivered. She didn't know which sight affected her more deeply: six plus feet of shockingly naked male, or the damage to his legs, in the form of multiple bruises and a deep scar that puckered the long quadriceps of his right thigh. The old Nell would never have reacted this way to the sight of a man's body, regardless of his wounds or state of undress—but the old Nell had yet to encounter William Hewitt.

Retracing her steps, she met up with Mathilde in what appeared to be a buttery connecting the main hallway to the dining room.

"Would you like some?" the actress inquired, holding up a decanter of hazy greenish liquid and a tiny gold-rimmed glass. "Don't worry, it's not absinthe—just an herbal liqueur. French—very good."

"No, thank you." Nell might have accepted the drink, if only to calm her nerves after that spectacle—why was it that only William Hewitt had the power, and the desire, to make her blush like a callow young girl?—but her post-cognac headache Tuesday morning was still fresh in her memory.

"A cup of tea?" Mathilde leaned back against a wine cabinet to sip her liqueur. Nell was surprised to find her in such amenable spirits so soon after her own little drama with Will.

"No, really. I'm fine."

Setting down her glass, Mathilde withdrew a box of matches from the pocket of her wrapper, and a hand-rolled cigarette, which she slid between her lips. Nell had never seen a woman smoke before. "So you're Nell Sweeney."

"He spoke of me?"

Mathilde let out a little huff of laughter as she lit the cigarette. She looked at Nell as she drew in and exhaled the smoke. "He was drunk on opium."

Nell nodded, wondering what he'd said but unwilling to ask.

"You're going to have to take him away." Another sip of the green liqueur, another puff of the cigarette. "He's in some trouble, eh?"

"He's been accused of murder."

Mathilde's eyes lit with interest. "Did he do it?"

"Do you think he's capable of it?"

The actress considered that. "I don't know. Maybe. If someone tried to take away his gong."

"Before the gong. When you knew him before the war."

"He did beat a man up once. I was waiting for Will and his friends one night in front of Tuttle's Restaurant— I'd wanted to get some air while they settled the bill— and a man stopped his carriage, got out and, well . . . propositioned me very crudely. I was in one of my best gowns, too—it wasn't as if I should be mistaken for some common *putain*. When I slapped his face, he slapped me back and grabbed me where he shouldn't have, and called me a . . . something very rude about my color. He was trying to force me into his carriage when Will came out of the restaurant." She smiled at her reminiscence. "Oh, he was furious, *très sauvage*. I never knew he had it in him. His brother Robbie and that one in there"—she cocked her head toward the bedroom—"they pulled him off this man, because they were afraid he'd kill him. It was very exciting."

"I imagine it was."

"My father killed a man, back in Martinique. He had it coming to him, but you would never have thought a gentle man like my father could do something like that. Sometimes I think anyone can kill if given enough reason." Mathilde tossed back the last of her liqueur and set the glass back down. "He can't stay here. Take him away—anywhere—but get him out of here."

"You're that put out with him?"

She sighed, raised the cigarette to her lips. "My gentleman friend is coming back."

"Your . . . *Oh*." Nell had wondered how an actress of no particular renown could afford to live in such luxury.

"Will cannot be here when Edmund arrives. That bed is big, but not big enough for three, you know?"

"No, I suppose not."

On the assumption that Will had had time to get at least partially dressed, Nell returned to the bedroom, peering through the beaded curtain as she warily approached it.

Will, still shirtless and standing with his back to her as he buttoned his trousers, was talking about Mathilde. "She's miffed because I can't rouse to her. It's not her, of course. It's the goddamned gong—it's got a stranglehold on my cock."

Jack, sitting on the edge of the bed facing the doorway, noticed Nell and hitched in a breath. Will turned, saw her, closed his eyes, and muttered something under his breath. Jack's embarrassment did not surprise her. Will's did—especially in light of his nonchalance about the nudity.

Jack rose to his feet as Nell entered the room. "I, uh, was telling Will that capital crimes are tried before the Supreme Judicial Court. Not all attorneys can argue before the SJC, but I can."

"Not on my behalf, you can't," Will growled as he yanked an undershirt over his head. "Not without my leave."

"If you won't let me represent you, the court will appoint someone."

"So, let it," Will said, buttoning on his shirt. "Why waste your valuable time when I can waste that of some public greenhorn with nothing better to do?"

"Because it won't be some greenhorn, Will. They can't argue before the SJC. If it's not me, it'll probably be somebody better and more experienced than me."

Will took his time tucking in his shirt and shrugging on his braces. He shook out his vest and paused, raking a hand through his hair. "Why are you doing this?" he asked Jack, his voice low and earnest.

Jack regarded him in weighty silence. "You know why." When Will didn't respond, he added, "I swore to stick with you once, and I didn't. This time I'm going to. How could I not, considering . . . My God, Will. *How could I not?*"

"Your papa won't be pleased."

"The hell with him."

After a moment's nonplused silence, Will burst out laughing. "It's worth putting up with you just to have heard that," he said as he buttoned his vest. "All right. Go ahead and represent me, for all the good it'll do. They want to hang me and I'll wager they will, regardless of how brilliantly you defend me."

"We'll see about that," Jack said, holding Will's coat open for him—not August Hewitt's hand-me-down, Nell noticed, but a new-looking black frock coat that fit him perfectly. "My first order of business will be to find out everything the police know, and hopefully a bit more. Miss Sweeney, I wonder if you would be willing to visit Flynn's Boardinghouse with me tomorrow—say, around noon? You can introduce me to our cast of players."

"Of course." Nurse Parrish was generally awake and alert enough to care for Gracie around then. Pray God she didn't cry and carry on when Nell left; it was excruciating to have to extract oneself from a sobbing child when all one wanted was to hold her and rock her until she calmed.

"I'd rather you stayed out of it," Will told her. "With Jack playing the intrepid champion, I don't see the need for you to be involved."

"Your mother sees it differently," Nell said. "She made it clear I'm to keep close tabs on you." *I want to know where he goes and what he does,* Viola had said last night after her guests left and Nell finally got the chance to relate her conversation with Jack. *But be careful. If anything happened to you, I'd never be able to forgive myself.*

Jack said, "You can tell her Will's going to stay with me till this all blows over."

"That will be a comfort to her," Nell said. "She's very relieved that you've agreed to help us. Where do you live?"

"The Back Bay—one of those townhouses on Commonwealth near the Public Garden. My father bought me one as a Christmas present. Mother had it all furnished before I even got here."

"That should make Miss Pratt happy," Nell said.

"Are you serious?" he asked with an incredulous little

laugh. "Nothing less than a forty-room chateau will do for a Pratt. The blueprints have already been drawn up."

"A wedding gift from your father?" Will asked.

"From hers. Come, let me walk you over to my place and get you settled."

Nell said, "I'll come with you."

"That isn't necessary," Jack said.

"Oh, but it is. Mrs. Hewitt insists that I actually see where her son is staying this time. I've got to go inside, look around with my own eyes, and draw a picture for her when I get home—literally. She said she's had enough Belmont Hotels to last her a lifetime."

"Speaking of my mother . . ." Will withdrew a well-stuffed envelope from inside his coat and handed it to Nell. "That's what she lent me last Sunday, plus a week's interest."

Nell felt the stack of bills through the crackling paper. "You've been gambling?"

He gave a little smile, as if it were a naive inquiry. "It's what I do."

"You really shouldn't while you're out on bail," Jack said. "If you're caught—"

"Miss Sweeney has already delivered this cautionary lecture, Jack. Don't worry—I won't be caught."

"Your mother never intended for you to pay this back," Nell said, holding the envelope out for him.

"The last thing I want," he said as he turned and held the beaded curtain open for her, "is that woman's charity."

THE war had slowed development in the Back Bay land-fill, envisioned a decade ago as a haven for Brahmins who hadn't managed to buy into Beacon Hill or Colonnade Row before they filled up. The broad boulevard dubbed Commonwealth Avenue was to have been, by now, Boston's very own Champs-Elysées, surrounded by a harmonious little enclave of Parisian-style mansions and townhouses. The landfill extended only two blocks west of Arlington and the Public Garden, however, and contained many vacant lots, giving it a rather sparse and melancholic aura. Commonwealth Avenue ended abruptly at the tidal flat that was shrinking all too slowly in the western end. Indeed, the effluvial reek of that great stretch of mud and sewage tainted every breath one drew in this section of the city. Thus, the most desirable part of the Back Bay at present was the far eastern edge, which was relatively built up, and this was where Jack's house was located.

Number ten Commonwealth Avenue was one of an attached row of four-story, bay-windowed brownstones with imposing flights of front steps disappearing beneath handsome porticos. Will limped only slightly as he carried his bag through the ornate iron gate and up the stairs, and the four-block walk over here hadn't seemed to trouble him—evidence that he'd dosed himself at Mathilde's with enough opium to deaden the lingering ache of that old bullet wound, at least for the time being.

"I assume Papa provided you with servants," he said as Jack twisted his key in the glazed, French-style double front door.

"A cook and a maid, but they're only here on weekday mornings, while I'm at the firm, because I can't bear having them underfoot. I take my suppers at the club."

"The Somerset?" The inquiry had a mocking little bite to it. The Somerset was the most prestigious gentlemen's club in Boston—the home away from home of such eminent personages as Leo Thorpe, Orville Pratt, and August Hewitt.

Ignoring the taunt, Jack ushered Nell and Will into the house, which was remarkable for the value and quality of its furnishings—matched sets of Hepplewhite and Sheraton, mostly—as well as for the utter absence of evidence that this was actually someone's home. Jack had presumably been living here for two months, yet there were no personal effects lying about, no untidy little corners, no open books or half-read newspapers, no lap rug tossed over the back of a chair, no kicked-off shoes next to a couch. In every room they passed, the carpets—Axminsters, Savonneries—were as velvety and pristine as if they'd never felt the tread of a shoe.

"My word," Nell murmured, pausing in the wide entrance to the formal dining room. Suspended over a gleaming mahogany table was the most spectacular chandelier Nell had ever seen—a monumental confection of crystal and brass that looked as if it weighed a ton. "It must be as bright as the sun when you turn the gas all the way up."

"I wouldn't know," Jack replied. "I've never lit it."

"I would have lit it once just to see what it looks like," she said.

He answered that with a disinterested little grunt. "Mother had it sent from Venice. She's terribly proud of it, calls it the centerpiece of the house. She tells me it'll be the talk of Boston once I start having people to dinner."

He smiled and shook his head, as if bemused by the notion that he would ever have anyone to dinner.

Chapter 12

"THIS is where it happened?" asked Jack Thorpe as Nell guided him into the alley next to Flynn's Boardinghouse at noon the next day.

"Right there." Nell pointed to a section of the cracked stone pavement—devoid now of snow—that was still slightly discolored. "He bled out fast once his carotid artery was cut."

Jack stared at the spot, one hand in a pocket of his overcoat, the other absently kneading his temple. He looked pale and wrung out today, and had complained of a headache earlier. "You viewed the corpse, you say?"

"Yes. The wounds were extensive, and rather savagely haphazard. I believe he tried to ward them off."

Jack looked up at her uneasily. "I'm sorry you had to see that. I don't know what that detective was thinking, bringing a lady into a morgue."

"He was only doing what I—"

"Miss Swee—er, Chapel? I *thought* that was your voice."

Nell looked toward the window into the back parlor, partially open as always, to find none other than Detective Cook himself leaning on the sill to peer at her through the glass, smeared with a dingy brownish stain from years of opium smoke.

"Speak of the Devil," she said. "Mr. Jack Thorpe, I'd like you to meet Detective Colin Cook, whose job it is to ensure that your client hangs by the neck until he's dead."

"You're Toussaint's lawyer?" Cook asked.

"I am. Pleased to make your acquaintance, Detective."

Cook speared Nell with an incisive little glance. He would assume, from what she'd had the thankful presence of mind to tell him last time, that retaining Jack was a sop for Mrs. Hewitt, and would have no effect on her husband's zeal to see his son hang—or on the payoff due Cook for paving his way to the gallows. The detective said, "You *will* be pleased, Mr. Thorpe, once you come on inside and find out how much more difficult my job has just gotten."

They joined him in the parlor to find Seamus Flynn standing in the corner, expression dour, arms crossed. Molly, the prostitute who'd talked her friend Pearl into working at Flynn's, sat on the leather chaise smoking a cigarette. Curious, after having gone her entire twenty-six years without seeing a woman smoke, that Nell should witness it twice in as many days. She wondered if the easy women she'd known on Cape Cod were smoking cigarettes now, or if the trend was confined to the big cities.

Molly had on the same low-cut purple basque and red-and-white-striped skirt she'd been wearing last week when Nell and Detective Cook had barged in on her servicing her customer in the pink room; her black-dyed hair was mounded high on her head. She eyed Nell and Jack with a studied lack of expression as she drew on her cigarette.

Tapping his bowler against his leg, Cook said, "I took it into my head to pay a visit to Pearl this morning, mainly to make sure she was trying to sober up for her court date. I found no one at home, and the neighbors saying as how one of the wenches that lived there had up and run off during the night. Since I knew that had to be either Molly or Pearl, I came here straightaway and found Molly hard at work upstairs. Quite industrious for so early in the day, Molly. You're to be commended for your work ethic."

Molly rolled her eyes as she smoked.

"Pearl disappeared with no word to anybody," Cook said, "including Molly here, who's shared a flat with her for . . . how long has it been, Molly?"

"Seven years," Molly said to the wall.

"Seven years, and she never told you she was leaving?" The detective propped a giant foot on the chaise lounge, hovering over Molly in the manner of a grizzly hovering over a rabbit.

Molly shrugged. "That's Pearl."

"That's Pearl, yes," Cook said. "That's Pearl. I suppose that will have to do. My most important—correct that, my *only* real witness who can pin this murder on William Toussaint has vanished into thin air, but hey—*That's Pearl.* Thank you for that insight, Molly. I can't tell you what that means to me. Well, I *could*," he growled, leaning over the whore, "but my ma taught me never to curse in front of a lady, and I tend to be very generous in my definition of 'lady.' "

Nell sat next to Molly on the chaise. "What happened?"

"I woke up this morning and found her gone," Molly said.

"All her things are still there?" Nell asked.

"Yep."

"She didn't leave a note?"

"She don't write too good."

"You didn't hear *anything* when she left?" Cook asked.

"She can be quiet when she wants."

Nell said, "Do you have any idea where she might have gone?"

"Nope."

Addressing the detective, Nell said, "She might not have left voluntarily, given that she didn't take anything with her, or tell Molly she was leaving."

"I considered that," he said, "but Molly tells me the two of them sleep in the same bed. Surely Molly would have woken up if Pearl had been abducted against her will."

Jack said, "She probably just decided she didn't want the trouble of testifying—or getting sober."

It was understandable that Jack chose to believe, as Cook did, that Pearl had left on her own, given that her disappearance was such a boon to his case. But Nell's conscience wouldn't permit her to so easily dismiss the more ominous possibility. "The abductor might have had a gun, or a knife, and threatened to kill her if she made any noise," she pointed out.

Flynn spoke up for the first time. "Roy Noonan's got a gun *and* a knife."

"So does every other ruffian in this town." Detective Cook churned that great jaw in thoughtful rumination. "Where was William Toussaint last night?" he asked, looking from Nell to Jack, and back again.

Jack seemed momentarily thrown by the question, but recovered swiftly. "He . . . he was in my house, asleep. He's staying with me."

"You're sure he didn't leave?"

"I would have seen him if he had. I was up all night reading in the library, with the door open." Reading and drinking, Nell assumed; she knew a morning head when she saw one.

"All night?"

"I have trouble sleeping sometimes."

That last bit, about Jack's wakefulness, was true enough. He'd told Nell while driving her over here in his smart little one-horse gig that he'd reread Mr. Fourier's *The Social Destiny of Man* start to finish last night. He'd been too uneasy to sleep, he'd explained, after hearing Will steal out of the house around midnight—presumably to gamble. Dawn was breaking by the time Will returned, groggy and disheveled and uninterested in Jack's advice that he adopt more circumspect habits, at least until his murder case was resolved.

Clearly, Jack was lying about Will's whereabouts last night not just because gambling was a violation of his bail conditions, but in order to prevent him from being implicated in Pearl's disappearance. Regardless of whether Will had anything to do with it—and Nell couldn't believe, didn't want to believe, that he had—it wouldn't do to ignore the possibility that Pearl was in terrible trouble. "I don't have to tell you how much I sympathize with your position, Mr. Thorpe," she said. "But I'm afraid common decency obligates us to look for Pearl. If she was abducted against her will and is being held somewhere—"

"She took her pictures," Molly said. So unexpected was it for her to volunteer information that Nell and the three men just stared at her.

The prostitute sucked on her cigarette, stained bloodred at the tip, held the smoke in her lungs for a few seconds, and blew it out in a stream. "She's got two pictures—photographs, in velvet cases. One's of her and her sisters, when they was all little. The other's of her babies."

"She has children?" Nell asked.

"They died within a day of bein' born, both of 'em. Little twin girls, Ernestine and Adelaide. She had a photograph made of the two of 'em in their coffin. They was buried together," she said with surprising wistfulness, "like two little china dolls in a box."

"Why did you tell us she didn't take anything?" Cook asked.

A negligent shrug. "I forgot about the pictures. Two pairs of shoes was missing, too, her favorites. Pearl, she loves them shoes of hers."

"She left on her own, then," Jack said.

Nell nodded in agreement; what kidnapper would let his victim gather her favorite things to bring along?

"I mean to find her," Cook said. "Does she have family somewhere?" he asked Molly.

"Her sisters are mill girls in Charlestown, but they won't have nothin' to do with her." She took another puff of her cigarette. "Can I go now? I've got a customer waitin' for me upstairs."

"One more question, if you wouldn't mind," Nell said. Except for that altercation with Tulley around eight o'clock, Will had spent the entire evening of the murder in the back parlor, dozing off between bowls of opium. Without Pearl to tell the jury about Will's fury toward Tulley and his resolve to "make him pay," perhaps Jack could make a case for Will being too quiescent to mount such a vicious attack—assuming they could scrounge up enough witnesses who'd seen him after he'd smoked himself into a stupor. "The night Ernest Tulley was murdered," Nell asked Molly, "did you happen to notice William Toussaint in the back parlor?"

"I was only in that part of the house once or twice," Molly replied, "and I wasn't there when they arrested him, so I'm not sure I'd know him if I saw him."

"Perhaps this will help." Nell retrieved from her chatelaine bag the embossed leather case housing the photograph of Will, Robbie, Harry, and Jack posing in the Red Room before the Children's Aid Ball in 'fifty-eight.

"Oh," Jack said when she snapped it open. "I remember that night. I'd forgotten all about that."

"This is him," Nell said, pointing.

Molly shook her head. "No. Sorry. Don't recognize him."

"*I* do," Flynn said. Pointing to the photograph, he added, "And that one, too." It took Nell a moment to realize he was pointing to Harry. "He's been in here regular. Molly, you've brung that one upstairs. I know you have."

Molly squinted at the photograph. "Oh, that one. Yeah, I guess I done it with that one."

Nell and Jack blinked at each other. "Harry Hewitt?" she said.

"Yeah, he's never one for the rats or the gong," Flynn said. "Just the cards, the dice, and the chippies. Brings his own bottle, always."

"He's not so bad. Smells like French soap." Molly stood, tucking both hands into her plunging bodice to plump her bosom. "I've got to go now, before my customer gets tired of waitin'."

Cook gazed at the stairway that squeaked with Molly's retreating footsteps. "She knows where Pearl is," he said.

"What makes you think that?" asked a nonplused Jack.

The detective sighed in Nell's direction. "You tell him."

Nell wished, not for the first time, that Colin Cook weren't quite such a good detective. "First, there's the fact that Molly didn't seem terribly upset by Pearl's disappearance. Considering they've lived together for seven years and are, by all reports, close friends, I would say it's quite significant. She certainly wants to keep us from looking for Pearl. Why else would she suddenly 'remember' those missing photographs and shoes when I suspected foul play and started insisting that we look for her?

If Pearl left of her own accord, there's a good deal less urgency about the matter."

"Not as far as I'm concerned," Cook said. "She's still my only witness."

"Your only witness who can point the finger at my client," Jack clarified.

"That's right," Flynn said. "I keep tryin' to tell you it was Noonan done the deed. Tulley wouldn't pay up, so Noonan made an example of him. You want witnesses as to what Noonan's capable of? Put the son of a bitch— sorry, miss—put the bastard behind bars, where he can't get at them he's done dirty to, and you'll have more witnesses than you know what to do with."

"He's got a point," Jack said.

Cook shook his head. "My gut tells me it's Toussaint."

Flynn said, "Your gut's gonna get an innocent man hung and let that no-account Roy Noonan off scot-free to keep on doin' like he's been doin'. Nice work, Detective." He spat on his own parlor floor and stomped off, muttering under his breath.

Detective Cook watched him leave, then turned to regard Nell and Jack with an expression of weary forbearance. "Tomorrow I'll send someone across the river to Charlestown to check out the sisters, though I don't expect that particular branch to yield any fruit, seeing as how Molly offered it up so easy. In the meantime, I'll be posting some men near Molly and Pearl's flat to keep an eye on Molly, shadow her if she heads anywhere but here."

It was exactly what Nell would have done—although she also would have followed up, and intended to follow up, on Noonan.

"Not that we won't convict William Hewitt regardless," Cook added, buttoning his tweed overcoat. "No reasonable jury could look at the facts and doubt his guilt."

"You choose to believe that," Nell said, "because you hate what he represents—that Brahmin sense of entitlement—and because it helps to alleviate your guilt over taking August Hewitt's money to assume—"

Cook's gaze flicked toward Jack, then back to Nell.

"He knows everything," she said, adding the fabricated reassurance, "Who do you think hired him? It helps to alleviate your guilt to assume that William Hewitt killed Ernest Tulley. You must have doubts—you're a smart man—but you hate to think you might be slipping the noose around the neck of an innocent man. Therefore he must have done it. Does any of this strike a chord of recognition in you, Detective?"

Jack was staring at her, looking stunned and, if she wasn't mistaken, a little impressed. Detective Cook shoved his bowler onto his head and executed a stiff little bow in her direction. "Miss Sweeney." Turning to Jack, he said, "Mr. Thorpe. A pleasure to make your acquaintance. If I may be of further service, you know where to find me."

With that, he was gone.

Jack wagged a finger at Nell, his eyes sparking in a way she suspected they rarely did anymore. "Why, you sharp-tongued little thing. I had no idea. Well . . . perhaps some."

"Come," she said with a chuckle as she motioned him toward the kitchen. "I think I hear someone. I'll bet that's Kathleen."

It *was* Kathleen, in her ever-present head rag and apron, peeling her way through a mountain of potatoes at the kitchen table. She glanced up when Nell greeted her, the little knife in her big hand stilling in the act of shearing off a tendril of skin, then resumed her work. The abrasion on her cheek was much improved, making her look a good deal prettier than she had last week, despite her broad face and strapping bones.

"Kathleen, this is Mr. Jack Thorpe, an attorney," Nell said. "Mr. Thorpe, Miss Kathleen Flynn."

"Miss Flynn." Jack bowed; Kathleen kept peeling.

"Mr. Thorpe represents William Toussaint, the man who was arrested for Ernest Tulley's murder. I wonder if we might ask you some questions."

The girl's shoulders twitched in what appeared to be assent of a sort. Nell and Jack seated themselves at the table.

Jack said, "Would you mind telling us what happened in your room the evening of Saturday, February eighth, between Mr. Toussaint and Mr. Tulley? We understand there was some sort of scuffle."

"Pearl told us about it," Nell said when Kathleen just kept peeling, little furrows corrugating her broad brow. "She said the two men seemed to be fighting over you."

The girl looked up sharply, seemed on the verge of saying something, then closed her mouth and looked down, color mounting in her milk-white, lightly freckled cheeks; even without seeing her hair, Nell knew she was a redhead.

"You can see how that would look pretty damning for my client," Jack said. "It would appear to give him a motive for killing Mr. Tulley. Jealousy and all that."

Kathleen's head shook—or rather, quivered—as she stared at the half-peeled potato in her hand. She opened her mouth a couple of times, only to close it. Finally she said, in her girlishly high-pitched brogue, "They wasn't fightin' over me. I mean, they was fightin', but it wasn't like that."

"What was it like, Kathleen?" Nell asked gently. "An innocent man may go to the gallows if we can't set the record straight."

"He don't deserve to hang. He didn't do it, I know he didn't. He ain't that kind of man."

Jack said, "We don't think so, either. What happened, Miss Flynn?"

Kathleen sat back in her chair, one hand fisted around

the potato, the other absently twirling the knife. Without
looking up, her voice low and strained, she said, "That
Tulley, he never could leave me be. I don't know why.
There's women round here who would of given him what
he wanted for the change in his pocket, but he used to
pester me somethin' fierce, didn't like to take no for an
answer." She licked her lips nervously.

"Did you tell your father?" Jack asked.

Kathleen gave a dismissive little grunt. "He said I must
be leadin' Tulley on, said I was no better than them
whores, but that ain't true."

"Of course it's not," Nell said. "Did Tulley pester you
that night?"

"Worse," she said softly. "He followed me up to my
room and tried to . . ." She glanced up at Jack, her blush
coalescing into ruddy splotches.

"Go ahead, Kathleen," Nell urged. "He's got to hear it
if he's going to defend Mr. Toussaint."

Frowning at the potato, her voice almost inaudible, she
said, "I was settin' on the bed, mendin' my hose. He come
in and . . . at first I thought it was that Roy Noonan, 'cause
they got a similar look, and Noonan's a rough customer,
too, but then I seen it was Tulley. He gets on top of me
and starts . . ." The knife jittered in her hand. "He grabbed
at me and tried to . . . lift my skirt. I hollered at him to
get off me. I tried to hit him, so he punched me in the
face." Setting the potato down, she touched the partially
healed scrape on her left cheek. "I seen stars for a minute,
and when I went to get up, come to find out he's tyin'
my hands to the headboard. I tried to scream, but he'd
stuffed a stocking in my mouth. He's got my skirt up, and
he starts undoin' his britches."

Nell reached across the table to squeeze her hand.

"I thought my goose was cooked for sure," Kathleen
said, "but then *he* come in, and—"

"He?" Jack said. "William Toussaint?"

"Yeah, him. It's like Tulley just . . . lifted up off me and flew across the room. He hit the wall pretty hard. The one that done it—Toussaint—he pulls down my skirt and unties my hands, but then Tulley comes to and they start throwin' each other around. That Toussaint, he landed some good punches, but Tulley, he just kept comin'."

"Did they exchange any words?" Nell asked.

Kathleen looked uneasily at Nell, then at Jack; she picked up her potato and continued peelin'. "I don't rightly remember."

"It's all right," Jack assured her. "I'm Mr. Toussaint's lawyer. Nothing you tell me will do him any harm. Did he say anything to Tulley?"

She stopped peeling. "He said somethin' like . . . You're gonna pay for what you done.' "

Nell and Jack exchanged a sober look.

"And he called him a bunch of names—I did, too, 'cause I had that stocking out of my mouth by then—but mostly they just fought. Tulley was takin' the worst of it, so he slams a chair over Toussaint's back and heads down them outside stairs, but that Toussaint, he was right behind him. I'm not too sure what happened then, 'cept I know the window in the pink room got broke, and Tulley got away."

"What about after that?" Nell asked. "Did you tell any-one what Tulley had tried to do?"

She nodded. "I sent Pearl down to the rat pit to get Frank, and I told him—"

"Frank?" Jack said.

"Frank Castelli. It's Franco, but I call him Frank. Him and me . . ." The girl's blush deepened.

"Did you tell your father?" Nell asked.

"Nah, he wouldn't care. He'd just say I brung it on myself."

"What was Mr. Castelli's reaction?" Jack asked.

"Oh, he was fit to be—"

"What do you *think* my reaction was?"

They turned to find Frank Castelli scowling in the doorway. His handsome, swarthy face was badly bruised, and there was a good-sized lump on his forehead.

"Are they bothering you, Katie?" he asked as he came to sit next to her, one hand curling protectively around her shoulders.

She shook her head. "This fella," she said, nodding toward Jack, "he's the lawyer for the one they arrested."

"Did Noonan do that?" Jack asked, indicating Castelli's face.

Castelli shrugged. "Ain't no big deal."

"Were you late in paying money back to him?"

"You kiddin'? I wouldn't borrow money from that snake."

Nell said, "You don't happen to know if Tulley did?"

"Wouldn't think so. He was a snake, too, but he wasn't stupid. You got to be pretty low on lamp oil to take money from Roy Noonan. Reason he went after me," he told Nell, "is 'cause I spoke up when you and that copper was here the other night. He thinks he owns the lot of us, but he don't."

Nell opened the leather photograph case and handed it across the table to Castelli. "Do you recognize any of these men?"

"Well, this one's him." The young man nodded toward Jack as he pointed to his image in the photograph. "Only younger."

"What about the man standing next to me?" Jack asked.

Kathleen, looking over her sweetheart's shoulder, said, "That's Toussaint."

Castelli nodded. "I saw him when they arrested him."

"Did you notice him before that?" Nell asked.

He shook his head. "Nah. I was down in the pit most of the night."

Nell felt a rush of disappointment; so far, the only witness to William Hewitt's narcotic ennui was Seamus Flynn, who'd sold him the opium he'd spent the night smoking. Given that, and Flynn's general dull-wittedness, it wouldn't take a brilliant prosecutor to turn his testimony against Will.

Kathleen said, "This other fella, in the fancy vest, settin' on the arm of the chair, he's been in here."

"Yeah, I seen once or twice," Castelli said.

Jack looked at Nell. Nell said, "It shouldn't surprise us. Harry spends his nights prowling the gaming hells and watering holes. He was bound to find this place."

"So what *was* your reaction," Jack asked Castelli, "when Miss Flynn told you what Ernest Tulley had done?"

"How does any man react to somethin' like that?"

Jack said, "I can tell you how *I* would have felt. I would have wanted to beat Tulley to a bloody pulp—or worse."

"Frank didn't kill him," Kathleen said quickly.

"I didn't say he did," Jack replied mildly. "I just said he might have wanted to."

"Of course I wanted to," Castelli said, "but he'd run off already, and there's no findin' anybody over by the wharves unless they want to be found."

"So what *did* you do?" Nell asked him.

"Wasn't much *to* do, not then, anyway. Figured I'd deal with him when he came back. Katie and me, we kind of talked for a while, and then she sent me back down to the pit before her father found us together."

"I wanted to be alone," she said. "I went back up to my room, but this time I locked the door."

Nell said, "I don't suppose you two arranged to meet in the stable later that night."

Castelli looked at Kathleen, who shook her head, as if to say, "I didn't tell them."

"Your father knows all about it," Nell said. "He's the one who told me. What time did you agree to meet?"

Castelli grimaced. "It don't have nothin' to do with—"

"We're trying to save a man from the noose," Jack said, a hint of impatience creeping into his voice. "A man we believe to be innocent. In order to do that, we need to reconstruct, in as much detail as possible, everything that happened that night."

"It's all right, Frank." Kathleen took her sweetheart's hand. "We was supposed to meet at midnight," she told them.

"So, at midnight," Nell said to Kathleen, choosing her words carefully, "or a little before, you stepped out through the back door and into the alley, only to find that Ernest Tulley had come back."

Kathleen hesitated a moment before saying, "What I seen was him laying there with blood pourin' outa him. I never seen him alive after he left my room earlier, if that's what you're gettin' at."

"And William Toussaint was there, too?" Nell asked.

"Yeah, he was down on the ground, crouching over Tulley. But I only seen him from the back. I never saw what he was doing."

"That's when you screamed?"

Kathleen nodded. "Everyone come runnin'."

Nell turned to Castelli. "Including you, presumably."

"Sure. The rest of 'em scattered, 'cause ain't nobody want to be anywheres near a dead body when the coppers show up, but I stuck around for Katie."

"Where were you when you heard her scream?" Jack asked. "The cellar?"

Castelli shook his head. "The stable. We was gonna meet there, remember?"

"So you'd left the cellar a few minutes earlier, then."

"I know what you're gettin' at," Castelli said. "You

think I could of come upstairs, killed Tulley, then headed over to the stable. Only I didn't."

"When you first saw Tulley's body," Nell asked Kathleen, "did you have any thought as to who might have killed him?"

Kathleen shot a telltale glance at Castelli before lowering her gaze and muttering, "Nope."

"Whoever did it woulda ended up covered with blood," Castelli pointed out. "And I didn't have a spot on me. Neither did Katie."

"What makes you think we're considering her?" Nell asked.

"Look, I ain't stupid," Castelli said. "I know what you're fishin' for, but you ain't gonna find it. I'm not saying I'm sorry Ernest Tulley got what was coming to him, but Katie and me, we didn't have nothin' to do with it."

"And you don't think William Toussaint did, either," Jack said.

Kathleen shook her head resolutely. "He couldn't of."

"Because he saved you from Tulley?" Nell asked. "I realize you're grateful to him, but if you know something you're not telling us—something that may implicate him in Tulley's murder—we'd rather hear it from you than from the prosecutor."

Castelli and Kathleen exchanged a look, but kept their mouths shut.

"Why do you suppose Toussaint was crouching over Tulley that way?" Jack asked. "What was he doing, if not finishing him off?"

Kathleen shrugged. "Trying to help him, maybe? He would of seen what happened from the parlor windows, and heard it, too. My da keeps them cracked open for air, and the curtains tied back."

"*Would* he want to help him, do you think?" Nell asked.

"After the way they'd fought earlier?" Even as she broached the question, she knew the answer. Physicians worked at saving lives. It was what they were trained to do, what they'd taken oaths to do, what they were driven to do, regardless of the circumstances. William Hewitt's protestations notwithstanding, and despite his dependence on opium, no former battle surgeon was likely to stand by and watch a man bleed to death.

"She's just guessing," Castelli said. "She don't know nothin'. Neither do I, and I'm getting pretty fed up with some of these questions."

"Mr. Castelli," Nell said, "why did you lie the other evening when I came here with Detective Cook and he asked if Tulley and Toussaint had exchanged words the night of the murder?"

"I don't know what you're—"

"You said they'd never spoken. But you knew that wasn't true. You knew they'd fought. And, Kathleen, you didn't tell the police about Tulley assaulting you, and Toussaint coming to your rescue and pursuing him down the back stairs."

Castelli and Kathleen glanced at each other.

"We know you're trying to protect him," Jack said gently. "We are, too. All we're saying is, it's important that you don't hold anything back."

Castelli said, "You should be talkin' to Noonan, not us. Try squeezin' the truth out of *him*."

"We intend to," Jack assured him.

"HELL no, I didn't lend Ernest Tulley any money!" Roy Noonan bellowed when they cornered him alone in one of the dormitory rooms upstairs. "I wouldn't have handed over a Bungtown copper to that stinkin' goober grabber."

The big, bearded sailor was sitting at the foot of his

cot cleaning his revolver. A navy blue Union Army haversack on the floor next to him had R. NOONAN, 14TH N.J. INF. stenciled in black letters across the flap.

"We've been informed otherwise," Jack said.

"By who?"

Not wanting to make Seamus Flynn a target of Noonan's famously vengeful wrath, Nell said, "That's not important. What's important is if it's true, and if it's also true that Mr. Tulley refused to pay you back."

" 'Cause that may have led me to kill him?" Noonan snorted. "Hate to ruin your little theory, sweet pea, but dead men are even worse at payin' off their debts than live ones."

Tossing aside his cleaning rag, he rummaged around in the haversack and produced a small book bound in oxblood leather, which he handed to Nell. "See if you can find Ernest Tulley's name in there. If you can, then you lead me off to lockup right now, and I'll go along like a lamb. Otherwise," he said, raising the gun and squinting through the barrel with one flat black eye, "I'd appreciate it if you folks would mind your own business, and I'll mind mine, and we'll all get along just fine."

The book was a ledger neatly inked—in surprisingly good penmanship—with the names of every one of Roy Noonan's debtors, the amounts owed, interest charged, and dates of payment. Ernest Tulley's name was nowhere to be seen.

"JAYSUS, it was just a rumor, is all," Flynn said when they interrupted his rat catching in the stable—clearly a favorite pastime of his—to ask why he'd fed them that tale about Tulley refusing to pay Noonan the money he owed him. "It ain't as if I swore to it on a Bible."

"You made it sound like the God's truth," Nell said.

Flynn grinned as he scratched his great, soft belly with

his curling tongs. "Us silver-tongued micks, we've got a gift for that. Don't we now . . . Miss *Chapel?*"

They always knew. . . . Ignoring the jibe, Nell said, "I don't think it was a rumor at all. I think you made it up, about Tulley owing Noonan money."

"And why would I have done a thing like that?"

"No mystery there," she said. "He's been a thorn in your side for a long time. You told us so yourself. You couldn't keep him from staying at your boardinghouse, or preying on your other customers, or threatening you with his knife, but you could get him convicted of murder and let the commonwealth take him off your hands."

"Well, now, that's right clever. Wish I'd of thought of it."

A slight rustle from the corner of the stall drew Flynn's attention. He kicked the straw; a rat darted out, only to be snatched up in a blur by the Irishman's tongs. "Oh, you poor, scrawny little thing. My Flossie'll make short work of *you.*"

Jack stared in wordless fascination as Flynn dropped his latest catch into the squirming sack and cinched it tight.

Nell said, "I believe you did think of it, Mr. Flynn. I believe you were trying to get an innocent man hanged for murder."

"Innocent?" Flynn barked. "Roy Noonan's about as innocent as Old Scratch himself. He may not have murdered Ernest Tulley, but I know in my gut he's done in others. Problem is, he's slick as goose shit—never gets pinched."

"Have a care, old man," Jack said. "There *is* a lady present."

"How could I forget, the way she rides me? Way I see it, if there was any justice in the world, Roy Noonan would of died jerkin' at the end of a rope years ago."

"Did you ever consider taking justice into your own

hands?" Nell asked. "A summary execution, as it were?"

Flynn knelt to tie off the sack. "Killing's a sin. Bible says so."

"It also says 'an eye for an eye,' " Nell reminded him.

"Even if I was tempted, and I ain't sayin' I was, Roy Noonan's still alive, ain't he? It was Ernest Tulley took that knife in the throat. Not that I'm weepin' into my pillow. For my money, he was just another good-for-nothin' water rat like the rest of 'em. He won't be missed."

"But William Toussaint may hang for his murder," Jack said, "even though he didn't do it."

"Mistakes happen," Flynn grunted as he stood, joints popping. "But there's a reason for everything. I firmly believe that."

Livid color mottled Jack's neck. "You're saying there could be some *justice* in an innocent man being executed for murder?"

"Maybe he ain't so innocent," Flynn suggested. "Just like Noonan ain't so innocent. This Toussaint—he may not of killed Ernest Tulley, but maybe he done somethin' else, somethin' just as bad. He *is* a pipe fiend. The good Lord has His ways—that's all I'm sayin'."

"You've got a lot of damn—" Jack broke off, reddening. "Excuse me, Miss Sweeney. You've got some nerve, Flynn, using the Lord to rationalize your cavalier disregard for the life of an innocent man. You may think it's all well and good if one man dies for the sins of another, but I hardly think God sees it that way. You may not comprehend His plan—I daresay a worm like you has never even tried to—but don't you dare drag His name—"

"A worm, am I?" Flynn dropped the bag of rats, stretched his fingers, and was in the process of curling them into fists when he paused, his gaze fixed on Jack. His wrath seemed to evaporate, supplanted by a slow, keen-eyed smile. "What the hell. You want to know what *really* happened that night?"

Jack, who had no doubt been anticipating a fistfight—if not a savage drubbing—took a moment to respond. "It's what we've wanted all along."

Flynn shook his head, cracked his knuckles. "It's what you *thought* you wanted. You may change your mind when you hear what I have to say."

Nell said, "Out with it, please, Mr. Flynn."

"I came upstairs around midnight to check on them gowsters, like I said, but I looked out the window *before* Kathleen screamed—before she even got there. I saw the whole thing."

"You saw Ernest Tulley murdered?" Nell asked.

"Yeah, and I saw who done it." He grinned at Jack. "Sorry to break it to you, but it was your client."

"Liar!" Jack spat out, taking a menacing step toward the Irishman.

"Jack," Nell murmured with a small shake of her head.

"He's lying! You son of a bitch, *tell the truth!*" Blood rushed to Jack's face; a distended vein bisected his forehead.

Flynn said, "It was William Toussaint I saw cutting Ernest Tulley's throat, and I'll swear to it in a court of law, so put *that* in your pipe and smoke it."

"That's a pretty vicious lie," Nell said, "just to get back at someone for calling you a worm."

"Ain't no lie. I seen what I seen."

"If that's true," she began as Jack seethed and muttered, "why didn't you tell us before?"

"It was like you said. I figured if Noonan took the pinch, he'd be the one to get hanged and I'd be left in peace—me and everybody that walks into this place. That's why I made up that tale about Tulley not payin' Noonan what he owed him, so's Noonan would have a reason for doin' murder. The cops, they're big on reasons, but me, I don't think your ne'er-do-well types always needs 'em, or at least not real good ones. I seen too much in my time." He spat into the straw.

"So you just stood there and watched through the window while a man's throat was hacked open?" Nell asked.

"What was I supposed to do, step in front of a blade for the likes of Ernest Tulley?"

"Did your daughter and Frank Castelli see the murder take place?"

"Naw, it was over by the time she came out the back door and screamed. Then all of 'em come runnin', including the dago."

Nell said, "You seem awfully sure of who and what you saw, considering there was almost no moon that night, and it's an unlit alley. And that window is filthy. Toussaint could have been any man in a dark coat. He could have been the other man from the back parlor, the one who was drinking whiskey while Toussaint was smoking opium. Even Tulley would have been hard to recognize. He could have . . ." It struck her then. "He could have been Roy Noonan. Didn't they look alike, Tulley and Noonan?"

Flynn scratched the back of his neck with the curling tongs. "Not to my way of thinking."

"They did," she said. "Even dead, Tulley resembles him. Did you think the man being attacked was Noonan? Was that why you didn't try to intervene?"

"I didn't try to intervene 'cause Tulley wasn't worth it. Not that I'd have lifted a finger for Noonan either, God knows, but him and Tulley, they was easy to tell apart."

"Even in that alley at night?" Nell asked. "If I were to encounter one of those men under those circumstances, I'm not sure I'd know which one I was seeing."

Somewhat testily he said, "Yeah, well, I got good eyes. Always have."

"Good enough to see in the dark?"

"I'm like a cat. Speakin' of which . . ." Flynn bent to heft the thrumming sack over his shoulder. "If there's one thing cats know, it's rats. Can't keep these little buggers in the sack for too long, or they'll take to tearin' each other apart before Flossie gets a go at 'em. I've even known 'em to gobble each other up, like them African what-do-you-call-'em . . . cannibals."

Jack eyed the sack uneasily as Flynn headed out of the barn.

Flynn turned to wink at him as he walked away. "Way I figure, it's all part of the good Lord's plan."

Chapter 13

IT was almost four o'clock the following afternoon before Nell could take a respite from her duties to pay a visit to William Hewitt, Gracie having been difficult about going down for her daily nap and Nurse Parrish having yet to awaken from hers. Nell relished the walk from Colonnade Row to Commonwealth Avenue, which took her past the Common and adjacent Public Gardens, transformed by last night's freezing rain into a glittering fairyland of ice.

Carefully mounting the slippery front steps of Jack Thorpe's townhouse, Nell knocked loudly—in case Will was upstairs in his guest room—and waited. The lace curtains on the glass-paned double doors were tied back, affording her a clear view into Jack's foyer and down the hallway that led to the library and dining room. Nothing hung from the hooks on the ornately carved, mirrored hallstand; the crystal calling card tray was empty and gleaming, as was the porcelain urn meant to hold umbrellas.

Nell listened for footsteps, but didn't hear any. She chafed her arms through her overcoat, chilled now that she wasn't moving—or perhaps it wasn't the cold making her shiver so much as the prospect of demanding, at long last, some straight answers from Will about the night of Ernest Tulley's murder.

Kathleen's account of Will's altercation with Tulley suggested that it wasn't jealousy, after all, that had provoked his fury toward the merchant sailor, but outrage over an attempted rape. It had been fairly early in the evening—too early for him to have lapsed into an opiated stupor—and he did appear to have a history of protectiveness toward women; there was that girl in Shanghai, and the beating he'd dealt to Mathilde's assailant. But would his rage have incited him to murder four hours later, especially after smoking opium all night?

Nell knocked again, muttering, "Come on, you must be home. You probably just woke up."

What had begun as a task undertaken grudgingly on Viola's behalf—to ferret out the truth of Ernest Tulley's murder and save Will from the noose—was turning into a rather more heartfelt mission. Notwithstanding Seamus Flynn's dubious eyewitness account, the more Nell learned of Dr. William Hewitt, the more she doubted his capacity for murder—especially such a brutal murder. Yes, he was a flawed man, but there was a spark of civility—perhaps even honor—that flickered stubbornly within the dissipated creature he'd allowed himself to become.

It was that, his willingness to trade the silver spoon he'd been born with for an opium pipe and a deck of cards, which baffled and disturbed Nell most. He'd chosen to embrace the low life, whereas she had striven for years to put as much distance as possible between herself and the morass of poverty and crime that had once held her captive. His path in life was the direct opposite of hers, a fact that distressed her more than it should.

Equally distressing was the extent to which she found herself tapping into old instincts and street lore she'd long assumed—indeed, prayed—she would never need again. How easy, and ingenuous, it had been to think of the old Nell as dead and buried. Like a grimy street blanketed by snow, her past could be cloaked in a pristine mantle of respectability, but it would forever be there, lurking just beneath the surface.

And sooner or later the snow always melted.

Stripping off one cashmere-lined kid glove, she rapped on the leaded glass door until her knuckles were red. Finally accepting that he either wasn't home or was choosing to ignore her, she tugged the glove back on and headed back the way she'd come.

She'd rounded the corner of Commonwealth and was halfway down Arlington—passing beneath the shop canopies to avoid a trio of fur-swathed matrons laden with hatboxes and shopping parcels—when she stopped in her tracks, turned, and retraced her steps about twenty feet. A flash of someone's black coat in a store window had caught her eye. It shouldn't have—nine out of ten Bostonians, male and female, dressed in black for the street—but there was a certain quality to the movement, a presence to the anonymous figure . . .

Yes, indeed. It was William Hewitt, in overcoat and low top hat. He stood at a glass-fronted counter with a huge scale on it, opening his wallet, as the proprietor wrapped up something small in brown paper. The gold-and-green sign on the shop door, shaped like a mortar and pestle, read:

JOSEPH MAYNARD & CO.
—BOSTON—

Offering all pure
MEDICINES, ESSENTIAL OILS, EXTRACTS, POWDERS,

French and English DRUGS *and* CHEMICALS *at* WHOLESALE
*to Druggists and Physicians, at the lowest prices
for goods of fine quality.*

*Open Monday through Friday, 8:00 a.m. until 8:00 p.m.
Saturday, 9:00 a.m. until 5:00 p.m.*

In the window to the left of the door was a placard that read:

Proprietors of
**COCOAINE, ORIENTAL TOOTH WASH,
SYRUP OF POPPIES, LAUDANUM, PAREGORIC,
DOVER'S POWDER,
WISTAR'S BALSAM OF WILD CHERRY**
for the treatment of coughs, colds, consumption,
and lung diseases,
PERUVIAN SYRUP, AN IRON TONIC
for the treatment of dyspepsia, debility, dropsy, and humors,
DR. WALKER'S CALIFORNIA VINEGAR BITTERS,
the great blood purifier.

Nell tapped on the window. Will glanced toward her, looked pleasantly surprised, and motioned for her to come in. The man behind the counter—white-haired and goateed, with a starched apron tied over his frock coat—smiled and nodded as she entered. Will removed his hat as he bowed, tucking it under his arm. The shop, with its floor-to-ceiling shelves filled with bottles and jars, reminded Nell of an Occidental version of Deng Bao's.

"Thank you, Dr. Toussaint," said the apothecary as he handed Will the paper-wrapped parcel. "I hope you'll rely on us for all your medical supplies."

Nell slid her gaze toward Will, smiling in that private way of his as he tucked the parcel into his pocket. "I expect I will. By the way, Mr. Maynard, this is my assistant, Miss Sweeney."

Nell mumbled something innocuous as the pleasant old gentleman greeted her. She waited until they were outside on the sidewalk to say, "So I'm your assistant now, *Doctor*?"

Will shrugged as he replaced his hat. "The professional discount is really quite remarkable, and they've started an account for me. It's not too difficult to convince people you're a physician if you know the right things to say."

Nell didn't bother pointing out that he actually *was* a physician, like it or not.

"I must say it was a pleasant surprise running into you today," he said. "Dare I hope you've wandered into the Back Bay in search of me?"

So courtly was the greeting—surprisingly so, given Nell's past interactions with Will Hewitt—that she was momentarily at a loss for words. It wasn't only his manner that was unexpectedly civilized, but his appearance. The cut near his eye had almost completely healed, and the bruises had faded to mere shadows on his smooth-shaven jaw. His hair was well groomed, his shoes like polished onyx, his attire neat and smart.

"You see?" He leaned close, as if sharing a confidence. "You're not the only one who can look disconcertingly respectable."

She took a step away, discomfited as much by his closeness as by the illusion that they were just ordinary acquaintances having a nice little chat on the sidewalk. There was nothing ordinary about William Hewitt, regardless of how conventionally he chose to dress or act. He might not have killed Ernest Tulley but that didn't mean he wasn't still dangerous.

"I *was* looking for you," she said. "There are some things we need to discuss. You should know that—"

"Would you like to take a walk in the Gardens?" he asked.

She hesitated, nonplused by the invitation.

"I'd wanted to do it before the ice melts." Taking her by the elbow, he started guiding her across Arlington, toward the entrance to the Boston Public Gardens. "You can interrogate me while we walk."

"THEY look like spun glass," Will said of the leafless, ice-glazed trees bordering the path along which they strolled, his limp keeping them to a leisurely pace. "The lower the sun sinks in the sky, the prettier they look."

There was, indeed, a crystalline majesty to the Gardens today, and a blessed sense of exile from the buzzing city that surrounded them; they'd passed only two other pedestrians since entering the park. Nell was glad she'd let Will talk her into coming here. Indeed, she was enjoying herself so much that she'd almost forgotten her purpose in seeking him out. "I don't know whether Jack Thorpe told you this, Dr. Hewitt, but Pearl Stauber has disappeared."

"I haven't actually seen much of Jack. We keep different hours. Who's Pearl St—" Recognition lit his eyes. "Ah. Yes," he said, a little sadly. "Pearl."

So. He *had* remembered her—not just from Flynn's, Nell realized, but from their encounter twelve years ago.

Nell said, "She left her flat, apparently of her own free will, late Sunday night or early Monday morning, and hasn't been seen since. Detective Cook is determined to find her, and it will go badly for you if he does. She's the one who heard you threaten to make Ernest Tulley 'pay with his life.' Her testimony could send you to the gallows."

"Look at the icicles on the fountain," he said, pointing. "They reach almost to the ground, and some of them have merged together. They put diamonds to shame, don't they?"

"Why did you tell me you were fighting over Kathleen Flynn," she asked, "when in reality, you were trying to keep her from being raped by Ernest Tulley?"

"You *assumed* I was fighting over Kathleen Flynn. Bad habit of yours, those assumptions."

"You confirmed them. 'Clashing horns over a woman,' you said. 'Oldest story in the book.' "

"Was I smoking gong at the time?"

"Yes, but—"

"Well, then."

"You must think I'm a very great fool, indeed, if you expect me to believe that it was the opium that made you say that."

"You have many and various facets to you, Miss Sweeney," he said with a smile, "but foolishness is not one of them."

"Seamus Flynn says he saw you murder Ernest Tulley."

"Really? The evidence certainly seems to be piling up."

"You deliberately misled me," she said testily. "You've been toying with me all along, withholding the truth and letting me stumble round in the dark—Jack, too—when all we're trying to do is keep you from being hanged."

"I told you once before, Miss Sweeney—some people are meant to hang."

She stopped walking. "Not you."

He turned to face her. Gravely he said, "Don't be so sure."

"Tell me the truth, for once!" she demanded. "Did you kill Ernest Tulley because of what he did to Kathleen?"

He closed the space between them, seizing both ends of her loose scarf to halt her when she tried to back up. Tugging her none too gently toward him, he bent his head until his face filled her field of vision, his gaze searing, his vaporous breath mingling with hers. "I am growing weary, indeed," he said quietly, "of your refusal to tuck in your scarf. One would think a grown woman would have more sense."

He crossed her scarf as if preparing to tuck it in himself. She snatched it away from him, stumbling back. "I am sick to death of playing these games with you, of begging for a shred of cooperation, only to have you laugh in my face! There are people who want to execute you for what they think you've done, Dr. Hewitt. You could *die*. If you do nothing to help yourself, you probably will."

"And you think I don't realize that."

"You don't seem to, not really."

He gazed upward, into a tangled network of ice-dipped branches ignited from within, spectacularly so, by the setting sun. "If only I didn't." Reaching into his coat pocket, he withdrew the little paper-wrapped bundle he'd purchased at the apothecary. "Do you mind if we sit?" he asked, nodding toward a nearby iron bench. "My leg. It's . . ."

"Of course." She sat next to him, not too close, and watched him unwrap the brown paper, revealing a little cobalt blue bottle. "What's that?"

"Black Drop." He held the bottle so she could read the label, engraved JOSEPH MAYNARD & CO. across the top. Handwritten beneath that in blue ink was:

Vinegar of Opium
1.5% Morphine
Dosage: 5–10 drops
2 oz.

Uncorking the bottle, he said, "It's the strongest opiated tonic I know of. I've run out of gong, you see, and it'll be late tonight before I can get back to Deng Bao's for more." Tilting the bottle to his mouth, he shook out a rapid stream of reddish brown elixir—far more than ten drops.

"Should you be taking so much?" she asked.

He chuckled drunkenly, his head lolling back as he recorked the bottle. "I shouldn't be taking it at all."

"You might consider—"

"Shh." Shifting sideways on the bench, he pressed his gloved fingertips to her mouth, his half-closed eyes as glassy as if they, too, were sheathed in ice. "Five minutes of peace, Miss Sweeney. That's all I ask."

Exactly five minutes later, she said, "You're a slave to that stuff. A man like you shouldn't be a slave to anything."

He opened his eyes, muttering "Jesus" under his breath when he saw her snapping her pendant watch shut. "I'd forgotten what a damnable shrew you turn into when I indulge this particular appetite. Don't you worry about seeming unsophisticated?"

"Is Mathilde Cloutier unsophisticated? She cast you out of her home because of opium."

"It wasn't the opium," he said through a yawn. "She always finds some excuse to stage one of her little melodramas when her current protector is due to return."

"You know about Edmund?"

"Is that his name?" Will tucked the bottle back in his pocket. "She isn't normally so forthcoming with strangers. You seem to have a way of drawing people out."

"It doesn't bother you . . . sharing a woman with another man?"

"How else could she afford to live in the Pelham?" Will laughed drowsily as he opened a Bull Durham tin. "Do you mind?" he asked, sliding out a cigarette.

"No, of course not, but don't let the police catch you smoking in a public park." A true gentlemen wouldn't ask; he would simply refrain. But it was a nod in the direction of courtesy, and a meaningful one.

He lit the cigarette and took a deep, tranquil draw. "I'm certainly in no position to keep Mattie in the style she deserves, even if I were so inclined—which I'm not. Why take on the care and feeding of such an exotic specimen when I can simply swoop in from time to time, disport myself for a few days or weeks, then fly away free and unencumbered? The arrangement suits her as well, and don't think for a moment that I'm the only diversion she seeks when the cat's away."

They both fell silent for a minute. Nell wasn't always good about holding her tongue, as Dr. Greaves had often pointed out. Yet even she knew better than to question whether William Hewitt was actually capable of "disporting" himself with any woman, given the apparent effect of all that opium on his body. *She's miffed because I can't rouse to her . . .*

He leaned forward, elbows on knees, the cigarette dangling between his fingers. That he'd been ruminating on the same thing she had became clear when he said, hesitantly, "The thing one must understand about this drug . . . Once it has its talons into you, you don't even care about the rest of it."

"The rest of . . . ?"

"One's needs, one's desires . . ." He glanced at her, then away. "All those hungers that demanded appeasing in one's former life fade into insignificance before the poppy. To smoke a bowl of opium is to . . . transport oneself, body and soul. The very ritual of cooking up a dose will make me drunk with anticipation. And when I finally take that smoke into my lungs, and it seeps into my mind and my body and works its magic . . . the flood of pleasure is the closest thing to heaven on earth. Physical passions become secondary." He sat back, exhaling a lungful of smoke. "As for emotional passions, well . . . they are certainly more controllable."

Something about that statement sounded familiar. When she realized why, she couldn't help observing, with a mischievous smile, "Wouldn't your father be pleased that you've finally learned to command your passions."

He stared at her for a moment, then burst out laughing. She laughed, too. It felt good, if strange, to share this moment with him, even if he *was* drunk on opium. She couldn't remember having seen him laugh before—really laugh, like this.

Will shook his head. "So all it took for me to finally live up to his standards was a steady ingestion of narcotics. Wish I'd known that when I was a boy."

Nell sobered, envisioning the photograph of Will at four, with his slick-combed hair, big eyes and guileless smile . . . and that arm curled so protectively over the golden baby boy on his mother's lap . . . the doomed Robbie. Little William had been doomed himself, in a way, not long after that photograph was made. *He begged me not to send him away. . . . He screamed and sobbed all the way up the gangway.*

"I know why you resent your mother as you do," Nell said. "I think you should know that she deeply regrets having sent you to live in England."

"Is that what she told you?" he asked. "She always did have a knack for saying the right thing."

"She was weeping when she told me about it. All she can talk about is how this is really all her fault—what's become of you, this arrest. She's consumed by guilt, views herself as a terrible mother."

"As I've said before, she's nothing if not perceptive."

"Jest if you must, Dr. Hewitt, but she's in pain for you, and she really does want to help you. It's not easy for her. She's displayed a great deal of cleverness—and nerve—in defying your father without his catching on."

"I daresay you've displayed more. I've known Saint August to sack a kitchen maid for popping too many cherries into her mouth while she was making a pie. You're taking quite a chance, doing Lady Viola's legwork for her—and brainwork, I might add. If my father finds out what you've been up to, you'll be right back to wherever you were before my mother took you under her wing—or worse. You do realize that."

"One does what one must," she answered evenly, though she'd lain awake just last night, fretting over that very thing. It was the prospect of losing Gracie, more than anything else, that she truly dreaded. "There's something I've been wondering," she said, eager to change the subject. "Why did you give a false name to the police when they arrested you?"

His shoulders rose as he brought the cigarette to his mouth. "The Hewitts are one of the oldest families in Boston—in the *country*. It would have been on the front page of every newspaper from here to San Francisco if someone of that name were accused of murder. Why invite the press to make an already grotesque situation even more lurid and complicated?"

"You did it to protect your family," she realized with quiet astonishment.

"I did it so as not to put myself at the center of some unseemly spectacle."

She smiled. "You must care about them a little."

"I care about my privacy, but believe what you like." Dropping his cigarette butt, he ground it out beneath the heel of his shoe. "Do you still have that photograph?" he asked, glancing at the slight bulge of her chatelaine bag beneath her coat. "The one you showed me the other day?"

"That picture of Gracie? No, I . . . No. I can bring it next time I see you."

"Don't."

"But you wanted to—"

"I just wanted to know if you had it. I was curious as

to whether you carried it around with you. Struck me as something you might do."

"I keep it on my night table."

He nodded thoughtfully. "You . . . care for her, I take it. I mean, not just as your charge, but . . ."

"I love her," Nell said, "as if she were my own daughter."

He looked at her, seemed about to say something, looked away.

"You should meet her," Nell said.

"Good Lord! And here I've been thinking you're such a sensible woman."

"Why not?"

"You have to ask? Look at me!"

She shrugged. "You look like a perfect gentleman today."

"You've got a strange definition of 'perfect,' " he said, underscoring that observation by helping himself to a second, if smaller, dose of Black Drop.

"Yes, well . . ."

"Let's walk some more, shall we?" Rising, he handed her up from the bench. His gait was, if not flawless, certainly less halting than before. "Present appearances notwithstanding, I happen to be a professional gambler and opium fiend who will almost certainly hang for murder before the year is through. Hardly what any little girl would want in a father. Far better if she never learns of my existence."

"You're much more than those things, Dr. Hewitt. Didn't General Grant once call you the best battle surgeon in the Union Army? Jack Thorpe praised your skill and fearlessness—he told me you saved countless lives."

"I sawed off countless legs," he said, "and if the cut wasn't too close to the hip, they had a better than even chance of making it. Any corner butcher worth his salt could have done as well. Jack wasn't at Andersonville,

Miss Sweeney. He doesn't know how pathetically useless
I became there. I was surrounded by filth and contagion,
with no medications, no tools—except for my folding bistoury, which I'd hidden in the hem of my trousers. Not
that it helped much. Four out of every ten men who
walked into that place were buried there, and I did little
to improve on those statistics."

"Jack told me you allowed yourself to be captured in
order to take care of the wounded men."

"It was Robbie I was mostly concerned with." He lit
another cigarette and blew a plume of smoke into the
frosty sky, stained lavender now that the sun had dipped
below the horizon. "The others weren't so bad off, but
Robbie had taken a Minié ball just above his right elbow, and it had ruptured everything—bone, soft tissue,
arteries . . . I didn't dare move him. I put off the decision
to amputate as long as I could, but I finally did it, while
our regiment was retreating. The other men had to hold
him down, because there was no chloroform, but he hardly made a sound, just gritted his teeth and took it. He held
his screams in for me so I could do what I had to do
without . . ." He shook his head, adding hoarsely, "So I
could get through it."

"My God," Nell whispered. "I didn't know he'd lost
an arm—and under such circumstances. Your mother
didn't tell me."

"I don't suppose she knows. No reason she should."

"I won't mention it," she said.

He nodded stiffly as he drew on his cigarette.

Interesting. "It's a credit to your skills that Robbie survived at a place like Andersonville after something like
that."

"It helped that it was February, and cold, which tends
to keep certain types of infection at bay. I remember, it
was snowing when we got there. I'd never realized it
snowed so far south. The men with no shelter lay curled

up on the ground, thousands of them, their bones showing through their clothes, no blankets . . ."

"Did *you* have shelter?"

"I dug a hole for Robbie and me—not a real hole, because the ground was half-frozen, just a sort of depression in the earth, but it was ours alone. Two raiders tried to take it over, but—"

"Raiders?"

"The Andersonville Raiders. They were a gang of prisoners who'd banded together to steal what they could from the rest of us, and they didn't stop at murder. The two who went after our hole had clubs, but I had my bistoury. I got one of them in the throat when he raised his club over Robbie's head—big blond fellow, looked like a Viking. They left us alone after that."

Got him in the throat? "Did he die? The one you . . . ?"

"I imagine so. That was the last I saw of him, in any event. We rounded up the rest of the raiders in July and put them on trial. The commandant let us hang the ringleaders."

"Ah—when we first met, at the police station, you told me you'd seen six men hanged at once."

"I often wish I hadn't."

"The commandant himself was executed after the war, wasn't he? What was his name? Something German, I think."

"He was Swiss. Henry Wirz. I saw him hanged. He died as hard as those raiders. Took a long time for him to stop struggling."

"Jack Thorpe was part of the legal team that prosecuted him. But he must have told you that."

"Yes." He smiled indulgently as he stamped out his cigarette. "I gather it was an attempt on his part to make up for having let Robbie and me go to Andersonville without him. He always did have a painfully earnest streak." Will dosed himself with a few more drops from the little blue bottle.

Nell said, "Wirz was hanged in November of 'sixty-five. You were in Washington then?"

He nodded as he shoved the cork back in the bottle, his eyes heavy-lidded. "I got there just in time for the victory parade along Pennsylvania Avenue at the end of May. Stuck around for a few months, till I felt like myself again. It had taken me the better part of a year just to make my way back north after I got out of Andersonville."

"That long?"

"Eight or nine months, anyway. Let's see, I escaped August ninth, the day after Robbie was killed, then I spent the next—"

"Killed?" Nell stopped in her tracks. "It wasn't dysentery?"

He stilled, his back to her for a moment, before turning and regarding her gravely, if a little blearily, given all the Black Drop he'd consumed. "No, Miss Sweeney. It wasn't dysentery."

"Then how did . . ." It came to her then. "He was trying to escape, too, wasn't he? You were going to get out together, on August eighth, but he was killed. That's when you were shot."

"Oh, that busy little mind of yours." He stuck his hands in his coat pockets, smiling as if at a precocious child. "And then?"

"I suppose you . . . Oh. You had a bullet in your leg."

"I also had a bistoury."

"Don't tell me you took it out yourself."

"Would have been untidy to leave it in. We surgeons loathe that sort of thing."

"How did you control the bleeding? You had no way to suture the wound."

"Cauterization—also with the bistoury, heated up a fire."

Nell winced, imagining it. "Handy little implement."

"Hence my sentimental attachment to it."

Nell shook her head. "Performing surgery on yourself in those conditions . . . You're lucky to be alive."

"You think I'm alive?" Turning, he continued down the path.

Lifting her skirts to catch up with him, she said, "How did you manage to escape, with a fresh bullet wound? Jack said the stockade was made of solid pine logs, with sentries standing watch."

"You're quite the relentless interrogator, Miss Sweeney."

"I'm just trying to—"

"There was a thunderstorm," he said as he fished the little bottle out of his pocket again.

"You're taking an awful lot of that," she observed as he tossed back a few more drops.

"Helps me to remember without reliving." Stuffing the bottle back in his pocket, he said, in a slightly slurred voice, "It was the worst summer storm I've ever seen, before or since. The sky went utterly black around noon, except for the lightning. You know what a mountain howitzer sounds like?"

"Um . . ."

"The thunder sounded just like that—a sudden, concussive *roar* that rattles your teeth in your head. The problem was, of course, that most of us had no shelter. Runoff had flooded the creek we used for drinking water, and it dammed up against the stockade wall till parts of it started collapsing."

"You mentioned Stockade Creek at the Charles Street Jail, when you were delirious."

He stopped walking. "I talked about Andersonville?"

She paused, wondering why he seemed so anxious. "I suppose. It was all pretty—"

"What did I say?"

"It's hard to recall. It sounded like gibberish at the time. It seemed there was something you wanted to do, or were willing to do. You said, 'I would have done it.' You seemed very upset. Oh, and you said the Stockade Creek was full of typhoid."

He grunted as he continued walking. "That and about a dozen other wretched diseases. The sewage used to back up in there."

Walking alongside him, she said, "I gather you saw an opportunity when the stockade wall started collapsing."

He nodded. "No one else would come with me. Most of them were half-starved and wasted from disease, and nobody thought we could make it back to the North alive—we were in the deep South, don't forget."

"What made you think *you* could?"

"I didn't think I could—I've always been fairly good at calculating odds—but I'd lost Robbie, and I knew my own days were numbered if I stayed there, so I took the gamble. I scratched my name and unit on the back of my belt buckle and exchanged belts with one of the corpses in the mud. There were scores of them, so I picked a fellow I happened to know had no family waiting for news of him. I darkened my skin with charcoal, but I had to swim through the creek to get out of there, so most of it washed off—but with all the chaos, I made it into the woods without being spotted. It was slow going, what with the leg, but by nightfall I was in an orchard a couple of miles away, feasting on peaches. They came back up immediately, of course—I was pretty malnourished myself by then."

"It took you nine months to make it up north?" Nell asked.

"Oh, it was quite the odyssey. In the beginning, I had

two major concerns—keeping my wound clean and stealing anything I could find that contained enough opium to keep me on my feet. Before long, I needed it not just for pain, but to avoid withdrawal. I learned I could imitate a passable Georgia accent—the inflections are actually quite British—and that helped. And I'd always been good at cards, so before long I was able to honestly purchase my laudanum and Black Drop—when it was available. The Confederate Army was so low on opium that they actually had farm wives growing poppies. There were times when I aroused suspicion, and I had a few narrow escapes, but mostly it was a matter of just limping northward. By the time Lee surrendered, I was in Washington."

"Why didn't you let your family know you were alive?"

"At first, I just kept putting it off. I couldn't bear the prospect of all their questions, their pity, their loathing of me because I was alive and Robbie was dead."

"They wouldn't have loathed you for that."

"Why not? I did." Will stopped, withdrew his Bull Durham tin, and flipped it open.

He still does, Nell realized. It may have been physical pain that first drove Will into the arms of Morphia, but it was a different kind of pain that kept him there. His self-imposed exile among the hop fiends and cardsharps was a sort of penance for having crawled out of the Hell that had consumed so many of those "pink-cheeked youths" he'd failed to save—most especially Robbie.

"Eventually it just got too late to go back, and I came to realize it was the last thing in the world I wanted." He lit the cigarette, expelling the smoke in a lingering stream. "God, what a relief it was to be dead."

He flicked the match out, and she realized night had fallen while they were walking. There were a few gas lamps in the park, but none close by. The nearest source of light was the orange-hot tip of Will's cigarette, and all it illuminated was his face as he studied her in the dark.

"You owe me now," he said, his voice so low that she felt it humming all along her skin. "I've allowed you to hammer me with questions, some quite personal, and I believe I've been admirably forthcoming. You, on the other hand, remain a creature of mystery. It's your turn to open up a bit."

Turning, he crossed in two long strides to a bench, and gestured for her to sit.

Not budging from where she stood, Nell said, "I'm afraid I've no mysteries to uncover."

"Nonsense. All I know about you is that you grew up on Cape Cod, and that your father was a day laborer on the docks. And of course, that you were apprenticed to Dr. Greaves for four years. I can only speculate as to what became of your family . . . and how you got that intriguing scar."

She rubbed her arms. "It's cold. We should—"

"It's been cold all along. If you'd minded, we would have left before now. What are you afraid of, Miss Sweeney—that I'll disclose your secrets to my parents? You must know there's no chance of that. And of course anything you tell me will die with me, so . . ." He sat and patted the bench next to him.

She hesitated a moment longer, then sat.

He finished his cigarette in silence, stubbed it out. "What was his name?" he asked quietly.

She turned to find him looking at her. It was too dark to tell for sure, but he seemed to be focusing on the tiny scar near her left eyebrow.

"Duncan," she said. The name came out sounding rusty, as if from lack of use; in fact, she hadn't spoken it in years.

"He was the man you were with before Dr. Greaves?"

So he knew about her and Dr. Greaves, or else it was exploratory surgery. In any event, she said simply, "Yes."

"For how long?"

"Two years. We met when I was sixteen." There was a dizzying sense of liberation, after years of taking such care not to reveal too much, in answering his simple questions with simple, truthful answers.

"Where is he now?"

"Serving a thirty-year sentence at the state prison in Charlestown."

That quieted him for a moment. "For what he did to you?"

"No, for beating and knifing a man during a robbery. He tied him up and . . . mutilated him. He did things he didn't have to do."

Will took out his blue bottle, looked at it for a moment, and put it back unopened. "How did you meet him?"

An interesting alternative, Nell thought, to *What were you doing with him?* "My brother Jamie introduced us. I knew he was a petty thief, like Jamie, but he was incredibly handsome, and he had quite a winning way about him, when he wanted to. And compared to the men I'd known growing up . . ." She steeled herself and forged on. "My father ran off with a barmaid when I was ten. A year later, my mother died of Asiatic cholera, along with two of my brothers and a sister. The rest of us—me, Jamie, and my baby sister Tess—we got sent to the Barnstable County Poor House. I lived there till Duncan took me away."

"Your knight in shining armor."

"It felt that way at the time."

"Where are they now, your brother and sister?"

"I don't know where Jamie is—behind bars somewhere, probably. Tess died of diphtheria in the poor house when she was about Gracie's age. She even looked a little like Gracie, with that dark hair and her impish little—" She was going to say "smile," but her throat closed up.

"I'm sorry," Will said with quiet sincerity.

"I've always felt there should have been some way for me to save her, something I could have done . . ."

"I feel the same way about Robbie. But diphtheria . . . No, Miss Sweeney, I'm quite certain there was nothing you could have done, so you should put your doubts out of your mind and just be grateful for the time you had with her."

She looked at him, but it was too dark to make out his expression. He lit a cigarette, briefly illuminating his face, but he looked away from her as he did so. They were sitting closer than before, she realized as she caught a whiff of Bay Rum mingled with tobacco.

"And how did you meet Dr. Greaves?" he asked.

"After Duncan . . ." There were no words to describe the horror of what he'd done to her. "He . . . I'd been . . . hurt, rather badly."

She heard Will take a breath and let it out, saw his free hand, the one not holding the cigarette, tense on his leg. He turned toward her, and she saw it in his eyes: he knew what she meant by "hurt." There had been that, yes . . . but so much more. It had been a nightmare she had no desire to recreate.

"I found myself in Dr. Greaves's care. He saved my life," she said, omitting the details, because it wouldn't do to tell him everything. "He let me stay in his house in East Falmouth because I had nowhere else to go, and Duncan was still out there somewhere. His cook and housekeeper lived there, too, so it didn't seem too improper. It took months for me to get back on my feet. He was very kind, very undemanding. Eventually he offered me an apprenticeship, and I jumped at it. I'd been living there for almost a year before . . . things changed between us."

She could still feel it . . . Dr. Greaves's tentative, surprising touch on the back of her neck as she sat on the floor in front of his drawing room fireplace that night, bent over her French exercise. *The last thing I'd want to do,* he'd said, *is force my attentions on you, after everything you've* . . . She'd touched her fingers to his lips. He'd closed his eyes, pressed her palm to his mouth.

The first time, it had been because he'd saved her life, and he'd been so kind and needful, and she couldn't turn him away.

The second time, it was because he'd been so tender the first time, so different from what she'd known before.

"I didn't begrudge it," she told Will. "I don't want you to think it was just repayment for what he'd done for me. It was . . . complicated."

"These things always are." Golden light suffused his face as he drew on his cigarette. "I'm surprised he let you go. He might have offered to marry you, if only to keep you there."

"He already had a wife."

"Ah." He sounded surprised, and a little dismayed.

"It's not what you think. She's been a psychiatric patient at Massachusetts General for about twelve years now. He loved her. He still loves her, I'm sure, but . . ." She shrugged sadly.

"Still, one would think he would have tried to hold on to you somehow, offered you money, anything . . ."

Nell bristled.

"Not that you would have taken it. I'm not implying . . . what you think I am. It's just, in his situation, I would have moved heaven and earth to keep you." An odd, unsettled expression shadowed his eyes. He turned away to smoke his cigarette.

Nell said, "He wanted the best for me. It was a kindness to let me go." He'd kissed her on the mouth, that night at Falconwood, which he hardly ever did. *God, I'll miss you, Nell. I'll miss you so much.* They hadn't written. She'd seen him twice in the past three and a half years, just in passing, during her summers with the Hewitts on the Cape. He still had that engaging smile and those warm, sparkling eyes that tended to follow her around a room.

"He sounds like a good man," Will said.

"He is." She took a deep breath and said, "I'm afraid to ask what you think of me now."

He laughed disbelievingly. "Should I think any less of you for your past? Look at mine! Look at my *present*! No, I'm gratified that you told me this, that you felt you could trust me. Rest assured your secrets are safe with me."

Nell looked away from him, shamed by his gratitude, by how touched he was that she would confide in him. She'd told him a great deal, of course, but she didn't dare tell him the worst. What she had revealed would scar her reputation if it got out, but her position with the Hewitts might survive the scandal; Viola had her ways, and hadn't Nell turned over a new leaf? But the rest of it, if Will were to blurt it out to the wrong person in an opiated daze, might very well destroy her.

He put out his cigarette and helped himself to more Black Drop.

"You might think about weaning yourself off opium," she said. "Slowly, so it's not so traumatic."

"It's a bit harder than you think, Miss Sweeney, when one is truly in Morphia's thrall. It's not just the drug one craves, but the smoky room tucked away from the rest of the world, the feel of the *chum tow* under one's head, the aroma of the gong as it bubbles over the flame . . . Not that I'm discounting the grim realities of addiction. When you've been on the hip as long as I have, you need a steady supply of the stuff just to feel normal. Weaning myself off it means feeling fairly dreadful for a fairly long time. Can't say as I see the point, especially given that I've got only a limited amount of freedom left. I do still have to stand trial and face the hangman. Although I suppose I shall have to give up gong rather abruptly when they put me on death row. Now that I know what that's like, I'm looking forward to it even less."

Shivering now—and not from the cold—Nell asked, "Have you considered . . . not standing trial? Just leaving? Going into hiding somewhere?"

"Sacrificing Mummy's bail money so that I can spend the rest of my life scuttling about in the dark, peering over my shoulder? I think not. In any event, pipe fiends have a hard time avoiding detection. The authorities know where we get our gong. And too," he said as he took a thoughtful puff of his cigarette, "there's a certain justice at work here. Some people are meant to die for their sins, don't you think?"

"Some people. Not you."

"What makes me so special?"

A hundred different things, but Nell held her tongue.

He smiled at her in the dark. "Tell me, Miss Sweeney. Will you be my angel of mercy after I'm convicted? Will you smuggle in laudanum or Black Drop when I'm on death row waiting to hang?"

Shaking in earnest now, head to toe, she said, "Yes."

Will's smile faded; he regarded her with a sort of drowsy intensity. Taking her hand in both of his, he chafed it gently, then just held it, lost in thought. She knew he could feel her trembling through the layers of leather and cashmere.

"I've kept you too long." Still holding her hand, he stood and raised her to her feet. She allowed him to escort her by the arm through the lamplit Public Garden and Boston Common to the corner of Tremont and West.

He bid her good night from beneath a shadowy copse near the edge of the Common, directly opposite his parents' home. Nell crossed the street and entered the front door, noticing, as she shut it, that he was still standing there. She hung up her coat, went upstairs to her room, and after a moment's hesitation, cracked open the shutter blinds on one of the windows facing the Common.

The orange pinpoint of a cigarette was barely visible from within the ice-sheathed thicket of trees. It winked out as a lamplit hansom cab came rattling down Tremont. A top-hatted, black-coated figure—Will—stepped into the amber nimbus of a gas lamp and raised a hand, halting it; he got in and the cab continued on its way.

Nell drew the blinds shut.

Chapter 14

"THERE'S someone to see you," announced Peter, the young fair-haired footman, from the doorway of the nursery as Nell and Gracie lunched on veal aspic, stewed carrots, and apple fritters. "Big mick in a bowler and tweed coat. Says his name's Cook—Colin Cook."

Just "Colin Cook"? Nell thought while picking globs of aspic off the dinner napkin tied around Gracie's throat, the child meanwhile aiming another heaping, jiggly spoonful at her mouth. *Not "Detective" Colin Cook?* She wouldn't have expected such discretion—but she was grateful for it. If it started getting around that a policeman had visited her, God knew what the repercussions would be. Every moment she spent in Gracie's company was a reminder that it could all be snatched away from her in a heartbeat.

She was grateful, too, that it was the affable young Peter—one of the few Hewitt servants who didn't openly loathe her—who had answered the door just now. The female staff were forbidden to entertain gentleman visitors—Mrs. Mott's rule, strictly enforced—and although Nell didn't answer to the housekeeper, she knew the old woman could make her life good and miserable if she wanted to.

"You got a sweetheart, Miss Sweeney?" Peter asked with a suggestively boyish grin.

Nell gave him a doleful look. "If I did, would I let him come to the house for all to see? Two more bites of carrots now, buttercup—then you may finish the aspic. He must be a tradesman of some sort. You'll have to send him up, Peter. I can't leave Gracie right now." Both Nurse Parrish and Viola were napping, the former because that was how she spent the middle part of every day, and the latter in order to rest up for tonight, when she, Mr. Hewitt, and her sons would finally see *Bluebeard* at the Tremont. Paola was busy altering the gown Viola would wear to the theater, and Mrs. Bouchard was eating her own lunch downstairs. There were a couple of maids Nell trusted to watch Gracie in a pinch, but mealtimes took a certain talent for high-level negotiation, not to mention a tolerance for godawful messes.

Three days had passed since Nell's evening in the Public Garden with Will Hewitt. She'd made no effort to seek him out, although Jack Thorpe kept her apprised of the comings and goings of his nocturnal houseguest via handsomely penned letters delivered by messenger every day around noon. Those letters—addressed, for the sake of discretion, to Viola—also related the various legal maneuverings Jack was undertaking on Will's behalf, in which, according to Jack, Will evinced not the faintest interest.

"Miss Sweeney?" Detective Cook loomed in the doorway, blinking at the nursery, which Viola, thrilled at having a little girl to pamper, had decorated with rococo opulence. Ornamental plasterwork adorned the mirror-lined, sea green walls, cherubs hovered around the gilded ceiling, and the windows were layered with elaborate puffs and swags of silk.

"Detective Cook," Nell greeted. "May I introduce Miss Grace Lindleigh Hewitt."

"Well, good afternoon, young lady," Cook said with a bow, holding his bowler to his chest. "Enjoying your luncheon there, are you?"

Gracie, still gripping her spoon, turned away with a coyly bashful smile to cuddle her governess, the aspic around her mouth smearing the day smock Nell always wore for meals in the nursery.

"What a bonnie little miss she is," Cook praised. "A good eater, too, I see."

"She'd eat a brick if it was chopped up into aspic," said Nell as she tidied the child's hair. "Have a seat, Detective."

Cook eyed the chair to which she pointed—delicately carved and upholstered in floral damask, like all the rest in this room—and declined. "I can't stay long. I just wanted to share the latest in the matter of the Ernest Tulley case. But if this isn't a good time . . ." he added, his gaze lighting on Gracie.

"No, go ahead," Nell said, breaking an apple fritter in half and handing it to Gracie. "She's more interested in this fritter than anything we might have to say. What's happened?"

Cook said, "I've had my men watching that flat on Milk Street day and night—the one Pearl shared with Molly? It was Keating on duty last night, a rookie, but sharp. He saw Molly get in a coal wagon this morning around dawn with a trunk and two carpetbags all but bursting, and hand the driver some money. Keating commandeers a milk truck and follows the wagon about six or seven miles as it heads south out of Boston, making deliveries. Around midmorning, they arrive in Quincy, which is where Molly gets out, in front of a little white house. The door opens, and who should be standing there, but . . ." He spread his hands.

"Pearl Stauber." Nell closed her eyes for a moment, dismayed by this development. If the prostitute were to testify in court about Will's threats to "make Tulley pay," he would almost certainly be found guilty.

"I asked Keating if the house looked like a . . . place of assignation, but he said no, it's on a nice little tree-lined street, very respectable. There's an empty shop on the ground floor—used to be a chocolate shop, the neighbors said. Keating left without announcing his presence, per my instructions, so Pearl has no idea we've found her."

"What now?" Nell asked dejectedly.

"I need to subpoena her as a witness. I'll get the subpoena today and deliver it personally tomorrow morning. Not that she's that critical to our case anymore. Something else came to light yesterday that you should know about. I don't imagine it'll make you very happy, Miss Sweeney—although August Hewitt will probably break out the champagne."

"What is it?" Nell asked dully as she swept fritter crumbs from Gracie's lap. And how could it be worse than Pearl's reappearance?

Tap, tap, tap went Cook's bowler against his leg. "You remember me saying as how I needed to get some background on Ernest Tulley, in case something in his past figured in all this?"

"Yes," she said, recalling their conversation in the morgue.

He scratched his jaw, as if both proud of his news and hesitant to reveal it to her. "Turns out Tulley had been a merchant seaman only since the war. Before that, he was a graycoat posted at Andersonville as a guard. That's the

prison camp where William Hewitt was supposed to have
died of—"

"Yes. I know about Andersonville. Are you sure?"

"He was infamous. The men I spoke to who'd been
prisoners there told stories that turned my blood cold. Him
and three or four other guards, poor Georgia trash like
Tulley, they'd get bored, pick out a prisoner—a sick or
injured one, usually, so he couldn't put up too much of a
fight—take him into the woods around the compound and,
well . . . basically, torture him. They had different things
they liked to do—bury him up to his neck and leave him
there, light him on fire . . ."

"Oh, my God."

"Their favorite game was to tell the poor soul he could
go free if he could outrun their bloodhounds, otherwise
they'd use him for target practice. They'd give him a head
start, but the dogs always caught up with him, and then
they'd do him in. Sometimes they took their time about
it, sometimes it was quick, depending on Tulley's mood—
he was the leader."

"He knew him," Nell said dazedly. "William Hewitt
knew Ernest Tulley."

"They all did, all the men who'd served time in Andersonville. How they'd cheer and carry on when I told
them he'd been murdered. The general consensus was
he'd got a taste of his own, and good riddance."

He'll pay for it, damn him. He'll pay with his life. It
hadn't been about Kathleen after all, or if so, only partly.

Cook said, "I'm on to you, you know."

She looked at him.

"I believed you in the beginning," he said, "when you
said you were doing August Hewitt's bidding. A pretty
girl, if she wants to play a double game, she can usually
pull it off pretty easy, and a pretty *Irish* girl, there's no
finding them out—unless the game goes on a bit too long,
'cause that's when you get to wondering about things late

at night when you can't sleep. And then one morning you wake up, and you nudge your wife, layin' in bed next to you, and you say, 'You know that Nell Sweeney I was telling you about? I don't think she's working for August Hewitt at all. I think it's the wife who's callin' the shots, and I don't think Hewitt has the slightest notion what she and the governess are up to behind his back. Do you think it's possible he was hookwinked like that? And not just him, but me?' And your pretty little Irish wife just laughs and rolls over and goes back to sleep."

"I'm sorry, Detective," Nell said. "Please don't think I regard you with anything less than the utmost respect, but I had no choice but to—"

"Save your breath, Miss Sweeney. If I was of a mind to get het up over it, I wouldn't have come here."

"Why did you?"

" 'Cause I know you've gotten a bit . . . wrapped up in this case, and in the notion that William Hewitt is innocent. I just thought you deserved to hear the truth from me."

She nodded. "Thank you, Detective."

He cleared his throat. "I, uh, happen to know Dr. Hewitt's been seen playing faro and poker in the wee hours. We haven't nabbed him yet, 'cause it hasn't been important enough—till now. I'm putting the word out among the boys to be on the lookout for him. If he wants to stay out of lockup, he'll turn homebody right quick. He doesn't even have to show up in one of his usual haunts. If he so much as lights up a cigarette on a public street, we'll get him, and this time he ain't getting out. Just a bit of friendly advice."

"Why are you offering it, if you want to catch him?" she asked as she gently deflected Gracie's attempt to feed her a chunk of fritter.

"Because I know he won't take it. His type, they're

only happy when they're prowling the streets between dusk and dawn."

If only it weren't true.

Cook said, "You should have heard the prosecutor, when I gave him the news about Hewitt knowing Tulley from Andersonville. He giggled like a schoolgirl."

"It never occurred to me . . ." Nell said. "I mean, I just assumed they were strangers . . ."

You infer too much, Miss Sweeney, Will had told her when they first met. *Far too many facile assumptions.* Even then he'd recognized the flaw that would, in the end, negate everything she'd learned, unravel all her clever theories and speculations . . . and send her hurtling right back to the beginning.

S HE saw him through Jack Thorpe's glass-paned front door just as she was raising her fist for a third battery of pounding. Will smiled as he approached, his braces dangling and his shirtsleeves rolled up, hair damp and uncombed, lower face flecked with shaving soap, a straight razor in one hand.

"Good afternoon, Miss Sweeney," he greeted as he opened the door. "What an unexpected—"

"Ernest Tulley killed your brother, didn't he?" Her voice quavered despite her efforts to steady it. "Tulley and his cronies took him into the woods and they . . . they . . ."

Will closed his eyes briefly; a muscle twitched in his jaw. He turned and retreated into the house, leaving the door open.

"You told me Robbie was shot trying to escape," she said as she followed him through the foyer and up the thickly carpeted stairs.

"No, Miss Sweeney, you told *me* that," he said without turning around. "You made an assumption, one of several which—"

"Do *not* blame my assumptions!" she demanded shakily, and a bit shrilly, although in truth, she knew she was the one at fault. "You allowed me to believe it. Just as you allowed me to believe that you didn't know Ernest Tulley—and God knows how many other erroneous things. You've been watching me stumble round in circles, trying to piece everything together with too little information, or wrong information, and laughing to yourself all the while."

He paused at the top of the stairs just long enough to say, "I never laughed," before heading down the hall, Nell right behind him. She followed him into a bathroom stuffed with ferns and paneled in darkly burnished wood, the air balmy and scented with Castile soap, warm water steaming in the marble sink. Guided by his reflection in the gilt-framed toilet glass, he craned his neck to scrape off the last few unshaven patches.

"The police know about Tulley and Andersonville," she said.

A drop of red beaded on his throat; he held a washcloth to it as he rinsed off the razor.

"And they've found Pearl Stauber. Even if they don't put two and two together about Robbie, they'll have little trouble proving to a jury that you killed Tulley simply because he'd been such a monster at Andersonville—especially if Pearl and Seamus Flynn testify against you."

"I told you from the very beginning that it was a waste of time to try to keep me from my date with the hangman." Will glanced at the spot of blood on the cloth, set it aside, and bent his head over the sink to rinse off the remaining shaving soap. "Hand me that towel, will you?" he asked, pointing.

She shook it out and gave it to him. "Did you do it?" she asked. "I need to hear it from your own mouth. Did you kill Ernest Tulley?"

He lowered his head and buried it in the towel, rubbing

it slowly, taking his time. Tossing it aside, he patted his face with Bay Rum, its tropical spiciness filling the little room.

"For pity's sake!" she exclaimed, her patience strained to the snapping point. "After everything I've been through on your behalf, I think I deserve a straight answer for—"

"Yes." Gripping the sink, head down, eyes closed, Will said, "Yes. Yes. I did it. I . . ." He opened his eyes and met Nell's gaze in the mirror, his expression rawly contrite—startling, shocking even, considering his usual self-possession. "I'm sorry, Nell," he said in a soft, strained voice. "I truly am. I didn't want to have to tell you this. I wish to God you'd never gotten involved."

Nell felt suddenly starved for air, as if her stays were tightening all on their own. The bathroom walls seemed to sway inward, upsetting her balance. She reached out for something to hold on to and felt his arms catch her up. "Easy, now."

Will walked her down the hall and through a door as her skull crawled with cold and her lungs heaved, every breath a labor. Divesting her swiftly of her coat and hat, he said, "Lie down."

It was an unmade bed—his bed, judging from the tray of opium paraphernalia on the far side. The little horn box, she saw, was nearly empty again.

"No," she said, even as her feet lifted off the floor and the room spun on its axis. Her head nestled into something dreamily soft that smelled like Bay Rum—a down pillow—and she closed her eyes, just for a moment, until the world righted itself.

NELL blinked as she came to in Will's bed, lying curled on her side with a quilt drawn up over her shoulders. She felt much more herself; if nothing else, she could take

a full breath again. The light through the curtains had that
late-afternoon look to it, so she knew some time had
passed. She smelled a whisper of cigarette smoke, heard
the squeak of a chair behind her.

"Are you awake?" he asked softly.

Nell rolled onto her back, crinoline rustling beneath the
quilt, and turned her head to find him in a Windsor chair
on the other side of the bed, leaning his elbows on his
knees.

"How are you feeling?" He set his cigarette in an alabaster ashtray and rose to sit next to her on the bed.

"Fine." She tried to sit up, but it made her head swim.

"Yes, well . . ." Easing her back down, he said, "Best
to give it a bit longer."

Nell nodded, her eyes drifting shut. She sensed him
reaching toward the ashtray; the cigarette crackled as he
drew on it.

When she reopened her eyes—it felt as if only a few
minutes had passed, but it might have been longer—she
found he'd shifted on the edge of the bed to look at her.
She held his gaze until he said, "They came for Robbie
just before sunset. They chose him—really it was Tulley
who chose him—because he was missing that arm. It
made him an easier target."

No, don't tell me, she wanted to say. *I don't want to
hear it.* But they'd come too far for that. He was, at long
last, offering the truth. He'd lived it; the least she could
do was listen.

"I tried to fight them off," Will said, "but there were
too many of them, and I didn't have much strength left
at that point. I screamed at them to take me instead. Tulley
just laughed. He said, 'Oh, yeah, he's your brother, ain't
he? All right, then, we'll let you watch.' "

In her mind's eye, Nell saw those photographs from
Harper's Weekly, the sea of emaciated men, the pine log
stockade, the surrounding woods.

Will said, "They tied my hands behind me and forced us at gunpoint into a clearing in the woods. I was still trying to convince them to take me instead of Robbie, but Tulley couldn't be swayed. His lackeys got tired of holding me back, so he shot me in the leg to disable me. They told Robbie to run, and then they set the bloodhounds on him. He wasn't used to running with only one arm, so he didn't get very far. It was all over rather quickly. They dragged him back to the clearing and shoved him onto his knees in front of me."

Nell realized she'd curled up into a tight ball, her arms wrapped around her.

"Tulley had a big brass-framed Reb version of a forty-four Remington. He put it to Robbie's head and cocked the hammer. He asked me if I still wanted to take my brother's place—if so, I had three seconds to speak up. Robbie said, 'Don't you dare. I couldn't live with it.' I figured he'd have to, like it or not, but just as I opened my mouth, Tulley said, 'Time's up,' and he pulled the trigger. The top of Robbie's head disappeared before he hit the ground."

Nell squeezed her eyes shut, crossed herself.

"You know the rest," Will said. "I removed the bullet from my leg that night, and the next day, when the storm came, I saw my chance and got out of there. Then, a couple of weeks ago, while I was buying gong from Seamus Flynn, who should walk past the parlor door but Ernest Tulley. I recognized him instantly, even without his Confederate uniform. It was like a kick in the stomach—I could hardly breathe. I followed him up to the third floor with no idea where he was going, or why. When I opened that door and saw what he was up to with Flynn's daughter . . ." Will shook his head. "It was clear he hadn't changed."

"No wonder you were so enraged." But could his rage

have turned murderous four hours later, especially in light of all the opium he'd smoked that night?

As if he'd read her mind, Will said, "I can be relatively alert between bowls, as you've observed."

"Alert enough to . . ." Nell shuddered as she recalled Patrolman Hooper's account. *You should have seen his eyes. They were like a wild animal's, and his face was spattered with blood.*

He looked down, clawed a hand through his hair. "I don't know what to tell you, Miss Sweeney. I was . . ." He seemed to be groping for words. "I'd been thinking about Robbie all evening, remembering. Christ, I've done nothing but remember for the past three and a half years, remember and wonder why I wasn't just a little quicker in speaking up, why I let him die like that. I can't go to sleep at night without finding myself in that bloody clearing in the woods, seeing Robbie's eyes when the bullet fired. So when I saw Tulley return, I suppose I . . . went a bit mad. I mean, obviously I did, to have . . ." He shook his head. "Christ."

"Talking to yourself now, Will?"

Nell and Will both turned as Jack entered the room, his smile dimming as he took in the two of them. Will's hair was as mussed as before, his shirt half-unbuttoned, braces undone; she was still lying next to him on the bed, wrapped up in the quilt.

Jack stared at her—at both of them. "Oh. I . . . I'm sorry," he stammered, backing out of the room. "I'll just be—"

"Stay," Will said as he rose and circled the bed. "It's a conversation you're interrupting, counselor, not a tryst. Miss Sweeney fainted. That's why she's lying down."

Nell was about to protest that she never fainted, when she realized that any alternative explanation was bound to raise untoward questions.

"You *fainted?*" Jack asked, crossing to her. "Are you ill?"

"Not at all." She sat up, the quilt slipping off her shoulders, her chignon uncoiling down her back as the pins slipped out. "I'm fine. I just . . ."

Jack was gaping at her.

She looked down at herself, only to find her bodice and corset cover unbuttoned and the steel busk that secured the front of her stays completely unhooked, revealing the linen chemise beneath. She gasped, tugging her garments closed, and shot Will a look of outrage.

"You couldn't breathe," he said. "I *am* a physician."

"When it suits you." Turning her back on them to sit on the edge of the bed, she snatched off her gloves and set about refastening her clothes.

"She's not ill," Will said. "She just had a bit of a shock."

"What . . . what kind of—"

"I admitted to her that I killed Ernest Tulley. I plan to make a full confession to the authorities and put an end to all this ridiculous—"

"What? *No.*"

Nell glanced over her shoulder as she fumbled with her busk to find Jack looking utterly stricken.

"No, Will," he repeated.

"I'm afraid so, Jack."

"Will . . ."

"They've got me, Jack. New evidence has come to light regarding my motive for—"

"No! This is insanity. You can't—"

"Let's step outside and give Miss Sweeney a little privacy, why don't we?" Will suggested, guiding his friend toward the door. "I'll explain what's happened."

*   *   *

NELL found them downstairs in the library, Will lazing back in one of a pair of leather armchairs flanking the hearth, Jack hunched over in another, one hand cradling his forehead, the other wrapped around a glass of whiskey. Both men rose when she entered the room, properly attired once more, complete with gloves.

"Ah, Miss Sweeney. All buttoned up now, are we?" Will took her hat and coat out of her hands and pulled a big velvet-upholstered wing chair over to the fire for her to sit on, prompting an expression of dismay from Jack. "Something wrong, old man?"

"It's nothing, just . . ." Sheepishly Jack said, "It's Mother. She likes the furniture to stay where she's arranged it. I can move it back later."

Will arched a bemused eyebrow for Nell's benefit as Jack paced away from them, drink in hand.

"What I'm trying to tell you, Will," Jack said, "is that you don't have to hang. There's no reason it should come to that."

"A drink, Miss Sweeney?" Will gestured toward a cabinet set out with decanters and glasses. "Sherry? Port?"

"No, thank you."

Will lowered himself back into his chair, crossed his legs, and brushed some dust off his trousers. "A murder's been committed, counselor. People like to see someone hang when that happens."

Turning, hands on hips, Jack said, "Will, listen to me. I'm a lawyer. I'm *your* lawyer . . ."

"And you don't like to lose. I realize that, but—"

"It's not about losing!" Jack crossed to Will in a few long steps, reddening. "Christ, Will, you know it isn't."

"I know what it's about, Jack," Will said. "And I know what I have to do. I've played my hand and lost. I chose to play it, knowing the risks."

"Yes. Fine. I understand that, but there's no reason you

should hang when we can still establish a reasonable doubt as to your guilt."

Will flipped open a cigarette tin labeled SPHINX. "How the devil do you propose to do that?"

"By presenting evidence that someone else may have been responsible. Whereas it's true you had the motive and weapon—"

"Not to mention having been caught in the act," Will said as he struck a match.

"Flynn's not a credible witness," Jack said. "I could eviscerate him on the stand, and the prosecutor will know it."

Nell said, "Yes, but the patrolman who was first on the scene says he saw Will . . . choking Tulley."

Jack stared at Will in stunned disbelief. "Jesus, Will. Why in God's name would you—"

"Why would I have done any of it?" Will asked on a stream of fragrant smoke as he shook out the match. "I never did want to have to think up answers for all these absurd questions. Everyone wants answers that makes sense, but there *are* no answers that make sense. Bloody hell . . . Is this what the trial's going to be like?"

"With any luck," Jack said, "there won't be a trial— assuming I can cast enough suspicion on someone else. No matter how good a case they've got against you, they'll have to drop it if I can make it seem just as likely that another man committed the murder."

"Whom do you plan to sacrifice," Will asked with a mild smile, "so that a reprobate like me can walk free?"

"We don't have to get this other person convicted," Jack said. "I just have to show that he was equally likely to have killed Ernest Tulley." To Nell he said, "I'm thinking about Roy Noonan."

"But Noonan's ledger proves that Tulley didn't owe him any money," Nell said.

"Perhaps not all of his debtors are listed in the ledger.

Perhaps he keeps a second ledger. If I offer up enough witnesses willing to swear that Tulley owed Noonan money, that's bound to carry some weight."

"What if it carries too much?" Will asked, tapping his cigarette ash into an exquisite Japanese bowl. "What if they try him, and he ends up being convicted?"

"Have you met the man?" Jack asked, taking a drink. "I wouldn't trouble my conscience too much on his account."

Will shook his head. "If it came to it, I couldn't allow it. I'd have to confess."

"It doesn't have to be Noonan," Nell said. "There was the other man in the back parlor. Who's to say he wasn't the killer? We can argue that he was the man the neighbors saw running away that night."

"Absolutely not," Will said. "I won't have an uninvolved man dragged into this."

"Those witnesses were drunk, in any event," Jack said. "That will cast doubt on their testimony."

"But we know he was there," she said, sitting up as the idea took form in her mind. "At least two people besides Dr. Hewitt saw him, but he's still completely anonymous. No one knows who he was, just that he was there that night—drinking heavily, I might add. We can make a case for him being the killer without exposing him to arrest, because no one knows his identity."

"Yes, but what if they go looking for him?" Will asked. "As you say, two people saw him. He might very well be tracked down and identified."

"That's an acceptable risk," Jack said.

Will shook his head resolutely. "Not to me. Suppose they find him?"

Jack drained his glass in one tilt. "Suppose they do? It'll be his problem then. Better him than you."

"I don't see it that way."

"I wish you'd try to," Jack said earnestly. "I want to

help you, but you make it so blasted difficult."

"Then stop trying so hard. Learn to accept the situation."

"Accept your being hanged? Never! Even if I have to—"

"You're to do nothing without my say-so, Jack, do you understand me?" Will demanded. "As my attorney, you can advise a course of action, but only I can authorize it. We've been all through this. I chose my path. I gambled and lost, and now I intend to take my losses like a man, without a lot of humiliating last-ditch efforts from you." Including Nell in his gaze, he added, "From either of you."

"Then I don't suppose you'd be receptive to a plea of insanity," she said.

"Oh, do spare me," Will groaned, stabbing out his cigarette.

"You went through some terrible things during the war," she said. "You wouldn't be the only man who's come back a bit . . . unhinged. And there's the opium on top of that."

"Not guilty by virtue of being an opium fiend?" Chuckling, Will stood and started rolling down his sleeves. "It might be worth mounting that defense just for the entertainment value of watching Jack try to argue the case."

"I considered it, actually," Jack said as he refilled his glass, rather generously, from a decanter of whiskey, "but it won't work. Everyone was driven a little mad by the war, and as for the opium, that was voluntarily self-administered. And then there's the fact that Will displays no overt symptoms of lunacy."

"Murdering a man by stabbing and choking doesn't count?" she asked incredulously.

"Not if it's the only time he's ever done such a thing. Even if I *could* get him declared *non compos mentis*, he wouldn't be sent to some nice, progressive hospital like

Massachusetts General, or the Friends Asylum. He'd spend the rest of his days in some ghastly public lunatic house, under lock and key."

"I don't have to tell you I'd rather be executed—even by hanging—than face that prospect," Will said. "I do wish you two would just relax and stop trying to clean up a mess that shouldn't be any of your concern. I know that's just what I'm going to do."

What a contrast, Nell thought, to Will's brother Harry, who was more than happy to let others follow behind him with a mop and pail. *He* wouldn't have any compunction about Jack pointing the finger at someone else, as long as he got to keep on whoring and drinking and losing at cards night after night.

"Lovely chatting with you two," Will said as he levered himself out of the chair, "but if you'll excuse me, I'm going to make myself presentable, then head out in my nightly pursuit of riches and intoxication."

"I wouldn't recommend it," Nell said. "Every policeman in the city will be watching for you, starting tonight. Detective Cook knows you've been violating your bail conditions. He means to catch you in the act—or at least have you picked up on a nuisance charge. It's not safe for you out there."

"What's a nocturnal adventure without a bit of risk?" he asked as he crossed to the door.

"Fine," she countered, "but don't expect any Black Drop if you end up behind bars before your trial. That offer was only for after your conviction."

Pausing in the doorway, he said, "You've got a streak of pure, cold-blooded venom in you, Miss Sweeney. I find that devastating in a woman."

"If I were cold-blooded, would I be willing to supply you with opium at all, under any circumstances? You know how I feel about it."

Suddenly thoughtful, he said, "Yes. I do."

"Please don't go out," she implored. "I'll be sick with worry."

"Will you?" he asked. "I'd rather like that."

"I'm serious."

"So am I."

"She's right, Will," Jack said. "You'd be taking a foolish chance, leaving the house tonight. Stay here."

"And what? Sit by the fire with my knitting?"

"Is that any worse than convulsing and hallucinating in some jail cell?" Nell asked.

He actually seemed to be thinking about it. "No, Miss Sweeney. Nothing is worse than that. You rescued me from that fate once, with bribes and paregoric, despite your misgivings. It would be ungentlemanly of me to ask it of you again—even on death row, regardless of your kind offer."

"I wouldn't let you go through opium withdrawal in a situation like that."

"I don't intend to."

"But—"

"Tell you what," Will said. "Just so neither of you has to fret on my account, I hereby promise to steer well clear of all gaming hells and hop joints tonight."

"Or any night until your trial," Nell amended.

"So sworn."

"And you won't leave the house," Jack added.

Will rolled his eyes. "All right. Fine. I won't leave the house." He ran a hand through his still-uncombed hair. "You're very irritating, Jack, and a great deal of trouble. But you're a good friend, to care what becomes of a wretch like me. As for you, Miss Sweeney . . ."

He bowed slowly, almost gravely, smiling at her as he straightened. "It has been a very real pleasure," he said quietly, then turned and went upstairs.

Chapter 15

"DID you notice how distraught he became," Nell asked Jack as she pulled on her coat, "when I brought up that other man, the one he'd been talking to in the back parlor?"

She'd stayed behind after Will's departure in order to discuss the case outside of his hearing—and his persistent attempts to hamstring their efforts. Unfortunately, Jack, who'd been tossing back whiskeys like water, was no longer in any condition to formulate legal strategies. He stood facing the library fireplace, arms braced on the mantel, staring into the flames with glazed, wavering eyes; hence Nell's decision to head home and finish this discussion some other time.

"Distraught?" Jack said thickly. "You think so?"

"For him. He's normally so self-contained." She withdrew from her chatelaine the leather case housing the photograph she'd been showing to witnesses—the portrait of Will, Jack, Robbie, and Harry in white tie before the Children's Aid Ball. Flipping it open, she studied Will's urbane, flawlessly groomed image. He seemed almost to be holding in a chuckle, as if something about being photographed had amused him. Try as she might to imagine him slashing a man's throat, regardless of the circumstances or motivation, the picture would not come.

She shifted her gaze to Harry, with his careless grin and his garish waistcoat. *I saw something of myself in him,* Will had said. *Those of us with an appetite for sin always recognize it in others . . . But I was too preoccupied, too disgusted by him, and by myself, to offer him any meaningful guidance.*

Viola shared Will's guilt at having failed Harry, and his concern over his excesses. *When he heard about Robbie's death, he went a little mad . . . I just worry that someday he'll do something money can't put right.*

"Jack," she asked, "do you know anything about your father's personal legal work for August Hewitt? The, um, private family matters that he attends to?"

Jack shook his head as he lifted his glass from the mantel. "That's all confidential, even from me. Very hush hush." He pressed a finger to his lips, swaying slightly now that he wasn't holding on to the mantel. "Nothing in writing, ever." Gulping down the last ounce or so of whiskey in his glass, he headed unsteadily to the liquor cabinet for more.

Nell considered and swiftly rejected the notion of sharing her speculations with Jack; that could wait until he was sober. "You probably shouldn't be drinking so much," she said as she checked her pendant watch. Half past six. Would Detective Cook still be at the station house?

"Just one more," he said as he twisted the glass stopper out of the decanter.

Crossing to him, she said, "It would be best if you remained sober tonight, so you can keep an eye on Dr. Hewitt and make sure he doesn't leave the house."

"He told us he wouldn't."

"But he's low on opium, so I know he'll be tempted." Perhaps she should bring him some laudanum or Black Drop later, after she met with Detective Cook, so that he'd be less likely to head out in search of gong. Regardless that it violated her principles to provide him with the stuff—a qualm he seemed, surprisingly, to respect—there was nothing to be gained right now from condemning him to opium sickness.

Jack hesitated, his gaze on the decanter's amber contents, shimmering in the firelight, then pushed the stopper back in. "What did you mean when you said the offer about the Black Drop was only good for death row?"

"Dr. Hewitt asked me if I would smuggle in opium tonics when he was waiting to be executed."

"Christ," Jack said, gripping the edge of the liquor cabinet. "I can't . . . I can't let him . . ."

"I know," she said. She reached out to pat his back then, for some reason, withdrew her hand.

"If he hangs, I'll have lost both of them, him and Robbie. And it'll be my fault."

"Even the best lawyer can't work miracles," she said. "Especially when his client is as difficult as—"

"It doesn't matter!" He wheeled to face her, that vein rising on his forehead, his eyes red-rimmed. "It doesn't matter how difficult he is. He's my friend, the only real friend I have left, and I can't . . . I can't . . ."

"You're upset because you've been drinking," she said evenly. "But we haven't exhausted all our options. When you're more yourself, we'll talk about—"

"More *myself*?" He laughed, but his eyes shone damply. "Oh, yes, I'm so terribly capable when I'm *myself*. You think that because of who *you* are, so clever, so imperturbable. I'm not like you, Miss Sweeney. God, I wish I was, but I'm not." Tears welled in his eyes; he scrubbed them away before they could fall. "Tell me what to do. Tell me what *you* would do."

"I . . . I can't. I'm not a lawyer. Please, Mr. Thorpe, just—"

"*Help me,*" he pleaded, seizing her by the arms. "Help me to not fail him. I can't do it on my own. I don't trust myself. I'll miss something . . ."

"You won't," she assured him as calmly as she could. "Of course I'll help you, but—"

"That's all I ask," he rasped, his hands tightening on her. "You don't know how much it helps, having your insight. I need that. I need you. You see so much. You see everything."

"Mr. Thorpe . . ." Nell tried to squirm away from him but he was surprisingly strong.

"It's meant so much to me, your perception, your . . ." He looked down at his hands clutching her upper arms. Easing his grip, he stroked her through her coat sleeves. "You're wise beyond your years, and so . . ."

"Mr. Thorpe." She pried his hands loose and stepped back. He teetered but managed to remain upright. "I really must be going."

Jack started to move toward her, seemed to reconsider that, and retreated awkwardly to lean against the liquor cabinet. "Yes, of course." He raked an errant lock of hair off his forehead, his gaze bleary and sad. "Of course."

"It's just that I want to catch Detective Cook before he—"

"No need to explain," he said, grabbing on to the edge of the cabinet as he turned to face it. "Go on. You've got things to do."

She hesitated, wondering if she should caution him again about drinking.

"*Go,*" he said.

She did.

* * *

A N hour later, having convinced Detective Cook to bring her with him tomorrow when he served the sub-poena on Pearl Stauber, Nell stepped out of a hack at the corner of Arlington and Commonwealth. Joseph Maynard & Co. was the only business still open on the darkened block, its windows radiant with the glow of a battery of pendant lamps hanging from the ceiling.

"Good evening, miss," greeted the white-haired apoth-ecary as he measured a mound of powder on his scale. Glancing up, he said, "Ah, it's Miss . . . Sweeney, is it not? Dr. Toussaint's assistant?"

"That's right."

"He wants those extra needles after all, does he?"

"I'm sorry?"

"For the syringe. I *told* him the one wasn't enough. It has to be cleaned between patients, after all, and they do break." Hauling a tray out from beneath the counter, he asked, "How many would he like?"

The tray had compartments for the display of hypo-dermic injection supplies: delicate silver and glass syrin-ges, sturdy steel ones, medicine vials, needles of various sizes, and portable syringe kits in cases ranging from util-itarian brass to ornamental gold plate.

"That's . . . not actually what I'm here for," Nell said, looking away from the rows of needles glinting in the bright overhead light. "He, um, asked me to pick up a few things this morning, but I couldn't get here till now, and it looks as if he might have beaten me to it."

"Ah." Mr. Maynard nodded sympathetically as he put away the tray. "Some days are so hectic, aren't they? One wonders where the time goes. Yes, Dr. Toussaint was just here about fifteen minutes ago. What did he ask you to pick up? Perhaps he got it himself."

"It's actually a fairly long list," she said. "Why don't

you tell me what he bought so I'll be sure not to get the same things."

"Just the syringe, the needle, and four grams of morphine sulfate."

"Four grams . . . How much would that be in—"

"Ounces? Less than an eighth."

"No, um . . . he mentioned doses. How many doses would that be?"

"It depends on the patient's body weight, of course, but at an average of ten milligrams per dose, that would be four hundred."

She stared at him. "Four hundred doses?"

"Average doses. A large man would need twenty milligrams—more if he'd developed a tolerance. And as for addicts, well, they can go through hundreds of milligrams a day. In fact, I once heard of a man who regularly went through as much as I just sold Dr. Toussaint in a single day—over the course of twenty-four hours, of course. Four grams is a lethal dose, injected all at once."

Striving to keep her voice steady, Nell said, "Did he mention what he needed it for?"

"It really only has the one medical application," Mr. Maynard replied. "Pain relief. I offered to put it on his account, but he insisted on giving me cash and paying off the account, seeing as he'll be gone."

Gone? Nell's heart felt as if it were trying to hammer a hole through her stays.

"I wish all my customers were as good about tidying up loose ends before long trips. You should see what some of them end up owing! It's a wonder I can . . . Miss Sweeney? Are you—"

She grabbed her skirts and bolted from the shop, heart tripping, mind whirling. Four grams of morphine and one needle . . .

Four grams is a lethal dose, injected all at once.

She raced around the corner to Jack's house, leapt up the stairs, pounded on the door.

No answer. It was dark inside. She tried the knob, but it was locked.

"Mr. Thorpe!" She pounded harder. *"Mr. Thorpe! It's me, Nell Sweeney. Answer the door!"*

This can't happen. Please, God, don't let this happen. *"Damn you, Jack, answer the damn door!"*

Nell heard a gasp from behind her and turned to see an elderly couple walking a tiny white dog. They averted their gazes and hurried away.

There came a yellowish haze of gaslight from within the house. Squinting through the glass, she saw Jack, in rumpled shirtsleeves, lighting a wall bracket in the foyer. He blinked when he saw her, tucked in his shirt as he approached.

"Where's Dr. Hewitt?" she asked, bulling her way past him when he opened the door. "Is he here?"

"Yes, of course," Jack said groggily as he finger-combed his untidy hair, one cheek imprinted with creases.

"Are you sure?" she asked. "Did you just wake up?"

"No." He hesitated guiltily. "Y-yes, I suppose I—"

"Oh, Jesus." She sprinted up the stairs, checked his room, the bathroom.

I wouldn't let you go through opium withdrawal in a situation like that.

I don't intend to.

No sign of him anywhere in the rest of the house, which she swiftly searched.

As for you, Miss Sweeney . . . it has been a very real pleasure.

Jack was waiting for her at the bottom of the stairs with a sealed envelope. *Miss Cornelia Sweeney* was written on the front in a masculine, economical hand. "He left me one, too," Jack said, holding up his own envelope. "I found them on my desk."

Nell broke the seal and read the note:

My Dear Miss Sweeney,

I have decided to sacrifice Lady Viola's bail money after all and take my chances in Shanghai, where a pipe fiend is less likely to attract notice than in any other city on earth. If we never meet again, please know that making your acquaintance has been a bright spot in a rather dark life.

And do watch those assumptions.

Gratefully yours,
Wm. Hewitt

"He's not going to Shanghai," Nell said. "He just wants us to think that. I was just at the druggist around the corner. Dr. Hewitt was there about fifteen minutes ago. He bought a great deal of morphine and a hypodermic syringe."

Jack stared at her, his eyes widening as the implication sank in. He shook his head. "No. He wouldn't."

"He doesn't seem to mind dying," she said. "But he loathes the idea of hanging."

"Let's not jump to conclusions. We know he was almost out of opium. Perhaps this is just a substitute."

"He uses Black Drop for that. But he once told me he'd prefer a syringe full of morphine to the noose." *Quick, fairly painless . . .* "And now that the case against him is pretty much airtight, and Detective Cook is threatening to lock him up again if he so much as steps out the front door . . ."

"Christ." He raked both hands through his hair. "It's my fault. I was just going to rest my eyes for a moment on the couch, and I . . . I . . ."

"We've got to—"

"I told you I'd fail him," Jack said, his voice taking on a frantic pitch. "You see? I told you. I *knew* it. Jesus Christ!"

"Mr. Thorpe, please calm yourself."

"I should never have let this happen," he said, kneading his temples with tremulous fingers. "I should never have let him—"

"Get hold of yourself," Nell commanded, although she felt perilously close to panic herself. "I need you. Dr. Hewitt needs you. We've got to find him before he . . ." *Don't think about it.* "We just have to find him, as soon as possible."

"What if he's left Boston?"

She shook her head as she thought about it. "Let's just hope he didn't."

Jack nodded mechanically, his face flushed, rubbing that vein on his forehead as if trying to erase it.

"We can cover twice as much ground if we separate to look for him," she said. "If we're right about his intentions, he'll want to be someplace relatively private, where he won't be disturbed. But not too private. I should think . . . I mean, if I were him, I should think I'd want to be . . . found."

"Yes . . . yes. A hotel room, perhaps."

"There are so many hotels in Boston. Where would we start?"

"I've got this year's city almanac. It lists them all."

Jack fetched the little green book from his desk in the library, where they sat to divide up the hotels, Nell taking the larger, more respectable ones—the Tremont, United States, Parker, Revere—while Jack assigned himself the more questionable establishments, as well as the flop houses and de facto brothels in the poorer quarters.

"You don't want to dress too well, where you'll be going tonight," she said, "or you might attract the wrong kind of attention. If you've got an old sack coat, wear that. And a slouch hat or a plain cap. Oh, and no tie."

"You're right," he said. "I wouldn't have thought of that." He offered to drop her off at the Tremont Hotel if she would just give him a few minutes to change his clothes and have them hitch up his gig at the livery stable half a block away.

"You can leave me just down the street from there, at the Tremont Temple," she told him. "The Hewitts are seeing *Bluebeard* tonight, and I need to speak to Harry."

"You think he might know where Will would have gone?"

"It's possible," she said, although she thought it best not to elaborate, given Jack's brittle state of mind; he needed to focus on the task at hand.

S HE was about to be sacked.

Nell drew as deep a breath as her stays would allow, let it out, and knocked on the door of the Hewitts' box at the Tremont Temple. From the other side, over the muffled music—a jauntily Gothic duet to orchestral accompaniment—she heard a deep male voice, August Hewitt's, say, "Who the devil is that?"

He would dismiss her for what she was about to do. It wasn't even worth praying to Saint Dismas over, or hoping for intervention by Viola—not that she wouldn't try, but her chances of success would be virtually nil. A servant—and that was what he considered her, regardless of her standing in his wife's eyes—did not meddle in her employer's private family affairs. She didn't work to undercut the express dictates of the man who paid her salary. And she certainly didn't barge into his private opera box to accuse his son of murder.

By this time tomorrow, she would have no job, no home . . .

And no Gracie.

A nervous impulse propelled her to step back from the door, screamed at her to turn, run! There was still time to save herself. She didn't have to do this.

But then she thought about Will, bowing to her with such solemn finality as he took his leave this afternoon. *It has been a very real pleasure.*

She raised her fist to knock again as the door swung inward, pulled open by Harry, who'd tilted his gilded chair backward at a perilous angle to reach the doorknob. "Miss Sweeney!" he chuckled as he righted the chair with a thump. "A secret fan of Offenbach, are you? You may have my seat." He stood, tugging at his tailcoat. "I've just discovered that I can't bear comic opera."

His father and younger brother, in white tie, like Harry—creamy orchids in their lapels, the three of them—also rose as Nell stepped hesitantly into the darkened loge. Martin looked startled, but pleased, to see her there; Mr. Hewitt scowled in bewilderment. On the gaslit stage below them, a man in an outlandishly tall European-style top hat, fur-trimmed great coat, and chalky face paint was singing in French to a cartoonishly pink-cheeked young woman in an ivory gown.

"Nell?" Viola, in jet-beaded aubergine velvet, an opera glass cradled in her white-gloved hand as it rested upon the railing, had turned to address her governess with an expression of anxious bewilderment. Her two ivory-handled canes, folded at present, were hooked over the arm of her chair. "Nell, darling, is something wrong? Is it Gracie?" she asked, making an awkward effort to rise.

"No! No, Gracie is . . . Nurse Parrish is watching her. I . . ." Nell pressed a hand to her churning stomach. "I need to speak to Mister Harry."

"What business do you have with my son," asked August Hewitt in his formidable baritone, "that would prompt you to interrupt us at such a time?"

Nell nodded toward the door and said, "I'd rather speak to him in pri—"

"You'll speak to him in front of me, or not at all," his

father intoned as laughter rose from the audience. "What is this about?"

Nell licked her lips. Everyone was staring at her. Viola looked terrified. "I . . ." Turning to Harry, she asked, "Do you . . . do you know where I might find your brother?"

"My brother?" Harry pointed to Martin, wide-eyed with confusion. "He's right—"

"Not him," Nell said. "William. Has he ever mentioned a hotel or rooming house? I desperately need to find him."

The only sound, a short intake of air, came from Martin, who must have thought she'd lost her senses.

"My brother William," Harry said slowly, "is in a graveyard in Georgia."

"I don't know what this is about," his father bit out, "but I'll have you know I do not appreciate—"

"How long have you known he was alive?" Nell asked Harry. "How long? Since before he came to Boston, or has it only been—"

"You're mad." Harry turned to his parents, hands raised in self-absolution. "She's mad. I have no idea—"

"Liar," Nell said. "You knew. You knew and didn't—"

"He didn't know," said Mr. Hewitt. "Nobody knew but Mrs. Hewitt and I."

"What?" Martin exclaimed.

"I'm sorry, Martin," Viola began. "We only found out—"

"He's *alive*? How could you know and not tell me?"

"That's enough," his father scolded as one or two audience members glanced up at them. "We'll discuss it when we get home."

"Ah, yes," Harry muttered. "Mustn't make a scene."

"You knew," Nell said to Harry. "But you kept it a secret. And how convenient it was, after they found Ernest Tulley in that alley, to have an older brother handy to take the blame for—"

"What are you implying?" Mr. Hewitt demanded.

Still addressing Harry, Nell said, "It was you. It was you in that back room at Flynn's that night, wasn't it?"

"Flynn's?" Harry shook his head in apparent puzzlement, as if he'd never heard of the place.

"It's a boardinghouse for sailors in Fort Hill," Nell said, "and you know it very well."

"Sorry," Harry said on a little huff of laughter. "Not my kind of neighborhood—or establishment."

"I think it is," she said. "I think you like whiskey and cards and whores, and I think—"

"My God!" Mr. Hewitt exclaimed, gripping his wife's shoulder. "Miss Sweeney, I'll thank you to leave here and—"

"No! Not until he"—she stabbed a finger at Harry—"admits what he's done and helps me to find William."

"I've never heard of Flynn's Boardinghouse," Harry said.

"That's funny," she countered, "because Seamus Flynn and a prostitute named Molly have identified you from your photograph, and they swear you're a regular cust—"

"See here," he said. "Out of consideration for my mother's sensibilities, if you're absolutely determined to pursue the subject, I really think we should do it out of her hearing." Harry looked toward his father, who nodded acquiescence, his mouth a grim slit, before turning his frosty gaze on Nell.

"Pack up your belongings tomorrow, Miss Sweeney," Mr. Hewitt said, to the accompaniment of a gasp of dismay from his wife. "And I hope you don't expect a reference, not after this little performance."

She had anticipated the dismissal. Still, a dull sense of shock deadened her legs as she followed Harry out into the hallway, closing the door behind her. She thought about Gracie, and felt a crushing jolt of grief. *God, what have I done?*

"I don't know what you think you're doing," Harry ground out as he yanked a silver flask from inside his coat, "but frankly, life in the Hewitt household is excruciating enough without you playing these sorts of games."

"You *have* been to Flynn's," she said. "You were there that Saturday night."

He lowered the flask, having taken a generous swallow, and recapped it. "Saturday night is Rat Night. I don't play the rats."

"No, but you thought you could still get in on a game of poker, or chuck-a-luck, and when you found you couldn't, you sat with your brother in the back parlor and drank. William told you about Ernest Tulley, and by the time Tulley returned at midnight, you were drunk enough to want to pay him back for killing Robbie. William had nodded off from the opium, I presume, but his bistoury was lying about, because he used it to scrape the spindle between bowls."

"His what?"

"The folding surgical knife, the one you used to slash Ernest Tulley's throat. William woke up, probably from the sound of Tulley's struggles when you attacked him. He offered to stay with the body while you made your escape, and you let him. You let him be arrested. And now you're going to let him hang—if he lives that long."

"What a remarkable imagination you have, Miss Sweeney. No wonder you're such a capable artist."

"Pearl was the only one who got a good look at you. Did you pay her to disappear, like you pay off your mill girls?"

"You tell me," he said as he took another drink. "You've got all the answers."

"I think you did. I think you'll do whatever it takes to make your problems go away, as long as it leaves you free to create more of them—even sacrifice your own brother."

"Dear me," he sneered. "I must be quite the cad."

"He's going to die for you! Does that mean nothing to you?"

"You're presuming he's doing it for me. Perhaps he's doing it for himself. Perhaps he wants to die."

"Did you kill Ernest Tulley?"

"Does it matter whether I did or not?"

"Of course it does."

His laughter had a ragged, drunken edge to it; he must have imbibed earlier, perhaps during intermission. "That only proves how naive you are, Miss Sweeney. You remind me of Robbie. He used to tell me that life had meaning, that one must try to be a good man and do the right thing, always, and everything would work out splendidly as a result. Well, that's exactly what he did, and now his twenty-five-year-old corpse is rotting under six feet of red Georgia clay. So forgive me if I'm a bit skeptical when it comes to 'doing the right thing.' "

"Nothing matters, then?"

"Why, I believe you're catching on, Miss Sweeney. Very little matters, certainly—aside from the pursuit of simple animal gratification. Once one has absorbed that essential truth, it's actually quite liberating. The rules that keep others on a short leash don't exist for you—as they shouldn't, because they're arbitrary and suffocating, most of them. Everything becomes possible. Nothing is taboo."

"As long as there's someone to clean up after you, or pay the price for your sins."

"That would be their choice."

"You're that sure you'll never have to pay the price yourself?"

He tucked away the flask, saying, "I'm a Hewitt, Miss Sweeney," as if that were answer enough.

Chapter 16

"**T**HIS is it," Cook said as he handed Nell down from the squeaky old police department gig in which they'd made this morning's journey from Boston to Quincy.

Nell yawned as she appraised the white clapboard house, its ground-floor windows fitted out with green-and-white-striped awnings, a painted-over shop sign on a pole in the tidy front yard. She'd been up the entire night, searching in vain for Will. Once, she'd stopped by Jack's house to see whether he'd had any luck, but there'd been no answer, so he must have still been making the rounds of the less reputable hotels.

Nell had spent most of the ninety-minute drive, while Detective Cook had chatted on, reins in hand, about this and that, imagining the relief she would feel when she knocked on Jack's door later this morning and found Will there. Even as he mocked them for wasting an entire night looking for him, Nell would see in his eyes that he was touched by their concern. She would still be without a job, without a home . . . without Gracie . . . but Will would not be lying dead in some hotel room, a needle in his arm, waiting to be found by the maid when she came in to make up the bed.

Wrung out as she was, emotionally and physically, she refused to consider any other scenario. If she did, she could not go on. And she must go on.

A curtain in a front window twitched as they climbed the porch steps. From inside came the creak of a floorboard, muted voices.

Detective Cook gave the brass door knocker—which looked to have been freshly polished—three quick raps; no response. He rapped again. "Pearl? I know you're in there. You, too, Molly. We're all a bit too long in the tooth for hide and seek, so kindly open the door, if you would."

More voices. About half a minute passed, and then the door creaked open, courtesy of Pearl, although it took Nell a moment to recognize her. Her formerly yellow hair, half-covered by a kerchief, had been dyed brown. In lieu of the too-tight green satin dress in which she'd once plied her trade, she wore a plain cotton frock, *sans* crinoline, and a bib apron. Perhaps the most surprising aspect of her transformation was her face, which, scrubbed free of paints and powders, looked remarkably soft and young.

Molly, standing next to her, had also redyed her hair—to a slightly darker brown than Pearl's—and was similarly attired and devoid of makeup. She glared at them. "I'd tell you you're not wanted here," she said, "but I don't guess coppers care much about that sort of thing, do they?"

"May we come in?" Nell asked.

Molly said "No" as Pearl opened the door wider, stepping back for them to enter. "They're already here," she told her friend. "They know where we are. What difference does it make?"

Nell and Cook followed the two women into the empty but freshly painted front room, equipped with a sales counter and shelves, through a storage room behind it, and up a narrow staircase. The second floor was modestly but neatly furnished as living quarters. Nell noticed a tidy little kitchen and a bedroom with prints of birds and flowers on the walls.

Pearl offered to take their outerwear and bring them tea as she ushered them into a cozy little front parlor, but Cook declined. "This will be a brief visit," he said, withdrawing a folded sheet of paper from inside his coat and handing it to her. "Just wanted to let you know that your presence will be required in court when William Toussaint is tried for the murder of Ernest Tulley. This here's a subpoena. It means you have to show up or go to jail."

She nodded resignedly as she glanced at the document, inked in a rather slapdash scrawl by some judge's clerk yesterday afternoon. "You sure about the tea? We've just had some, me and Molly, and the water's still hot."

Nell said, "I'd love some, actually, if we can spare a few minutes." She looked at Cook.

"I don't suppose one little cup will take that long," the detective said.

Pearl, seeming gratified, sent Molly to fix the tea as she hung up their things on a coat tree in the corner. "Have a seat," she invited as she took one herself, seeming for all the world like any ordinary matron receiving morning callers. Nell couldn't quite believe this was the same booze-steeped whore she'd known in Boston.

"This is a lovely little house," Nell said, feeling the weight of the pint of rum she'd tucked into her chatelaine before coming here; somehow she didn't think she'd need it.

Pearl smiled, her cheeks warming with color. "I been fixin' up the downstairs for a shop. We're gonna be dressmakers, me and Molly. Well, I'll be doing the sewing—

Molly, she can hardly thread a needle. But she's got a real good business head, so she'll be handlin' that end of things. She'll get me my raw goods from the mills up in Charlestown, and she's gonna paint us a sign for out front, and take out some ads in the newspapers. Oh, and she's fixin' to buy me one of them sewing machines, like they use in the big garment factories."

"That's wonderful," Nell said. "Sounds expensive, though."

Pearl's smile dimmed a bit. "I . . . I been savin' my money."

"Enough to buy this house?" Nell asked. "And provide capital for a new business? Pearl, I know you were paid to leave Boston."

Cook cast a quizzical glance at Nell, who hadn't yet disclosed to him her true reason for wanting to accompany him here.

"It was the man from the back parlor, wasn't it?" Nell asked. "He found you and offered you money to disappear so that he wouldn't be identified."

"You don't have to answer that," Molly said from the doorway, holding a tray of tea and cookies. "You ain't in court yet."

"I will be soon enough," Pearl said. "It don't matter anymore. Don't you see that, Molly? They found me."

"You'll have to testify," Nell said, "but the man who paid you the money will be locked up, most likely, so you won't be in any danger from him, and the money will be yours to keep."

"Good thing." Molly snorted as she handed Nell and Cook steaming cups of tea. "It's spent already, most of it. Can't get blood from a stone."

"I don't know about that," Pearl told Nell. "I mean, what you said about this fella bein' locked up. It's not like he done anything wrong. He didn't kill that man. He just didn't want anybody finding out he'd been at Flynn's that night, is all. He come to our flat there on Milk Street about a week after the murder—it was a Sunday morning, early. I remember me and Molly was still sleepin' when he starts knockin' on the door. Saturday nights are late nights for us."

"Used to be," Molly corrected.

"I threw on my shawl and let him in," Pearl said. "He hands me the fattest roll of greenbacks I ever seen and tells me he knows the cops are sniffin' around for witnesses, but his old man'll skin him alive if he finds out he was at a place like Flynn's drinkin' whiskey and . . . consortin' with the likes of me."

"So it was supposedly just a matter of avoiding his father's wrath?" Nell asked.

Pearl nodded. "So he said, but I could tell that wasn't the full story. You know how sometimes you just *know*?"

Cook grunted.

"I reckoned maybe there was a wife in the picture," Pearl said, "or a sweetheart."

"Or a pending murder charge," Nell conjectured.

"Not this fella," Pearl said. "He was a real gentleman— handsome, well dressed . . ."

"I wonder if you'd mind looking at this." Nell retrieved the photograph taken before the Children's Aid Ball from her bulging chatelaine, opened the leather case, and handed it to Pearl.

"Oh, why, it's Doc," Pearl said, squinting as she held the picture close to her face. "Toussaint, I mean." Wistfully she added, "That's what he looked like back when I first met him."

"Do you recognize the man from the back parlor?" Nell asked. "The one who paid you to leave Boston?"

"Yeah, that's him right there." Pearl pointed, Molly looking over her shoulder. "He was even better lookin' back then, or maybe it's just what he's wearin'. Men look so elegant in white tie."

"I'm not so sure about that waistcoat," Nell said.

"Ain't nothin' wrong with a plain white waistcoat."

"No, I meant—" Nell stopped breathing. She'd meant Harry's flashy brocade waistcoat. It was the other three men—Will, Robbie, and Jack—who'd worn classic white vests with their tailcoats that night.

"You know how I said I thought he was in the city government?" Pearl mused. "I remember why now. It was 'cause the other one, Toussaint, kept callin' him somethin'. What is they call them fellas—the ones on the Common Council? Councilman?"

"Councilor, usually," Cook said. "Course, they call lawyers the same thing, only it's spelled different."

Counselor.

"Holy Mother of God," Nell whispered.

N ELL jumped out of the gig, nerves buzzing, as Detective Cook tugged on the reins in front of ten Commonwealth Avenue. "You will wait for me, Miss Sweeney!"

Light glared through the leaded glass door of Jack's house, too much light, especially for this early in the day; it was barely 11 A.M. Who would light the gas jets at this hour, and on such a sunny morning?

Leaping up the front steps, her skirts clutched in her fists, she peered through the glass, eyes shaded, to find the hallway off the foyer choked with furniture and blazing with light streaming from the wide dining room entrance. That huge mahogany table had been pulled halfway into the hall in what must have been an arduous undertaking. Most of the matching chairs were shoved haphazardly against the wall, but one had been drawn up to the table before the crystal decanter and glass Jack had been drinking from earlier, both now empty, and an inkwell with a pen in it.

"What the devil . . . ?" muttered Cook from behind her. He knocked a few times, then jiggled the doorknob. Whipping off his bowler, he balled his big fist in the crown and rammed it through a pane of glass next to the knob, shards raining on the tiled entryway inside. He reached carefully through the jagged gap, unlocked the door, pushed it open. There came a steady, snakelike hiss, and the unmistakable smell of death. "Stay here."

A futile command. Nell followed him as he sprinted through the foyer and down the hallway, surprisingly light on his feet. The hiss grew louder, the smell stronger, a thick stench in the back of Nell's throat that made her nostrils flare, her gorge rise.

Cook stared unblinkingly into the dining room, closed his eyes, crossed himself.

"Oh, God," Nell moaned as she approached.

"Miss Sweeney—" Cook turned and seized her, kicking and flailing, in his bearish grasp. "I don't think you want to—" He swore as one of her fists caught him in the nose.

A wail rose from her when she saw him, hanging by a belt from that titanic, searingly bright chandelier, his body limp and reeking, his blackened face grotesquely distorted. He wore the old sack coat he'd had on when he'd let her off at the Tremont Theatre last night, no tie. One of the dining chairs lay on its side beneath him, along with his cap, which he'd no doubt tossed off during his death throes.

"*Jack!*" The scream, hoarse and despairing, seemed to come from somewhere else, from all around her. It reverberated in her skull, squeezed her stomach until the floor slammed into her knees and she found herself wretching onto that beautiful Axminster carpet.

"There, now, Miss Sweeney," soothed Detective Cook as he helped her to her feet and walked her, jittery and weeping, to the front stoop, where the air was bracing and

the sun almost as bright as that hellish, hissing chandelier . . .

But not quite.

"Sit here," he said, pushing her gently downward onto
the top step. "Don't move. I'll be right back."

He returned less than a minute later, sat next to her,
and handed her a letter.

"What is this?" she asked numbly.

"It was sticking out of his coat pocket."

Feb. twenty-two 1868

> *I, Jonathan Leopold Thorpe, hereby declare that I
> am solely responsible for the death of the merchant
> sailor known as Ernest Tulley, as well as that of Dr.
> William Lindleigh Hewitt, also known as William
> Toussaint, who took his life rather than be hanged for
> a crime I was too craven to acknowledge as my own.
> I make this declaration freely and attest to its veracity
> before Almighty God. May He have mercy on my un-
> worthy soul.*

> > *Jonathan Leopold Thorpe*

April 1868

Cambridge, Massachusetts

H E was still there.

Nell had first noticed him about five minutes into the graveside service, a spectral figure in the dense morning mist, shadowed by a massive, newly leafed oak at the far edge of Mount Auburn Cemetery. He'd stood unmoving as Jack Thorpe's coffin was lowered into the earth, although he was much too far away to hear Reverend Nicholson's remarks.

Six weeks had passed since Jack's death, but the ground had been too frozen until now for him to be laid to rest in the family plot. Leo Thorpe's influence was such that the nature of his son's passing, not to mention his written confession of murder, never became public knowledge. Indeed, his own mother and sisters had been spared the unseemly details, having been informed, along with the rest of Boston, that Jack had succumbed to a ruptured appendix. The murder charge against William Toussaint, missing and presumed dead, had been dropped and the case quietly shelved.

Viola, although dismayed by Nell's having wrongly accused Harry of murder, was grateful enough for her efforts on Will's behalf to beg her husband to rehire her. He subbornly refused; this, Nell had expected. What she hadn't expected—what had stunned her as much as it had stunned Mr. Hewitt—was for Viola to threaten to divorce him and return to England, even going so far as to consult an attorney. It would be scandalous, but when had Viola Hewitt ever minded being talked about? Nell had her job back within forty-eight hours of losing it.

Harry was a good deal less forgiving than his mother, despite Nell's formal apology delivered in the presence of his parents and Martin. Outraged over her continued employment in the Hewitt household, he bucked Brahmin tradition by moving out of his parents' home and into number ten Commonwealth Avenue, which he rented on very favorable terms from Leo Thorpe.

"It's the perfect day for this," said Viola as Mrs. Bouchard wheeled her down the brick path toward their waiting brougham, both women in black mourning gowns, as was Nell.

Mrs. Bouchard cast a dubious glance at the back of her employer's head. "I'll take New Orleans in April *any* day."

Mr. Hewitt, normally not one to tolerate Mrs. Bouchard's casual impertinences, added a bemused little *hmph* to that assessment. "Only an Englishwoman would call such a dreary morning perfect."

"A young man has just been laid to rest," Viola said. "One ought not to do such a thing when the sun is shining."

"Point taken, my dear."

In fact, Nell thought, it was as if two young men had been laid to rest this morning, for William Hewitt was almost certainly just as dead. In fact, many of Reverend Nicholson's observations about Jack—particularly the

tragic irony of his having been taken so young after sur-
viving the war—were just as applicable to Will, for whom
there had almost certainly been no eulogy. In all likeli-
hood he lay in some pauper's graveyard somewhere, an
unidentified corpse with no one to claim him, his death
owing as much to crippling regret as to morphine. Nell
had lit dozens of vigil candles at church these past six
weeks, offered up scores of prayers for Will's immortal
soul—yet still she wept at night.

But when at last she drifted into sleep, he would be
reborn, in uneasy, complicated dreams from which she
would awaken in a state of feverish melancholia, a whiff
of opium lingering in the air like perfume.

Such an extraordinary man, felled—as Jack had been—
by his darkest memories, and the self-loathing that came
of having survived them.

"Viola . . . August," greeted Eugenia Thorpe through
her nearly opaque weeping veil of black crepe—the most
voluminous Nell had ever seen—as she approached them
on the arm of her husband Leo, who looked remarkably
old and stooped. "Thank you so much for coming."

"We loved Jack as if he were our own son," said Viola,
one of the few people who knew the true circumstances
of his death, because Nell had told her.

The two couples exchanged condolences and com-
ments about the service and the weather while Nell and
Mrs. Bouchard, both long accustomed to de facto invisi-
bility, stood quietly by. Cecilia Pratt, chatting with her
parents about twenty yards away, drew Eugenia Thorpe's
attention with that glass-popping giggle of hers. Lowering
her voice, Mrs. Thorpe remarked that a young woman
attending the burial of her fiancé should know better than
to wear sapphires with her mourning black—especially
sapphires given to her by the deceased's replacement.

A movement in the distance caught Nell's attention as
the Thorpes were taking their leave. She looked that way

to find the man who'd been standing under the big oak coming toward them. A tall, lean figure in black cutaway and top hat, he had a slightly stiff, almost stately gait that made Nell's lungs pump a little harder because it was so familiar, so much like . . .

"Oh, my God," she whispered as he came nearer, his gaze shifting from her to Viola, then back to her. "Oh, my God," she repeated on a tremulous, disbelieving little laugh.

"Nell?" Viola reached out to her. "Darling, what's . . . ?" Tracking Nell's gaze, she watched her firstborn son, the son she'd twice given up for dead, materialize out of the gloom. She breathed his name, braced her hands on the arms of her Merlin chair, and struggled to rise.

"Careful there, Mrs. Hewitt." Mrs. Bouchard helped Viola to her feet, unfolded the two canes one-handed, and crossed herself, her gaze fixed on Will as he approached.

"Ladies." Will tipped his hat and bowed to the three women, his eyes lingering a moment on Nell, then nodded to his grim-faced father. "Sir."

A slight thinning of the mouth was August Hewitt's only response.

"Will." With the aid of her canes, Viola took a quavering step toward the son she hadn't seen in over four years, her eyes damp, smile wobbly. Taking both canes in one hand, she reached out to Will, who hesitated a moment before stepping forward.

"Ma'am." He allowed her to touch his cheek, remove his hat, stroke his hair.

"My baby . . . I don't believe it." Viola laughed as the tears fell. "I thought you were dead. Nell said . . ." She turned toward Nell, upsetting her balance.

Will caught his mother by the arms before she could fall. "Easy," he murmured, lowering her gently into the Merlin chair as Mrs. Bouchard pushed it forward. He unfolded a handkerchief and handed it to his mother.

"It's been a shock to her," Mr. Hewitt said, "seeing you again. You might have thought of that before you decided to just reappear like this, out of the blue, with no warning whatso—"

"Oh, honestly, August," Viola said as she dabbed her cheeks with Will's handkerchief. "I've never been so thrilled to see anyone in my life. It wasn't the shock that made me stumble—it was these withered old legs of mine."

"Do you still keep a wheelchair on every floor of the house?" Will asked.

"Yes, and it's bloody tiresome, I can tell you, hobbling up and down stairs with those canes. The older I get, the harder it seems."

"That might just be a delayed effect of the infantile paralysis. Some people become weak and achy years later." Turning to his father, Will said, "Have you considered installing an elevator for her?"

"In the *house*? No, by Jove, I certainly have not! They tried to get me into one of those contraptions at the Fifth Avenue Hotel last year, when I was in New York, but I climbed to the top floor on the strength of my own legs, thank you very much. Wouldn't be caught dead in one."

"How fortunate for you, then," Will said dryly, "that you've got such fine, strong legs."

Viola and Mrs. Bouchard both looked to be biting their lips, as was Nell, who exchanged a quick, amused glance with Will.

Blood flooded August Hewitt's translucent white skin, turning it a rather startling pink. "You're as insolent as ever, but I don't know what else I would expect. I confess I'm at a loss as to why my Robbie should have been taken so young, while someone like you gets to live. God knows you're not half the man he was."

"On that, at least," Will said, "we can agree." He nodded in turn to Viola and her nurse—"Mother . . . Mrs.

Bouchard"—and then to Nell. "Miss Sweeney," he said
with that coolly intimate little smile of his, "always a pleasure."

"You aren't leaving!" Viola exclaimed as he turned
and left. "Will, please! At least tell us where you're staying."

Smiling over his shoulder, he said, "You should know
by now not to ask me that."

Nell watched him walk away until he was just a small
dark spot against a wet-on-wet ink wash of trees at the
edge of the cemetery . . . and then she couldn't make him
out at all. How could he just appear from the mist and
then dissolve back into it, she wondered, with no expla-
nations, when for six long weeks, she'd thought he was—

"Look," said Mrs. Bouchard. "He forgot his hat."

Will's top hat, the low-crowned, roll-brimmed type he
preferred, lay on the brick path where it had fallen earlier;
he'd walked away bareheaded, and everyone had been too
preoccupied to notice, even him. Mrs. Bouchard picked it
up and dusted it off. Taking a step in Will's direction, she
said, "I'll just—"

"Nell will bring it to him," Viola said.

"But I don't mind—"

"Neither does Nell." Snatching the hat out of her
nurse's hand, Viola gave it to Nell. "Go! We'll be waiting
in the brougham."

Nell returned her smile, lifted her black skirts, and
sprinted across the cemetery, dodging headstones, until
she reached the small patch of woods that had swallowed
Will up. "Dr. Hewitt!"

She wandered farther into the thicket, out of breath,
heart hammering, trying to make out anything in the damp
haze. "Dr. Hewitt!" She groaned in frustration, muttering,
"Damn it, Will . . ."

There came a deep chuckle from behind her.

Wheeling around, she saw him several yards away,

standing with his weight on his good leg, a cigarette in his hand.

"Such unladylike language, Cornelia. Good for you."

She walked toward him, still breathless, the hat in her outstretched hand. "You forgot this."

"Nonsense." He took it from her, tucking it under his arm with a smile. "A gentleman never forgets his hat."

It took her a moment to digest his meaning, and then she smiled, too. The hat had been a ruse; he'd wanted to see her alone.

She said, "It's good to see you, Dr. Hewitt. I thought you were dead."

He crushed his cigarette underfoot. "You called me 'Will' before."

"Yes, well . . ." She looked out through the trees at the irregular rows of tombstones, dry gray stumps fading into a watery gray background.

"Yes, well . . ." he gently mocked. "When one has gone through as much trouble as you have to save a man's life—even if it's as pointless a life as mine—it seems rather silly to be on such formal terms." A quiet gravity replaced his smile. "Please give me this. I know I haven't earned it, but . . ."

"Yes." Something in his demeanor—that earnest, frank request, his eyes so boyish, almost needful—touched her with unexpected force. "Yes—" Her throat closed; she cleared it. "I would like it if you called me by my Christian name."

He smiled, gave her a little bow. "Thank you, Nell."

The implication was that they'd be dealing with each other again, but Nell couldn't imagine under what circumstances their paths would cross.

"Why did you come here today," she asked, "if you weren't going to stand close enough to hear the service?"

He ducked his head, rubbed the back of his neck. "I wanted to be there when Jack was buried. I just didn't . . .

I didn't think I could deal with seeing my parents again."

"What made you change your mind?"

Will shrugged, looked away. "Perhaps it was seeing you there, knowing I wouldn't be facing them alone." He looked back at her.

She looked down, fussed with her glove buttons. "Where have you been these past weeks? You bought all that morphine and disappeared. I thought—"

"You *knew* about the morphine?" he asked. "How . . . ?"

"Mr. Maynard told me."

He closed his eyes, muttered something under his breath. "I didn't want you having to bring me Black Drop on death row. It wasn't fair to you—I knew how you felt about it. So I concocted this oh-so-scientific plan to wean myself off opium before the trial. Decreasing doses of its primary active ingredient—morphine—by injection."

"Did it work?"

He rubbed the back of his neck. "I'm still dependent on it, but I've reduced my need, and I've stopped smoking gong altogether."

"I'm pleased to hear it," she said, wondering if he would slide back into his old ways now that there was no stint on death row to prepare for. "Where did you go? Jack and I looked all over Boston for you."

He gave her a surprisingly diffident little smile. "Don't think me bourgeois, but I actually have a little place out in the country—upstate New York, the Finger Lakes."

"You?"

"I won it in a game of lansquenet. It's just an unassuming little cottage, but it's right on Skaneateles Lake. I rather like the sound of the waves slapping the shore when I'm falling asleep at night."

Lansquenet? She said, "I assume you know that Jack's father has managed to obliterate all trace of his confession. No one will ever find out what really happened."

"That's as it should be. Jack paid the price for his sin, as did Ernest Tulley. That should be the end of it."

Interesting, she thought, that a man who seemed relatively contemptuous of religion should speak so casually of sin. She said, "I've worked some of it out in my mind, but I can't quite figure out what Jack was doing with you at Flynn's that night."

"Drinking whiskey." Will leaned back against a tree, lit a cigarette.

"No, I mean—"

"I know what you mean. The first time I ran into Jack after Andersonville was the day they hanged Henry Wirz at the Old Capital Prison in Washington. They were issuing tickets for that particular show, and I'd made it my business to get one. Ernest Tulley could never have worked his evil if Wirz hadn't looked the other way. Jack noticed me in the crowd, and later, after a couple of beers, I asked him if he wouldn't mind forgetting he'd ever seen me. He said, 'Of course, old man,' without even asking why. He understood instinctively. I always appreciated that."

"So you stayed in touch and ended up spending that Saturday evening together at Flynn's," she said.

"The early part of the evening went pretty much as I've already told you—seeing Tulley, pulling him off the girl . . . But then Jack showed up—I'd asked him to meet me there. By that time I was pretty far gone on gong, and I blurted out the whole story—about Tulley killing Robbie, and how he'd been there earlier and left. I pointed out that other fellow who looked like Tulley . . ."

"Roy Noonan?"

"Him, yes. I said, 'That's what he looks like. Let me know if he comes back.' I wanted Tulley tried and hanged by the War Department. I thought he should die as Wirz had died—publicly shamed, kicking and choking. Jack, though . . ." Will shook his head. "He was drunk even before he got there, and my story about Robbie really lit his fuse. He'd loved Robbie like a brother, and he always felt as if he'd abandoned him when he retreated with the regiment instead of letting himself be captured."

"That's absurd, though."

On a plume of smoke, Will said, "People are absurd, Nell. Anyway, Jack was . . . not himself that night. He thought we should take matters into our own hands."

"Kill Tulley."

"Avenge Robbie ourselves, like men—that was how he viewed it. I think he wanted to prove something, and he saw this as the way. He was so soused I didn't think he could possibly pull it off—that was my second mistake. I smoked myself into my usual coma and awoke to the sounds of a scuffle out in the alley. It seems Jack had been looking out the window and saw Tulley come back. He grabbed my bistoury, went out to the alley, and . . ." He shrugged and took a draw on his cigarette.

"And you let yourself be arrested in his place?" Nell asked incredulously.

"That wasn't quite what I'd initially intended—although I probably wasn't thinking straight, what with all the gong. I do remember telling Jack to get out of there. No matter what transpired, he was to tell no one that he'd been there, and certainly not with me."

"And then you tried to save Tulley's life by applying pressure between the wound and the heart."

"If one's victim doesn't die, one can't very well be charged with murder. And I still wanted Tulley to have to make that long climb up to the gallows. Clever you, figuring that out."

"It didn't make sense that you would want to choke him while he was spewing blood from a severed carotid, no matter how intoxicated you were."

He let out a little huff of laughter as he tossed down his cigarette and ground it out. "How dead can one man get? In fact, I had to be careful not to press on his windpipe while I was compressing the artery. And I didn't want to take the bistoury out in case—"

"—it worsened the bleeding," she finished. "When in doubt, leave knives in."

"Dr. Greaves was thorough."

"I didn't learn that one from him." Before Will could pursue that, she said, "Why didn't you just tell that patrolman what you were doing, when you realized he thought you were the killer?"

"Oh, I doubt anything I'd said at that point would have been very convincing. He'd caught me in the act! And, too, I wanted Jack to get away. If they even suspected it had been someone other than me, they would have gone looking for him."

"So you let yourself be arrested and charged with murder." Just as he'd let himself be captured and sent to Andersonville. "Pretty self-sacrificing of you."

Wearily he said, "Not if you don't have that much to lose in the first place. Jack *did* have something to lose—a career, a fiancée, a family that could not only stand the sight of him, but actually wanted him closer. Why not trade an empty life for a full one? I'd hesitated about that once—I wasn't about to make the same mistake twice."

Nell got it: Will hadn't been able to save Robbie; he wasn't about to lose Jack.

"Why didn't you just plead guilty, then?" she asked.

"I was trying to do a friend a favor, not martyr myself. Oh, I was willing to see the sentence through if it came to it—I do believe in playing out one's losing hand—but why just present it to them on a silver platter? Make them work for it, by God."

"Fine, then," she said. "Why didn't you plead *not* guilty?"

"Because they would have investigated in earnest then, and it wouldn't have taken much for them to home in on

Jack. It's not as if he'd been particularly careful about the whole thing. And the reason I didn't want a lawyer," he continued, anticipating her next question, "was because *he* might very well have investigated, stumbled on Jack, and used him to get me off whether I liked it or not. Are you done? Can we flirt now?"

"Not quite. That's why you didn't want *me* snooping around, either, because I might find out it was Jack all along."

"Ah, you're finally catching on," he said with a smile, "now that it doesn't matter anymore. You *were* a damnable nuisance, but you have a certain prickly way about you that I find diverting, and those galloping assumptions of yours helped to keep you from doing too much damage."

"Why did Jack let you take the blame this way," she asked, "especially considering what was at stake for you?"

"He didn't realize I was doing it until you recruited him for legal services. And then he convinced himself he could get me off and we'd both walk free. We had a couple of long, fairly passionate arguments, he and I, about what would happen if I was sentenced to hang—he advocating for a last-minute confession on his part, I for the manly playing out of the hand, and all that. So, you're saying we *can* flirt, once—"

"He never wanted me to pursue that other man in the back parlor," Nell murmured. "The one you were talking to, the one Pearl . . ." She looked away, her cheeks warming. "Because it was him. It was Jack. It was all right to frame Noonan, though, because Noonan—"

"—was a blackguard. There's something about a beautiful young woman in mourning attire . . ."

"He probably would have done it," she said thoughtfully. "He would have admitted his guilt. He would have snatched away the sword you were trying to throw yourself on and shoved it into his own chest."

"Yes," Will said, suddenly sobered. "He would have. Which was why I had to . . . 'leave for Shanghai.' "

She looked at him. The sun must have been burning through the mist while they were talking, because a ray had penetrated the foliage overhead to infuse his face with a golden radiance. A glance through the trees into the cemetery revealed the truth of this; it was awash with sunlight.

"I'm glad you were worried about me." He replaced his hat on his head, nudging it to precisely the correct infinitesimal slant, something Brahmin males learned to do in the nursery.

Nell wanted to ask what he would be doing now, where he would be living, what his plans were, but she didn't. She didn't want to hear him say "cards," or "Shanghai," or "morphine." And God knew she didn't want to hear the name of some fictional hotel based on his "current actress's" play.

"You'll never learn." He reached out to take hold of her green woollen scarf. She didn't resist him, but instead let him take both ends and pull them even. "It may be April, but it's nippy."

He tucked it in, first one end, which he snugged beneath her right coat lapel, taking his time to make it smooth, and then the other, overlapping the first. For the briefest of moments—a second perhaps—he let his hand linger there, pressing it to her upper chest as if to gauge the thudding of her heart.

"You should listen when a physician gives you advice about your health," he said, allowing his fingertips just the lightest graze along her bare throat before withdrawing them. "I'll be seeing you, Nell."

He turned and walked away, into the morning sunshine.

First in the Victorian Mystery series featuring
Dr. Alexandra Gladstone

This country doctor thinks she's seen everything.
Until she finds an earl who's
been murdered—twice.

SYMPTOMS OF DEATH

Paula Paul

0-425-18429-3

When the old country doctor of Newton-upon-Sea
passed away, he left his daughter Alexandra the
secrets of his trade. Now, the village depends on its
lady-doctor Gladstone for its births, deaths, and all
the inconveniences inbetween.

"Don't miss it." —Tony Hillerman

Available wherever books are sold or
to order call 1-800-788-6262

B035